HUNTED

THE GATES LEGACY,

BOOK 1

Books by Lorenz Font

The Gates Legacy Series

Hunted - Book 1

Tormented - Book 2

Ascension - Book 3

Reckoning - Book 4

Redemption - Book 5 – Coming soon

Indivisible Line

Feather Light

Pieces of Broken Time

The Prodian Journey Series

Rise of Alpha

Hunted

The Gates Legacy, Book 1

By
Lorenz Font

Dad - I know you're watching over your little girl.
Mom - You can believe it now. I love you.

Glossary

Incomis Sippanus—A disease that can be transmitted from vampire to vampire or vampire to human through feeding or sexual intercourse. Symptoms are similar to leprosy or AIDS, including painful lesions and clouded white irises. Consumption of human blood alleviates visible symptoms but also speeds the disease's progression. Harrow Gates is the first known carrier of the disease.

Vampire Council—Governing authority of the vampire world, consisting of ten purebred vampires called Elders.

Harem—Goran's mistresses, beautiful redheaded vampires who are trained in combat.

Dangeran—Metal with the strength and weight of titanium that has been infused with diamond bits, used in the construction of most vampire weapons. Vampires cut by Dangeran will disintegrate unless the wounded area is cut from their bodies.

Arnis—Three-foot-long wooden sticks used as a sparring weapon.

Kalimetal—Metal version of Arnis. Three-foot-long sticks infused with Dangeran. Animal pelt is woven to the handle to provide a safe grip.

Blanch Room—A large secured area inside the Vampire headquarters that houses humans before and during transition.

Mentha—A plant extract believed to have a calming, numbing effect on vampires.

Great Vampire Revolution—Uprising by a group of revolutionary vampires seeking freedom from Goran's rule in the 1960s.

Pure-Blooded Vampires—Elite class of vampires on the verge of extinction, they are able to reproduce and can read minds. Each possesses a unique gift, and they must feed from pureblooded vampires of the opposite sex to survive.

Tack Enterprises—A company owned and operated by Pritchard Tack that manufactures guns for the military and private companies. Profits are used to support a large group of fighters, researchers, and medical personnel who are working on finding a cure for the disease *Incomis Sippanus*.

Vampire Rebellion—A small resistance by vampires in upstate New York. Reason for the uprising is unknown.

Harrow Gates knew the types of characters that surrounded him. Although unknown to most humans, vampires had coexisted with them for a very long time, and the musty smell of the club was a clear indication that both human beings and his own kind were cloistered together in the dank room. Mindful of his predicament—hunted and on the run—Harrow darted his eyes left to right. While he scanned his surroundings for any possible threat, he took in the general mood of the population around him.

The usual human emotions swirled around him—the anticipation of finding a lay for the night, the excitement of scoring drugs, and the de-stressing after a long day over a glass of alcohol. Vampire emotions were well represented, too. Both males and females came with a heavy dose of lust for blood and sex, but exterminating a sick vampire was always a vampire soldier's top priority.

"Another drink for you?" the bartender asked, eyeing him with interest.

Nothing much had changed as far as his appearance went. The disease had only affected his eyes so far. Gone were the baby blues, replaced by the horrid white irises that begged to be concealed. Apart from being emaciated from lack of proper nourishment, he could still pass as normal. His blonde hair needed trimming, but that just lent a grungy look to his otherwise average form.

"I'm good."

Harrow pulled down the hood of his sweatshirt to cover his face and adjusted his sunglasses, making sure his disguise could withstand the watchful eyes intent on taking him down. A warrant had been issued for his arrest, but he was certain that it was closer to an order to kill. The VC would prefer to have him dead rather than alive.

The illustrious Vampire Council had been tracking him, never relenting, and he'd been on the run for months now. The constant hiding was beginning to wear him down.

It had been a week since he'd last fed. If he intended to run and evade, he needed blood to keep going. There was no question that he could find someone here tonight—after all, money could buy anything. However tempted he was to rip away his hoodie and let his pursuers do away with him, his survival instinct was too strong. He must keep trudging along, continuing to try to right whatever havoc he'd left in his wake.

He was a carrier of an unknown disease, one that he'd doubtless contracted during his transition. Harrow needed blood, now. The sooner he got it, the faster he'd be out of there, free to run and hide until hunger forced him to resurface again.

A woman slinked in his direction, wearing a mini skirt that fell just short of showing her ass. Her fake blonde hair swayed in rhythm with her body's movement until she stopped next to him at the bar and eyed him with interest. She could very well be the one to service his need. Feeding had grown trickier when he'd learned that even careful sucking at a vampire's vein was a sure-fire way to transmit the disease. The one way he could live with himself was to feed less often. Harrow was a vampire with a conscience—a sick irony, if he said so himself. He would withdraw just enough blood to get him through another week or so, and human food could buy him at least a few days before his hunger for the real deal would begin gnawing at him again.

At this rate, there was no doubt that he would be dead soon.

Returning the woman's stare through his dark glasses, he checked out her Collagen-infused lips and flashed her a tight smile.

"Looking for some action tonight?" she asked in a piercing pitch. Her smile promised hours of fun.

"Yeah. Do you have any X?" Harrow replied.

If she were drugged, it would be easier for him to draw blood from her without biting. A single needle, like the one he'd pocketed earlier, would do the job.

"Of course," she answered with enthusiasm, grabbing his hand from the counter.

"No." Harrow's voice was explosive. The lesions he was sporting were active, and the last thing he wanted was to spread the damn disease. He didn't want to take a chance tonight by getting touchy-feely. Smirking, he shook his head at her now-fearful expression. "I'm good. Just show me the way."

His body rebelled, weakened by the slightest movement, but he got up from the bar, leaving enough dough to cover his drink plus tip. With every passing day, his lesions became more pronounced. Until he fed, the wounds would continue to open, and he'd slowly waste away. Not a party. He'd seen it firsthand, and he was not jumping for joy at the prospect. The pain was no picnic, either.

All of a sudden, he picked up a nasty emotion, more potent and hateful than the rest, rolling in thick waves from behind him. *Something wasn't right.*

He narrowed his eyes and sniffed the air around him, sensing an immediate threat. Just as he whipped his head around, an axe whizzed past his face, missing him by a narrow margin. It lodged in the wall, splintering the wood on contact.

Time to run!

His head wouldn't stand a chance if that axe touched it. *Dangeran.* It was obvious that the blade, though corroded, had been constructed of the one metal that would kill vampires in an instant. Anyone who wanted to waste a vampire would be sure to use the best blade out there. Rusty or not, it was good enough to sever his skull in few seconds, tops.

Harrow swung around and made a beeline for the exit, knocking down several people in his haste to get out of the club. The wind picked up, and the lashing cold bit at his skin. In his weakened condition, being killed was a big possibility. The clicking of his boots was loud on the damp pavement while he tried to outrun his pursuer. It wouldn't be easy.

Harrow's feet took him to the subway, where he might be able to lose his attacker. The well-lit underground station seemed to be an ideal place to hide with the large number of people still milling about. Maybe he'd get lucky and the vampire wouldn't continue to follow him in view of the human population. It would be a gamble—none of these vampire soldiers ever cared about witnesses or unintended casualties.

He slowed down to a brisk walk, trying to act inconspicuous and avoid eye contact. The last thing he needed was curious humans watching him. Anyone could discover what he was if he wasn't careful. After making it through the turnstile, he was turning the corner when massive hands clamped around his neck, holding him in a vice-like grip. He staggered backward and lost his footing in an instant. The hands tightened, beginning to choke him.

His mind worked feverishly. Harrow spread his legs and planted them firm on the ground. With quick motions, he slid to his left and twisted his body, locking his arm around his attacker's torso. He leaned forward and threw the vampire over his shoulder. The vampire hollered in pain when he hit the ground with a resounding thud, but his recovery was quick. The assailant grabbed Harrow's leg before he could break away, twisting it and yanking him back until he fell on the ground. Grunting with pain and exhaustion, Harrow felt a thick arm slide around his neck to put him in a headlock. He struggled to free himself from the man's death grip, twisting his body and trying to pry the hands off his neck, but his weakened state made it close to impossible.

Harrow gasped. "What the hell do you want from me?"

"I want you dead," the vampire answered.

"A . . . lot of people . . . want me dead." He had to choke out the words.

"You're a son of a bitch who has infected many." The vampire squeezed Harrow's neck harder. He felt his grasp slipping away, and his eyes began to roll back. People were watching them now, the struggle having attracted bystanders' attention. Some were even bold enough to move closer, intent on their battle for supremacy. Most of them doubtless assumed that the smaller man was dead meat.

"Someone call the cops!" one bystander yelled.

Then a shot was fired, and the surprise of the sudden noise distracted the grappling vampires for a moment. Startled people ran in every direction at the sound of the gunshot, ducking to the ground and seeking cover. The sound ricocheted off the concrete walls of the enclosed space while the two men continued to skid and roll on the pavement. Harrow was losing ground, but he kept trying to fight off his attacker.

"You two—get on your feet and follow me. If you don't, I will blow your heads into oblivion!" The order was given in an authoritative tone that brooked no argument. The man aimed the gun at them.

What the hell?

The big vampire shot his head up, zeroing his glare on the party crasher, but he didn't loosen his grip on Harrow's neck. Distraction was key if Harrow wanted to get away. Mustering a sudden burst of energy, he jammed an elbow into the vampire's ribs, making him loosen his grip. Harrow then rammed his fist into the vampire's face before struggling to his feet.

Another warning shot rang in the air.

Several men dressed in black leathers and gloves, their faces covered with ski masks, appeared out of nowhere and surrounded them. Each one was armed with a Dangeran blade. The massive vampire struggled to his feet, wielding his axe and ready to fight. The original combatants were outnumbered, no doubt about it. Harrow eyed the single escape route, but the men closed in on them, blocking their exit.

"The cops will be here in two minutes, tops. If you both want to live to see tomorrow, you'll come with me without causing a scene." The threat was clear. The man turned away, and the other vampire struggled, his resistance was rewarded with the butt of a gun pounded against his head. The dark-garbed men seized and handcuffed them both before covering their heads with black burlap cloth.

"Where the hell are you taking us?" the massive vampire roared, struggling with his cuffs. Harrow knew better and didn't resist further. If the cops were to get a hold of him, he was as good as dead. How much worse could it get?

Several men surrounded them. Harrow knew escape was impossible. He could attempt to break free, but his condition, he wouldn't get far. He'd be dead in no time, considering all the ammunition the group was packing.

Harrow forced himself to relax, a feat that was close to impossible. The hunger gnawed at him. He needed to feed, and soon. It didn't make things any easier that he could feel the lesions on his arms throb, stinging each time the cuffs rubbed them. Under the black sack that covered his face, he used his heightened sense of smell to distinguish each of the men surrounding him, including the vampire who moments ago had tried to kill him. They were all humans, he deduced. What in the world did they want from him and his attacker? How did these men know who they were? From the manner in which the leader spoke, it sounded like he had a good idea that they were vampires.

He could tell that their captors were excited by their breathing and the surge of electricity emanating off their skin. What were they so keyed up about? And why?

More questions.

Jordan had been following the group, tracking their every move and listening to their conversation. These two were no ordinary vampires, and she watched them with interest. She'd heard everything the man with the gun said and what his threat implied. It wasn't clear whether the speaker was human or vampire, but he spoke like someone used to power and authority. Intrigued, Jordan followed the group while they dragged the two vampires out of the subway in haste.

She ran after them, allowing a safe enough distance to escape notice. Her Kalimetal hung across her back, concealed by the trench coat she wore. Moving to match their speed with the agility and silence of a panther, she darted in and out of hiding places whenever one of the men did a spot check. The distant sound of police arriving at the scene competed with the rumble of subway trains zooming by.

When the group stopped in an almost vacant parking lot, Jordan hid behind a thick lamppost, a ghost in the dark. The group approached three black SUVs that stood waiting. She saw the leader slide into the front passenger seat of the nearest vehicle, while the remaining masked men loaded the vampires into separate cars. The gang was large enough that each vampire was surrounded.

Following a car on foot could pose a problem for her. Looking around for a better alternative, Jordan spotted a motorcycle across the street, parked in front of an apartment building.

Bingo! She smiled to herself. Without wasting time, she crossed the street just as the convoy began to move. Hotwiring a vehicle had never been a problem for her, but stealing was something she preferred not to do. However, Jordan knew that if she wanted to get some leads, she was better off kicking her beliefs aside. She punched the graphite engine cover, pulled free the wiring, and touched two wires together. With a little spark of electricity, the motor roared to life. Jordan jumped on, closing the distance in no time.

Jordan sat on a bench overlooking the Hudson River, the Manhattan skyline providing the perfect backdrop. The view never ceased to amaze her, and she made it a point to watch the breaking of dawn in this particular spot every day. The entire picturesque cluster of skyscrapers with their twinkling lights danced before her eyes, creating a vision of abstract paintings inside her head. She had done this every single night since leaving her lowly little town of Eureka, California. The vast vista soothed her wretched soul. She had turned into a creature of habit, as well as a woman hell-bent on finding answers to her questions.

Her mind wandered back, remembering what she'd lost and what she hoped to gain. Jordan promised herself that she would stop at nothing to avenge her parents' deaths and punish the monster that had turned her life upside down, condemning her to this eternal hell.

She'd had a normal childhood, the only child of doting parents who viewed the outdoors as their backyard. Marceline and David had been avid campers, hikers, and whitewater enthusiasts, and they had brought up their daughter to be familiar with living outdoors. They often spent entire weekends driving to the wilderness and exploring the forest. This was the lifestyle Jordan had known and embraced for as long as she could remember. Their rituals had gone through some changes when she went to college, but her parents had made sure they made up for lost time when her schedule allowed her to get away. They'd been content with their lot and had no wish to obtain more than they needed. Who would have thought that the life they'd cherished would be stolen from them in such a vicious manner?

Jordan's nightmare had begun in a forest not too far from their home. It was the camping trip that had ended her life as she'd known it. Their three-hour drive had taken the family close to the North Klamath River, where they'd intended to raft for the next few days and try fly-fishing for the first time.

Jordan and her parents had been filled with excitement that this much-anticipated trip was underway at last. Their campground was about a hundred miles away from the nearest civilization, nestled in the northwest tip of the Siskiyou Mountain, and it provided the peaceful and serene environment they'd sought. The area had been primitive and isolated, just as they preferred. Finding the campground deserted had been more than they'd hoped for, and Jordan had been glad to have her parents all to herself. The air was a little warm for California in April. At noon, they'd found their spot, and the promise of a glorious day had hung in the air.

"This is great, Jordan, don't you think?" Marceline asked as they piled out of their old truck. Her mother had been beside herself with happiness.

"It is, Mom. I'm glad we got the chance to get away," Jordan answered, before walking to the rear of the truck. "Hey Dad, what do you want me to unload first?"

David was scanning the perimeter of the area, looking up at the trees and deliberating on the perfect spot to pitch their tent to maximize the shade provided by the overgrown trees. "I'll take care of the heavier gear. Just grab the lighter bags and the portable stove. You and your mom can hang out while I put up the tent," he replied.

It took several hours to get everything in order, and by the time dinner was finished, dusk had settled. They found themselves staring into the fading light while they lounged in front of the campfire David had started.

It was a gorgeous evening. Jordan sighed as she sat next to her parents by the fire pit. It was a clear night. The stars and the moon were out, adding a little light to the otherwise pitch-black campground. The glow from the fire illuminated their campsite, giving it an eerie feel.

"You think it's a good time to tell scary stories now? Just like we used to do when I was younger?" she asked her father. In response, David contorted his face in a way that used to scare her when she was little. His stories had always ended with her in her parents' bed, unable to sleep. She laughed at her father's attempt to frighten her. "Dad, that's not going to work anymore, but go ahead and tell a story."

Marceline had her eyes closed while this banter was going on, breathing deep. "Ah, this is the life!"

"It is, isn't it?" David agreed, putting loving arms around his wife's shoulder and drawing her close to him to plant a tender kiss on her forehead.

"Ah, you guys, cut that out!" Jordan teased, adjusting herself on her chair. "I'm waiting!"

Without making the slightest sound, a silhouette emerged from the darkness. The figure appeared ominous in the illumination of the fire. It was a tall and gangly man, around his early thirties. He didn't say a word, but the hunger in his eyes was unmistakable. His menacing expression made the hair on the back of Jordan's neck rise. The eyes were almost onyx black, intense, and filled with desire. She could tell, even in the dark, that she and her parents were in trouble. Not uttering a word, he leapt in David's direction and picked him up by his collar. A loud crack echoed in the silence of the night when he hurled her father against a tree, David's body slumping to the ground. The man next turned to Marceline, who bolted from her chair in her husband's direction, crying in fear. With ease, the monster caught up with her and grabbed her neck, yanking her back.

"Get away from me! What do you want from us? Do you need money or food? We have it. We could give it all to you. Just leave us alone, please!" Marceline begged, her eyes fixed on David.

"I don't want anything but this," the man responded in a low voice, and it was clear that Marceline was in trouble. He sank his face into her neck and tugged hard.

Jordan felt like she was stuck in a bad dream. The man took her mother's head between his hands, and without any sign of remorse, he twisted her neck until a crack sounded. Her limp body slid to the ground. Marceline made a gurgling sound, but then fell silent.

The man still had his back to her, and Jordan had very little time to react before he turned. She darted out of her chair and charged at the man, willing to kill him with her bare hands if she could. What was he? Why was he doing this to them?

"You are a monster!" she screamed at the man, who pivoted at once to face her. His mouth was smudged with her mother's blood, and Jordan's anger doubled. "I will kill you." Her martial arts training kicked in, and she took a swipe at the man with her fist. She hit nothing but empty air and fell to the ground. The monster moved fast, blurring before her in quick movements that were impossible to follow.

Out of the corner of her eye, she saw her father get to his feet, unsteady, and stagger toward their attacker. His head and face were covered with the blood that dripped down from a huge gash in his head. He grabbed a thick piece of wood from the pile near the fire and pounded their attacker in the head. The monster staggered under the sudden blow but did not lose his footing. Instead, he turned around to face David, his expression reflecting his anger. He picked up David by the throat and lifted him, mocking him.

"You think you can hurt me? You have no idea what you're dealing with," he said in a tone that still sent chills up Jordan's spine.

David was choking to death. Jordan had no time to lose. She grabbed the piece of wood from the ground, and with all her might, she struck the monster in the legs. The man lost his grip on her father, and they both fell to the cold, hard earth. Her father didn't move.

The stranger regained his footing and shot in her direction, moving fast and leaving her no chance to react. All she could register in the next moments was his fangs elongating. Two unbelievable canines flashed at her before he bit her in the neck, just as he'd done to her mother. She felt her veins catching fire when something thick surged into them. Her body convulsed, and every muscle contracted, but his mouth remained latched on her throat. She knew at that very moment that he was sucking the life out of her.

As quickly as he'd arrived to unleash his terror on them, he dropped her on the ground and was gone.

Death was imminent, her breaths coming in irregular gasps. She could hear her broken sobs waning while darkness enveloped her. In the last moments of that gruesome nightmare, she looked into her father's eyes.

"I love you, Jordan." After speaking those last words, he coughed, and blood oozed from his ears and mouth. His strangled breath ebbed away, torturing her final moments with a deafening silence. She'd released a loud, piercing cry before succumbing to her own oblivion.

Jordan flinched at the memories. This was her life now. She was alone and miserable, but it wouldn't be for long. She swore on her parents' memories that she'd find the bastard and make him pay. He'd rot in hell for the way he'd sent her parents to death and sentenced her to this horrific existence. Many questions still haunted her to this day. Why had he let her live if he did not intend to turn her? Why did he leave her if he had? She needed answers. Soon, she hoped to find them.

Shaking away the dark clouds that blanketed her, Jordan got up and dusted invisible lint from her coat. She sighed while she took one last look at the glittering display of lights, then broke into a run, heading back to the place she'd discovered when she followed the group the night before. Her curiosity had been piqued, and she wondered what type of business humans would have with vampires other than as blood donors. She planned to check the entire perimeter of the establishment, mark all exits and entrances, and wait to see if these people would lead her to the beast she sought.

"Pritchard, I think you'll want to see this," Dante called out to his employer through a walkie-talkie, his eyes never leaving the monitor. Alert and focused, he watched while a woman streaked past the gates of their property. Dante positioned each camera to follow her every move, punching buttons with the efficiency for which he had been hired. A burly man in his late thirties, he hadn't seen much action since he took the job. He'd been offered a hefty salary in exchange for his expertise and silence, ending his career with the NYPD. His boss, multi-billionaire Pritchard Tack, strode into the room, his face red from exertion.

Although he was a laid-back type of guy, Pritchard was nowhere near relaxed. His sparkling blue eyes were sharp, and his wide shoulders were tensed. He nodded to Dante, who tapped some keys on the keyboard to

Hunted – The Gates Legacy, Book 1

reveal several shots that had been taken outside the property from different angles.

"Get Cyrus and Lambert in here quick," Pritchard ordered after reviewing the footage.

Dante called over the speaker system while Pritchard continued to track the woman's movement. His brows furrowed, and he wondered aloud. "Who is she, and how did she find us?"

"Sir, you called?" Cyrus asked. He was the heftier of the two large men striding into the room. Everything around them seemed dwarfed by their presence.

Pritchard stood up from his seat next to Dante, an inscrutable expression in his face. He glanced toward his best men, the pride and joy of their little unit. Both were bounty hunters he'd employed many years ago when his life had been threatened. The duo had stayed on his payroll. Their services had been more invaluable than ever since Allison had become sick. The thought of Allison brought with it an onslaught of unbearable pain, but Pritchard repressed his tortured emotions, forcing his mind to shift back to the task at hand.

"Watch this," he said.

Dante flicked a button, and several cameras started playing the different views of the woman prowling outside the property. Cyrus' eyes narrowed, and the veins in his neck tightened. Lambert, the quiet one, pressed his fists together. "Just say the word, boss," he quipped.

"Look at her, the way she moves . . ." Pritchard pointed to one monitor. "See that thing bulging underneath her coat?" The men nodded. "That's a pretty big weapon she's got there. I don't think she's human. You guys better arm yourselves with Dangeran and some sleeping beauties. Ask the big vampire if he wants to make use of his prowess for a good cause."

"Sure thing. Regardless of his answer, Lambert and I are going," Cyrus said.

"If he says no, take several men with you and a net." Pritchard smiled. "And I want her alive, okay?" With those orders, his two most trusted men left the room in a few quick strides, leaving Pritchard to entertain questions about the woman. Could she be a Vampire Council soldier? If so, she'd regret ever stumbling upon them.

The drive to their destination was short. Harrow could tell by the reverberation of the engine and the echo of rubber hitting asphalt that they were moving underground. The sound of enormous metal gates whirring and rollers grinding resonated in the close area that surrounded them, and several vehicles entered before the gates were shut.

Doors opened, and he was yanked from the middle rear passenger seat and hauled to his feet.

"Take them to the I-room," the commander said.

What's an eye-room? Harrow wanted to ask, but he wasn't given the chance. Several hands began shoving him forward, and he marched with the rest of the footsteps toward an unknown destination. The sounds of the city were muted. Nothing but the buzzing of fluorescent lights and the heavy sounds of their footfalls could be heard. The air was clean—sanitized, almost. Although he could discern faint light through the sack that covered his face, he couldn't tell if they were in a hospital or a laboratory.

They walked about one hundred feet, through a set of doors, and down several steps before he was taken inside a room and made to sit on a cold, steel chair. "Wait here," one man commanded.

"Like I could go anywhere," Harrow said. This was taking too damn long. He needed to feed. The longer he had to wait, the more probable it was that things would turn ugly. His lesions were already burning. The blisters would soon follow, and God knew what was next. Harrow had never dared to let his condition get that bad because he was aware that death would not be far behind. He'd seen corpses of vampires, their skin looking like they'd been exposed to the sun, and their flesh rotting, reeking of death, and seeping with purplish liquid. The sight was gruesome enough that he did not want to go there. Ever.

"Don't be a smartass," the vampire next to him said. "You have the balls to talk when you brought this on us."

"What the hell are you talking about?" Harrow bit out.

"You have to ask? Can't you tell you've done enough damage already? Why don't you just shrivel up and die, you pathetic motherfucker!"

"Shut up, you two." The voice of the commander bellowed inside the room. They hadn't heard his footsteps approaching. "I will remove your face covers, and I expect you to behave. I will do the talking, and you guys will listen. Got it?"

Harrow stayed silent, waiting for the other vampire to speak, but the silence stretched unbroken.

"Okay?" the commander repeated.

Harrow forced out his answer through gritted teeth. "Fine." He wasn't combative by nature, but his frustration was simmering, and he could feel his anger rising. If he didn't get blood soon, he'd be happy to introduce the goddamn commander to his fangs.

Before the head cover was removed, he felt metal scuff his ankle and an anklet snapped in place. The same sound came from the other side of the room where his original assailant was, and the vampire's growl filled the room in response. Harrow's hood was lifted, and it took a few moments for his pupils to adjust to the light. He blinked several times, trying to focus his sensitive eyes on his surroundings.

There were about ten brute-sized men positioned around him and the other vampire, including the commander of the group. They were in an oval-shaped, well-lit room with metal chairs and tables. Everything looked like it was standard military issue, and Harrow had a sinking feeling that he'd been captured by a group of renegade humans who might have knowledge of vampires' existence.

Great, just what he needed. More complications to his already fucked-up existence.

The walls were devoid of ornamentation. Instead, cameras were placed in every spot imaginable, all pointed in their direction. Harrow took his time studying his environment before focusing on the commander, who was watching him with an intent stare. He looked nothing like the men with him. His neat blond hair was pressed to his skull, and his crystal blue eyes watched Harrow's movements with calculating intensity. He had a beak-shaped nose and a prominent jaw, giving him more of a GQ appearance than the rogue persona he projected.

"You. What's your name?" the commander asked Harrow.

"Why don't you tell me yours first, since you seem to know what you want from me," he answered. He was still wearing his sunglasses and doubted the man knew he was shooting death glares his way.

"I think it's best for us to see eye-to-eye here," the leader commented before nodding to the man standing on his right. The man took two big steps forward and knocked the sunglasses off Harrow's face.

With the handcuffs still in place, Harrow could only fume and wait to dish out his own brand of hell later.

"Ah, just what I suspected," the commander said at the sight of the whitening irises that glared back at him. He cast a brief glance at the other vampire before he spoke. "My name is Pritchard Tack, and I run this facility." He looked at Harrow and waited for him to give his name. "You wanted a name. Now it's your turn."

"Harrow Gates."

"And you?" Pritchard turned to the big vampire.

"Tor Burns," he replied through clenched teeth.

"It's a pleasure to meet you both," Pritchard said, although his expression didn't look pleased at all. "And this right here is Cyrus," he continued, pointing to a big human with a severe crew cut and tattooed biceps. "Lambert." Pritchard indicated another muscular guy with a flattop and chestnut-colored hair, who glared in the vampires' direction.

Although Pritchard introduced the rest of his men, Harrow stopped paying attention.

"Why have you taken us? What do you want from me?" he demanded, unable to hold back his impatience. His body started quivering, and the wounds burned his skin.

"We have been following you, Harrow. My intel has given me enough information to conclude that you are indeed the host—the Alpha—the producer of this disease we have named *Incomis-Sippanus*.

"It's a mouthful, I know. As we're all aware, it's a lethal disease that is transmitted from vampire to vampire and also has a virulent effect on humans who have been bitten. You can't deny anything, Harrow. We have been following you for some time now. We studied most of your victims and knew that if we ever wanted to find a cure or stop the spread, we'd need you to cooperate with us.

"If you're wondering how this came about, our research has led us to a couple of possible conclusions. The first of those is that you were carrying this dormant disease before your transformation. The gene mutated when your human blood and the vampire poison mixed, and you became the originator of this disease."

Harrow lifted an eyebrow. It sounded ludicrous. He figured he'd infected many people, but he had always thought that the vampire who'd handed him his ticket to hell was the one who had passed on the curse.

Without waiting for any response, Pritchard continued. "Yes, I imagine that you're on sensory overload here," he said in a dry tone.

"Why are you doing this?"

A somber expression flitted across Pritchard's face before he masked it. "My reasons will be given later." He paused and drew in a long breath. "You're probably wondering how this could happen after so many humans have undergone the same process during transformation without the same result, right? Well, they don't carry the same disease that you have. The process began when you started pumping blood back into your system. The oxygen from the influx permeated the diseased cell, bringing it to life and thus ending its quiescent state. The more human blood you drink, the more active the disease becomes. Although blood alleviates the visible damage to your skin such as the burning and blistering, it never quite goes away.

"Now, these manifestations of yours are like AIDS lesions, and the wounds are also very similar to the symptoms of leprosy. Those are the sole commonalities. This is its own disease. We haven't witnessed a vampire dying from the lesions—we don't welcome death here. I realize that the wounds at this stage are painful, and the one respite is through feeding. The fact remains that vampires cannot die except through prolonged exposure to the sun and from the weapons made from Dangeran. Death won't come as easy as you might think. The suffering, though, is cruel enough to make you wish for it. It can drive you insane."

"What's my other option?" Harrow asked. His body had begun to shake, and his need was clear as the light of day—he must feed very soon before he turned into a rampaging maniac. He eyed the humans present and zeroed in on their necks, dying to latch his fangs onto their veins and alleviate his misery.

"There isn't a real second option. We're certain that our first hypothesis is correct." Pritchard chuckled.

Harrow hissed under his breath, unable to control his hunger any longer.

"You need to feed. I know Tor interrupted your dinner. Intel confirms that you have a needle in your pocket. I take it that means you're not advocating the spread of the disease. Am I right?"

Harrow shuddered before nodding. He could feel his strength fading, and there wasn't a damn thing he could do about it. This human, in all his infinite wisdom, should give him his neck and be done with it.

"I know what you're thinking, Harrow," Pritchard said. "I'm not the enemy here—or your dinner. I will take you to a cell for now, where you will be fed donated blood until we can find a cure for your ailment. Neither of you are prisoners here, but until we are certain that you're not a threat to humans, you will not be allowed to move around without restrictions."

Pritchard rose to his feet and beckoned Harrow. "Follow me."

Tor's voice thundered through the room. "What about these damn cuffs on our legs? We're not animals, you know." He was already up on his feet and facing off with Lambert, who was sporting a push dagger of Dangeran material.

"They are trackers, in case you are out there," Lambert motioned with his hand. "We will know how to find you."

"Just like we're dogs, right?" Tor said with distaste.

"Yes, but very *special* dogs," Lambert taunted as he grabbed Tor's elbow and shoved him forward to follow Pritchard and Harrow.

They walked down the long corridor, which led them to a windowless suite. The furnishings were top-notch—lavish, even. There were two king-sized beds, a state-of-the-art sound system sitting next to a giant television, expensive-looking art adorning the wall, and plush carpeting to boot.

"A great dog house." Tor grinned. "This is a definite step up from the slum I call home."

At this point, Harrow was brought to sit on the bed, and his handcuffs were released. He noticed that the human wore gloves as a precaution. He snorted.

"If you open the refrigerator, you'll find blood bags in there. Have a feast, and we'll talk more later. For now, I have something pressing that requires my immediate attention."

With this, Pritchard and his men left the room. The sound of the deadbolt engaging erased all ideas of a possible escape. There was no way out. Harrow and Tor glared at each other, debating whether to get their brawl on or satiate their thirst first.

Somewhere deep in the core of Manhattan, the Vampire Council rested for the break of day. The place they called home was a stone's throw away from the human world, buried under the most populated area in the city. They remained hidden in the very heart of the city whose people everyday walked above their sanctuary. Their hunt continued. The Council wouldn't allow their way of living to be altered by a group of infected derelicts, those deadbeats who tainted their gene pool.

Goran would make sure of this as the peerless head of the Council, which had taken great pride in policing and enforcing the laws in the vampire underworld for centuries. He continued to watch over those who chose to surface and coexist with humans. His position had been granted to him by votes and by birthright, and he loved the control and savored the power.

The Council's millennial existence, even with its close proximity to their human counterparts, was a well-kept secret. Scouts and soldiers mingled with both races to deliver news, gather information, and execute orders. It was better that way. Secrecy, even amongst their own kind, was an integral aspect of preserving their way of living. If they intend to flourish for eternity, their whereabouts must remain a mystery.

Vampires who served the Council were considered privileged and were rumored to be above the law, which was laughable in Goran's opinion. He was the only one above the law. He took pride in the fact that while he ruled, peace would be maintained and rules would be followed. He didn't concern himself about the execution of his orders. His people carried out his bidding. The extent of his punishments had been established centuries ago, and no one had been willing to test him for quite some time, placing him at close to untouchable status.

There was Demetrius, his son. The bastard, who hung on his every word like a lost puppy, was good enough to carry out orders to the letter. Goran's interest laid elsewhere. He was consumed with a new breed of vampires he'd created. This was the one of the few times he'd venture outside the safety of the Council chambers alone. Goran was obsessed with his hunt for a redhead to add to his growing collection of female warriors and lovers. He smirked at the label of "collection." Indeed, they were selected based on the color of their hair. He always had, for as long as he could remember, a fixation on red hair. Every time he looked around and saw a woman with ginger, auburn, reddish, or strawberry locks, his mouth would salivate and his body would begin to quake and quiver. He was driven by the urge to possess them.

Throughout history, redheads were known and believed to possess a fierce temperament. The Scots, who had the largest number of redheaded people per capita, were believed to be far better warriors than most. Historical accounts all agreed that the red tresses were the most feared, loathed, glorified, venerated, and tainted of all. Even in the present day, people with red hair elicited strong, often conflicting emotions—either you loved them or you hated them. For Goran, they were unforgettable. His obsession went deep, to an extent that he couldn't even begin to describe. He put great faith in the myths about these fiery-headed people, believing that where there was smoke, there had to be fire. This fascination led him to theorize that redheads would make the best vampire soldiers, Goran decided to test his theory, and was he ever glad he had.

Now, the best warriors he had were his ginger-haired creations. They were fierce, terrifying, and loyal, but most of all, they were attractive. The psychological effect they had on others remained their crowning glory. Goran often used them as a scare tactic. Vampires who would enter confrontations without hesitation under normal circumstances were scared almost shitless when in the midst of the group of these special fighters.

Not so bad considering he had about more than twenty of them in his harem, ever ready to abide by his every wish, regardless if it be a crazed whim or sexual favor. He had it made. He was a powerful and revered man with a group of the most beautiful warriors at his disposal.

A pounding on the door roused him from his feel-good stupor. He straightened from his desk, where he'd been surfing the Internet for the one that got away. No news was good news, so they said. It had been over a year, and he hadn't seen her. His mind tricks hadn't produced her—*yet*. They all answered when he beckoned them, running to him when he called. Where was she? Did she survive? In hindsight, he shouldn't have left her. He should've taken her when he saw her pass out. Instead, he'd left, salivating over the prospect of calling her to come to him. He was, after all, a libidinal sadist. The thrill of seeing her coming home to him was too much of an enjoyment for him to miss.

Another series of loud knocks sounded, and Goran shut the lid on his laptop with reluctance. "Come in," he hissed.

The knob turned as the door opened with a creak, and the room was bathed at once with light streaming from the hallway. A dark figure walked in, the spitting image of Goran except for the red hair, which had come to him courtesy of his mother Melissa. Goran's son Demetrius possessed the air of invincibility, which was bestowed upon him by birthright. Despite his noble features that could be mistaken as weak rather than fearsome, neither Demetrius nor Goran would hesitate to use force and cruelty, if necessary. Goran was pleased with his ruthless heir, though he'd never admit it and thereby show weakness or favor.

With his father's black eyes, strong and defined jaw, and magnetic personality, the one difference between their physical attributes was the color of their hair. Goran's was the color of midnight, reaching to his waist, its movement often uninhibited. Tall and muscular, Demetrius took a few steady and powerful strides toward Goran's desk. His dark expression was listless, and Goran had an almost precise idea of what was going on inside his son's head—discernment was a useful gift in this existence.

"Father." Demetrius bowed low, his voice a low drawl in the silence of the room.

"Demetrius, what news do you have with you?"

Hesitation and fear rose like the stench of decaying bodies, too obvious to ignore and making Goran scowl with disappointment. To his credit, Demetrius met his gaze, fair and straight.

"We have tracked some resistance in the upstate region, which we subdued and dealt with." There was a slight hesitation. "We lost a few men in the clash. Our weapons were evenly matched. Although our unit was bigger, they were able to flee just before dawn. I had to order everyone to return here. We'll regroup at sundown to hunt them down."

"Do you have any idea what brought about the uprising?" Goran rested his elbows on the desk and leaned forward, studying his son's expression and noticing the slight twitching at the corners his mouth.

"No Father," he answered, shoving a hand inside his jeans pocket.

"I think, before you head out there again, you should get that information first. We cannot afford to lose any more men, unless you're ready to let Hamilton lead the party and work on getting the information for me. You, on the other hand, can have the pleasure of getting more men inducted as soldiers. It's your call."

"I will handle the selection of vampires, Father, and I will let Hamilton find out the cause behind the resistance. Once it's done, I will lead another group to squeeze the motherfuckers out." Demetrius' composure quivered a fraction, and Goran couldn't help but smirk at his son's conviction.

"Do what you think will elicit the best results," he said, his tone dismissive. "Summon your mother, will you?"

With those words, Demetrius took his leave. Goran knew his son wanted more from him, considering their associations were minimal and most often concerning the trivialities of the Council. He recognized his son's conflict and could see the fire in his eyes. Goran would be watching his back, even from his own-blooded son.

Jordan had been sitting for several hours, paying close attention to the unknown establishment. She had monitored the entire area for any signs of life, any movement, but none came. With the sun peeking over the horizon, she made sure that she was well-hidden from the rays that were guaranteed to burn her into oblivion. After mapping out the structure with care, her intuition told her that the two mile, squared facility was packing a punch inside.

Whatever was in there, she bet it would lead her to her creator. Most likely, these humans were cronies of influential vampires, considering their familiarity with the recently captured vampires. She had no idea who'd created her, but her transcontinental travel had taken her to New York, the seat of the Vampire Council she'd heard so much about. She had bumped into many vampires who had led her to believe that she might be closing in on him sometime soon. She was confident that he was in the area and that she would be able to exact her revenge. It was just a matter of time.

Leaning against the wall, she sat down on the cold pavement and waited. What she was waiting for was beyond her. The sun had risen, and its burst of heat and brightness burning at full blast meant she had to wait it out. In the underground tunnel, her instincts told her that she should be expecting an ambush anytime. Jordan unbuttoned her coat and secured her weapon in her hands, ready to pounce at a moment's notice.

Inconsequential associations with another vampire in the past months had led to a productive friendship. Rohnert, her mentor, gave her the best possible weapon and training imaginable. Dangeran was a blade made of metal and likened to the strength and weight of titanium infused with diamond bits. It could cut through a vampire's skin, disabling and making it impossible for the body parts to meld back together. The material was fitted in most weapons, including swords, arrows, knives, throwing stars, and axes. Most important, it worked well with her Kalimetal weapon, which she preferred because of her martial arts background.

Her father had been a strong advocate of self-defense, and he'd made sure she was equipped with knowledge of hand-to-hand combat and how to disable an enemy, whether it was a two-legged human or a four-legged animal that they might encounter during their wilderness expeditions. She had been a martial artist during her high school years, and she had been found to be very adept at using the Eskrima weapons. With the help of Rohnert, her very own weapon had been made, and then they'd parted ways with hopes of Jordan finding the man who had ended the lives of her parents. She shielded her mind from thinking about him. Instead, she focused on the matter at hand.

Jordan knew she was being watched, though there were no cameras showing and no covert, hidden gadgets stood in place to back her theory.

She bounced off the walls, hoping she could expose any concealed device, but none was revealed. These people were more ingenious than she had given them credit for being.

A faint scratching noise sounded all around her, bringing her back to her feet, her hands tightening on her weapons. When she darted her eyes across the expanse of the tunnel leading to the massive metal gates, there were no signs of movement anywhere, nothing out of the ordinary.

She pointed her nose up to catch a whiff of any scent that would offer her any leads to go by. The hair on the back of her neck began rising, a confirmation that something was about to happen. But where? She moved a few steps, like a lion on a prowl honing in on its prey. She had nothing. She couldn't see anything. Then whirring noises sounded, followed by clapping like thunder, and before she could react, the ceiling opened up above her and a net came down to trap her where she stood.

The walls then turned into something from a cartoon, opening in several places at once. Men carrying every imaginable weapon came out and ran toward her. Jordan tried to launch her own weapon, but was struck by darts in several places on her body. The effect was instantaneous. She knew she'd been shot with a drug, one that was potent enough to put her to sleep. Could it be strong enough to kill her? Those were her last thoughts before her mind crossed an invisible line of blackened haze.

Hours later, Jordan's eyes fluttered open, and she found herself tied to a chair, which was bolted to the floor. *Smart people!* She smirked as she tried to squirm free from the bindings. She felt a metal cuff around her ankle when she tried to kick around. Tracking device, perhaps?

"Let me go!" she yelled, her voice sounding hoarse and foreign to her ears. It had been a while since she'd last spoken, since she hadn't had anyone to talk to, preferring a solitary existence. She kicked and screamed, trying to draw attention to herself in the stark white, empty room. Except for the chair she was sitting on, another chair, and small table, the place was quite bare. The cameras mounted on the wall were pointing in her direction. She would've flicked her middle finger at them if she could have as her anger started rising in waves.

The doors abruptly opened, and several men entered the room. Jordan recognized one of them as the same guy who had held the shotgun in the subway station, as well as the man who had commanded the abduction of the two vampires. She inhaled the air, which stunk of human sweat and blood. The thought of being in the midst of humans intent on bringing her down infuriated her. It wasn't supposed to be this way. She had to get out of there and find *him*.

"Well, well . . . our sleeping beauty has awakened," the man said.

Jordan sized up the man, and it was obvious that he was doing the same thing. She held his gaze in defiance, baring her fangs and hissing. The man appeared undeterred as he stood in front of her. One kick and his body would be laminated on the wall. It wasn't a bad idea, but her curiosity led her to restrain herself. She'd kill him after she got her questions answered.

"If you are thinking of harming me, you'd better shut down the idea, girly. Even if you kill me, you're not going anywhere. I don't think you'd like to die with your skin fizzling before your eyes and your guts melting like a marshmallow on fire. So it would be in your best interest to can whatever scheme is brewing inside your head so we can talk."

Jordan shot the man a murderous glare and kept trying to squirm out of the tight bindings on her wrists. It wasn't going to be easy with half a dozen men surrounding her, all armed with darts and lethal blades. She knew when to concede and when to challenge an opponent. This wasn't the time to push her luck.

"What do you want from me?" Jordan challenged, feeling her fangs elongate and press hard against her bottom lip.

"I have the same question for you. What do you want from me? Why are you snooping around here?"

"I'm looking for someone," she answered.

"Do you think we have him here?" The cryptic reply gave nothing away. He must have known that it was always better to answer a question with another question to keep your opponent confused.

"No, you're human. I have no business with you," she rasped out. Glancing at the men surrounding her, she singled out one who was beginning to irk her. He was big, brawny, and decorated with extensive ear piercings. Jordan threw an if-looks-could-kill glare in his direction.

"Then I guess we need to talk. Tell me about yourself."

Jordan huffed, feeling like a caged lion. A question-and-answer session wasn't what she'd expected. If there was anyone who would do the interrogating, it was going to be her. This was wrong on all levels. She was on the wrong side of the table.

"I don't have to talk to you or to anyone," she answered in a challenging tone.

"So be it. You will be kept here until you are ready to talk."

After gorging himself on several bags of blood, courtesy their jailer-slash-benefactor, Harrow slumped on the comfortable bed. It was so comfortable, in fact, that he felt his body begin to relax, his once-taut muscles loosening despite his present dilemma. The feeding had done wonders for him. The burning sensation started receding, and the throbbing stopped.

He had no idea where he was or if he'd ever see the outside world again. The man who took him and Tor sounded like he knew what he was doing, or at least what he was looking for.

Harrow wondered what the personal reason was behind Pritchard's quest to find a cure. What was in it for the human? The vampires had been told they weren't prisoners since they hadn't showed any aggression toward the humans when their safety was compromised. Harrow gave a hearty laugh at the thought, causing Tor to scowl at him. He was a theater actor, for Christ's sake, with loving parents and two sisters who missed him. He didn't possess a mean bone in his body. He wasn't aggressive by nature, although an immeasurable anger had begun to seep in after his transformation, when he'd realized just what he'd become and the life he was now tied to.

He scowled back at Tor. The vampire sat on one of the recliners, looking like he'd just won a million dollars. It was clear that he was enjoying the freebies and the sweet set-up. His feet were up, an action movie was playing on the television set, and a glass of blood waited for him on the little table next to his recliner.

Tor was big. At least a head taller than Harrow with sharp eyes in the darkest shade of purplish-red, his arms and legs were thick and massive. He carried himself with an air of confidence—in actuality, it seemed like misplaced arrogance. The deep lines in his face showed the strain of past hard labor. His brown hair was a tangled mess of dreadlocks, mangy and in bad need of a shower. Everything about him showed his toughness and grit.

He edged his body over to lean on the headboard and wondered why Tor had been after him. It wasn't because he was infected. There were no visible signs of wounds on his skin. His eyes didn't manifest the signs of the infection. Yet he'd said he wanted to kill Harrow for what he'd brought upon them. Who had he been talking about? Not just himself.

Tor shifted his attention to Harrow and caught him staring. His features darkened, and his irritation was obvious from across the room as he pounded his fist on the table, sending his glass clattering to the floor.

"What are you staring at, freak?" he asked, baring his fangs.

Harrow had been called many names—asshole, son of a bitch, and motherfucker—but this was something new. Tor was right in a way, Harrow had to acknowledge, but the accuracy of the label didn't make it any easier to hear out loud.

"I'm looking at you, *moocher*!" Harrow stressed the word and wasn't surprised in the least bit when the vampire hurled himself at him in an instant. With his now-fed body, Harrow felt light on his feet and was able to dodge away in time for Tor to hit the headboard, splitting the wood in half. Tor pivoted and spotted Harrow on the other side of the room leaning on the wall.

"You'll regret you said that," Tor threatened and lunged at Harrow again.

"Make me." Harrow laughed, jumping out of the way as Tor barreled into the wall, bouncing off the concrete material and falling to the floor. "You're making it so easy for me, my man."

"Not anymore." Tor got off the floor in a flash and plowed in his direction, getting his hands clamped around Harrow's neck. Yanking him closer, Tor breathed down into his face. Harrow twisted his body to squirm out of the firm grasp and jabbed an elbow into Tor's stomach, and the vampire struggled with the blast of pain.

A few hours ago, Harrow had been weak and unable to fight back, but now the tables had turned—it was his time to kick some vampire butt. To send his message loud and clear, Harrow kicked Tor away from him so hard that the vampire ended up ass-planted against the wall.

"Don't write me off yet, big guy. You were able to push me around earlier just because I hadn't fed." Harrow laughed.

Tor seemed to think for a moment before he got up, reaching to palm his axe and finding the holster empty.

"You don't deserve to exist," he said, and Harrow expected another outburst. Instead, Tor sat down on the sofa facing the television and stared at it.

"I thought about that, too, but until I find a cure, I think I'll try to survive a little longer," Harrow answered. He knew now more than ever that he needed to help find a cure. More important, he needed a method to stop the symptoms. If Pritchard's theory was indeed correct that Harrow started it all, then by all means, he owed the people he'd infected a fighting chance to exist. They deserved a chance to survive without the Vampire Council murdering them as if they were parasites without living privileges.

"You were so reckless in spreading this disease. You infected many, God knows how many . . ." Tor's accusation hung in the air, and Harrow's shoulders sagged in defeat.

"Tell me something I don't know."

"You have no right to live if you condemn others to this way of life."

"You're not infected. Why are you so adamant about getting rid of me?" Harrow shifted the conversation to get his answers. He walked to the sofa where Tor was seated, daring to sit closer to the volatile vampire.

"You infected a friend of mine . . . well, indirectly."

Tor scooted as far as possible away from Harrow, continuing to show how hateful and ignorant he was. But then again, Harrow had no real proof that he was contagious through direct contact. His lesions didn't secrete liquid, and he'd kept his arms and body well-covered. He had been cautious and hid most of the wounds from plain sight, avoiding any kind of skin-to-skin contact.

Harrow was thankful that his face showed nothing more than a few unpleasant scars now. The lesions across his body, though hideous, were quite dry and varied in form. Some were scaly, others were warty-looking, and some were clustered together. But make no mistake, these wounds caused terrible pain, often driving the afflicted to insanity. The pain could be made bearable with the intake of blood—the single known therapy to alleviate the torture.

"I know you won't believe me, but the moment I realized I was spreading this around, I started to substitute using needles for my fangs," Harrow commented in a matter-of-fact tone. In truth, he didn't care if the vampire believed him. It still boiled down to needing to find the cure.

"I don't know—"

A loud pounding next door stopped Tor from finishing his sentence. The two looked at each other, bolted to their feet, and raced to the wall from where the sound had come. They pressed their ears against its surface to listen. The walls were thick, but their vampire hearing enabled them to catch a few words from an enraged woman, who was screaming and hammering the door.

They both made out a few words. *Let out, Idiots, not supposed be here* were some of the more discernible ones. Harrow listened close, trying to decipher the voice to see if it was someone he'd come across in the past.

He was good at remembering voices. Since his eyesight had its ups and downs, his hearing had become enhanced to make up for his decreased vision. But this one was new. Was she *human*? He couldn't tell, but the likelihood wasn't great, considering the powerful and continuous pounding he was listening to. Humans tend to tire much sooner than vampires, who had infinite energy if they were well-fed.

Harrow had the sudden urge to meet the woman next door—he felt it in his bones. He wanted to see the owner of the distinct voice, the one who sounded like she was ready to take on any dumbass who crossed her path.

Pritchard delivered a soft knock to the closed door next to his own bedroom. The home he'd built within the underground facility was sufficient enough for him and Allison for the time being. It had nothing on their Fifth Avenue penthouse or their mansion upstate, but it would do until they found . . . It was much too painful to think about. Before he could land his knuckles on the door knocking second time, a soft voice called for him to enter.

"Ally?" he said as soon as he walked in the door. As usual, the curtains were drawn, not that there was anything outside the windows worth looking at except endless concrete murals. On a whim, he had ordered several artists to paint different city scenes, including Central Park and tall buildings. The paintings were good enough to fool—well, no one, really. He had just wanted her to feel more "normal" within these walls.

"I'm here, Dad," Allison answered from the darkest corner of the room, where she sat on the gleaming Calamander wood with an open book on her lap. Pritchard's heart ached as he walked over to his daughter.

Looking at Allison brought back painful memories of his dead wife, Cassie. Along with Allison, she had been bitten by a vampire, and an infected one at that. This two-for-one deal had resulted in a lifetime of suffering for them all. Allison, once as much a kindred spirit to him as her mother had been, had retreated into the darkness upon realizing her eternal death sentence.

Cassie, instead of fighting to survive, had opted to take her life and end her suffering. A diseased life was better than no life at all, Pritchard reasoned with himself time and time again. He missed his wife terribly and would have done anything to bring her back. But he'd be damned if he'd let anything take his daughter away from him, too. So he'd put together the best team of doctors, scientists, and soldiers. No matter what their character, he was willing to hire even the shadiest people if he deemed them vital to help find a cure that money could buy.

Allison reminded him of Cassie, except for the color of her hair, which she'd gotten from him. Otherwise, she was a carbon copy of her mother, her svelte figure carried with the grace of a ballet dancer. The term *beautiful* wouldn't even do her justice, from the oval-shaped face and blush-colored lips to her small but well-proportioned nose. Her blonde hair crowned her head like the princess that she was to him. She had been an aspiring actress in her last year at NYU when tragedy struck. At twenty-two, Allison's future had been promising indeed, not solely based on her exemplary grades, but also because of the business she was going to inherit. He would do anything in his power to keep her alive and happy, even if he had to sell his soul to the devil. This was his vow to himself and to his wife.

Allison looked up at him with her doleful damaged eyes he couldn't quite meet. Her gaunt face told him she was ready to let go and give up, but he wouldn't. He just couldn't.

"Sugar, how are you this morning?" he asked and settled himself next to his daughter. Crossing his legs at the ankle, he leaned against the wall before placing his arm around her shoulder. He felt her shrink from his touch, recoiling not because she loathed him, but out of fear—fear of infecting him with her terrible disease. It broke his heart, because he missed her so much. He missed his once-vibrant daughter, so full of life and promise. He tightened his arms around her and pulled her to his chest. She might be a vampire, a creature of darkness, but she was still his baby girl.

He felt her sigh against his chest, relaxing after a few moments. "I'm fine, Daddy," she said, a clear attempt to reassure him.

"What are you reading?" he asked, running his fingers through her hair and caressing her as he always had.

"It's, um, *A Heart is a Lonely Hunter.*"

"Ah, I've heard about that. Such a poignant story, underrated almost," he whispered.

"Yeah, I'm almost done with it."

"Does that mean you need more books?" He smiled. She was a voracious reader, just like her mother. Reading was a habit Cassie had instilled in Allison even before she could recite her alphabet. It had been a ritual both mother and daughter had enjoyed each night. They would read to each other or just keep each other company while they enriched their minds and feasted their eyes with any material they could get their hands on. Books had been Allison's companion back in the bleak days that had followed her mother's death. It had been her lifeline in the lonesome existence into which she'd been thrust.

"Yeah, is it okay if I buy some more?" she asked, a shy smile breaking the corner of her mouth and spreading a luminous glow across her face that warmed his heart.

"You have a card. Charge away, my princess, but promise you'll read to me one of these days."

"Of course, you know where to find me." She laughed.

"That's right," he agreed.

Pritchard did a quick survey of her room and how she'd decorated it. Bookcases filled with all the material she and her mother had collected over the years lined the walls. It gave one the impression of being in the library rather than a bedroom. Without needing to sleep as much as humans did, Allison spent most of her time reading books, be it in print or an electronic version. She'd decided to cut her ties to the outside world and was intent on keeping to herself, closeted inside her room as much as possible.

Pritchard often encouraged her to mingle with the other people in their underground residence, but she would rather spend her time cooped up in her room, exploring the outside world through the World Wide Web.

"Dad, I heard a commotion earlier. What was that about?"

Pritchard had been giving her regular updates on their efforts in the experimentation laboratory, offering her any source of hope he thought could keep her going. She had shown very little interest, though Allison had always thanked him for keeping her safe at all times.

"I believe we have in our midst the vampire who started it all."

"You do?"

A gleam of interest sparkled in her eyes. At last, he'd gotten a positive reaction after almost a year of disinterest and detachment. This was a welcome development. Something told him that everything would be all right now, and he believed it. He had to—not just for himself, but also for Allison.

Harrow and Tor's heads were still pressed flat against the wall when they heard the bolt on their door disengage. Lambert strode in a few seconds later. He stood in the middle of the room and stared at the two vampires. Instead of paying attention to their visitor, their whole and undivided attention was claimed by the furious pounding coming from the room next door.

"Didn't your parents teach you that eavesdropping is rude?" Lambert mocked.

"For lack of anything better to do in this dog house, we resorted to another form of entertainment," Tor fired back. He crossed the room with lithe movements, coming close enough to Lambert to kiss. However, Lambert's demeanor remained one of amused detachment. They sized each other up, human to vampire, but Harrow knew the man was armed and dangerous. If Tor tried to attack, he'd have to fight the human with his bare hands, and Lambert would retaliate with everything he had. The balance of power was lopsided for sure, which provided enough motivation for Tor to hold his temper. He continued staring at the equally muscular man who stood unwavering face-to-face with him.

"Be careful, Tor, you might find yourself attracted to me," Lambert chided. A smirk marked his weathered and grungy face.

"Don't bet on it, Romeo," Tor retorted, his voice even.

Harrow had continued listening to the hammering next door. The woman was relentless. Within the confines of their cell, there was nothing better to do anyway. However, the bickering between Tor and Lambert now managed to claim his attention, and he moved away from the wall to stand between the two.

"What's going on here? What's with the visit? Ready to take us to Disneyland?"

"Not yet. Maybe soon, if you get an A for good behavior." Lambert chuckled.

"Then it'll be sooner rather than later." Harrow snickered. "I want to talk to Pritchard. Be a good boy and fetch him for me."

Lambert's eyes flickered, and he laughed, a good-natured laugh that filled the room. "I like you already. You have a sense of humor, Harrow. You'll last longer with that attitude."

"Ah, I'll keep that in mind." Harrow bowed in a mocking fashion before moving over to the sofa and flicking through the channels on the television with the remote. Pictures flashed across the screen.

"Let's take a walk," Lambert said to Tor.

"Do we get to hold hands?" Tor mocked.

"If you don't attempt anything foolish, you'll be able to do so." Lambert walked to the door and turned when Tor didn't follow him. "What are you waiting for?"

"Why do I feel like something nasty is going to come out of this walk?" Tor sounded doubtful, but he walked straight to the door without a backward glance at Harrow.

"You're too pessimistic," Harrow heard Lambert say before the door closed and the bolts locked into place.

"It's going to be a goddamn long day," Harrow muttered to himself. He leaned on the leather sofa and settled on an action movie, seeing, but not really watching.

The pounding from the other room subsided. Wondering what the woman's story was, Harrow walked to the wall closest to the source of the noise and pressed his ear against the bare wall once more. The thick walls didn't offer him much, just a rapid heartbeat. Definitely a vampire, he concluded.

"Hey, anyone in there?" he shouted to the wall before turning his head to listen.

He heard a snort from the other side, but nothing else followed. He knew he had to try again. "That was not an answer," he said out loud.

He heard a snigger this time.

"Are you here against your will?" Harrow went for another tactic. Since he had been taken against his will, that similarity would place them in the same boat, although he didn't consider being offered refuge imprisonment. In truth, this sounded more like a beneficial arrangement for him, for now.

He waited for an answer. Just when he thought he wasn't going to get one, he started walking back to the sofa when he heard a faint answer.

"Yes."

"What's your story?" he asked as he walked back and pressed his face against the wall. He cupped his mouth with both hands to be heard better, but he doubted it would be a problem. She'd hear him just fine.

"I don't talk to people I don't know," the woman responded.

Fair enough, Harrow thought. Let's engage her in a little conversation. There was nothing else to do in this goddamn place anyway except watch TV. Might as well pass the time in a fruitful conversation.

"My name's Harrow—Harrow Gates. I was captured yesterday in the subway. I was turned about fifty years ago." Safe information to begin with, Harrow thought. It sounded like eons since he had been introduced to the dark world of vampires.

It had happened one night after one of the biggest successes as a theater actor. He had been given a stout part in a musical, which showcased his talent for music and singing. The opening night was packed, and at the curtain call, his name had been chanted for the first time in his career. When he stepped forward to bow, the entire auditorium had risen to their feet to give him a standing ovation.

This was every actor's dream, and his was just beginning. After an impromptu celebration at a nightclub with his peers, he'd set out on the long walk to the subway. The temperature had dropped that night, and he remembered hurrying in the direction of the station, anxious to arrive home.

Home was in Brooklyn, where he'd been born and raised. Although he'd maintained constant contact with his aging parents and older siblings, he'd wanted to pursue his dreams in acting. He had dropped out of college, a step his parents had frowned upon, and then joined a touring classical repertory theater. They'd toured smaller cities, towns, and rural communities of America. The main goal was to reach the thousands of people who had few opportunities to experience live professional theater. Harrow considered this a wise step toward learning the ropes of the theater business before he went for the big time. Broadway had always been a big marquee in his mind. He hadn't discussed his plan with the family. His father in particular had seen acting as a trivial passion and not a means of livelihood that would allow him to feed his own family in the future.

Harrow had known that he was on his own with this venture, and he had done whatever he could to attain his goals. However, in common with the many other struggling actors out there, the best roles were always given to better actors. "Always the best man but never the groom" was a running joke with his little group of theater friends.

On a darkened patch of his route to the subway, a man had appeared out of nowhere, blocking his way. Harrow had tried to step away from the vagrant to continue on his way, but the man had grabbed him by the shoulders and hurled him to the ground. He'd skidded about fifteen feet before his movement was brought to an abrupt halt when his body smashed into a lamppost.

Harrow remembered seeing stars, followed by a momentary blackout. He'd tried to get up but the pain had been excruciating, blood was oozing from a cut in his head. He had fallen back to the ground, only to be picked up by the man he was sure would end his life.

Sneering at him, the man said, "My parents told me to never play with my food, but I enjoy it too much." These were the last words uttered before the man sank his teeth into Harrow's throat, thereby ending his human life and handing him a new beginning.

This had been just the beginning of the darkness, an eternity of damned existence, and unending pain.

He remembered the torture of his transformation—the anguish burning in his gut, in his veins, and everywhere. Following the pain of what had been done to him, there were long moments of madness. It had been sheer torture. The stranger had leered at him before leaving him to die on the cold, hard pavement. He'd found himself being hurled into a stretch of oblivion, then yanked back and thrust into another round of torturous pain that made him think his insides were melting. It had been an inferno of agony.

The searing pain continued until the sun began to rise, and a new brand of pain had him scrambling for cover. That was the moment when it dawned on him that the sun would not be a part of his existence again. From that day on, he'd moved and lived in obscurity. He was no longer a part of the human race, but a meager child of the shadows, taking cover when he should have been living. When the first wave of gnawing hunger hit him, he knew the inevitable would happen and he'd have to take a life in order to survive.

Hunger listened to no reason—it didn't obey logic, but operated on instinct alone. He had taken down his first victim, and to this day, he could still remember the fear and self-loathing that had followed. He had taken a life to serve his own dark purpose—a purpose he knew would lead to more death, anguish, and pain. The blood of his victim's life had not only satiated him, but it also marked the first manifestation of the hell-bound pain he would experience from that moment on. The first blistering lesions appeared, and the more he picked at them, the more they grew and spread across his body. The burning continued until he fed again, and the more he did, the less visible their appearance was.

The vicious cycle continued, and the more lives he'd taken, the better he felt about himself. After years of such existence, it dawned on him that in addition to turning his victims, he was also infecting them. Many in turn hunted him down, marking him for dead—or deader. He developed a great sense of preservation and had a gift for evasion, as well as Hermes-infused speed. This was his lone means of survival. Within a few years, the Vampire Council was hot on his trail and his exposure had been cut to a minimum. He hid all the time, trusting no one and talking to no one unless necessary, and his feeding became less frequent, which often left him emaciated and weak.

The solitude gnawed at him hard. He had gone to visit his family several times over the course of the following years and had witnessed firsthand the sorrow in their faces when they thought they'd lost him. It had been painful to watch his parents from the shadows and see how their hearts had been broken by the mystery of what had become of their son. Soon after, they'd passed away, and Harrow had felt loneliness like a permanent knife speared in his heart.

He was indeed a freak, as he'd been branded by Tor, but not for the reason Tor had concluded. Harrow was a vampire with a conscience, a disease, and a shaky future ahead of him. He was fucked—as fucked as he could get.

"Jordan, just Jordan." The woman's voice ruptured the bubble of tortured memory in which Harrow had been floating.

He blinked his eyes and tried to rein in his emotions. His eyes refocused, but the blurred fragments didn't improve. This was one sick effect of the Incom-whatever scientific bullshit Pritchard called his disease. His once-sparkling blue eyes were now a murky gray with a whitish tint around the edges. He could still see through them, but his peripheral vision was his best bet, and he had to wear sunglasses to avoid detection.

"Just Jordan, that's an unusual name," he said and smiled.

"You asked for me?" Melissa glided into Goran's bedroom in her usual ethereal fashion. Wrapped in the finest silk, she wore a gown cut in the style he favored—this time, in a lavender tint. Melissa stopped short when she reached his bed. Her eyes did not even roam the room, but zeroed in on where he and Stephania were going at it. "Goran, I'm here," she announced in a don't-fuck-with-me-now tone.

Goran didn't turn his head to look at her. Instead, he spread his bare upper body under the satin sheets and lolled his head to the side. The woman underneath the sheet giggled and surfaced after a few moments. "Leave us." Goran gave a dismissive gesture with his hand, and the woman scampered out of the room with her clothes in her arms. He patted the now-empty space next to him. "Come, my lady. Tell me about your trip."

Melissa rolled her eyes, conscious of what a big sucker she was, but did as she was told.

Peering at her, Goran pulled her by the waist. "Let me look at you." He tipped her chin with his fingers. "What's going on, Melissa?"

"Nothing is going on," she answered. Goran knew how Melissa felt about his women, his *many* women, and how he preferred them. Nevertheless, she was also aware that she was his first mate, the first female who gave him an heir, a son destined to follow in his footsteps.

Goran fingered the material of her gown, rubbing it and feeling the richness of the fiber as well as the flesh underneath it. She was a perfect vampire and a beautiful woman with beguiling and regal features, feminine on the outside, but as fiery as her red hair on the inside. Her hair was her best feature, just like the others. Melissa was a fine woman, and the very first time he'd laid eyes on her, Goran had known she was the leader he'd needed for his army. He sired their firstborn, and once the baby was delivered, he changed her, sealed and ready to do his bidding.

Melissa arched her back, her flesh aching to meet his touch—the one touch guaranteed to send her emotions reeling with heated passion and shoving them in a confused turmoil of desire.

"Tell me, how is the mother and the baby?" Goran asked, knowing Melissa would give him everything he wanted, including the joyful news that he fathered yet another bastard. "Are they ready for me?"

Sleep was overrated. If only he could summon sleep to take him away to dreamland, to a place where thinking was needless. Harrow would go there in a heartbeat. He didn't need it as much as he wanted it. Sleep and the welcome refuge it represented were what appealed to him.

Harrow was growing restless. It had been several hours since the hulking human invited Tor out for a walk and since *Just Jordan* had given him her name. He'd been left to his own devices with nothing but a remote control to bridge the gap between restlessness and significance. As much as he welcomed the respite and shelter of the facility, Harrow realized he wasn't in any position to make demands, yet he needed to see a justifiable reason for being there.

Reflection on a former life no longer available to him never failed to bring back memories of his rather happy childhood, when an undeterred stretch of time provided him countless hours to dream of what he wanted to be and what he wanted out of life. Thoughts of a loving household filled with happy times made him want to turn back the hands of time, to erase the horror of his change and the despair that shadowed him wherever he went. Was it too much to ask for a rewind? To get things back to the way they used to be?

Nowadays, the single remarkable aspect of his life was that he'd been able to survive to see another day, feeding and keeping the frightful disease at bay. Being a vampire came with a lot of understandable surprises, in particular for someone who was hunted by the rest. So far, all he'd seen in his fifty or so years of existence was nothing but evasion, the fight for survival, and violence.

This was the one promise each new day held for him—the promise of more attempts on his life and vengeful acts against him brought about by his direct participation in the disease's transmission.

A knock on the door roused him from his self-induced stupor. Harrow stood up, but didn't proceed to open the door. He'd been locked in, and the door was controlled from an unknown location.

After a few seconds, the bolt on the door disengaged and Pritchard walked in. The human looked like he'd had a good day. Well-groomed and sporting expensive leathers from head to toe, he seemed like a man on a mission. Pritchard reached inside his leather jacket, produced a sunglasses case, and tossed it in Harrow's direction. He caught it with no problem.

"What's this?" Harrow inspected the black case before opening it.

"I took the liberty of getting rid of your crappy sunglasses. That's a replacement. If you're going to be working with me, it's good to do it in style," Pritchard explained.

Harrow took out black Oakleys with slim temple arms. The lenses were dark, although that didn't matter to him as long as they hid his eyes well enough. He could see very well in the dark, if the blurry patches in the middle would clear out. The dark lenses were intended to conceal the color of his eyes, which were a dead giveaway of an infected person. Trying them on for size, he slipped the sunglasses on his face and was pleased to find them snug and comfortable.

"Thanks," he muttered. "Working with you? Please explain that part."

Pritchard just nodded, but he seemed pleased. "Follow me," he said.

Once outside the hallway, there were countless doors that resembled the quarters that Harrow and Tor had been assigned. The long hallway stretched at least as long as a football field, bisected by another hallway at the end. Each door was made of a strong, steel-like material. They were identical, massive, and foreboding. There were no significant markings except for numbers like those in a hotel hallway. Harrow noted that each number had a corresponding Braille translation. He also took note that his room number was number fifty-eight and that the female vampire was being held in number sixty. Their rooms were almost at the end of the corridor.

Walking side-by-side, they proceeded toward the stretch of concrete flooring and fortified walls.

"We are on the third level of this underground facility. This is where employees and guests reside." There was a glint in Pritchard's eyes when he said the word guests. "There are more than one hundred rooms on this floor alone. Every room has the same floor plan and same accommodations. There are about fifteen rooms similar to yours. Human rooms sleep three, while vampire lodgings can hold four or more, for obvious reasons."

Harrow nodded. "Do you have a lot of *guests* here?" Harrow asked, thinking of *Just Jordan*.

"We have ones who are infected, like you. They began as reluctant guests but warmed up to the idea of working with us in exchange for the promise of a cure. They are first assigned to rooms just like yours with bolted doors until we know they don't pose any danger to others. We hate to think of this place as a prison, because it is not. We take safety seriously here," Pritchard said.

"Humans who work for us are free to go outside on their days off, which are once every month. We have several infectious disease experts, a resident doctor, kitchen personnel, and maids, and the rest are all security personnel, who we've dubbed 'freedom fighters.' "

They reached the end of the hallway, where the stairwell and the elevator were located. "Let's take this one." Pritchard pointed to the elevator, which opened with a punch of a button. They walked in, and Harrow noticed that there were mirrors all around them. For the first time in a very long while, he saw his image and what he had turned into.

Pritchard remained silent during the short ride to the second level while Harrow took a good look at himself through the dark lenses of his sunglasses. The dirty tangle of his blond hair was in complete disarray, hidden beneath the hood of his filthy sweatshirt. His skin had a white pallor, and the tip of his fangs peeked through his closed pinkish lips.

"A fresh set of clothes will be waiting for you when we get back," Pritchard said as soon as they walked off the elevator. "This floor is where most of the work is done." Just like the third level, the entire area was a maze of hallways and doors. A few people could be spotted walking in and out of rooms.

They began walking and stopped at the first door to their left. Pritchard punched a number on the keypad by the door, and it swung open. Pritchard walked in, and Harrow followed close behind. Several people looked up from their workstations the moment the pair appeared.

"This is the laboratory, where specimens are stored and worked on. That man right there"—Pritchard pointed to a balding and aging man with thick glasses who was sitting at a table in the middle of the room—"is our disease specialist. He has been working with us since day one."

"Hello, Mr. Tack," the bespectacled man greeted Pritchard.

"Hey, Leroy. How's it going?" Pritchard nodded.

"It's going," the man named Leroy answered and got on his feet to walk toward them. "We're testing some samples, but I'm afraid we're still hitting dead ends."

Pritchard's lips thinned before he responded, "Okay, we'll keep working on it, right?"

"But of course. We won't stop, Mr. Tack," the other man replied with confidence.

"How many times have I told you to call me Pritchard, Leroy?"

"I'm a creature of habit, I guess." Leroy smiled and peered at Harrow, his bushy eyebrows rising above the rim of his glasses. "And who do we have here?"

"This is Harrow Gates, Leroy. Harrow, this talented man here is our very own mad scientist, Dr. Leroy Marauder," Pritchard said by way of introduction, which seemed to please the old man.

Harrow nodded and slipped his hands inside his jean pockets. If Leroy recognized the refusal to shake hands as a sign that the vampire was infected, he didn't show it.

"It's nice to meet you, Mr. Gates."

"You can ask Leroy anything you want, and I'm one hundred percent sure he'll have some sort of answer he can give you." Pritchard patted the man, who seemed rather pleased with his statement, on the back.

"Anything you want to know," Leroy echoed.

"Thanks."

No doubt, Harrow would be paying the mad scientist a visit soon. All these years, he'd been dying for answers. There was no way he'd waste this opportunity to get some.

"Well, don't let us keep you from your work, Leroy. We'll be out of your hair soon," Pritchard said.

As the doctor moved away, Harrow stayed in his spot and glanced around the room. It was a typical medical and research laboratory, with modern equipment he hadn't seen before. Despite the enclosed space, there was ample lighting, bright enough to light a stadium. The room was airy and sterile, with a faint scent of ammonia. Stainless steel countertops lined the opposite walls, as well as graphs, charts, and chalkboards. Computer workstations took the spaces at the end of the room, where the steady sound of a printer buzzed. Several machines groaned on another side of the room where tests were in progress.

"Shall we?"

Pritchard was already at the door when Harrow caught up with him. About the same height, both men carried themselves with a purposeful gait as they walked into each room. Pritchard showed Harrow the I-room, which was the interrogation room where they had been taken yesterday.

"I-room?" Harrow couldn't remember the name of the disease Pritchard had mentioned. All he could remember was a mouthful of words.

"Incomis-Sippanus. It's the name we termed your mutated disease. Since its discovery, we named it based on what we thought had caused it and how fast it spread. It is a name Leroy coined." Pritchard laughed. "Told you he's mad."

Harrow blinked at the terminology that was being thrown at him. He was a goddamn theater actor who had no knowledge of medical terms. The few things he could remember were immunization from his childhood, as well as common colds and occasional bouts of the flu. Other than that, it was all Greek to him.

As if Pritchard had read his mind, he said, "Yeah, it's all Greek to me, too," and chuckled.

After they had visited a training room that was filled with different gym equipment such as treadmills, elliptical machines, weight machines, and stationary bicycles, they checked out an adjoining room that was dedicated to boxing and martial arts training.

Then there was the shooting range, available for any weapons there were. This was the place Harrow was most interested in. Most of the fights he'd been in in the past had involved fighting with his bare hands and grappling. He had no idea how to handle a weapon because he'd never seen the need to learn once he became a vampire. Another area they visited was the weapons room, which held innumerable armaments and tools for every imaginable offensive tactic and fighting strategy. Rows of cabinets were filled with guns, rifles, knives, axes, swords, throwing stars, nunchakus, shakras, bows, and daggers.

This was an area where Harrow could imagine himself. Times were changing, and he knew the Vampire Council would stop at nothing to find him and others. The sooner he learned how to fight back, the better his chances were of surviving long-term.

Their next stop over was the security room. This was where Dante, the security expert, was introduced to Harrow. The room boasted a wall-to-wall television, camera monitors, and high-tech computer system. Dante glanced at Harrow before returning his attention to the monitors that surrounded him. Several people manned the cameras and monitors while tapping at the keyboards with utmost efficiency. Continued clicking and ticking noises sounded as Harrow and Pritchard stood in the middle of the room, observing every camera angle and the area segments each displayed.

Several big monitors occupied the middle of the room, which was dedicated to the exterior of the underground facility. Every angle was covered. Every subject, corner, and section was being monitored.

Harrow checked each monitor as fast as he could manage, zipping through the pictures at the angle from which his vision was clearest. He noticed Pritchard watching him with keen interest while he scanned each monitor, looking for someone in particular. He had no idea what she looked like. All he had was the sound of her voice, but he kept looking.

He zeroed in on the monitor showing a woman who was seated on a bed in apparent contemplation. She looked out of place, wearing a trench coat and knee-high combat boots. Her face was turned away from the camera, but Harrow had a feeling she was the woman who called herself Jordan. He moved closer to the monitor to get a closer look, and all he could make out was the color of her hair.

Red!

Tor walked a few steps behind Lambert to get a feel for the man's intentions. It occurred to him that this might be a tactic to get rid of him or to send him to kingdom come. He was unarmed, and he would bet a rat's ass that the human was armed with every weapon imaginable. The bulge underneath Lambert's leather jacket stood out, and his legs couldn't have grown thicker in the few hours since Tor had last seen him, which confirmed what he already knew. Lambert was packing some serious ammo all over his body.

The human was tall and almost as burly as Tor. The flattop hairstyle didn't go well with his beard, creating a mixed militarized grunge. Lambert's almond-shaped eyes indicated an Asian background somewhere mixed with a Caucasian heritage. Go figure. He held an air of confidence that irked Tor.

He could take the human and wouldn't hesitate to do so. Tor had a fifty-fifty chance of ending the human's life, even with all the weapons the man could throw at him. With his speed, he could disarm Lambert without a hitch. No use trying, since he knew the place was rigged with cameras everywhere and that reinforcement would come without delay. There was no doubt he'd be taken out, fast and quick.

Tor's hands twitched at his side when Lambert made a sudden movement and turned around to face him.

"Easy, buddy," Lambert said. His body was taut and his eyes alert. "Let's head to the chow hall instead of walking around. I could use a cup of coffee."

"Lead the way," Tor said, not giving himself a chance to relax. He followed the human to the stairwell, where they took the stairs two floors up.

The cafeteria was close to empty when they got there. Just a few people remained since the breakfast fare had been served an hour earlier. Lambert walked to the buffet table to check what was left, while Tor took a seat at the far end of the room. The churning sound of a dishwasher and the clatter of pots and pans were a muted background sound in the rather quiet space. A few employees glanced at Tor with open curiosity. He glared at them, exposing the tips of his fangs to discourage them from gawking at him.

"What's on your mind?" Tor asked the moment Lambert took the chair opposite from him, watching as the man dumped three packets of sugar and a generous amount of creamer into his coffee. Tor shuddered, imagining what the coffee would taste like.

Lambert sipped his coffee and took his time before responding. "You're not infected." It wasn't a question but a statement.

Tor grunted, not only because he had nothing to say, but also from the stench of human food, which was making his stomach churn, doing enough flips and turns to make him want to gag.

"Why were you after Harrow?" Lambert asked.

"He transmitted the disease recklessly. I believe those were my exact words." Tor knew they had been recorded and that all his answers had been observed.

"So that tells me you're doing it as a vendetta?"

"You got it," Tor answered.

"And now? You still want to take him, if you can?"

Where this conservation was leading was beyond him. So what if he did? Why did it matter?

"What's with the twenty questions? Are you trying to piss me off?" Tor asked, making a growling sound and feeling hostile.

Lambert raised both hands, making sure it was understood that he didn't want to start a fight. He was just the messenger, which meant that nothing about this whole thing was his decision, although he was clearly a willing participant.

"I promise there's a point to the question . . . but you have to answer it straight. How do you feel about the whole thing now? After hearing what Harrow had to say, would you still consider taking him out?"

"You people ought to be ashamed of yourselves for listening to a private convo. I ought to sue your asses for invasion of privacy."

"Not an issue when you're within our property's jurisdiction. We can and will do any damn thing we want," Lambert answered in a forceful tone.

"I am here because you abducted me, or have you forgotten that detail?" Tor answered with a question, annoying the hell out of Lambert by the look on his face.

"And you are enjoying every minute of it," Lambert countered.

"That's beside the point. The question is, why are we here? Why are you wasting my time? You can't make me stay, and you damn well know that." Tor felt his muscles flexing with the slow build-up of rage. He hated being pushed into a corner.

"Answer the damn question," the human ordered. It was all too evident that Lambert was getting frustrated.

"No, I wouldn't kill him. But . . . if he so much as hurts another human being again with his disease, there won't be any hesitation on my part at all."

"If I didn't know any better, I would think you're beginning to like the leech."

"And your point?" Tor was closing in on losing his last ounce of patience. The human had better get to the point of this whole conversation before Tor introduced his knuckles to his face.

Lambert seemed unfazed by Tor's display of aggression. He took his time in answering despite the show of impatience. "This is between you, me, Cyrus, and the Boss. They want me to offer you a chance to work with us."

Tor cocked an eyebrow.

"You . . . as a part of our team."

"You're offering me a job?" Tor was incredulous. Talk about unexpected. All the while, he had been thinking that this *Twilight Zone* episode was going to get down and dirty.

"Well, the terms of payment would come in the form of board, lodging, and free unlimited drinks. You would be a part of the security team, as well as being offered protection, too. It's a win-win situation for you, considering the alternatives." Lambert rubbed his palm on his head, watching Tor weigh his options.

What were the alternatives anyway? Freedom was the first thing that came to mind. Tor wanted to come and go as he pleased. True, he had better accommodations here than he'd ever had, even as a human. His life hadn't been easy, moving from one foster family to another. He had never seemed to fit anywhere. And then there was . . . nah, he wasn't even going to go there. He had his fair share of tough breaks, but he had always been free. *Scratch that thought. That was a lie. Free to do whatever he wanted, any time he chose to do so. Yeah, much better.*

"What about this accessory?" He lifted his pant leg to show the cuff wrapped around his ankle.

"What about it?" Lambert asked.

"It has to go. If I were to be a part of the team, then I'd expect to be treated as an equal, don't you think?"

"But you are," Lambert answered. To prove his point, Lambert lifted his own pant leg to reveal an identical cuff on his own ankle.

"What in the hell is going on?" Tor couldn't believe humans were treated the same way, like pets that might need to be reined in at the master's discretion.

"This is our means of tracking each other when we're out and about, in particular when we're out there doing our surveillance and recon and when we're fighting. It's not meant to watch your every move because of trust issues. No, man. When you're in, you're expected to care and give a shit about the others."

Tor took in the information. This was all new to him. He'd never known what it felt like to belong to something important, to have someone watch his back and call him a part of a team. Where he'd come from, he had always been on his own. It was a dog-eat-dog world. He had to watch his back, or he'd be eaten alive. This could very well be what he'd always hoped for. Luck never smiled down on him, and this sounded too good to be true. Would anybody be waking him up from this dream anytime soon? "Are we free to come and go? Go and no one asks or gives us shit?"

"You're a damn bastard, aren't you?" Lambert accused, but his scathing tone didn't hold any malice. He was calling it as he saw it.

Tor punched his fangs on his lower lip to prove a point before smirking. He was a bastard, all right—a smart bastard.

"You get days off every month. It's a rotation. Nobody gives a damn what you do and where you go on your time. So fuck, smack, and be happy. The sky's the limit." Lambert chugged the remaining contents in his cup.

"And weapons?" Tor added. He was enjoying this. He hadn't agreed to the proposal yet, but he'd be a fool to turn down the best offer ever to come his way.

"We'll strap you to a rocket launcher, capiche?"

Tor chuckled. It was all good. He'd be sporting weapons and an ankle bracelet. Couldn't get any better than that.

Harrow couldn't take his eyes off the monitor. With his peripheral vision taking in every movement the woman made inside her holding cell, he followed her with great interest and mounting curiosity. Now there was another question he wanted answered.

"Tell me, what motivated you to put all this together?" Harrow asked when they mounted the elevator to go to the third level.

"You'll find out soon enough," Pritchard said. They got out of the elevator, and much to his surprise, there were many people walking around, just like a normal work environment. The third level held most of the facility's vehicles.

Half the third-floor structure was dedicated to different modes of transport. It was the type of collection that made your mouth gape open and your drool drip in massive amounts. Harrow couldn't believe his eyes. Two

Bentleys, a Rolls Royce, an Aston Martin Vantage Roadster, a Hummer Limo, and a red Corvette Stingray were there, along with some other less notable cars that a normal person would die for. There were some off-road vehicles in the far side of the lot, as well as the bulletproof SUVs.

"These are some of the cars I don't get to use anymore," Pritchard said with apparent nonchalance.

It all made Harrow think that there was more to this operation than what he was being told. Pritchard talked about wanting to find a cure. For whom, and why? The question had been burning in Harrow's mind since they'd started on this tour.

After they had visited the chow hall, the offices, and lobby, Pritchard took him to another long hallway, except this one was in a shape of a tube. It led to a single exit. Once they got to the end, they rode another elevator that took them to a floor marked "TE." Judging by the speed and the duration of the ride, Harrow's best guess was they had gone to a higher elevation. Once they got out of the elevator, a set of glass double doors greeted them. Pritchard keyed another set of numbers on the keypad, and the door swung to a new and different world.

Two armed security guards dressed in jeans and black shirts rose to their feet at the sight of Pritchard. Both of massive physique and snarling attitudes, they regarded Harrow with suspicion, just like any nightclub bouncers would before letting in favored customers.

"We're going to be in my office." Pritchard nodded to them and led Harrow to a hallway, the shiny wood paneling adorned with tasteful artwork. Harrow could tell that this was still a part of the underground facility but that it was somehow detached for a purpose. The concrete walls and floors, fluorescent lighting, and rigid construction of the facility were all a total contrast to the other areas he'd seen.

This wing had a different feel and vibe that made Harrow think there was more to Pritchard Tack than met the eye. The soft glow coming from the recessed lighting and the muted thump of their footsteps in the plush carpet gave the space a classy and professional feel. The one constant he'd noticed in the whole set-up was the video cameras, which were present everywhere. Dante must have his hands full, Harrow thought

They stopped in front of a rich, thick, mahogany door. Pritchard pulled out a card and slipped it in a slot. There was a swishing sound followed by a blinking green light before Pritchard pushed the door open.

"This is your office?" Harrow asked. He stood in the middle of a room with a magnificent view of Manhattan at night. They were close, but not too close. Floor-to-ceiling windows surrounded them—no obstruction between them and the breathtaking view. The entire room was filled with a mix of expensive mahogany and black leather furnishings. The plush, white carpet was a stark contrast to the furniture, its rich texture complimentary but not overwhelming. A large portrait of an elegant woman was perched on the mantle by the fireplace, where more framed pictures of a happy family completed the decor.

"Yes, I need my work to follow me wherever I go." Pritchard deposited himself behind the massive desk and sat down in the imposing black leather chair. "Please, have a seat."

Harrow sat down on an odd-shaped but comfortable-looking chair opposite Pritchard. He looked very much at home in the impressive business surroundings. This was the type of environment in which Harrow had pictured Pritchard from the first time they'd met.

A picture on the desk of two beautiful women caught Harrow's eye, and he studied it with interest. "Wife and daughter?" he asked.

Pritchard drew a long breath before letting out an even longer exhalation, his eyes filled with utter sadness. "Cassie and Allison," he whispered. His body slumped against his chair before he leaned forward, resting his elbows on the desk and raking his fingers through his blond hair with obvious gloom.

"Money can't buy everything. The billions of dollars I worked hard to make for my family are just sitting around and cannot bring Cassie back." His voice trailed off.

"What happened to her?"

Pritchard began the painstaking task of telling Harrow what happened to his beloved wife. "Losing her was another stab in the heart for me. The pain never leaves, and I miss her more than ever."

Harrow could see the wretched pain clutching at Pritchard's soul when he talked about his daughter Allison and her present predicament.

"Digging up our happy past and recounting old and cherished memories are the only beacons of hope I can hang on to. I need to keep hoping and pushing to find a cure for Allison. That's why I needed to find you and ask you to help me in finding the cure," he concluded. Pritchard's expression was that of a desperate, pleading man.

"I don't know what I can do for you, but I'm here and I will try," Harrow heard himself say. He may not have had anyone to live for, but he wouldn't stand in the way of Pritchard's happiness or that of Allison's.

"You won't be sorry for helping us." Pritchard bowed his head.

As soon as he walked out the door, Harrow couldn't help but think of his conversation with Pritchard. It seemed that he'd found himself a home. He headed straight for the laboratory, quite surprised that he wasn't lost in the maze of hallways and elevators. First things first, he needed answers to some questions, and it seemed like good old Leroy was his best bet for getting them.

He knocked on the door, pushed it open, and let himself in. Leroy looked up from the mountains of papers littered on his desk and smiled.

"Back so soon?" he asked.

"Yes. I have some questions."

Leroy motioned to the empty chair across his desk from him, and Harrow sat. There were still a few other people in the room, but they kept to themselves except to cast a few glances his way.

"I'll try to give you answers." Leroy sat back and watched him.

The man was your typical science geek who looked like he'd forgotten about everything else pertaining to a presentable appearance, concerned with finding pleasure in his work alone. He had an intelligent gleam in his eyes as he waited for Harrow to speak.

"I thought vampires didn't eat, bleed, or have heartbeats. Why are we almost like humans?"

"Myths. Believe me, I thought that was the case, too, until I was able to perform some tests. And your friend Tor was my latest lab rat. These results are all based on what I've gathered or based on findings given to me by our resident doctor Shelly Anderson."

Harrow waited.

"My first findings relate to vampires in general. You're a completely different species from humans, although you breathe, perspire, bleed, and shed tears. Your bodily functions are just like ours, except your organs are far more robust, which explains why you heal faster and why Dangeran-laced weapons are the only sure way you'll get killed."

Harrow swept his fingers through his hair, unable to hide his surprise. "What else is there that you can tell me?"

"Vampires' central and peripheral nervous systems are far superior to that of humans, which might explain why you are fast thinkers, have keener eyesight, and have better hearing. Your genes, though similar to ours, are more complex. I'm not even close to finishing my research. There is so much to learn from your kind, and I can't wait until we start working together."

Harrow smirked. *Yeah, working together. A good relationship between a scientist and his guinea pig.* "Why do we have to feed on blood? Why can't food sustain us the same way as it did when we were humans?"

"I'm not sure." Leroy scratched his head and pushed his glasses up onto the bridge of his nose. "This is what I think. I suspect that vampires might be attracted to human blood just because they feel that humans fire up their neurons, giving them more power and energy, not because they want to kill in the first place."

Harrow grimaced when he thought about the conversation long after he had gone back to his room, pondering how good it could have been if food and water alone would have sufficed. Leroy had suggested that this has been going on as long as humans had existed, which, of course, had led Harrow to another question.

How long had vampires been in existence?

Jordan sat on the edge of the bed, all too aware of the camera trained in her direction. She tried shielding her face with her body, making as little movement as possible. She could sit unmoving for a long period. Heck, she could do it all day, but who was she fooling? They'd still be watching her, no matter the time that elapsed.

After several hours, she decided to move around the room, checking every angle, every possible opening for her escape. She had no idea where she had been taken, but from every sound she'd heard as they moved her from one place to the other, she was deep beneath the earth's surface. This was no ordinary facility. Even when blindfolded, she could discern from the echoing sounds, the intermittent silence, and the scent in the air that whatever was brewing here had something to do with humans and vampires.

She pounded on the walls, tapping and probing, looking for possible signs of hollow areas to punch through to find a way out. Later, she discovered that the room she was taken into was fortified, sealed, and not easy to breach. The massive steel door with its ominous-sounding bolts told her that this would be a waiting game. She had to sit tight until they came for her. *They* wanted her to talk.

She'd been alone for too long to want to have company now. She talked to no one about her plans and how she intended to get there. The sole person who had been able to get through to her was Rohnert, and she'd used him for what he had to offer. He had been unlike any other vampire she'd come across. He was decent enough, but without needing romance to complicate her life, she'd set out and moved on, leaving him and his good intentions behind.

She walked into the little bathroom, which housed a standing shower, a pedestal sink, and toilet. This was the bare minimum based on a vampire's needs. Shower or no shower, it didn't matter to her. She'd been out too long. Mere physical needs were easy to ignore. Jordan gazed at the little square mirror to check herself out. It had been a while since she had last seen herself in a mirror. She found herself not liking the woman who stared back at her. Her red hair was dull, matted, and dirty. There were urges over the past few months to chop it off and get rid of any connections to her old self and bring out the new Jordan. It had been just one year since she became what she was now, and yet, it felt like she had lost so much of herself already.

She still looked the same, except for the hard lines around her mouth that had replaced the laugh lines her mother had always loved. Her amber eyes retained the same color except they had gotten murkier, but her vision had improved tenfold. The mouth that had always held a smile for everyone before was now twisted into a grim line. She hadn't found a reason to smile in a long time. Her father had called her gorgeous with a face of a sweetheart. He was always bragging to friends how she got most of his features, such as his red hair and a small nose that fit Jordan but seemed at odds with his bigger face. But her luscious and full lips were a gift from her mother, as well as her curves–in–the–right–place figure.

Maybe the day would come when she'd see the man who'd ended her human life, see him down on the ground and begging her for the same fate that he had inflicted on her parents. Maybe then she'd have a reason to smile.

A nagging urge to wash off the year's accumulated grime and dirt from her body had her reaching for the shower knob to get the running water started. With no other clothes to her name, she figured she'd just have to wear the same ones again. Commando and all.

A tapping from the wall sounded just when she was drying herself off. Jordan pressed her ear against the flat surface to listen.

"Do you need fresh clothes?" The vampire next door asked.

Jordan huffed at the thought of the vampire listening on her business. Angry, she replied, "Go to hell."

"I can't. They're not ready for me," he retorted, followed by a chuckle.

"Then shut the fuck up and mind your own business," she shouted. Donning her dirty jeans and long-sleeved, black cotton shirt, she then tied her damp hair into a ponytail with a thread she'd pulled out of the towel.

Stomping out of the bathroom, she put on her boots, sank on the sofa, and flicked the television on, raising the volume to the highest level to drown out any conversation coming from Harrow next door.

When he returned to the room he shared with Tor, Harrow finally had a chance to get out of his grubby clothes and into a shower. The clothes Pritchard had promised were waiting for him. They were made of finest material, something Harrow imagined the billionaire would wear himself. Pritchard, he realized, was a very influential character, based on what he'd put together as far as the facility was concerned. The human's billions worked for him in every step he took. Money was no object, and Pritchard seemed to be the kind of person who spread his wealth around. More than a dozen set of leathers, sweats, and even boxers were lined in the closet, waiting for Harrow. All were put together with good taste, matching colors, and even tasteful styles. Several pairs of running shoes, sneakers, and leather lace-up boots in his size were stowed in the bottom rack. Impressive, but to be honest, quite unnerving.

This arrangement was still one-sided, though. Harrow felt like a giant leech for taking all that was given to him in exchange for being their prized guinea pig, which if taken into careful consideration, didn't mean much. He'd brought this upon them, the appalling disease that was his own freak of nature. It felt wrong that he was getting the royal treatment just for being the scum that he was. He'd have to figure out a way to pay them back, one way or another.

The shower was more than he'd bargained for. When was the last time he felt a drop of water to soothe his aching and tired muscles? The spray of steam rising to his nostrils cleared his grimy pores, and his mind, as well.

Vampires in reality, as opposed to myths and legends, resembled humans. They breathed, they bled, they suffered hunger, and they ached and reeked. This much-needed cleansing had been long overdue, considering the mileage he had collected with his years of running— running away from all the aggressors poised to destroy him. Harrow lathered several times, feeling clean for the first time in ages. As soon as he dried himself off, he checked the wounds that covered his body. The lesions disappeared the moment he fed. The once red and throbbing wounds were now dull and latent. It was a temporary reprieve until his system required another dose of human blood, an unending merry-go-round unique to his existence.

Throwing on a crisp pair of black leather pants and a white cotton T-shirt, Harrow inspected himself in the small bathroom mirror. His lesions, though muted in appearance, still had a repulsive effect. He donned a matching leather jacket to cover his arms before lacing up the pair of leather boots he'd found in his closet.

Tor hadn't reappeared yet from his walk with Lambert. Harrow hadn't seen the other vampire since he'd left at the rather questionable invitation of the human. He wasn't by any means worried about the vampire. Tor was capable of holding his own, as Harrow had seen firsthand. If anything, he thought Lambert might be on the losing end if a brawl were to break out. If there was one thing that would go against Tor winning, it was his impulsive and explosive nature. He seemed to act before thinking in his approach to situations. Harrow had noticed it the first time their paths had crossed.

Still, he would want to know what had happened to Tor. It would be interesting to find out if his mouthy attitude had gotten him into trouble. Although Harrow wouldn't trust him with his life, he had seen a glimmer of understanding in Tor's eyes when they'd last spoken.

With nothing else to do, Harrow picked up the intercom and buzzed Dante, as instructed by Pritchard. Dante picked up with a grunt, not that there was anything they had to talk about. Harrow looked straight in the camera, where he knew Dante was watching him. "Would you let me in to room number sixty, please?" Harrow asked.

It was an impulsive decision on his part and a foolish request that might be turned down.

"Wait."

The receiver crackled in his ear while he waited for a several minutes. Dante came back on the line as soon as the bolt on his door unlocked. "Whatever you do, close the door right away," Dante instructed and hung up before Harrow could ask why.

He didn't waste any time, grabbing the signature sunglasses from the table and securing them on his face before he ran out of his room. Making a quick right turn in a few strides, he heard the door hiss and open, and he slipped right in the tight space it allowed. He kicked the door shut just as he entered. Before he had a chance to check out where the woman was, a hard sweeping kick hit the back of his knees and he fell to the ground ass-first.

"What the hell . . ." Cursing, he leapt to his feet in one quick move. He pivoted to face Jordan and charged forward, but she bent down and rammed her hip into his midsection. She grabbed his shoulder with one hand, and her other hand went around his back before she whipped him across her shoulder, shoving upward with both legs. The surprise attack rendered Harrow helpless on the ground with his arm locked to the joint, her knee resting on his neck in a chokehold.

"Who are you, and what are you doing here?" Jordan roared, her amber eyes blazing with unspoken fury. Harrow gritted his teeth as he tried to break from her hold. She was strong, he had to give her that, and she'd had the element of surprise on her side. Harrow felt his breath sputter when she pressed her knees harder. He wouldn't dare strike a woman, but desperate situations called for extreme measures, so he did something he thought might work.

Mustering enough power despite the choking sensation spreading across his body, he moved his hand fast before she could react, and the ball of his palm smacked her right across her forehead in between her eyes. The loud crackle of bone meeting bone resonated in the room, and Jordan stumbled back, her knee releasing Harrow's neck. With a quick acrobatic move, Harrow jumped to his feet. Jordan recovered at once and poised herself to attack.

They faced off, lips curling back to expose their fangs and their growls reverberating in the small room. They circled, moving from side to side, sizing each other up.

"You're a lousy people-person," Harrow said.

He inclined his head to get a better look at her. Eyes fixed on her, he absorbed all that he could as waves of anger rolled off her. She was a few inches shorter than he was, a tall woman with her flaming-red hair tied in a ponytail. Her amber eyes were blistering with fury as she glared at him, not hiding her distaste for his sudden appearance. She was stunning, with her soft features, freckles dusting her face, her small mouth, and full lips that peeled back to expose her fangs and perfect white teeth.

With his eyes concealed beneath dark lenses, she couldn't know that he was looking straight at her. Their movements as they continued circling were calculated. She moved when he moved, anticipating another attack.

"And you have no right to barge in here," she snarled back before gunning forward with a fist meant to connect with his face.

Harrow sidestepped, avoiding the contact, but her leg swept to the side and delivered a kick to one of his knees, breaking it backward and whipping him down to the floor like a rag doll. Reacting quickly, Harrow grabbed her leg and pulled her down before she could trap him again. Harrow didn't have any martial arts in his background but he knew how to grapple, and bringing her to the ground sounded more like his type of fight. He locked his arm around her neck and held tight as she squirmed and thrashed around like a wounded animal.

"I'm not here to fight, but I won't let you kill me," he said, pulling her body closer to his, where he could feel her rage vibrating like a surge of electricity. With both hands, she tried to pry his arms off her neck, but he kept his hold tight enough to disable any movement on her part. He inhaled and took in her scent before he leaned close to her and hissed. "You're Jordan?"

Instead of giving an answer, Jordan jabbed an elbow to Harrow's ribcage, hard enough that several ribs cracked, but Harrow kept his vise-like grip on her neck, refusing to ease up until he was certain she wouldn't attack him anymore.

"We can stay like this for a long time. It's your call." Harrow couldn't resist sniffing her hair. Her remarkable scent took him to a place he hadn't been for a very long time. He felt the urgings straight from his loins, and a groan escaped his lips before he could stop himself.

Jordan felt it when his body shuddered against hers. Repulsed by the Neanderthal act, she made a last ditch effort to free herself from the man whose body hummed like a livewire, alive and disturbing. She jammed her boot onto his foot and wrenched herself free from his hold. She twisted the arm that had held her while he hobbled in pain. She smacked her fist into his face, shattering his sunglasses.

The moment they locked eyes, hers flashed in recognition. She had realized that he was one of the diseased ones, the hunted. She stared before she staggered backward, while Harrow removed whatever was left of the sunglasses that had covered his face and threw them on the floor. He looked at her, challenging her to say something. He'd seen it before, the ignorant fear and the indisputable disgust—one time too many.

Jordan backpedaled away from the vampire she believed to be infected with the disease that has been causing havoc in their world. Humans weren't safe from the wrath of the disease either. Every single one who was bitten was guaranteed to catch it on contact.

She recognized the man she'd seen a few days before, but he seemed different now. He was emaciated still, but he cleaned up pretty well. Though his eyes were murky and disconcerting, she knew he could see her well with the way his head inclined while he watched her.

She saw the myriad emotions flicker in the man's eyes when their gazes locked. If one's eyes were the mirror to one's soul, this man had everything out in the open for everyone to see. Pain, torture, mortification, loathing, weakness, and desire—and yet, he held his head high as he stood before her. A primal growl tore through him, and she jerked farther away. Repulsion was a natural reaction, but she felt another unusual emotion tug from within. No, it couldn't be. Not pity or compassion. There was no room in her life for trivial emotions. She was a woman on a mission. The core reason for her existence was all that mattered.

Her brain told her this man was dangerous. Every fiber of her being warned her to stay away out of sheer self-preservation. However, something in his eyes told her she wasn't in imminent danger. He wouldn't hurt her. Torn between conflicting emotions, she braced herself and snarled at the man. She had nowhere to go, even if she had wanted to flee.

"Stay away from me," she warned. Her lips curled, exposing her fangs.

His face clouded, his lips thinned into a straight line, and without saying a word, he glanced at the camera situated on the north side of the room and nodded. The door opened, and he let himself out without sparing a backward glance in her direction. As quickly as he had come, he disappeared with the roar of the closing door.

Stunned by the turn of events, Jordan sat down on the edge of the bed and glared at the camera. She mouthed a curse meant for whoever was watching her, and she made sure she got her message across, loud and clear. Confusion distressed her. There must have been a good reason why he had come to see her, but instead of letting him speak, she had attacked him. Why had she reacted in such a violent manner? Frustration could muck up one's better judgment, and being held against her will inside this godforsaken room was messing with her.

Focus. You have to focus, she told herself. She needed to think of ways to escape before she lost whatever was left of her sanity. How could the one thing she wanted to do be so elusive? All she wanted was to kill the monster who had ended her parents' lives, plain and simple. There was nothing much to it, and she wouldn't care what happened next.

Looking up to the camera, she said, "Let me out, and I'll tell you what you want to know." Jordan waited. This was her only escape route.

Muted sounds of approaching footsteps brought her up to her feet. She felt for the missing Kalimetal. Without it, she felt incomplete and naked. She pulled her trench coat closer and readied herself. The duo of Mutt and Jeff came for her, as well as the big vampire who days ago had been taken from the subway along with Harrow.

No one said a word as they led her into the same room she had been taken to for questioning when she was first captured. Covertly eyeing every single exit, doorway, and hallway, she studied the floor plan, feeling ill at ease with the huge vampire watching her every move. The humans, even though they seemed fierce and strong, were still humans. Their strength still paled in comparison to hers, but the vampire was on to her, watching her like a hawk.

"Sit," Mutt ordered. Jordan soon found out he answered to the name Cyrus.

Prudence would be her saving grace, and she followed the order, even though she was seething inside. She sat and waited, studying the three men who surrounded her. Mutt and Jeff stayed silent, leaning against the wall across the table, arms across their chests. The big vampire hulked by the doorway, blocking the one exit available to her. Not long after, the same man who interrogated her walked in the room. With movements of an uptight predator, he eyed her with interest.

"You wish to speak now?" he queried and lowered himself down at the head of the table. Without knowing the gripes the man harbored, Jordan could tell by the expression on his face that he carried the weight of the world. No aggression could mask the pain that riddled his eyes and caused the droop of his shoulders.

Jordan nodded, still eyeing everyone around her. "You wanted to know why I was snooping around," she said.

"Yes," the man answered, looking at her in a clear attempt to get a read on what had driven her into their midst and hoping to unravel the secret of the female vampire who now sat across from him.

"I'm looking for one particular vampire to kill," Jordan stated and wasn't surprised when the room erupted with laughter. She hissed, shifting her gaze from Mutt, then to Jeff, and then back to the man questioning her.

"And you thought you'd find him here?" he asked.

"I've been watching some of your men, and I saw everything that happened at the subway station when you took the big guy"—she pointed to Tor—"and the other vampire a few days ago."

"You mean Harrow?" the guy replied.

It dawned on her that the man who had come to her room, the one she'd tried to kill with her bare hands but had been unable to subdue, was the same one who had asked for her name. As recognition turned to awkwardness, Jordan tried her best to hide her expression. To her chagrin, the man seated across the table laughed.

"Yes, that one," she answered. "What is it that you find amusing?"

The laughter continued, and her blood pressure spiked to the max. It was one thing to laugh without a reason, but to be made a laughing stock was not something she'd signed up for. Shooting dagger-like glares at the man, Jordan rose to her feet in a threatening manner. Firm hands clamped on her shoulder and pushed her back down.

"Easy, woman," the vampire blustered behind her. His fingers dug into her skin. Jordan winced internally, not giving the vampire the benefit of knowing how his hands on her made her want to scream.

The laughter died out, and the man watched her with honest-to-goodness interest, close enough to make her cringe. Jordan returned his open regard with a glare. She decided against making the slightest movement and stayed still.

Know which fight you can win. This isn't one of them, she reminded herself.

"I'm sorry. I didn't mean to make fun of you. In fact, we're all watching when you kicked our dear Harrow's butt. I must say, I'm impressed. Where did you learn how to fight like that? I swear, Selene would pale in comparison," the man said, referring to a fictional character from a vampire movie.

How cliché. Jordan fought the urge to roll her eyes. "Does it matter?" she asked in a disdainful tone.

"Well, yeah. You hurt our boy's feelings. I bet he's licking his bruised ego right now." He chuckled. "But let's get down to the nitty-gritty. Who are you looking for?"

"I don't know his name. All I know is that I won't stop until his blood is spilled and I watch him take his last, evil breath."

"That's a mighty tough hatred you got there, Ms . . .?"

"Jordan, just Jordan." Her last name didn't matter. To everyone who had known her before, Jordan Foz had ceased to exist. She was dead, along with her parents. Now, she was just Jordan.

"Ms. Jordan. I'm Pritchard Tack. I'm sure you're not interested to know it, but I run this facility. We are one big happy family here."

"Yeah, that's what it seems like. You got Mutt, Jeff, and the Hulk over there." Jordan pointed at Cyrus, Lambert, and Tor, who growled in unison at her tactless reference to them as comic book characters.

Pritchard gave a hearty laugh at the expense of his men. They all glared at him with contempt but said nothing.

"You have some balls on you, Ms. Jordan. I like that. You have spunk."

"I'm glad you find me amusing, Mr. Tack. Believe me when I say that you wouldn't be amused once my hands were tightening around your neck," she spat.

"Pritchard, call me Pritchard. We don't stand on formalities here." He laughed some more. "I'm sure you would love the idea, Jordan, but I'm not the enemy here. Our vampires here are your typical infected beings looking for a cure."

"A cure?" Jordan's curiosity was piqued, and for a moment she forgot about her own agenda.

"Yes, but that's not the reason why you're here. Tell me, what does this man look like? The one you are dying to kill?"

Jordan began to describe the monster who had ravaged her mother before handing her a death sentence and bringing her father's ultimate demise. The looks and subtle glances exchanged between Mutt, Jeff, Hulk, and Pritchard didn't escape Jordan's observant eyes.

"You know who I'm talking about?" she asked, quite certain the people around her knew of the man she'd described.

The vampire was the one who answered her question, walking closer to the table. "Tor." He reached out his hand with the obvious intent to shake Jordan's hand, but she recoiled. Tor's eyes flickered with amusement, followed by a throaty chuckle. "Impossible feat, my lady," he mocked.

"What is impossible?" Jordan asked.

"If the vampire you're looking for is the same man who is responsible for keeping the vampire world *safe*, then you're in for a very long haul."

The way Tor said the word safe was suspicious, Jordan thought. "His name. Tell me his name." Jordan's voice rose, and she jumped from her chair. She was getting closer to finding him. With a name, things would be easier. She could feel it in her bones.

"Goran—but it won't be as easy as you think. I've heard things about him. Rumors." Tor had the nerve to look uncomfortable about admitting to listening to gossip. "He is the head of the Vampire Council, the big Kahuna, and the master of disaster himself. If the rumors are true, he has a healthy appetite for redheads."

"Goran . . ." Jordan rolled his name on her tongue, relishing the small victory of getting a name to go with the face she remembered so vividly. Now, the only thing standing between her and the monster she sought were these people.

"What are you holding me here for?" Jordan asked, and Pritchard leveled heavy eyes on her. "I haven't done anything to be kept here as a prisoner."

"Indeed, we don't intend to hold you here against your will. Our intention was to protect ourselves since you were caught prowling on private property," Pritchard said.

"Then you shall give me back my weapon and set me free now."

Pritchard nodded to Cyrus, who took his leave and returned after a few minutes with Jordan's weapon. All eyes were transfixed on it, but no one could have felt as relieved to see it as Jordan.

"It's an interesting weapon," Pritchard remarked and rose from his seat. He glanced at Jordan, as if asking for permission. Jordan felt no threat at the moment, so she nodded her head. She hovered next to Pritchard when he took the two metal rod-like sticks with reverence from the table and examined it. "Is it made with Dangeran?"

"Yes," Jordan replied. "Made by a friend of mine."

"We are very much interested in this fine weapon you have."

Pritchard swept his gaze at the three foot-long metal sticks, the gleaming metal suggesting solid and excellent craftsmanship. He traced his fingers on the intricate inscriptions in an unknown language on the blade. The grips were made of animal pelt woven to the handle. With the addition of Dangeran to its makeup, the weapon possessed an intimidating and lethal quality.

"What does it say?" Pritchard pointed to the inscription *Ang Mamatay ng Dahil Sa'yo*.

"Rohnert, the one who created this, has ties with martial artists from Asia, where he learned the art of Kali-Eskrima. It's a form of stick fighting that uses any rod or stick material, even blades or knives. He mastered and perfected the art. He is the one who taught me how to fight and to protect myself. He trained me by using different weapons, but we concentrated on Kalimetal—it's what he called this improved version—which is infused with Dangeran to be more effective against vampires."

Jordan had no intention of divulging the meaning behind the inscription. Rohnert had engraved the weapon with his sentiments. "To die because of thee," Jordan said the words that couldn't hold more meaning for her. And this she vowed to do in the name of her parents.

"Should the blanching commence?" Giancarlo asked, exhibiting excitement at the slaughter that was about to happen. Demetrius glanced at his most favored minion and nodded.

The Blanch Room, a big and secured section located on the farthermost wing of their headquarters, had been created to house the many humans, most of them unsuspecting, to undergo the change. A few came of their own accord, most were shady characters or bottom dwellers willing to trade their worthless existence for a chance to participate in the woven lies of bountiful returns.

Once an answer was given, none of the damned could get away. Suffice it to say that many of them were unwilling participants in a ritual they had been led to believe was a part of an initiation to a favored position within a secret community. These humans, snared by the gift of persuasion or by sheer brute force, were all taken into the room where they would fall under the spell of a promise of great adventure and the lure of a better life. It was a necessity if the vampires wished their way of life to go on and to flourish. Feeding was a different scenario altogether. They could feed off each other, but they needed new vampires to keep their legacy stout and strong.

Demetrius surveyed the room full of fledglings gathered together in the Blanch Area, a name he'd coined after he launched the very first induction of a group he'd taken many years ago. Alas, not everyone was cut out for the job. Some were too stupid, some too placid to carry out an order, and a few lacked the initiative. To keep his father happy and their army sturdy, he must produce soldiers to replace those they lost in battles or conflicts.

The name referred to the cleansing ritual performed, a purging of intentions before delivering the blow to the vein. Fledglings spewed blood from every orifice imaginable to attain a physical death and would later be reborn to a new way of life, as well as a new wave of mindsets.

Tied to a beam with arms outstretched, each one was stripped of any clothing, and the only sound audible to anyone who would listen was the wails of fear, uncertainty, and doubts of the unknown. Most of the humans were male, although a few females were also chosen by Demetrius's group to be mates.

Demetrius sat on an aging Bergere chair with indifference as Giancarlo unleashed a coiled whip in his hand, making a slashing sound in the air. The rest of the vampire soldiers did the same, creating a tense atmosphere as humans began to recoil, pulling away from the very people they'd thought would hand them a desirable destiny. As the whipping ensued, curses of agony and cries of pain lapped against each other, followed by gnashing of teeth and woeful petitions for their lives to be spared. With a satisfied smirk, Demetrius leaned back, propping one leg over the arm of the chair. He let his eyes wander, looking for a suitable human to serve as his meal for the day.

As each soldier took their turn in handing out the death sentence, continual pleading and tortured cries saturated the premises, yet no one listened.

The evening was young, but Demetrius was in a hurry. Begging and cries of horror hung in the arid air, mixed with the stench of blood, sweat, and tears. "Hose them down," he ordered, and then water poured out from the tubes that ran horizontally and vertically from the ceiling.

Giancarlo grinned like a dazed madman, having the time of his life as Demetrius looked on, hoping for the process to end soon and thinking of better ways to spend his evening.

Tor walked into the bedroom he shared with Harrow. They were now assigned to a no-lock door and were free to come and go as they pleased. It had been a week since they had been taken against their will, but after an unexpected turn of events, Tor had found himself with a purpose, a job, and a place to stay, whereas Harrow wandered the facility without purpose. After the day he had been embarrassed by Jordan, he'd become a laughing stock. It was a place Tor didn't want to go, feeling the reckless anger simmering in his roommate's blood.

"Harrow, you in here?"

Silence was thick as a cloud, and after looking for Harrow in the last hour, Tor could feel something was amiss. He had been tagged as Harrow's protector—his babysitter, as Lambert called him. Reluctantly agreeing to the arrangement as a part of his assignment, Tor followed Harrow around the facility, often finding him in the training room hurling weapons at stationary targets or drumming up scores of bullets on the firing range. He knew Harrow's self-esteem had taken a nosedive when Jordan whooped his ass, unfolding before everyone's watchful eyes.

"Shit," he muttered to himself, breaking into a dead run toward the direction of the camera room, almost pulling the door off the hinges when he flung it open. Dante shot him a look meant to reprimand. Not caring about the damn door, Tor bared his fangs and demanded to check all the cameras intended to track Harrow.

"He's just on the deck. He needed fresh air," Dante quipped, punching a key and several screens showed Harrow sitting on the ledge of the upper deck. It was located at the top section of Tack's office building, inaccessible to most and only utilized should Allison decide she needed fresh air.

The low and steady beeping from Harrow's ankle bracelet sounded on the board, blinking his name. "Whatever." Tor frowned.

"You have nothing to worry about, my man. It's all good. Just allow him to lick his wounds, and he'll be all right in a few days." Dante smiled.

"He's a vampire, for crying out loud, not some little Ms. Nancy."

"Why do you care? What's with the sudden compassion for your ward?"

"Shut up. Don't let me introduce my knuckles to your face." Tor threatened. Though he wouldn't strike the human, he wasn't about to show that he had grown a soft spot for his human counterparts.

Chuckling at Tor's misguided attempt to intimidate, Dante relaxed against his chair but shot to his feet when the harsh alarm sounded off, a signal that the barrier had been breached. One look at the monitor showed Harrow jumping off the ledge, triggering the alarm that meant he was out of the camera range. Jacking up the monitor from every angle, Harrow was nowhere to be found.

Tor jumped up. "Clear me to follow him now," he demanded. Dante waved a wand-like instrument at Tor's ankle cuff, deactivating the alarm, and punched several keys to open the nearest exit for him.

"Each door will open as you get closer. Just follow them 'til you find your way out!" Dante shouted before Tor cleared out of the room.

He palmed the Glock hidden underneath his leather jacket and the axe secured in its holster next to the throwing stars Lambert had supplied him. Tor packed enough ammo to take on the world. He bolted out of the metal door and took the stairs to the outer layer of the facility, where another door led him to more stairs before he climbed out of a stairwell as long as the freakin' Great Wall. As each door opened and closed for him, Tor had a feeling that he'd be running for a good length of time tonight.

Despite the speed at which his feet enabled him to reach the last line of doors, Harrow would be well on his way, given that he'd had a few minutes leeway. The humid air assaulted Tor as he stepped outside the confines of the facility. They were deep underground, situated within the city but ghosts to the naked eyes of the unsuspecting people. Navigating through the muddy terrain that surrounded the exit of the facility, Tor scanned his surroundings. A quick intake of breath filled his nostrils with the pungent aroma of the earth and his surroundings before he singled out Harrow's distinct scent.

He couldn't be too far away, Tor surmised. A faint trail of Harrow's scent alerted his sensitive nose, and he broke into a free run toward the city. What in the hell would Harrow want in the city?

Different scenarios came barging into Tor's mind as he took the side of the freeway, leaping over muddy piles, trash, and whatever godforsaken waste was out there. All he knew was that he wasn't going swimming. If Harrow chose to swim the river, he would trail the bastard through the safe and dry harbor of the ferry. It wouldn't take as much time. Drenching his new get-up in river slime wasn't a part of the plan.

Though he and Harrow didn't gab like a bunch of women, he felt he knew the machinations in the vampire's brain. He was wired differently.

Harrow was more of a gentle creature, not inclined to fight if words were available. He wouldn't kill if at all avoidable. Heck, the fucker carried a needle so he could feed off humans without infecting them. This misplaced goodness was a stinker to their reputation but also a breath of fresh air. Instead of throwing a dagger or knife, Harrow could kill by throwing a piece of bread to his opponent, masquerading as kindness. What sick irony to their mythical dynamics.

Hauling ass to get to the city as fast as he could without getting his outfit wet, Tor used his speed to blur himself from human eyes, an unrecognizable figure whizzing by and leaving a cloud of dust in his wake. He could still catch the weak scent of Harrow when he crossed the busy street of Times Square, snaking through bodies and creating a gap as he ran in between the hordes the length of several blocks.

The trail ended in a dinky dive bar on Broadway Street. Pushing the grubby door open, he spotted Harrow at the corner of the bar, his back to him. Tor made his way inside the club with no intention of blending in. People stopped to gawk as he walked by. He sneered but kept his fangs hidden.

"I don't need a babysitter," Harrow growled and sounded a hiss when Tor was within earshot.

"I resent the title," he answered as he inched his body into the little space between Harrow and another bar patron, almost knocking the human off his barstool.

"Hey, watch it!" the human yelled and applied a little elbow action on Tor's ribs.

"Be a good boy, give me your seat, and get lost. Ya hear?" Tor lifted his mouth and grinned at the guy, exposing the tips of his fangs without mercy as the poor human scurried away like a wet kitten given its first bath.

Turning to Harrow as soon as he secured his winded ass on the now-vacated seat, he asked, "What's with the disappearing act?"

Harrow shrugged, raising a hand to get the bartender's attention. "What's your poison?" he asked in a gruff tone.

"Are you drowning something, Harrow?"

"Mind your own business. What will it be?" Harrow asked again as the bartender parked himself in front of them, wiping the counter while waiting for Tor to order.

"Patron-Silver," Tor said.

"Make that two," Harrow seconded.

"You realize liquid goes right through you, right?"

"It's just psychological," Harrow retorted. His lips were thinning by the second, and he did not seem interested in engaging in meaningless chatter.

"I don't want to piss on your pity-party here, but this is the last place you want to be, ya know, being hunted and all."

The reminder was enough to elicit a rumbling growl from Harrow. Tor just chuckled at the anger seeping from Harrow's pores. He decided to get off the vampire's back. He turned around to check the place out when a few raised voices caught his attention. Bodies parted like the Red Sea as two rather imposing figures began walking toward the direction of the bar, their gaze directed in their general vicinity.

Without prelude, one of the men reached inside his jacket, and Tor heard alarm bells ringing in his ears. *Vampires!* Reacting on instinct alone, he drew a throwing star and wielded it in one of the vampire's direction, aiming straight at his chest. Without much fanfare, the vampire's face contorted, locked eyes with him before a popping and crackling sound followed. He soon was rendered a useless pile of broken limbs and torso on the floor, fast disintegrating into a heap of ashes.

Responding to the sound, Harrow swung around just in time to find a knife swishing by his face. Felt like déjà vu. Been there, seen that. Tor threw another throwing star at the other vampire but missed. Grabbing Harrow by the shirt, Tor pulled him to his feet and pointed him to the back exit of the club, not before another knife missed him by a whisker.

This wasn't the time or the place to use his gun if he wanted there to be no human casualties.

"Run!" Tor ordered as Harrow pushed the back exit door open. The door alarm sounded while they skittered along the darkened alley. "This is the fucking reason why you shouldn't be out in the open."

"Damn it," Harrow retorted, indignant.

Another knife whooshed by as they zigzagged across the street. Too many people meant a lot of cover for them, but could also mean casualties. These characters wouldn't avoid killing. Ducking low, Tor led Harrow to another alley before breaking out at a dead run, looking over his shoulder several times to check whether they were being followed. The last thing they wanted was to lead the man to their hideout.

Tor decided to slow down and wait for the vampire while Harrow sped ahead. A few seconds later, their pursuer closed in on him, aiming at Tor with another knife. With precise movements, Tor tossed his beloved axe in the air before the vampire drew his blade.

The same popping and crackling followed, disabling the vampire. Before falling to the ground, he snarled, "More will be coming, I swear."

"Say hi to Lucifer for me." Tor sneered, jamming his foot in the vampire's face while pulling his axe out of his chest and running away from the scene before a crowd could start to gather around the mound of ashes on the ground.

Catching up with Harrow, Tor roared. "Next time you pull a stunt like that, fuckin' arm yourself!"

When Harrow and Tor slowed down to a jog, they were winded, pumped, and pissed at each other. Looking over their shoulders, they checked the stretch of darkness to see if they were being followed or if reinforcements were hot on their trail. The last thing they needed was to lead the Vampire Council to their present lair.

Harrow shot a glance in Tor's direction, not certain if he should blast the vampire for ruining his night out or thank Tor for bailing him out. He had no intention of sounding like an ingrate, but one thing was for sure. He'd sound like one the moment he opened his mouth.

"Did you hear what I said? No disappearing shit. If you ever decide to pull a stunt again, make sure you can protect yourself."

A lecture was the last thing he needed. Harrow growled in frustration. What had happened to the peace and quiet? Time alone to listen to his thoughts without Tor falling short of calling him an idiot for venturing out on his own. "I heard you."

"If I hadn't showed up, you might have bitten the dust. Fun, right?"

Harrow flinched at the reminder of scene at the bar and their narrow escape.

"God, Harrow, you had no weapon but a T-dagger. You expected to come out of that club alive?" Tor bristled, his heavy footfalls pounding against the pavement.

"As I said before . . ." Harrow paused, making sure Tor was listening. "I don't need a babysitter." He wished the vampire would give up the idea of following him like a doggone bloodhound.

" 'Thanks' would be a more appropriate thing to say right about now," Tor replied sarcastically. Wiping the bloodied axe on his jeans, he grimaced at the grime he'd have to scrub away later. After giving his weapon a careful inspection, Tor replaced it back in its holster.

"I don't mean to sound ungrateful, but you gotta admit, I'm capable of taking care of myself just fine." Harrow parried, not even close to saying how thankful he was that the other vampire had saved his hide.

"You don't mean to sound like one, but you are an ungrateful bastard," Tor said, slowing down to a walk. The city's vivid lights burned bright in the distance while they made their way through alleys, preferring darkened pathways not frequented by humans.

"I've been called worse."

"Boo hoo." Tor mocked. "So the woman beat the crap out of you. Get over it."

"What the hell are you talking about?" Harrow stopped in his tracks. He yanked Tor by his shoulder, and they glared at each other.

"Get your fuckin' hands off my leather, and you know what I'm talking about. So this woman—you dig her, huh?" Tor shrugged him off, smoothing his jacket before he walked away.

Harrow followed. His mind was caught in a tailspin, neither happy nor sad. Just an endless circle of cluttered emotions. His thoughts wandered to an attractive woman with flaming red hair. "And mind your own business."

Sure, Jordan had caught him off guard. He hadn't been expecting a fight when he entered her room unannounced. She had whooped his ass to high heaven, and he'd ended up on his butt twice but had held his ground. Hadn't he? He thought he had done well against her, considering she was a female. Christ! What sort of a loser would measure and even consider fighting against a woman and then gloat with satisfaction?

But if he was being honest with himself, Jordan shoving his face to the floor several times and humiliating him was only a little wound to his ego. Heck, he wasn't a fighter by nature, and being a damn vampire didn't change his outlook one bit.

What was bothering him was her reaction when she had seen his eyes. Her response told him what he already knew. He was a freak, a diseased monster not even his own kind could stand to be around. His appearance repulsed her. The way her face had contorted told him without words that she couldn't stand being in his presence. She had shrunk away. The unspoken rejection had been so thick it had suffocated him with the realization that she wanted nothing to do with him.

He wasn't under the impression that he could charm any female, but he was hoping to get to know Jordan. Get a fresh start, maybe make a new friend? Who had he been kidding? The mere sight of him disgusted her, and the way she'd ordered him to stay away from her had kicked him in the gut so hard, he couldn't even think.

He had no idea why her reaction had bothered him. It shouldn't. This was something he was supposed to be used to after years of dealing with it. He shook his head as if the thoughts and the cloud that hung around would somehow disappear, and then let out a sigh. To make matters worse, he'd reacted like a caveman when he had pinned her body with his. The unexpectedness of the act she'd prompted from him was embarrassing and downright mortifying. He'd felt like a pervert the way his body had tensed, and his hardware getting all woody on him was unexpected, but not surprising. She was a very attractive woman, and any male would salivate at the sight of her.

Tor chuckled next to him. "You're sulking." He observed. The vampire might be strong and considered himself a guardian of some sort, but he was getting on Harrow's nerves. "Wanna talk about it?"

Harrow cocked an eyebrow. "Do I look like I want to talk?"

"It's your call." Tor paused. "Just so you know, you're as stuck with me as I am with you. There's no way around it. So if you plan on getting killed anytime soon with your stupid escapades and wanting-to-clear-my-mind shit, you're dragging me with you. So do me a favor and get your head out of your ass, think, and maybe get some mighty powerful toys to back up your silly ass and find someone to train you to fight."

"Is that all, Dr. Phil?" Harrow huffed. His mind was racing. Maybe the stupid vampire to whom he owed his life had a point. It wouldn't hurt to get some basic training in martial arts, arm himself with fancy weapons, and kick some Vampire Council soldiers' butts in style.

At that point, they had reached the lip of the tunnel.

"I'll take the left, and you take the right area," Tor said with a nod.

They separated and scouted the entire perimeter to be certain they hadn't been followed. After giving the entire periphery a quick check, they descended to the little trail meant for foot traffic. Camouflaged with bushes and wild hedges in a sloping formation, the entrance to their underground facility gave nothing away, not even the slightest sign that such an establishment existed in the area.

"Do you want me to call on Cyrus to give you some pointers?" Tor teased as soon as the metal entrance door shut behind them.

"Consider this the last time I'll say this—mind your own goddamn business and stay away from me. Go find yourself another person to annoy."

"No can do. As I said, we're stuck together like fuckin' sweethearts. And besides, you can't get rid of your roommate."

Tor had the audacity to wink, which sent Harrow's patience to its limit. How good it would feel to wipe the smirk off the other vampire's face.

"Screw you, Tor." Harrow made a beeline to the elevator, intent on finding the man who might be able to sew his shredded ego together. That alone would help a wounded cat like him.

"Man, I love this job." Tor chuckled and went the opposite way.

Just before Harrow reached the training room, the door of the I-room swung open and Pritchard called out to him.

"Hey, would you come in here for a minute?"

Pritchard's voice was even, Harrow noted. He wondered what it was all about. He shrugged and walked toward the door Pritchard held open for him. As soon as he walked in, Cyrus got up from the chair in which he had been sitting and pushed it in Harrow's direction. The man for the most part preferred standing up, in the shadows if possible. Harrow caught the chair with his foot and sat down with a grunt, looking down at his dirty boots.

"I don't want to scold you like a mother would—"

"Then don't." Harrow's eyes lifted to challenge Pritchard. The sound of several knuckles crunching came from where Cyrus stood. Harrow cocked a brow in his direction and hissed before returning his attention to Pritchard.

He continued. "We talked about you being free to come and go as you please. Maybe I forgot to mention one little condition. You cannot leave the facility without giving us information on where you're headed, and whether it soothes your soul or not, Tor is going to be your babysitter."

"That's not acceptable, at least the latter part. I will inform you of my plans, but I don't need someone watching me like a goddamn kid."

"Some things aren't negotiable. I need to give your best friend something to do, and besides, you almost got yourself killed out there." Smirking, Pritchard rose from the table and walked to the front of the room, where several keypads where located by the wall. He punched in some numbers before stepping back. In a blink of an eye, a quarter of the wall started to turn, revolving to display a rack full of libations. He picked up a bottle, a glass, and a bucket of ice, and then poured a drink for himself. "Care for any?"

Harrow nodded, but Cyrus declined. Pritchard returned with two glasses of scotch. Handing one to Harrow, he lifted the glass and downed its contents in one gulp.

Harrow tilted his glass in Pritchard's direction and followed suit. The drink coated his throat and slinked down to his gut, numbing it in the process. *Sweet,* Harrow thought.

"I can't stress it enough that I want you here with us alive. You may not like it, but you have no choice in the matter. Tor was instructed to follow wherever you go. It's a manner of protecting my investment. I've come a long way in finding a cure, finding you, and I'm not going to let you ruin it."

"Is that what I am, an investment?" Harrow felt anger rising from within. This was a new low—he was now considered a venture?

"We can name it whatever we want. Just the same, we have something much more important to worry about here. You believe that you can run all the time and that nothing or no one will catch you. That may be the case for now, but I guarantee you, they will catch up one day, and God forbid, they will not only skin you alive, but also offer you to Apollo for good measure."

Pritchard dragged a hand through his hair and watched Harrow's reaction, which was masked by a grim face and thinning lips.

Harrow realized that the Council had stepped up their hunt for all diseased vampires, not just him, and so far, they had been cleaning house in a big way. There was no doubt in his mind that it was just a matter of time before they caught him. None of it scared him. He almost welcomed the inevitable when he was upset—upset because he felt rejected. Damn him to high heaven, he was beginning to sound like a sour puss.

"Fine," Harrow snapped. "One condition."

"Name it."

"Cyrus will train me with all weapons known to man, and I get to pick any toy I want."

"You said one. You just quoted two conditions."

Harrow scowled and glanced over his shoulder in time to see a grin spreading on Cyrus's face. He fought the urge to roll his eyes at both men. Even knowing that he had no real leverage to demand any conditions, he couldn't back out now. They wanted their guinea pig? Then they needed to give him something in return. "Those are my conditions."

"Cyrus?" Pritchard shifted his gaze to Cyrus, who was leaning on the wall with a bored look on his face.

"Bring it," he said, flashing a big smile in Harrow's direction. He was no doubt thinking that Harrow would make a nice target for his wicked ideas of punishment, pain, and pleasure.

"Then it's settled." Pritchard placed both palms on the table. "I expect you to follow our simple rules, and we'll have no problems."

Rising up and walking to the bar, Pritchard poured another glass of scotch and took a quick swig. Instant gratification marked his face. "I will leave you guys to figure out the finer details in your training." With a half-smile, Pritchard exited the room and left Harrow looking up at Cyrus.

"I'm ready when you are," Cyrus said.

"I am."

"Then follow me."

Jordan sighed for what must have been the hundredth time that day. After the rush of information, the sea of new faces, and her introduction to the facility's operations, she was riding on sensory overload highway, finding herself caught at the junction of wanting to flee and hoping to stay, wishing for nothing more than to fulfill her goal and be done with it and wanting to stay to help a worthy cause. She found Pritchard's project significant enough to rouse her curiosity.

Then she was introduced to Allison. Talk about hitting it off from the get-go.

"Jordan, are you okay?" Allison had settled on the concrete ledge, her legs dangling below her. They had been sitting for the last four hours talking after their introduction. If there had been anything in the year following her transformation that had resembled normalcy, talking to Allison was it. As different as their lives had been in the past, it seemed like their paths were going along the same route now.

"Yeah, I have no idea how I got here in the first place." Jordan sighed again. Looking over the dark horizon in the moonlight, the shadow of the lit buildings cast an eerie glow, rendering the sight haunting—foreboding, even. Somewhere out there lived the man she was looking for, the one who had altered her life forever. Haste and impatient motivation would have to take a back seat if she wanted to find him and carry out her revenge. Careful planning was in order. Taking out a man as powerful as Goran without solid preparation was suicide at best.

"Can't you stay?" The pleading in Allison's voice was unmistakable. Jordan had known the woman for several hours, and yet, she felt drawn to her like the sister she'd never had. Talking to Allison seemed so easy, and Jordan found herself pouring her heart out for the first time. Taking another sweeping breath, she pointed her chin up toward the sky, drawing strength from the simple act.

"I suppose I can," she replied. "No promises, though."

The thought of Harrow crept into her mind. The vision of his wounded expression never left her. It niggled at the recesses of her subconscious, reminding her how hasty she had been and how far she had let her anger take her, when she'd dumped all her frustrations on him.

She remembered with vivid clarity the wordless derision she'd felt and had manifested in her eyes, the timbre of her voice as she'd ordered him to stay away from her. Ignorance was bliss, and if she hadn't known what was wrong with him, she might still be able to keep herself aloof from the whole situation. Having learned from Allison and Pritchard what the disease was all about armed her with disgust for herself and took away the possibility of the detached approach she would rather have kept out of sheer self-preservation.

The one thing she had room for in her life was exacting her revenge, nothing else. This newfound friendship, the worthy cause, and finding another vampire interesting would derail her plans, and this was unacceptable. It would just complicate her already-complicated life.

Erecting walls around her emotions had been easy. She'd let her anger and rage dictate her course. Rohnert had been able to chip away a small chunk of her armor, and that was all she'd ever allow. She had left. Staying would have been a bad decision since she knew that if she'd stayed any longer, her goals would've change. Jordan was not ready to give up her plans and her hatred. She had to find that man before she could let life and its providence take over. Enter Harrow. With all his vulnerability, he must be kept at arm's length. Steeling her resolve, she got up, dusted herself off, and walked the expanse of the ledge, letting the crisp wind blow her hair.

Turning around, she found Allison watching her with a twinkle in her eyes. "Daddy said you are free to come and go as you wish. You can share my bedroom if you'd like."

Wrapping her arms around her body, she held herself together, willing her mind to translate her refusal into words. Jordan found the offer both sweet and dangerous at the same time. Staying in the facility would make her feel connected, and if she knew herself well enough, she'd find herself involved, which would make leaving difficult.

Sensing Jordan's conflict, Allison with a nimble movement jumped to her feet and walked closer to her. Jordan felt more exposed than she wanted to appear when Allison stared at her with pleading eyes.

"I don't know if it's a good idea. Attachment is a luxury I can't afford right now, because when it's time to leave, I know I won't even think twice."

Allison spoke in her soft, soprano voice. "Cross that bridge when you get there. You have nowhere to go anyway. Maybe we can even help."

"That's what I don't need," Jordan replied, pushing the windblown hair away from her face and tucking the strands behind her ears. "More lives affected, involved. This is my business, and I don't wish to drag any more innocent lives along."

"You may not see it now, but there's a reason behind your stumbling upon us. I know there's a purpose for everything . . ." Her voice trailed off.

"Even if you, yourself, refuse to believe it?"

Allison nodded her head. "Who would sign up for this life of darkness?" It seemed as though she had spoken her thoughts aloud before realizing it.

"No one, but we're going to make the best out of it, right?"

For the first time, Jordan found herself wanting to believe that there was more to live for after she killed the monster. It was a thought she hadn't allowed herself to entertain before now. Her purpose would cease once her task had been carried out—the only thing that had kept her going, day in and day out.

"I guess . . ."

A hint of a small smile tugged on Allison's lips.

"Well, then, I'll stay until I find the monster or until we find a cure for you . . ." And Harrow, Jordan added silently, even though the name and the man scared her, for whatever reason that was still unfathomable to her. "Whichever comes first."

Once in a while, Goran would venture out of his chambers if duty called for his own involvement or if the need to harvest another woman carrying his child beckoned him. This was one of those times. He stalked the premises of the woman's house, keeping his figure hidden behind the confines of the shadows until she was alone. The house sat in dead quiet before he let himself in, just like the way he had slid into her house when he'd impregnated her.

Scaling the walls to her apartment, he moved to the first window where the babe, his baby, lay swaddled in blankets inside her crib. Willing the latch on the window open, he moved through the opening with ease, letting himself in without making a noise.

Straightening his body near the crib, he hovered and glanced down at the sleeping newborn, his heart swelling with pride. She was beautiful, just like her mother. Her carrot-colored hair peeked out from under her little bonnet, and her little lips moving in a sucking motion even without the presence of her mother's lactating breast. Bending down, his lips caressed the baby's forehead, inhaling her pure scent, food for his soul, before giving her a feather-light kiss.

Turning his attention to the other room, Goran let himself out of the nursery and proceeded with caution toward the mother's bedroom. Moving across the room without a sound, he stopped by the bed and inhaled, letting her scent saturate his senses. Goran picked his victims well, studying their patterns and their lifestyles before choosing who would bear his seed. It was too easy. He preyed on beautiful women. The sole prerequisite was the shade of their tresses. His long-standing fixation on redheads fueled his need to take them as the sacred vessel to bear his offspring, planting a seed with every thrust and every pound of his male pride into them. He derived deep satisfaction from every child who carried on both his name and the mother's hair. Goran wanted them crying out his name, moaning in ecstasy as they pictured him in their minds. He called upon them, weaving a sweet and mesmerizing spell to complete their satisfaction.

What's her name again—Milla? He racked his brain. There was no keeping up these days. The bed dipped under the weight of his body. The languid length of the woman's figure stirred, and then turned in his direction. He stilled himself, unmoving until she settled in a new position. He stayed still while her beautiful face relaxed under the glow of the light that streamed through the window from the outside lamp. Her sensual lips parted, and her even breathing was a provocative rhythm to his ears.

A part of his ritual was to ravish them with his eyes while they lay in innocent slumber before he used them to service his need. Time was up, and he was ready.

His gaze traveled down to her chest, which rose and fell with the cadence of her heartbeat. Goran slid his hand inside her parted legs, spreading them wider and getting her in position. He'd planned to take her again before he changed her. His gentle fingers ran through the soft curls splayed on her goose down pillow. It was a crown of red fire that framed her face and provoked his inner lust, which was gaining momentum and wouldn't be denied a moment longer.

Unzipping his trousers in one quick motion, he unleashed his already throbbing arousal and sheathed himself in her without any preliminaries. Her tight but languorous walls embraced him as he pumped into her again and again. Blissful sensation enveloped him as he worked at her, whispering waves of calming incantations in her ear. She moaned, prompting him to hurry while she was still caught under his spell. The old language he seldom uttered tumbled from his mouth as surging waves of euphoria hit him.

Wiping his shaft with her sheet, he pushed his proud length back into his trousers. Minutes later, he pressed his face closer to her neck, giving it a thorough lick and tasting her human sweetness before latching his fangs to the largest vein available to him. On contact, her eyes fluttered open, confusion spreading across her like wildfire when she saw him. There was a flicker of fear in her eyes, and he smelled her anguish as sweat beaded from her pores. She began thrashing her hands and legs, flailing under the weight of his body, which pinned her against the mattress. The pain that came was unavoidable. Change was tortuous, but the glory after would be worth it.

"Sshh, settle down, my lady," he whispered in the dark.

He cupped a hand on her mouth to trap her screams. His fangs throbbed with delight when he began drawing her blood, suckling and mixing enough of his own brand of poison and blood into her. Within a short time, her eyes rolled into the back of her head, her thrashing stopped, and she turned limp against his touch. Smiling at his latest conquest, he let his fingers trail along her velvety skin, savoring her not only with his hands, but also with his eyes. She was beautiful and would make a perfect addition to his harem.

With one swift movement, he lifted her almost-lifeless body, her head resting on his chest. The flimsy material of her nightgown settled like a feather on his arms, and her sweet scent wafted around him. She was coming home with him, another treasure he'd be adding to his growing collection. Her scent excited him even more. He proceeded to the nursery, carrying the woman's body as if she weighed nothing.

Bending down over the crib, he scooped up the sleeping baby, cradling her in her mother's arms, and proceeded to jump out of the window the same way he'd come.

Deep in the shadows, a lone soul waited for Goran to emerge. Not daring to exhale a single breath, the figure lurked in the darkness unmoving, taking every precaution to stay hidden and watching him with zealous eyes and unwavering interest when he landed on the pavement with a soft thud, a woman and infant cradled in his arms like precious cargo.

Goran's movements were lithe and purposeful, and a satisfied smile dominated his expression. Another successful venture in turning an innocent soul to the darkness and adding a bastard infant to his unlimited number of sired impervious Halflings.

"Spread your legs farther apart." Cyrus grunted in annoyance during sparring practice with Harrow. He stepped aside, checking Harrow's form, leg positioning, and posture. "Widen your stance, damn it."

It had been a week since they'd started Harrow's lessons, and despite gaining enough wisdom as far as martial art moves and tactics, he wanted more.

Moving his left foot an inch wider, Harrow did what he was told. It had been a grueling day under the watchful eyes of Cyrus, who he thought was worse than a drill sergeant. They'd started with stretching exercises he believed were more for Cyrus's benefit than his. Exhaustion wasn't part of his vampire makeup, far from it, but repetition could burn one's patience dry. They had been working on the same moves and techniques over and over. Harrow sometimes wondered if Cyrus was a perfectionist based on his request to repeat a stance or a leg block, or if he just sucked at it.

"Practice makes perfect." Cyrus had repeated the saying over and over, and it was beginning to drive Harrow stir crazy. Sure . . . whatever. He was beginning to believe otherwise. Practice could also lead one to realize that they had what it took to excel at something—or not.

"Now show me a roundhouse kick," Cyrus barked, crossing his arms over his chest.

Harrow bowed before executing a near-perfect kick. Cyrus inclined his head. A muscle in his jaw pulsed a little, but he said nothing.

"Do it again," he ordered.

Harrow narrowed his eyes, growing quite tired of doing the same thing over and over, but he knew better than to say anything. He repeated the kick, lifting one knee, arching it behind, and bringing it around in a large arc with his foot and knee at the same level. His hip and knee moved together before he extended his knee at the last minute, resulting in a powerful strike to the invisible target.

Cyrus walked in the direction of the rows of cabinets at the end of the room without uttering a word. He retrieved a rectangular wooden board and came back to face Harrow. With a hint of a smile, he held the board out for Harrow's inspection.

"I think you're ready for this. Let me remind you to control your kick. We humans are not as sturdy as you are. Just remember, in a real life scenario," he paused when Harrow smirked, "you can do whatever you want and kick as hard as you can. Now, do it again, and this time, the board will be your target."

Harrow spread his legs, bowed in Cyrus's direction, and with restrained movements, executed the same technique. This time he had a target. His leg extended, and his instep landed on the board, smashing it in the middle. A loud crack echoed as Cyrus staggered backward from the sheer force of the contact.

With a satisfied grin, Cyrus clasped the board together and handed it to Harrow.

"Here you go. That was good. I'm impressed. Now that you've perfected the Dollyo Chagi, I think you're ready for more." It was a definitive statement and was meant as a compliment.

"Thanks." Harrow smiled and took the board from Cyrus, who turned toward the drinking fountain. Harrow followed him. "I want to learn more as fast as you can teach me."

Cyrus lowered his head to the drinking spout, taking big gulps of water while Harrow waited for his answer. Wiping his mouth with the back of his hand, Cyrus looked up at him. "What's the big hurry?"

"I don't enjoy being idle. The sooner I learn, the better I'll feel." *And get this monkey off my back and let him hop onto the next loser,* Harrow thought acidly. He cast his memory back to the incident during which Jordan had not only kicked his rear but also his manly pride, and the bar fight in which he and Tor had been involved a week ago, when the vampire had to save his ass. God, could vampires have complexes these days?

"I have no problem with that, since you'd be doing all the work. Just do me one favor, will ya?"

"Shoot."

"Lose the sunglasses around me. I want to see who I'm talking to. And besides, don't want the boss to have to spend more money if I shatter them by accident." Cyrus chuckled.

"My eyes aren't pretty." It wasn't a lie. "I don't want to see a grown man running for the hills and calling for his mommy."

"My stomach's strong. You have nothing to worry about."

True to his word, the man had a strong stomach. He looked straight into Harrow's eyes when they spoke, not showing any indication that what he saw repulsed him.

The rest of the afternoon stretched into a blur of sparring, hand-to-hand combat techniques, instructions on throwing knives, and familiarizing himself with the use of throwing stars and daggers. There was much to learn, Harrow realized as he tried to keep up with Cyrus.

Then there was the question about his lesions, the wounds he covered with long-sleeved shirts. Harrow was still under the impression that he could infect people by mere touch. This was something he had to discuss with Leroy. Though Cyrus never mentioned anything about it, Harrow often questioned the human's frame of mind. If he had a silent death wish, Harrow would never know. Thinking it was best to keep his mouth shut, he made sure the wounds weren't visible to create distraction and discomfort.

Cyrus appeared winded, sweating, and panting like a horse by the time their session was over. Harrow, on the other hand, felt like a champion, and he basked in the afterglow of another fruitful session.

The shutters that blocked the sun's lethal rays in the office building began retracting with a loud whirring sound, marking the end of the day and the beginning of the evening for creatures such as him. With nothing better to do, Harrow wandered the now-empty corridors, taking a restful walk without a destination in mind.

He heard faint sounds of laughter when he reached the top floor that led out to the deck. Those giggles of pure mirth he hadn't heard for a long time. Harrow did not intend to barge into people's space, and he was ready to turn away when the women both looked in his direction. He stopped, hand gripping the doorknob, and he sensed a pair of amber-tinted eyes belonging to the redhead he hadn't seen for days watching him. It came as a surprise to see her still lingering in the facility when the gossips claimed that Jordan had been dying to get away.

She had a stout goal, considering she was planning to do it alone. *Stupid and ambitious*, he thought. It was death sentence, if anyone cared to ask for his opinion. Yes, males gossiped, too. Too late to leave now. Damn his antennae for failing to gather the much-needed information or maybe even just to warn him that she was still around. He would have tried harder to make himself scarce, knowing how his presence made her uncomfortable.

Stay away from me! The order still rang in his ears, echoing through the recesses of his mind and poking fun at his blasted ego. Harrow felt his insides tighten. He wasn't sure if it was anger or pleasure he felt at that moment. Stilling, his feet refused to move as he watched her behind the refuge of his dark sunglasses. There was no sign of the revulsion he had seen in her eyes before. Instead, she stared back at him, her expression blank.

"I don't think we've met," the other woman said, breaking the silence his presence had created. He hadn't seen her before, but he recognized her from the picture in Pritchard's office.

"I've seen you in pictures," Harrow replied, still poised to flee.

"And I've seen quite a few of you, too," Allison answered, dimples showing. She rose from the ledge and walked toward Harrow. She offered a hand. "I'm Allison."

"Harrow." He took her hand. It was soft, a hand that told you manual labor hadn't been a part of her past. It was the softness belonging to a child of wealth and good fortune. "Seen me?"

"Nice to finally meet you, Harrow. Yes, you know how Daddy is fond of his cameras and such. Nothing bad, don't worry." Her dimples deepened.

"Same here, Allison. I didn't mean to interrupt your conversation. I was just hoping to get a whiff of fresh air." He began backing away.

"It's free for all. Why don't you join us?" she asked.

From the corner of his eye, he saw Jordan squirm a little. Not wanting to crash their little party, he shook his head. "It's okay . . ."

"Got anything better to do, Gates?" Jordan derided him.

Harrow whipped his head in her direction, forgetting for a moment that Allison was standing in front of him. He regarded Jordan, trying to find any malice behind the aloof question.

"No, but . . ."

There hadn't been many times when Harrow had found himself tongue-tied and groping for a smart comeback, but this time, he had nothing to say.

"C'mon Harrow, we're just talking about our childhood antics, stuff we did in the past. Nothing heavy. I'm sure you have some stories to tell." Allison began tugging on his arm.

The simple touch was a welcome change, no matter how impersonal it might have been. With some reluctance, he let Allison lead him to where Jordan sat perched on the edge of the ledge, her feet swinging beneath her. Harrow waited for Allison to claim her spot before he settled next to her, leaving a considerable amount of distance between them.

"I was telling Jordan about my exploits during my second year at NYU. I was taking a Shakespeare acting class—"

"You're into acting? Shakespeare?" He looked surprised. *Now we're talking. Another Bard fan.*

"Yes, I am." Allison's eyebrows rose, sensing the excitement in Harrow's tone. "Do you like his work, too?"

"In fact, the night I was—" He abruptly stopped as memories came flooding back. The standing ovation, the fateful walk, the pain, and the bitter change he had gone through, all in the same night.

Sensing his distress, Allison prodded. "Go on."

Sighing, Harrow raked his fingers through his hair and waited until the memories abated, leaving him with scrambled thoughts. "Well, the night I was changed, I had just finished the biggest performance of my career as a theater actor." He winced as if having trouble conjuring happy memories amid the bitter thoughts that muddled his mind.

"Theater actor, huh? Must have been nice," Allison said, her voice wistful, as if she were reining in her own memories.

Harrow studied her with covert glances, as well as Jordan next to her. Both women had a faraway look in their eyes, as if they were fighting their own memories—the ghosts of the past that they'd rather forget, given their present predicament.

"Believe me, it wasn't as grand as it sounds. I had enough letdowns to last me a lifetime." Harrow stood up and jumped away from the ledge. He walked a few steps away and headed back in their direction, repeating the movement until he was walking in circles.

"Tell me, what type of production was it?" The interest in Allison's voice was unmistakable, and Harrow obliged.

"Well, it was a modern-day take on Midsummer Night's Dream. The director, who also doubled as the musical director, had adapted modern music to the play, creating a contemporary feel by mixing it with Billy's old-fashioned language."

Allison laughed at Harrow's nickname for the playwright. "Which character were you?"

"Lysander." Harrow snickered. It had been a character he'd enjoyed portraying. "I am, my lord, as well deriv'd as he. As well possess'd, my love is more than his, my fortunes every way as fairly rank'd."

Allison's genuine, delighted laughter reverberated in the quiet evening and bounced off the walls. Jordan, amused by Harrow's animation and his depiction of the character, couldn't help but join in Allison's jollity. She was quite familiar with Shakespeare's work, having taken an elective in college just for the heck of it. Hard as she tried not to show her interest, the vampire was good.

"You're amazing!" Allison's voice took on a vibrant tone.

"Thanks," Harrow replied, feeling quite pleased with himself. It had been a long time.

❧

Pritchard sat straighter on the chair in his office. It had been a long day. His back ached, and his head pounded from the day's work after meeting with potential clients. He could hear the sound of the helicopter blades as they buzzed from the helipad, taking the Japanese businessmen back to their hotel. This was the special mode of transportation via which he would allow his business associates to arrive at the facility. Safety was still his main concern. His business continued to need personal attention, even though he had capable people working for him. There were some aspects in the business he'd rather do himself.

The intercom buzzed. "Sir, General Krever is here."

God, how long had it been since he had seen his good friend? The man was as punctual as the beating of his heart. Good. "Let him in."

Pritchard fixed his necktie, finger-brushed his hair, and plastered a professional smile on his face as the door squeaked open, and his broad-shouldered friend walked in.

"Long time, Pritchard." Leo grinned as they exchanged handshakes and slapped each other on the back.

"A very long time, indeed. How have you been?" Pritchard relaxed. "Have a seat."

"Fine." Leo watched him, all too aware of the worries that plagued his friend. "How are you?"

"Everything's good. Just fine." Pritchard might as well be lying because Leo wouldn't buy it, but instead of prodding, he moved on to his favorite topic.

"How's my goddaughter?

"She's doing great." It wasn't a lie, for a change.

During work hours, he let Dante monitor the cameras and the activities in the facility. Dante was under strict orders to inform him of Allison's whereabouts. Since she seemed to be taken with Jordan, he'd followed the budding friendship with keen interest, paying close attention to their movements. This was no secret to his daughter, though conversations were muted as much as possible since he didn't want to invade his daughter's privacy more than he'd already done.

He had been watching them on and off from his laptop during the meeting, finding himself glued to the monitor and watching the life seep back into his daughter's facial expressions and behavior.

Excusing himself, he left Leo leafing through photo albums of their newest product. This was a visit for both business and pleasure. It had been a long time coming, a meeting they both had been planning. Leo was his contact in the military, the decision maker when it came to weapons acquisition, the sole outsider who knew about their operation, and a man he could trust with his life and his secret.

Pritchard walked to an adjoining room and increased the volume on another monitor to listen in on the trio's conversation, just in time to hear Harrow's recitation and the sweet sound of Allison's laughter. Pritchard felt his heart melt at the sound of a genuine giggle he hadn't heard since her mother had taken her own life.

Allison not only seemed full of life now, but she also began emerging from the walls with which she'd surrounded herself, coming out of the room she now shared with Jordan more often, and even paying him a visit several times in the past week. He marveled at the changes and thanked the gods for her positive transformation.

If he could persuade Jordan to stay, maybe even Harrow, Pritchard knew there was hope for Allison. It was now up to him to concoct reasons for the vampires to find it irresistible and worthwhile to stay. He hoped that Leroy would come up with something optimistic from all the blood samples Harrow had supplied to them for testing and studies.

Pritchard cranked the volume back down and scrutinized the gray-suited man who stared back at him in the mirror. There was the smile that had been absent for such a long time. It was a smile swelling with love and pride that only a father could feel.

He rejoined Leo at the business table after a few minutes. With a grin still lingering on his face, he said, "I want to show you how good your goddaughter looks nowadays," and Leo eagerly nodded his head.

Demetrius arrived at the vampire headquarters a few seconds before his father did, hiding in his chambers and trying to make himself scarce to avoid questioning. Not that anyone would question him, except his father. The Council members were known to closet themselves, preferring the confines of their chambers and opting to come out only when called upon. They weren't social creatures. It was unheard of to mingle with the humans-turned vampires, or as they were callously called, the Mongrels—who he had dubbed half-baked vampires.

Each member had his or her own duty. August, for one, was in charge of their finances. A female named Marania kept the records on full-blooded vampires, the ones who were able and expected to procreate. Randolph was the liaison to other existing Vampire Councils spread worldwide. And there was Bretania, the Council's tactical and weapons expert, a position that had been abruptly vacated by Rohnert.

The Council could be likened to the human government. Each branch served a purpose, whether it was administering laws, promoting justice, or upholding their way of life. Running the U.S. Council and its population was by far one of the most lucrative positions there was. Most vampires would love to be in Goran's shoes, because he held one of the most coveted positions. Goran's family bloodline would continue to rule until he was unable to produce a pureblooded heir.

These purebred vampires were considered an elite class and were on the verge of extinction. Their numbers were dwindling, and it was part of their mission to produce heirs and to keep their bloodline thriving. Why Goran hadn't produced a purebred offspring was a mystery to many.

Demetrius eased out of his coat and clothes before walking to the shower, feeling rather raw with his mind running in complete turmoil. His mother provided all information about his father's exploits and extracurricular activities. He had no problem with it, and even if he did, there was no questioning Goran. This was his show, and others, including Demetrius, were mere puppets.

He poured a generous amount of shampoo on his palm before massaging it into his hair. The hot water was soothing his tired and aching muscles.

Demetrius was aware of the redhead army Goran was creating. After some time, the secret had gotten out, not that his mother could keep it a secret from him. The army was increasing in numbers. They needed to go out after having been cooped up in a section of their headquarters so long, not to mention that their services had been called upon when the revolution he'd spearheaded had failed to produce a victory that measured up to Goran's standards. His father was impatient and had sprung into action soon after.

In a few days, the rebellion had been squashed. Demetrius saw his rank shoot down to the lowest grade imaginable. The one saving grace had been his mother Melissa, the headstrong leader of the harem. After containing the rowdy group of vampires, she had persuaded Goran that their son's failure wasn't his fault. The young vampires Demetrius commanded were volatile and erratic at best. Many of them were easily swayed, and some were terrified, running away from their positions even before facing the enemy. By chance, Melissa had called it, when Demetrius and Giancarlo and a few others were able to fight back and get away with their lives intact.

Failure was unacceptable, not an option. Goran had accused Demetrius of failing to live up to his standards, and he'd believed his father, vowing to do better next time. From then on, Demetrius tried to stay out of Goran's way, opting to do the menial work of choosing hardcore souls to fortify their ranks.

He walked out of the bathroom, still feeling ill at ease. He rummaged through his vast collection of clothing and picked out a pair of dark-washed jeans and a black Henley before strapping a holster full of Dangeran weapons across his body. He picked a dark brown bomber jacket and pulled his shoulder-length hair into a low ponytail before striding out of his room to meet Giancarlo.

Demetrius was resolved to leave as soon as night fell and start scouring the streets and establishments for humans to convert. The candidates he sought were those who exhibited willingness to follow orders and those who possessed inherent darkness of the soul. These were the traits he needed to harvest in order to regain the trust and praise of his father again.

As soon as nightfall claimed the skies and darkness loomed over the outskirts and fringes of the city, Demetrius and Giancarlo set out the in the night as planned. Armed with wickedness, loathing in their hearts, and prime Dangeran weapons, they entered a shady bar that was frequented by bikers, druggies, and pushers alike.

Demetrius fingered his medal, a necklace that bore the Council's seal and had been gift from his father, something he'd worn all his life. It was a simple, octagonal piece of metal the color of faded gold that read We Will Prevail in the old language, encircling an oak bush. According to Goran, the plant was as old as the last ice age, a symbol of strength, endurance, and worth. The plant withstood the test of time, surviving in the most extreme climates, prevailing, just like them and their way of life. They had as much right to exist as their human counterparts, and they would go through adversities and weather the test of time.

He had doubted his place in his father's life and questioned his position in the hierarchy of succession. Demetrius was his father's firstborn bastard, but the first one nonetheless. It had to mean something, and he had to assert himself if he wanted a bite of the big cookie. Good graces—that was what he was aiming for, where he wanted to be.

The probability of Goran siring a purebred vampire remained a threat to him. For sure, Daddy-O or the Vampire Council wouldn't even consider Demetrius, much less look at him as a front-runner candidate to ascend the seat when the time came. But he wasn't losing hope. There were other ways . . . if he had his chance.

His mother could help and had been aiding him every step of the way. Make no mistake, he wasn't a mama's boy, but anyone who wanted to be someone needed a boosting once in a while. However, Melissa often wondered about her own position in his father's life. As of late, Goran had been spending an exceptional amount of time with the other vampires in his harem, electing not to call on Melissa to satisfy his needs. Being threatened was a sad reality for his mother.

Demetrius inhaled air deep into his lungs before pushing his domestic concerns aside. He swept one quick glance through the bar, hating the task to which he'd been reduced.

Sensing his irritation, Giancarlo pointed at a corner table. "Boss, go sit, let me do the dirty job. Just spot for trouble, okay?"

Demetrius nodded and strode to the corner table. The lights had been dimmed as much as possible in that the corner, making it a good spot to be. He could watch without being noticeable. He unbuttoned his jacket before he sat down, making sure his weapons were within easy reach. Maybe they could also snag and kill a few infected lowlifes in the process. After all, Maynard's was rumored to be frequented by the sick bastards who were hoping to get a quick fix and infect others.

It was a sick, vicious circle. The sooner they got rid of the parasites, the better the whole vampire population would be. Their numbers, he hoped, were dwindling from being hunted. Others had gone into hiding, surfacing only when the need to feed arose. But there were still some dumb enough to mingle with the rest of them, hoping that they would blend. Their eyes were a dead giveaway. Not to mention, they stunk to high heaven. Demetrius made it a point to pay close attention to those beings who preferred to wear dark lenses despite the almost pitch-black interior of the bar. The foul odor was another thing. Each time a lesion was in its active state, the stench was hard to miss.

Glancing around the smoky room and tapping his fingers on the table to the beat of a slow rock tune that was playing on an aging jukebox, he watched several couples sway to the music on the parquet flooring in the middle of the room, devouring each other like hungry, rabid dogs. *Pathetic losers,* Demetrius thought as he switched his attention to Giancarlo, who seemed to have befriended several lowlifes at the bar. Giancarlo was slapping empty shot glasses on the table with a few men as they finished yet another round of drinks. It was a surefire way to earn the respect of humans and gain easy access as soon as the unsuspecting fools were beyond inebriation.

"Hey, good looking, can I get you something to drink?" A bleach-blonde wearing a micro mini and four pounds' worth of silicone implants asked.

Instead of answering right away, he raked his eyes over the waitress's body with deliberation meant to make her uncomfortable enough to leave. Instead, the woman pushed her chest forward, inviting and full of enthusiasm. There was no question that she liked what she was seeing.

Demetrius was pleasing to the eye. The opposite sex stood no chance when he decided to turn on the charm.

"I'll have a glass of scotch, no ice," he said, losing interest in the woman, who was looking like she was ready to sell herself to the devil just to get Demetrius's dick inside her almost nonexistent skirt.

Recognizing the expression so well, Demetrius smirked and waved his hand for her to disappear from his presence. He wasn't interested in bedding someone at the moment, and he wasn't hungry either. There were a lot of things he needed to think about, the scenarios running through his mind. The woman frowned at his blatant disregard at her offer and left.

Just as another song started on the jukebox, Demetrius noticed a lone figure hunched at the bar, head bowed down. He knew the tendencies. He could spot it from miles away. If being invisible was a possibility, he knew the person would have opted for it. With undisguised interest, Demetrius observed the man, who was unmoving at first, deep in thought while trying his best to stay inconspicuous.

A few minutes later, the same waitress who had taken his drink order strolled over to the man. He whispered something to her, and the woman threw back her head in laughter. There were a few more exchanges between the two before the man got up, following her toward the rear of the room. Demetrius couldn't hear the conversation. The loud music atop the warring laughter, banter, and chatting made it impossible to hear the exchange.

Giancarlo was still buried in shot glasses, vying for the trust of two bikers whose droopy eyes and slurred speech were guarantees that they'd be falling like flies soon. Demetrius got up and followed the stranger in time to see the door to the women's restroom swing open and closed, swallowing the two from sight. The lock clicked into place.

Knowing what to expect and with his dagger aimed forward, Demetrius kicked the door open, tearing it from its hinges. He found the two carousing by the sink. With the woman's legs straddled around the man's waist, her head thrown back in apparent ecstasy and the vampire's fangs bared and ready to pounce, neither one looked up.

Without hesitation, Demetrius threw the dagger straight into the vampire's head and watched him convulse before falling forward and taking the woman down with him. She landed on her back and burst out screaming upon realizing the man above her was dead. Blood gushed from his head down to the woman's face, creating a pool of crimson liquid on the white tiles as the woman frantically pushed and shoved to get the body off her.

Before she could push the dead vampire aside, there was a loud crackling noise, and the body started disintegrating before their eyes, blood and all. The only remnants would be a heap of ashes and Demetrius's dagger.

Annoyed at the noise she was making, Demetrius flashed to the irritating woman and pulled her aside to reveal his dagger on the floor.

"Shut up," he ordered and pulled his dagger from the pile of ashes. Scowling at the stain of blood on his blade, he lowered the dagger toward the woman's face as she continued to scream bloody murder and wiped the blades with the strands of her hair. Laughing at the terror in her eyes, he slipped out the back door and into the pale moonlit night. Giancarlo would soon realize that he had left. He heard footsteps approaching the crime scene as he darted out of the parking lot and blended with the rush of foot traffic.

Some nights produced results they cared about, and some nights didn't. But he had to remind himself that one less infected rat was as good as creating another one.

Goran closed the door to the adjoining room, feeling rather pleased with himself. He went straight to his closet and pulled out a robe, then proceeded to the bathroom for a much-needed shower. The night had proven to be another fruitful endeavor, he thought, smiling to himself. The baby was beautiful, just like her mother. Esmeralda would grow up into a lovely vampire, no doubt. Fathering several Halflings was his way of spreading his bloodline, even if they wouldn't ever be deemed worthy.

He was too proud to ask the elders for help. Ancient rules about creating pure vampires had been buried since his father Cantor's reign, so he'd opted to seed bastards with human females instead of seeking the help of purebred females who could give him pureblooded offspring. Goran was as pure as they came, and he wasn't planning to relinquish his seat in the Council, so no one had the gall to challenge his supremacy or question his actions. This worked best for him.

Standing under the steaming spray of hot water, Goran thought of his newest creation. Milla. Her name alone evoked a wave of lust in him. The woman, still slumbering, was the epitome of the kind of young blood he craved. She was perfect for him, a source of feeding pleasure for days and nights to come.

A slight movement outside the shower door alerted him of company. Just one woman—one vampire—dared intrude his solitude. Only one vampire was bold enough to test his patience, and more often, he had let it slide. She was good to him, a very good warrior and leader. Every single one of his orders was adhered to with utmost obedience and respect.

"Mind if I join you?" Melissa's lustrous voice drifted in when she opened the shower door, her naked form facing him in all its glory.

Goran spread his arms wide in welcome, raking his eyes over her taut breasts, their pink tips glorious and perky, before sliding his gaze to her flat yet firm stomach and down to her hot center. "Join me, my dear," he answered with pure pleasure.

With grace, Melissa slipped inside the shower and wrapped her arms around his waist, the gentle slosh of water grazing her skin. He folded his arms around her, feeling her soft skin rubbing against his skin and marveling at her delicate beauty.

"How did it go?" Melissa asked, pulling herself away to look at him. Her voice was even, not showing any hint of how she felt inside. Restraint was one of her best qualities.

"The mother and babe are both doing well . . ."

"As they should be," she replied.

Her hands went up to his chest, spreading them to feel the expanse of his skin as he lifted her hair to nuzzle her neck, breathing in her incredible scent. They all possessed distinct scents that drove him wild. Melissa's particular aroma was that of sweet vanilla, a rarity in Goran's book. Tilting her head, she captured his mouth and slithered her tongue inside, teasing, exploring, and desiring. She purred, creating a delicious sensation in Goran's body. His hand explored the length of her back, caressing her before his fingers raked her hair, toying with the ends.

Melissa arched her body and pressed against him. Goran felt himself getting excited. Grabbing her hips, he guided himself into her with one thrust. That was all it took for Melissa to be filled with unadulterated desire, falling under his spell. With a series of shoves and pulls, Melissa's ecstasy burst, moaning and heady with intense passion. With a final thrust, Goran rasped out an ecstatic groan.

She melted into his arms, spent and giddy with satisfaction. "You're incredible," she said after a moment.

"As you are, my lady," Goran responded, drawing the curtain then handing her a towel. "You will see to Milla and the baby?"

"As always."

Melissa stepped out of the shower and wrapped the towel around her body. She tilted her head in deference before walking out of the bathroom, holding her head high.

Time passed quickly if it was spent with purpose. Such was the case for Harrow, who spent all his time training with Cyrus. This, of course, was being dictated by Cyrus' ability to get away from his responsibilities at the facility. As much as Cyrus wanted to share his wealth of fighting tactics and skills with Harrow, he joked that he needed to sleep, too, unlike vampires, who required less.

Weeks had gone by during which Harrow soaked in instructions and methods like a sponge, and he was surprised to find himself eager for more. In the process, mutual respect had grown between the two men, falling just short of giving verbal praise. Except for the usual grunts and nods of approval, not much was uttered between them. In spite of their differences, an easy camaraderie had been forged between them. Cyrus no longer felt it a duty to train Harrow but took pleasure in helping a friend.

With his confidence mounting with each passing minute, Harrow practiced with conscientious patience and diligence, even without Cyrus. He found the throwing stars and daggers among the weapons he most favored.

"What part of 'rest and relaxation' don't you get, my friend?" Cyrus asked, securing goggles to his face right next to Harrow at the shooting range.

It had been one day since they'd last sparred against each other, Cyrus huffing and out of breath when he declared Harrow to be "good and ready" while his body was pinned to the ground. The human had asked for a break, claiming sore muscles and a bruised ego. Harrow had laughed it off and sauntered away with a renewed sense of pride and humor. But at the end of the day, he still wanted to learn more, for lack of better things to occupy his time.

This was in sharp contrast to his roommate and appointed babysitter. Tor had taken an extreme liking to the DVR, often spending his supposed sleeping hours in front of the television, recording films as he feasted his eyes on every action movie available.

Harrow found it impossible to sit still. There was a nagging feeling of being a complete freeloader for not being able to give something back for all the gifts and favors he'd been getting. Short of waving him off, Pritchard had assured him several times that his help came in terms of being an experimental subject in finding the cure and that this was more than enough payment. He had nothing to worry about as far as Pritchard was concerned.

Then there was the issue of Jordan. Jordan . . . the vampire he had avoided since the night they'd spoken atop the deck with Allison. Although he and Allison had done most of the talking, he'd caught a glimpse of Jordan's sympathetic side, when she'd smiled and listened with interest, even without speaking.

Harrow realized he wouldn't be able to resist the attraction he'd felt from the first moment he'd seen her if he was often thrust into her presence. Avoidance was his greatest ally, and hiding in the training room was his escape.

Harrow emptied the round of bullets into the target. The ear-splitting bangs of empty shells came as they pinged to the ground while he continued to fire with fierce concentration and murderous aim. The target stood no chance as the bull's-eye hole got bigger and bigger.

He smiled to himself, pleased at the outcome. Placing the gun down on the table in front of him, he acknowledged Cyrus with a nod as the human positioned himself, closed one eye, and took aim at his target. Gunshot erupted and empty shells grazed the floor, and Cyrus let out a whooping fist pump the moment he replaced his gun on the table. His target, with its gaping hole in the middle, was evidence of how accurate his aim was. With a cocky grin, he turned to Harrow.

"I don't require sleep like you do, my man, and besides, what is there to do here except watch TV, aside of course from avoiding Leroy and his needles." Harrow chuckled, not hating the doctor for his obsessive habit of drawing all the blood Harrow was willing to supply.

Cyrus snorted. "Tor is hogging the tube again?"

"The vampire is tireless. I think he has a secret aspiration to be Clint Eastwood, Charles Bronson, or even Tom Cruise."

"Go ahead, make my day." Cyrus mimicked the famous movie phrase while pretending to shoot his gun, cowboy style.

Reloading their guns with another cartridge, Harrow and Cyrus, who were separated by clear fiberglass, fired their weapons simultaneously. Neither stopped until it was time to reload or change the target, firing until the guns were ready to blow smoke, only to repeat the routine over again.

"Why don't you let me join your patrol tonight?" Harrow asked after replacing his gun in the ammo cabinet at the corner of the room. Several members of Cyrus's team came through the swinging doors and glanced his way. Although the humans were still wary around him, they treated him with polite indifference.

"No can do. Strict orders," Cyrus replied, reaching into his back pocket for a stick of gum. After popping it in his mouth, he tossed the wrapper in the wastebasket. "Sorry."

Harrow shook his head, feeling trapped even with the go-as-you-want policy. "I'm not delicate china, you know. I think you can vouch for me."

Lifting an eyebrow at Harrow as they strode out of the shooting range, Cyrus shook his head. "Even if I think you're good enough to go, Pritchard would skin me alive, take my hide, and burn it to a crisp while I watched. No, sir! Don't want that for myself."

"Damn it, Cyrus. This is a Beverly Hills prison." Hating the whiny tone of his voice, Harrow slipped his hands in his pockets and shrugged.

"You know I wouldn't hesitate to take you in a heartbeat." Cyrus chuckled. "No pun intended. But the boss would need a very good reason to allow you to go. A routine patrol won't cut it."

"Yeah, whatever."

As head of security, Cyrus went out on a routine run each night, scouring the general vicinity of the facility and roaming the neighborhood for additional down-and-out infected vampires to play Robin Hood for.

Reaching the first floor, they stopped outside Cyrus's door. "I'll see you at nine tomorrow. Bring your best spinning kick."

Harrow grunted his answer, feeling like a benched ten-year-old who's being punished for bad conduct. He heard Cyrus's good-natured laugh as he closed the door behind him.

"Hey, Cinderella! Where have you been?" Tor hollered as Harrow strode into their shared quarters. Harrow rolled his eyes at the other vampire, who was busy strapping his weapons holster across his chest.

"Where the hell are you going?" He flopped on the sofa, brought his feet up, and propped them on the coffee table.

Harrow knew what went down during those patrolling nights. Either Cyrus, Lambert, or other people from their team, whether vampire or human, scouted the bars and trolled pool halls, lounges, and dance clubs to find infected and hunted vampires and saving them from the wrath of the Vampire Council.

Why Pritchard aimed to save every vampire out there was beyond Harrow's grasp, but he wasn't about to complain. He was one of the lucky recipients of Pritchard's kind heart, and for that he was grateful. Still, this being left behind was getting to him like never before now that he was feeling stronger and better.

"Lambert's off tonight, so I'm taking his spot along with Drake and Holt." Slipping his jacket into place and patting his chest, Tor peered at Harrow's face. "I think you need to feed soon. Your cheeks are hollowing out."

Jest or not, Harrow flashed his fangs at Tor. Sick of being treated as if he was made of porcelain, Harrow leapt nimbly and was at Tor's neck before the other vampire could react. Grabbing him by the collar of his jacket, Harrow hissed in his ear. "Don't tempt me, I don't like male vampire blood, but I just might make an exception tonight."

Tor staggered backward, but he was not surprised. "Heard you were training hard," he said, lifting his hands palms out and yielding to Harrow's sudden attack. "I better tell Cyrus your temper isn't a good match with all that combat training he's giving you."

Harrow relaxed his grip on Tor's jacket and continued glaring at him. "Go," he muttered, releasing Tor after he'd calmed down a notch.

"Just so you know, Lambert's watching you tonight."

With those words, Tor left the room, chortling. Harrow felt like he was about to burst. He was sick and tired of the ninny jokes that had been going around long enough. There had to be a way to show the others what he was made of. Yeah, maybe one of these days, he would.

For lack of anything better to do, Harrow resorted to wandering the hallways. He was, after all, a benched student. He continued walking until his feet took him to the rooftop. There was nowhere else to go in the facility. Watching the news made him more depressed with all the killings, accidents, and coups d'état. The facility was pleasant, yet it could be stifling at times. The same faces and activities day after day sure could drive a person mad.

He needed air, and this was a place where he could get as much as he wanted. Harrow pushed his sunglasses off his face and rested them on his head. He was alone anyway and could get away with exposing his appalling eyes.

But of course, time wasn't cooperating with him. When he reached his usual spot on the ledge, he found that Jordan was sitting on the concrete as if her name had been stamped on it.

He knew it was too late to back out when she turned and looked at him.

"Out again, for your usual repose?" she asked.

Taken aback by the cordial inflection in her voice, it took him a moment to respond. "Someone has been taking the cameras seriously."

"It's a pity to leave them gathering dust. I took it upon myself to use all the technology available to me." Jordan regarded him for a moment. Whatever she was thinking was not betrayed by the blank expression on her face.

If she was making small talk for his benefit, it was working. He was thirsty for company. Tor was not the conversationalist, with his wise cracks and low-blow teasing, who Harrow was looking for.

"Mind if I join you?" he asked.

"Do as you wish," Jordan answered.

Now, wasn't that a perfect answer? If he could do what he wanted, she'd be wrapped in his arms, moaning his name as he kissed her all over. Yeah, maybe add a little blood play somewhere in there, too. These were dangerous ideas to even consider. Harrow pushed them to the back of his mind and attempted to clear his head.

With a sigh, he sat down a few feet away from her but did not speak. He was aware that he needed to refrain from saying anything that might ruin the moment. Jordan did the same. They stayed silent, content to just stare out at the lure of the city lights. The only sound that reminded him she was still sitting in his favorite spot was the swishing of her feet while they swung back and forth underneath her.

Not bad. No conversation was necessary so long as they could stay close to each other and didn't get the urge to tear each other's heads off. *This was a start.* Harrow smiled to himself.

As the foursome entered the already-crowded pool hall, they noticed a tense atmosphere charging the air. After exchanging quick glances, they made their way toward the rear of the room where the bar was located. The pool hall, a long-standing destitute hangout, was located in a raunchy part of the city. Most of the people who visited the place were derelicts themselves. According to Holt's intel, both humans and vampires frequented the joint, and this was their target for the night.

With Holt and Drake flanking Cyrus, Tor walked in behind them. This was the vampire's first night out with the boys, and by the looks of things, it would be a long night. Holt stepped forward and waved his hand at the bartender. A brawny ex-marine and a man of few words, he exuded confidence and good instincts.

"Order up," he barked at them when the bartender bounded in their direction.

"I'll have a Coors Light," Drake called out.

"Same here," Cyrus said, settling on the last available barstool. "How about you, Tor?"

"Patron Silver," Tor told the bartender, who hurried away to fill their order.

While the others looked around, Cyrus focused on a scantily clad woman in a tank top, her breasts almost free-for-all to ogle. Completing her hooker outfit was a tight, frilly skirt that left nothing to the imagination as she worked on a man standing a few feet away from them.

"Wanna have some fun?" The blonde hoisted her arms around the man's shoulder to get his attention, before grabbing his crotch in a playful manner. Cyrus smirked at the sight. Women in these types of joints were hookers as a general rule. No human woman in her right mind would hang out at a place like this otherwise. Either that or she was looking for a quick fix, a snort, or a pill to pop.

"I'm hungry," The vampire drawled, exposing a pair of canines that seemed sharp and dangerous. Cyrus straightened and leaned closer to listen without being too obvious. The man, he noted, was a face he'd seen before, but he couldn't quite recall the details.

"Oh," the woman giggled. "What's on your mind?"

"I'd rather not talk about it here."

"Wanna follow me to the back?"

"Sure," the man answered and grabbed her around the waist, pivoting her toward the neon exit sign. "Let's go."

The stranger paused for a moment and looked around before walking out of the room with the woman in tow. Cyrus got up with the intention of following them, not relishing the idea that a vampire would be created, bottom dwellers or not.

"Gotta take a piss," he told Drake who just nodded, eyes glued and intent on watching a basketball game on a little overhead television.

Cyrus let the pair get a head start before he exited through the back door. The air was still humid, prickling his skin as he adjusted his eyes to the dark alley with the barest glimmer of light coming from the lamppost on the main street.

He spotted the man and woman a few seconds later. The woman had her legs straddled around the man's waist, and he was pumping his body hard against her, with her leaning on the concrete wall of the club's grimy exterior.

Trying not to conceal himself but not appear as if he were watching them, he pretended to fish for something inside his pocket. He heard the woman's moans and mewls as the vampire thrust harder into her. For a brief moment, Cyrus saw him flash his fangs when the woman arched her neck in apparent ecstasy, exposing her veins in an open invitation.

Before the vampire could sink his teeth into her skin, Cyrus bolted into action, flicking his knife in the man's direction. Vampires were fast, he realized in the millisecond that passed. The vampire whipped his head in Cyrus's direction, sensing the attack, and he was able to dodge the first knife but the second one buried itself into his arm. With a growl loud enough to startle the dead, the vampire skittered in his direction too fast for Cyrus to be able to change his direction, much less grab another weapon from his holster.

By then, the knife he'd used on the vampire was being plunged right into his own gut, the blade twisted with considerable force into his body. He fell to the ground just as an explosive pain shot through his abdomen. Cyrus caught the sight of the vampire trying to slash his own arms off before the process of poisoning and disintegration brought about by the Dangeran blade finished him off.

But before Cyrus could so much as twitch the corner of his mouth in a satisfied grin, the world as he knew it darkened, and he blacked out.

"Is there anything you wanted to ask me?" Pritchard asked as soon as the meeting adjourned. He sat on his usual seat at the head of the table with Harrow to his left and a glass of scotch in hand.

Harrow looked up and met the man's eyes. "You gave a lot of us a chance to stay and reform here. I know you don't ask for much." He watched while Pritchard knitted his eyebrows, trying to follow his words. "What I'm trying to say is . . . there are vampires who I'm sure at one time wouldn't be able to contain their bloodlust and who would make a mistake. What do we do with them?"

Pritchard put the glass to his lips and downed the entire thing in one gulp. The man didn't care for doing anything halfway, that much was certain. Just like his approach in life—take the world by the balls, run with it without stopping until questions were answered, problems were solved, and goals were reached. He might have been enigmatic, but he was fair in every aspect of his dealings. Harrow couldn't help the respect he felt for the man.

"There have been many accidents in the past, and most of the victims were people we love who were here working for us. We have a strike team, a group of vampires and humans, who hand out judgment to those who carelessly end a human life."

"Please explain that part," Harrow requested.

"The process is led by the victim, the human-turned-vampire. They have a guideline to follow to determine if leniency would be appropriate. Strike one is given a first chance if the victim deems it forgivable. If not, then we destroy the vampire."

Harrow winced at the thought. He realized such things were possible. With two such beings trying to coexist, and their half having a nasty tendency to drain humans, there had to be some form of repercussion aside from just a mere slap on the wrist.

"Tell me if I've got this right. The vampire is given a chance if the victim deems it forgivable? There's a lot of convincing involved, I'm sure."

Pritchard leaned against the supple leather chair and shot his gaze upward before closing his eyes and resting his head on his entwined palms.

"Yes, before they are hired, our human employees are given the possible scenarios, and they can leave if they want or remain. No one is staying here against their will and without full disclosure."

Harrow laughed. "Now is that the truth?"

"Well, maybe not quite for you, Jordan, and Tor. You people have no idea what's good for you, so I had to step in. You all have vendettas or an agenda, which I know are important but very misplaced. I'm just here to provide directions and financial assistance."

"And what's in it for you?"

"People always ask me that question." Pritchard shifted in his chair, opened his piercing blue eyes, and focused them on Harrow. "Is it so unbelievable that I have no hidden agenda except wanting to find anything that might help Allison and the others?"

Harrow felt compassion toward the other man, but still wary of his ulterior motives. "Not at all. I understand where you're coming from. But all this money you're spending on the facility, I'm sure it's going to drain you dry soon enough."

"What you really want to know is how I sustain the operation."

Harrow nodded. He was not one to pry, but his curiosity on this point had to be satisfied. He suspected that there had to be a basic part of the operation Pritchard could use to support the upkeep, payroll, and maintenance of their facility.

"Tack Enterprises is a designer of weapons, like the sniper rifles the military uses. I have had their business for some time now, and this facility is a tax deduction for me. I used this as an expense to produce the income —"

"Oh, enough of the income mumbo-jumbo." Harrow cut him off and laughed. "I'm not big on numbers. Never was my strongest subject in school."

Pritchard laughed as well. "I do have a *very* close friend inside who is aware of this operation, and in fact, some of our intel is coming from him."

"Whoa, are you telling me that the government is aware of our existence? Vampires?"

"The government, and the military in general, have information based on things they are finding out there. Believe me when I say, they are keeping a close eye on things, but they find it necessary to keep their info on the down-low because an all-out war isn't productive and would be very dangerous. And what most humans don't know won't hurt them, right?"

Harrow nodded, and Pritchard continued. "Knowledge of other beings requires tolerance and restraint. After all, Earth isn't under the sole ownership of humans. Vampires, and whatever else is out there, deserve the chance to coexist, so long as the imaginary line of decency isn't breached."

"Damn, this is much bigger than I thought. I hate to think that the government is allowing humans to be slaughtered without feeling the need to spring into action." Harrow shook his head. Now, things were clicking into place like a Rubik's cube. "I'm curious about the blood supply."

"Ah, I've been wondering when you were going to ask me about that." Pritchard smiled. Pushing his body off the chair, he covered the few steps toward his built-in wall bar and refilled his glass. Instead of heading back to the table, Pritchard began a listless walk around the expanse of his office space.

"You guys can eat human food, but it doesn't give the nourishment like blood does. It buys you a little time, a day or two maybe just to hold off the hunger, right?"

Harrow nodded.

"We have a blood donation hotline to which people donate their blood, and they get paid for it. Believe me, there are a lot of people who need the money and are willing to donate a pint or two."

"Where is all this being done?"

All the information was quite new to Harrow. He had figured there was more to the whole operation than what Pritchard had led him to believe. This had to be a massive undertaking on the human's part, considering he was dealing with precious lives. Harrow took his sunglasses off his face and rubbed his eyes. Information overload was creeping up on him again. The feeling of whiplash his endless questions caused him had been increasing ever since he had become a part of the operation.

"It's done outside the facility. We have several collection sites masquerading as health centers for the down-and-out of our society."

Harrow's eyes narrowed. "*Are* you helping the down-and-out?"

Pritchard laughed. "Yes, we are. And we are a big benefactor for the Red Cross. We get most of their rejects since we are not concerned about diseases other than what we are facing here right now."

"Isn't that a little reckless? What if a new disease, another strain, is born out of it?"

"God, Harrow, where is this entire compassion and do-good attitude coming from?" Pritchard teased him.

"You have to give me more than a jab at my personality."

"Hold your sensitive heart, my boy. Of course, we test each one. Why do you think we have all those machines in the laboratory? I'm sure you didn't think those were all yours." Pritchard laughed again. As annoying as he could be, Harrow joined the laughter.

He knew the immensity of the disease he'd created, and it was a big enough problem to worry about. Harrow wished Leroy could do his miracle crap and find a cure or a method to stabilize the damned disease.

"True, that."

"We have an abundant blood supply for everyone. The reason for that is to discourage human attacks within the facility. Newly created vampires who aren't infected are the doings of the other vampires out there, and we are not concerned with them. So far, the uninfected ones that we are associating with in here are just Tor and Jordan."

"Yeah, I know."

Jordan—the name elicited a different response from Harrow. His system was doing flip-flops inside, giving him a fuzzy, warm feeling he wasn't sure about. He felt like a lovesick puppy dog and hated himself for it.

"So it goes without saying, if they're bitten or in any way involved in . . . well, you know what . . ." Embarrassed, Pritchard left the sentence dangling in the air. "They could get infected, too."

Harrow grunted a response. It felt like the man could read into his actions, more than he was willing to admit. "I know what you're saying, Pritchard."

"Um . . . I know it's none of my business. I can see it, Harrow."

Pritchard's skin color turned beet red, as if embarrassed by the revelation. He downed his glass and sat back down.

"God damn it. Am I that transfuckinparent?"

Harrow hated this wear-his-heart-on-his-sleeve deal. He not only felt like a pansy, but also a laughing stock to all the fuckers watching his life evolve on camera.

"Just to me and Dante." Pritchard snickered.

"Dude, seriously. I'm getting tired of you pussies gossiping. You had better knock it off. It's an invasion of privacy. I'm sure I have some rights here, don't I?"

"Sorry, H, those rights were revoked when you took the first sip of our blood here."

Pritchard had the nerve to laugh aloud, making Harrow's blood start its boiling process. "Believe me, one of these days, I'm going to stick gum on those expensive cameras of yours, and you'll be sorry."

"Don't even think about it." Pritchard grinned at the threat, but after a few moments his expression turned thoughtful. He gave Harrow a lingering stare. It held Harrow's attention and told him that there was a revelation coming up.

"You know, I treat you like the son I never had."

"Whoa, Daddy, I don't like feeling special." Harrow quipped and laughed.

"Yeah, yeah. Believe me, this is making me feel like I want to throw up, but it needs to be said." Pritchard waited until Harrow had stopped laughing. "If there comes a time when I am unable to continue this project, I want you to help Allison."

The request came as a big surprise to Harrow. Of all things to happen, this was the last he would have expected. For Pritchard to even think of tying him down to the operation, to the facility, was a shock.

"Why me? And where are you going?"

"Because I see the goodness in you. You retain a lot of your humanity, and you don't think with your muscles or your dick. You're not impulsive, and you treat people, humans and vampires alike, with respect. And besides, you and Allison are in the same boat. No one will understand her better than you. You have the same pain and carry the same burden. I know you will treat her like a sister and help her through tough times."

Harrow shook his head, unable to grasp the weight of Pritchard's request. "So give me a Nobel Peace Prize or something, but don't expect me to help run a facility or be kin to your daughter. You hardly know me. I'm just a lost cause you picked up off the street. You can't be serious about this."

"Cut the joking, Harrow. I'm dead serious. Call me crazy, but I trusted you from the moment you came here."

Harrow snorted in response. There was nothing he could say at the moment. Pritchard's trust overwhelmed him.

"I will have it all written down soon. I don't know when my time will be up. This is my wish, and I want you to promise me you'll see it come to fruition." Pritchard leaned closer and put his hand on top of Harrow's arm. Although there was a fabric that separated their skin, Harrow could feel the warmth and sincerity in the Pritchard's touch and see the burning authenticity in his eyes. As much he wanted to deny the man his request, Harrow found himself giving a pledge of solidarity and dedication.

"Damn it, Pritchard. This is a tall order, one I don't think I'm worthy or capable of fulfilling, but I'll try not to fail you." Fuck, now that he'd said it, there was no going back. He was at the crossroads, the point of no return.

"Thank you," Pritchard whispered.

Harrow saw the lines in the man's face disappearing, as if a huge weight had been lifted from his shoulders.

"There are two people who'll be coming to see you soon—Jeffrey Smith, my lawyer, and Claude Shafter, my accountant. Nothing heavy, just some run-of-the-mill information about my holdings, my investments, projects, and associations, and my will."

The way Pritchard mentioned the details made Harrow cringe.

"Now you're making me regret saying yes." He shifted, feeling uncomfortable.

"Allison will be there with you, and so will I. I'm sure she'll agree with my decision. Cyrus and Lambert will be happy with my call."

"Just where do you think you're going?" Harrow asked, suspicious.

"Nowhere, just making sure all my bases are covered. Death has a way of sneaking up on us, so I want to be prepared. That's all."

"If you say so, but God help me, if I find out you're hiding something from me, I will renege and kick your ass."

Pritchard chuckled, and Harrow could only shake his head. This was getting too weird for him. Just plain weird.

Sometime during the night, Jordan found it hard to stay still. She had been in the facility for what felt like years. It only had been several weeks, but she was itching to go, to do something—*anything*. For the past year, she had been on her feet twenty-four/seven. Rest or inertia hadn't been part of her vocabulary. Sleep had come in spurts. Running from one place to another, looming in the darkness, and observing were more to her liking.

As much as she enjoyed her budding friendship with Allison and the refuge and comforts the facility offered, she'd been on her own for far too long. Most times, she felt caged and unable to breathe, like she was going to suffocate. The humans, though pleasant, still regarded her with caution, as if she was going to drain them of blood at any given moment. Jordan had to laugh, because none of them enticed her in any way.

After waking up in a pool of her own blood one year ago and believing herself dead, she'd buried her parents at an unmarked spot. She'd then wandered through the forest, not knowing what she had become. The first attack of thirst had gripped her with fierce intensity. She'd stumbled upon a good-sized elk grazing. Armed with nothing but a small pocketknife, bare hands, and unbelievable hunger, she'd wrestled the animal to the ground within minutes and twisted its neck. Surprised by the strength she possessed, she began cutting the downed elk along the belly. With no plan and no idea what she was doing, she punched a hole in the middle of the stomach to create an opening.

Blood began pouring out of the skin like a faucet gone haywire, and Jordan got the distinct feeling that she was more enamored with the blood than the meat itself. Without stopping to think about what she was about to do, her face dove to the stomach, sucking at the blood oozing from the hole with a thirst that couldn't be ignored.

Unable to satiate the hankering in her throat, she tugged and pulled on every vein she could locate and bled the animal dry. For several minutes, she operated on confused instinct, following her thirst rather than reasoning.

It wasn't until after gutting another animal that it dawned on her what she'd become. She had become the same as the monster that had created her. Jordan had hidden in the forest for several weeks, trying to make sense of it all.

Vampires weren't real, she had thought. They were myths and legends meant to scare children into submission. Known to be vicious and blood hungry, they still weren't supposed to be real. They were just fabricated fiction to sell the idea of supernatural beings that crept in the night. And yet, she realized, she was real. When the first morning rays started dusting the horizon, she fled for cover, feeling the sizzle of her skin and the burning in her eyes.

Fear, hatred, and confusion had mingled with loneliness as she'd spent countless hours trying to piece her broken life together. After the last piece had settled in her ever-stirring reasoning, she knew what she had to do. She would deny her nature, denying the blood that had buried her parents and created a monster within her.

Halting the sad passage of memories, Jordan jumped to her feet, unwilling to spend another minute doing nothing when sleep evaded her. She glanced at Allison, who looked up from her book.

"I'm going to get some blood pumping."

Allison nodded, understanding the unspoken restlessness radiating from Jordan. She'd seen it many times and commented on few occasions, advising her once to channel her aggression into something constructive rather than burn her energy seething over revenge yet to be delivered.

Jordan left the residential wing into which Allison and Pritchard had welcomed her with open arms. It was a place Allison coaxed her to call home, even if it was just a temporary one. The whole place was quiet, the humans snoring the night away, whereas their vampire counterparts were most likely out of bed, breaching the night or finding entertainment where they could.

Jordan reached for her Kalimetal behind her and fingered the blade, a habit she'd developed some time ago. Whether it was to assert her need for vengeance or to rest a perplexed nerve, the act often sent a calming sensation to her raw spirit.

She heard movement inside the training room before she shoved the door open. It was always a possibility to find a few people still awake, wanting to push their limits at the treadmill or on the elliptical machine. Jordan wasn't planning on staying long. In and out after a brief contact with the boxing bag would do the trick.

Once she rounded the corner, she spotted Harrow at the far end of the room. His gloveless hands were going at the punching bag with gusto. Jordan stopped in her tracks, unable to turn around and head out the way she'd come in.

Harrow was punching the bag with fierce determination and unabashed energy. What stopped her, she grasped in an instant, was the carefree way he'd shed his ever-present sunglasses and long-sleeved shirts he often sported. Without meaning to stare, her eyes took note of every portion of his shirtless body.

Her curiosity prompted her to stay and watch as his muscles rippled, contracted, and flexed with every movement. Harrow was thin, but he wasn't emaciated like he had been the first time she'd seen him. His narrow waist twisted as he moved, and she couldn't help her eyes from darting down to the tight jeans he wore. Everything about the man exuded virility, and Jordan couldn't bring herself to accomplish the simple task of looking away. There were traces of the lesions and varying degrees of healing wound marks across his torso and on his arms, but most now appeared benign, nothing more than harmless, pinkish scabs.

His mop of wild blond hair swayed with every movement, and the clench of his defined jaw mesmerized her. Harrow was, as she already knew, a good-looking man. In a way, she found herself drawn to the vampire, but she reminded herself as she had many times in the past weeks that Harrow was a no-go. He was the source of a disease that could eradicate their kind, whether by infecting others directly or indirectly as a result of actions taken against them by the Vampire Council. Struck dumb, she stayed glued to her spot, wanting to tear her gaze away but unable to do so. That was mistake number one.

Jordan often wondered if something was wrong with her. Throughout high school and college, there was not one person who appealed to her. She'd watched couples walk by holding hands and had asked herself whether there was a possibility that she might be a lesbian. She hadn't had an attraction to anyone of the same sex, either, but the opposite sex had held no appeal, until now. Standing here right now, she was sure as hell attracted to him. She was enthralled and fascinated with him.

Wrong! It was all wrong. Not now, and not this man. She had better things to do than occupy her mind with whimsical thoughts meant for teenagers. She needed to get real. Better to stick to the former emotions he elicited in her. Repulsion would be her lifesaver. Jordan groaned before she could stop herself.

The pounding ended, and Harrow looked in her direction, narrowing his eyes at her. From where she was standing across the room, the electrified atmosphere couldn't be denied. Jordan shook herself from the trance she'd been consumed by for the last several minutes.

"Didn't mean to intrude," she said. Jordan turned her face, hoping he wouldn't see her embarrassment at being caught staring.

Harrowed answered, "You're not intruding. I'm done here." While he picked up his shirt and sunglasses from the chair, he seemed to be enjoying her discomfort. He walked up to her on his way out the door, close enough that she could almost taste the sweat beading on his body. "It's all yours."

She stared at his form while he swung through the door and walked out before she stuttered, "Thanks."

An hour later, Jordan made her way to the deck after going at the punching bag like a woman possessed. *Possessed? By what?* She couldn't shake the image of Harrow from her mind—the way he regarded her, the expression meant to tell her she was mistaken. Short of gutting the punching bag, she'd stopped and decided to go outside to breathe some fresh air and clear her head.

Tomorrow, she told herself, she'd go out and start looking for the vampire leader. She'd put it off long enough. The sooner she found and killed him, the sooner she'd be able to determine how to live the rest of her existence.

As soon as she opened the door, she recognized mistake number two. His scent gave away his location. Harrow sat on one of the patio loungers next to the facility's massive, throttling air-conditioners.

"Are you following me?"

Though his tone wasn't hostile, she detected a hint of unwelcome in his voice. What had happened since the night they'd spent sitting next to each other as friends? Were they back to square one again?

"Not intentionally," she retorted without looking at him. "As I recall, someone said this was free for all."

Stuck on the decision between leaving and staying, Jordan stood with her back to him. She heard the rustling of metal over concrete when several loungers were pulled back, and then quick footsteps approached her.

"Sure it is. You can go, or you can stay here and enjoy the quiet night— with me." His mouth was close to her ear, and she felt his breath graze her skin when he spoke.

Jordan gritted her teeth. Not one to shy away from a deliberate and obvious challenge, she decided to stay. No conversation was necessary, although it would help if she could stop the rapid beating of her heart and surging energy that pumped within her at his close proximity.

Harrow moved away as if he'd read her mind and sat back down on the lounger. "There's another chair here if you want to sit."

Jordan let out a sigh before walking to the lounger and slipping it farther away from where Harrow had positioned it. She sat down, her back rigid, feeling uncomfortable knowing he was watching her and seemed to be enjoying it.

"Tell me, what's your story?" she blurted out before she could stop herself.

There was a curt laugh. "Why do you want to know? So you can hate me even more?"

"Who says I hate you?"

"Actions speak louder than words, *Just Jordan*." The name was spit out with strong emphasis, and Jordan jerked her head in his direction.

"That was you?"

There was no answer, but she didn't expect any. It was obvious that they had started off on the wrong footing here, but she wasn't about to admit to mistakes she didn't know how to defend. Why should she? It would only bring complications she didn't need. The more the vampire thought she hated him, the better her chances of coming out of this unscathed.

"You didn't answer my question."

"You're a vampire. You're supposed to be able to judge and know based on your senses," he replied without giving a real answer.

"I was referring to your story," she bit out.

"Why talk about me when we can talk about you? You seem to have an interesting background. All fired up, guns a-blazing. You're beautiful, feisty, and determined. What could be a better story than that?"

Did she just hear him say she was beautiful? Jordan felt fluttering deep in her stomach at the undisguised compliment. God, this was so juvenile. In her present position, she shouldn't be acting all giddy just because someone had complimented her.

"It's not something I enjoy rehashing. Mind if we talk about something else?"

Harrow chuckled, an honest–to–goodness laugh that emanated from deep in his throat. "The woman wants to talk. Yippee."

Not big on humor these days, Jordan glared at him in the darkness. She knew well enough that he could see her, at least some of her, through his murky eyes—eyes that, well . . . if she thought about it, they made him look delicate, dazzling almost.

Jordan caught him looking at her sideways, as if he could see her better in that position. She made a note to ask about it later on, if time permitted.

"Yes . . . and you don't have to be nasty about it."

"Write me at the bottom of the nasty list. I—" Harrow stopped mid-sentence, interrupted by loud banging and curses coming from within the facility. Both of them heard the noises, and without a word, they shot up to their feet and ran toward the door leading back into the main wing. Harrow was fast, Jordan noticed. She tried several times to outrun him but found it impossible to overtake his long strides.

They took the stairs, following where their senses led them. The loud, ominous sounds echoed throughout the hallway.

"Fuck," Harrow cursed when it became clear to them what had gone down tonight.

They reached the infirmary just as Holt and Drake were transferring Cyrus to the examination table. A rather sleepy female doctor barged into the room, her eyes bulging out after seeing the man on her table, as well as his condition.

While she barked orders to some of the arriving staff, Harrow pulled Holt aside. His face, arms, and clothes were splattered with blood. "What the hell happened to him?"

"I don't know. Tor followed Cyrus after he said he was going to take a leak and didn't come back right away."

"Who's responsible for this?"

"I wish I knew, but I suspect it has something to do with the vampire he was scouting inside the pool parlor." Holt sounded almost breathless, blinking his eyes, in an obvious attempt to keep his tears at bay.

"And where the hell is Tor?" Harrow asked, clenching his jaw.

Before Holt could answer, they heard the doctor shout, her voice ringing in the once-quiet building.

"Clear!"

Harrow's sole focus at that moment was the man on the table who was fighting for his life, so it wasn't a surprise that he didn't notice the commotion happening around him until he felt a hand tugging on his arm, trying to get him to step aside.

"Gates, we have to wait outside," Jordan repeated several times before Harrow's brain registered the words. Glancing over his shoulder, Harrow looked at his human friend on the examination table while the doctor worked at a feverish pace on him. Pale as a white bed sheet, he could see from the small cracks between the bodies of people working around him that Cyrus had a big fight ahead of him. The sound of the defibrillator thudded, and Cyrus's limp body heaved up when the paddles jolted him.

Nothing.

Without saying a word, Jordan guided Harrow out of the crowded room and into the hallway where Holt and Drake leaned against the wall. Their faces were masks of sorrow and weariness. They looked up when Harrow leaned on the wall next to them, but neither said a word. Both were caught up in their own grief and dealing with their confusion over the evening's events.

There wasn't much to be done except wait. Harrow caught the scent of blood in the air, and even if the aroma gripped him, he disregarded his desire as trivial. His hunger could take the back seat. It was something that could wait under such conditions.

Jordan paced as the men stood, following her restless movements with unseeing eyes. All were lost in their own thoughts.

Harrow couldn't shake his sense of dread while he listened to the frantic voice of the doctor and her resuscitation efforts. He hovered on the thin line between the hope of seeing his friend alive and well, and the grim reality of losing him.

His fists clenched and unclenched at his side, and he wanted to pound the wall or scream his lungs out. Yet he kept his calm, fighting to rein in the bristling anger within him.

The elevator at the end of the hallway opened with a ding as Pritchard hurried out, his hair disheveled from being woken up. He wore a black satin robe, with his bare chest and pajama pants peeking out through the openings.

Pritchard raced through the hallway like a man on a mission, his jaw clenched and his mouth set in a grim line. He reached the door, but instead of walking in right away, he looked at the people who were waiting outside.

"Can someone tell me what the hell happened?" he demanded.

Pensive, Holt and Drake looked at each other before Holt answered, "We don't know what went down. We were on a routine scouting run at the pool hall in the south-side. There were a few vampires here and there, but nothing out of the ordinary. Cyrus said he was gonna take a leak and didn't return right away. That's when Tor decided to check on him."

Holt's voice held a tinge of misplaced guilt, a feeling it was obvious Drake shared. It was clear that they both wondered if they could've done more to prevent the incident.

"And where the hell is Tor?"

Drake answered this time. "He said he'd scout the place to see if he could get some answers."

"If he doesn't return by the break of dawn, get some men together and look for him. Can you call Lambert in right now?" Pritchard's tone was hard. Cyrus was not only a trusted employee but also a friend, and this was a common knowledge in their small, tight-knit group.

"Yes sir." Drake pulled out his cell phone and clicked on a speed-dial button. It was obvious, from the second Lambert was given the news, that the man on the other end of the line had gone berserk. After a few seconds, Drake replaced the phone in his pocket. "He's on his way."

Pritchard grunted before pushing the door open. His voice mingled with the noise coming from the all the people crowded inside the small clinic. "How bad is he?"

It was difficult to hear the doctor's response over the blaring music as she filled Pritchard in on the details. Harrow felt his stomach grinding with fury. The bottled-up rage began to morph into an immense frustration.

Jordan eyed him warily. She looked like she wanted to offer kind words but had thought better of it.

Holt broke the silence after a few minutes. "I knew I shouldn't have let him go by himself."

"Isn't that the reason why you guys go out as a team? So no one is by himself?"

The accusation was hard to miss, and this brought a reaction from both men. Drake whipped his head up and glared at Harrow.

"It was Cyrus's call. We followed orders." Drake's jaw clenched. "You should know better."

Harrow couldn't help it. His misdirected anger had bubbled to the surface. If Cyrus had relented and let him go, this wouldn't have happened. He would have stuck by the man like glue.

There was no answer. Drake sighed, and Holt couldn't even hold his head up. They were as much victims in this as Cyrus was, but Harrow wasn't about to ease up on them. He was certain that it was the work of another being—not a human. He had no doubt that a human would not be tough enough to crack Cyrus, much less leave him wounded and fighting for his life.

"Was there any particular person or vampire of interest?" Harrow asked.

Drake closed his eyes, leaning against the wall and sliding down to the floor as if his legs could no longer support his weight.

"I remember one man he paid close attention to. Come to think of it, he did look and act like your kind." Drake paused his brown eyes flickered. "No offense."

"None taken." Harrow glowered at him.

"The guy was playing with a hooker, and I think Cyrus left around the same time they went out through the back door. I'm not sure."

"And?"

"I don't know . . . Tor took off after about ten minutes when Cyrus didn't come back, and then we followed. We found him on the ground. There was a screaming woman next to him, and the knife was still lodged in his stomach. There were no sign of the guy. Damn it."

Drake pounded the tiles with his fist, while Holt sat with a helpless expression next to him. It wasn't every day that one could find grown men looking so vulnerable and useless. Incidents like this could render even the toughest of men powerless, especially when the downed comrade was their leader.

Holt continued the story as if in a daze. "We brought him here because that was what we'd agreed on since the beginning. He'd already passed out, but we still got a faint pulse while we were rushing him back here. Tor . . . well, he wanted to stay behind. He said there was nothing he could do for Cyrus except hunt the bastard who took him down."

Harrow knew he wanted a piece of the action. As soon as he could talk to Pritchard, he was going to broach the subject, and no was not an acceptable answer. He'd been cooped up long enough, and a man could stay obedient for only so long.

Jordan leaned on the wall. Harrow shot her a quick glance. Although he couldn't see her as well as he would like, he could tell by the slump of her shoulders that she was as shaken by the whole thing as the rest of them were. Cyrus, though a man of few words, was the kind of person everyone took a liking to, often forgoing his downtime to help others hone their skills, just like he had done for Harrow.

"Are you okay?" he asked, turning his attention to Jordan.

"Yes. Are you?" Jordan looked up, trying to peer through Harrow's dark lenses, but she was forced to settle for seeing her reflection instead.

"I don't see why you'd ask me that," he answered.

"He's your friend, isn't he? That's why." She placed a comforting hand on Harrow's arm, and despite the layer of cotton that separated them, he could feel the warmth of her touch burning through his skin.

Harrow jerked his arm, shaking her hand off him. He didn't want her to think she had an effect on him, in any way.

"He is . . . Fuck . . . The son of a bitch should have known better."

Holt and Drake stared at Harrow when he cursed. They seemed to feel the same way but were too tired to agree. Morning was already upon them, and humans needed sleep more than vampires did. Exhaustion had taken its toll after the adrenaline had receded.

"He was doing his job. You can't fault him for that."

"Yeah, and there'll be a monument erected on his behalf." Harrow had no idea where the sarcasm was coming from, but he felt himself dripping with it. He clamped his mouth to keep himself from saying anything more.

"Dude, that's not fair," Drake warned.

Harrow turned to him. "You're talking about fair? You people are hunting for infected vampires, right? Who do you think could do the best job, huh?" he mocked.

"Right—But still, it's not our call. If you're hot on the idea, why don't you pitch it to Pritchard and lay off Cyrus. I swear you're a whiny son of a bitch sometimes." Alert once more, Drake stood up, looking like his exhaustion had just walked out on him.

With blurry movements, Harrow towered over Drake and gripped his neck with one hand. Holt jumped to his feet, but Jordan held him back.

"Let them duke it out," she cautioned.

"I just might do that. Don't even think I'd back down from your bony ass," Harrow said. His fangs elongated while his hand tightened around Drake's neck. Sputtering from the chokehold, Drake attempted to fight him off, but Harrow didn't budge.

"Gates! Take your hands off him."

No one seemed to have noticed Lambert until he was already a few feet away. His hand rested inside his jacket as he held Harrow's gaze.

"Relax it, Gates. I'm warning you," Lambert repeated.

Harrow flashed his throbbing fangs before he relaxed his grip a little, allowing the color to return to Drake's paling features. As the human coughed and gasped for air, Lambert pried Harrow's firm hold from around Drake's neck.

"I swear to God, Gates, I won't think twice about gutting you if you try this stunt again," Lambert threatened, and by the looks of it, he wasn't bluffing.

By no means was Harrow afraid of the human. In fact, he liked Lambert, but he wasn't going to be intimidated by any order, not from him or anyone else.

"Stay out my business," he growled, walking a few steps away.

Jordan let go of Holt's arm and moved toward Harrow. At that moment, it seemed like she was taking his side. This was not a surprise to Harrow, since he could tell the woman was itching to fight, too.

"I'd be happy to, but we're not here to fight each other. Get that through your thick skull, will you?" Lambert barked.

The door to the clinic opened. Dr. Shelly Anderson and Pritchard emerged after what had seemed like a lifetime, both looking spent and halfway out of their wits.

"There's nothing we can do but hope that I was able to stop the bleeding in time," the doctor advised them, wiping the sweat from her forehead with the sleeves of her white coat.

"Don't even think of sleeping, Shelly. Watch my man until he gets better." Pritchard seldom used his position to make demands in such a manner, but if it came down to his men, they all knew he would do anything in his power to keep them safe and alive.

Shelly drew a long sigh before nodding her head. She glanced at all the people in the hallway with a disparaging expression before walking back inside the clinic.

"How is my man?" Lambert asked.

"Shelly stopped the bleeding and gave him a blood transfusion. Now we'll have to wait and see." Pritchard pinched the bridge of his nose.

Harrow huffed. He was itching to check Cyrus out for himself, but he didn't dare move until he'd had a word with Pritchard.

"He's alive. That's all that matters." Lambert let out a sigh of relief, but the uncertainty in his eyes remained. They all realized that Cyrus's condition could take a turn for the worse at any moment. Only time would tell whether he would survive.

"Give yourselves time to catch some sleep, and we'll meet at nine. We have some things we need to talk about," Pritchard ordered as he began walking toward the direction of the elevator. "You can join, too." His gaze was directed at Harrow.

Harrow returned to his quarters as soon as Lambert told them to go. He saw Jordan bounding up the stairs going the other way. He guessed she'd been staying with the Tacks, which would be the reason why he hadn't seen much of her.

Left to his own devices, he had nothing to do other than to mull over the information Drake and Holt had given him and the fact that Tor wasn't back yet. Harrow reminded himself that the vampire was big and strong and able to hold his own in any given situation.

Worrying wouldn't do them any good. He doubted Tor would welcome the thought of Harrow coming to his rescue. That would be a big laugh, when all anyone could see was his weak, diseased condition. Nobody viewed him as capable, hard, or strong enough to fight alongside them.

No one, except Cyrus, had the full info that he'd been doing well, learning every move and tactic with every weapon imaginable. He could fight with the best of them now, if he was given the chance. To Pritchard, he was precious cargo, a commodity to realize his dream of finding a cure. *A treasure*. Harrow snorted.

Shaking his head, he walked over to the table where a computer was taking up an awful lot of space. Pritchard had been glad to give him one when he'd asked. Instead of spending countless hours watching TV, Harrow had started scouring the Internet for news, disasters, and up-to-the-minute information—anything he could find to overcome his boredom.

In the morning, he'd checked on Leroy to see how the quest for a cure was going. He hadn't expected the man to come dancing to his door with news of finding a cure. Not *yet*, anyway. He just expected him to be making steady strides with the gallon's worth of blood he'd produced upon the doctor's request.

Harrow moved the mouse a little, and the powerful computer roared to life. Inclining his head where his peripheral vision was at its best, he glanced at the page he had been looking at the last time he'd used the computer. It was the website for the theater company where he'd been working before he vanished.

The colorful page greeted him with faces of new actors and the latest shows the theater was involved in. He looked into their archive of shows in the past, moving the view ruler on the right side of the screen until he found what he was looking for.

The costumes they'd worn and the faded colors, even if the photo was digitally restored, made the age of the picture clear. It had been taken a heck of a long time ago. Had it been fifty years ago?

Harrow saw himself in the middle of the group, smiling wide and proud, as if he was telling anyone who was listening that he'd conquered the world. He was so young. His blond hair had been tied in a loose ponytail, and he could tell his eyes were blue, even if the picture barely registered the color. They had such a sparkle that even the rarest gem would have paled in comparison. He had always been on the thin side. Never one for gluttony, his eating habits were dictated by need alone. He'd rather do what he loved best and read lines of script or rehearse with his co-actors until the wee hours of the morning.

Then there was a small newspaper article about his disappearance. "Harrow Gates—Broadway's Brightest Star—Disappeared," the headline read. There had been no leads, and no one could offer a solid clue because he was, as the article claimed, a likeable character. He sniggered. Why did everyone see him as weak, puny, and incapable? It almost sounded like they were discussing a female, not that he'd ever seen the opposite sex as anything close to weak. Take Jordan. The woman did not possess a single frail bone in her body. He snorted at the thought. The way she'd managed to creep into every thought he'd had in the past week was disconcerting.

The article offered speculations by both the authorities and other people connected to him in the theater business. His family refused to grant an interview, and the little tidbits written about them only claimed they were devastated by his disappearance.

Harrow felt his insides crawling with regret and yearning for his parents and sisters. Being yanked away from their lives, even if he had been absent in the two years prior to that, still wasn't fair. Groaning at the lashing memories of his past, Harrow closed the tab and opened a new one.

He Googled the word vampire and snorted once more. Movies, legends, and Wikipedia's take on vampires flooded the screen. The entertainment of each article helped him stretch the time until dawn peeked over the horizon. Nine o'clock was still almost four hours away, and he couldn't go to sleep. He knew he wouldn't be able to, not only because he wanted to find out what the meeting was all about, but also because he had to see how Cyrus was doing.

The door swung open, and Tor walked in, looking like he'd been through the wringer. The vampire's haggard appearance was startling, as if he'd been on the run for the last century. Harrow stifled a laugh just in time, while Tor proceeded to flop his body onto the sofa.

"Where in the hell have you been?"

"To hell and back," Tor replied.

Grunting, he spread his legs across the coffee table, sending some magazines and the remote on a free-fall to the floor. He unzipped his leather jacket but didn't take it off.

"Define hell." Harrow turned and gave Tor his undivided attention. The man looked a mess, his hair dampened with sweat and glued against his skull, not to mention he looked hungry. At least his weapons were still strapped across his chest and around his waist, clean and still polished—a sign that he hadn't been involved in any altercations.

"Damn it, Gates. What's with the newscaster interview?" Tor rested his head on the chair rail and stared at the ceiling for a moment before his eyes fluttered to a close.

"Fuck, man. Cyrus is hurt and may not even make it. You left the group without giving any information. I think that warrants some questioning. Besides, you'll be asked the same thing in a little over three hours. Consider this your dry run."

Tor muttered a curse and pursed his lips. It took several minutes before he spoke, even with his eyes closed. "I followed Cyrus to the restroom when he didn't return after ten minutes. The stalls were empty when I walked in, and that's when I heard a woman screaming outside.

"I ran out and saw the woman leaning on the wall, blaring like a goddamn siren, staring at Cyrus on the ground. Our man had passed out by the time I got there. I called Holt and Drake for back-up, and they brought him back here."

Tor threw his arms out in the air in a helpless manner. "I decided to stay to check out the remnants of what I knew used to be a body part on the ground. If my guess is accurate, which I think it is, Cyrus was up against a vampire. Believe me, the motherfucker didn't expect Cyrus to bring him down single-handed. The burn marks on the ground were from the disintegration process. In this case, it was Cyrus' knife that got him. I'd bet my balls the fucking vampire cut off the injured part of his body so it wouldn't spread, before running for cover."

"Damn, I missed the action," Harrow quipped.

"You're one sick bastard, aren't you?"

Instead of validating Tor's apt description, Harrow urged him to go on. "What happened next?"

"I'm fuckin' tired as shit. Can't you tell?"

"Damn it Tor, tell me what you did next." Harrow moved across the room and sprawled next to his roommate, crowding the already-full sofa.

Tor groaned. "I tried following the vampire's scent like a fuckin' bloodhound, but it ended somewhere in the middle of the city."

Harrow lifted an eyebrow. "In the middle of the city? What do you mean?"

"Rockefeller Center—that's where the scent faded." Tor opened his eyes and shot a look at Harrow. "I'm not kidding. Something's going on in that vicinity, though I can't put my finger on what."

"Then we should scout the area, don't you think?" Harrow asked, itching to get some action soon.

"You wish, my man. You wish." Tor laughed without humor.

Jordan slipped inside the bedroom she shared with Allison as quietly as she could, not wanting to wake up the other vampire. She squirmed out of her jeans and sweaty T-shirt and threw them on the chair, hoping to walk into a hot shower right away.

She padded across the room to the closet, which now housed the clothes the Tacks had given her—a closetful of clothes, shoes, and even accessories that she didn't think were necessary. She was happy with her faded jeans, black baby tees, and trench coat. These had been the staples of her wardrobe for over a year now. When you're always on your feet and running around, you couldn't be hauling luggage filled with clothes, or even the bare necessities. And no way was she tromping around in the Jimmy Choo, peep-toed, 3-inch heels that she'd gotten caught "glancing" at online. She had learned to live with the basic stuff, which consisted of her weapon, the clothes on her back, and her lace-up combat boots.

Pulling a black silk robe with purple embroidery from an expensive, cedar wood hanger, she slung it over her shoulder and chose boxer shorts from the drawer. With careful movements, she made her way toward the elegant bathroom. Jordan lit a candle close to the sink and turned on the hot water at the tub.

After the water had reached the right temperature and the tub was half-filled, she dipped her foot in, testing the water before immersing her body in its inviting wake. She rested her head on the lip of the claw-footed tub and stared at the ceiling.

What a day. Just when she'd thought she could escape to clear her head, she had walked in on Harrow, of all people. She hated her reaction to him, to his presence. Like a love-crazed schoolgirl, she couldn't help ogling him with curiosity, surprising and embarrassing herself.

It didn't help that Harrow sported the kind of body that she found most attractive. His face screamed masculinity but was softer around the edges, like he was some sort of delicate porcelain she needed to protect. God, what had gotten into her? And those lips . . . She couldn't tear her eyes away even if she tried. Must she remind herself that he was sick, with a disease known to make every afflicted individual beg for death or kill without mercy to survive?

But those lips were meant for something else. To possess her own, maybe?

"Damn it." Groaning, she splashed some water on her face to keep herself glued together and get the damn image of Harrow out of her mind.

A light tap on the door sounded, and it pushed open before she could respond. Allison walked in, but she didn't look in Jordan's direction, keeping her head averted to give her some privacy.

"Mind if I keep you company?" she asked. "Sorry to barge in on you like this. I can't sleep."

"It's okay. I'm just soaking before I head to bed." Jordan sank deeper into the water, feeling a bit vulnerable.

Allison walked barefoot toward the toilet, pushed the lid down, and sat. She was wearing a pink tank top with BITE ME written across it and matching pajama bottoms. Jordan had to laugh at the blatant reference to their feeding preferences.

"How did your workout go?" Allison still didn't glance in her direction, preferring to look at the wall across from the toilet seat. Her slight and delicate frame looked relaxed in the dim light of the room.

"Hell if I could say it went great." Jordan huffed, recalling her encounter with Harrow and the image of his shirtless body flashed in her mind again. "Harrow was there when I got in. Then—"

"Correct me if I'm wrong, and tell me to mind my own business if I'm out of line, but I can see a little attraction between the two of you." Allison held back a giggle.

Jordan sat straighter in the tub, gripping the sides to keep her from slipping down, and her body began quivering at mention of his name.

"What are you talking about?"

Allison chuckled and looked her way. Her pasty eyes danced with mischief. "You know what I'm talking about. You and Harrow—I can see it."

"See what?" Damn, she'd thought no one would even notice, but she had forgotten that her roommate was as sharp as a tack. Jordan couldn't help but snicker at the appropriateness of the idiom, considering Allison's surname.

"Gosh, I'd have had to be blind not to notice the body language. You two are a love affair waiting to happen." Allison said teasing.

The laughter that followed made her want to pull her hair out, because she felt it, too, but she'd never admit it. "Ally, what the hell? There's no love affair that's going to happen. First of all, I'm planning to leave soon. I don't want this shit going on in my life. I have some business I have to take care of, and there's no time for something like that," she protested. Even though she'd kept the tone of her voice even, there was a slight uncertainty behind her words.

Harrow and Tor bolted upright at the sound of rapid and furious pounding on the door. In the last hour, they'd fallen asleep despite their inclinations to fight the droop and exhaustion that gripped them. Even freaking vampires had to sleep.

When Harrow answered the door, Lambert stood outside, well-groomed, with his hair still damp from a shower.

"You ladies better get your asses to the I-room in a few minutes. Pritchard isn't one to be kept waiting." Eyeing Harrow before he turned on his heel, he added, "Five minutes, ladies. Vampire speed, chop-chop."

The air in the room carried a somber quality that latched onto Harrow and Tor in a vise grip as soon as they walked in the door. Everyone glanced up from their respective places but didn't say a word. Noting the silence in the room, which was filled with humans and vampires alike, Harrow and Tor took the last two remaining seats at the back of the room.

Some people Harrow knew by name, and others he recognized from passing them in the hallway or bumping into them in other areas of the facility. Not knowing why Pritchard had called the meeting, Harrow sat in silence and observed while Pritchard talked to Lambert. With the way their shoulders sagged, Harrow anticipated that some bad news was coming down the pipeline.

After a few minutes, Pritchard walked in the front of the room. A few stayed seated, but others preferred to lean against the wall, which Harrow felt like doing as well. He got up to stand next to Knox, a human he'd only gotten to know a short time ago. They nodded to each other while Tor also moved and stood next to Harrow.

Pritchard was in his usual leathers, looking regal in spite of the clothes he sported. The man made an argument for leathers as business attire. He wore them with ease and menace rolled into one sweet package. Lambert stood next to him with his arms crossed and his expression unreadable. Pritchard eyed each man in attendance before he addressed the group. "Some of you may be wondering why I gathered everyone here tonight." There were murmurs of agreement. "Our dear and fearless friend Cyrus was attacked last night."

A hush fell in the room like a thick blanket while every face registered surprise, rage, anxiety, and sadness.

"He is alive, thank God. However, the extent of his injuries is still unknown. He is in a medically induced coma, which Dr. Anderson deemed necessary considering the massive blood loss and the shock to his system." Pritchard paused as if trying to pull himself together. "So with that said, Cyrus will be out of commission until he's recovered." There was a tinge of uncertainty in his voice that was hard to miss, and everyone reacted with grunts, groans, and curses.

"Who will be calling the shots in his absence?" someone asked from the middle of the room.

Pritchard raised his hand again to quiet the noise that erupted when everyone began speculating. Harrow remained silent, watching everything with detached interest.

"Lambert will be calling the shots until, and if, Cyrus is back on his feet."

There was a round of applause at this news. There wasn't any doubt Lambert could rise to the occasion. The human was more than capable of leading an army. Besides, he was just as cunning, aggressive, astute, and skilled a fighter as Cyrus. If you didn't know any better, you would think he and Cyrus were twins separated at birth.

Lambert acknowledged the applause with a smile. In light of Cyrus' condition, taking the helm was not something he would happy about.

"It goes without saying that we'd be stepping up our goals a notch. We need you all to help with rotations, but we must proceed with caution. Our intel could very well reveal that the vampire who got our man is a member of the Council soldiers.

"So I have a feeling that they might be seeking blood as payment, considering Cyrus seems to have done a number on that vampire. He left with less than he came with." Another round of supposition broke out, and Pritchard waited for everyone to quiet down before he spoke again.

"We'll be pairing you guys up in groups of four. We'll have two vampires and two humans on each rotation. Two groups will be out each night doing the scouting and patrolling preplanned routes. I'm looking at increasing our numbers, but this has to be done with utmost discretion, now more than ever. We have to go through the same rigorous screening process we have used in the past."

Pritchard took a step back and let Lambert take the floor. Lambert took a deep and strangled breath before he addressed the crowd, seeming to be choosing his words with care.

"I know most of you already have some sort of training with weapons in one way or the other." Heads nodded in unison. "But I have to reinforce some basic training and methods for recognizing danger when it's staring at you in the face, appropriate ways to react, and what weapons are best suitable for your adversary.

"I will conduct sessions with interested parties as soon as I can arrange it. So for the meantime, I won't be participating in patrols. I have to be here to provide the training, and going by what Cyrus told me a few days ago, he had one student he felt would be able to help out in the field of martial arts."

Crap. Shit. For some reason, Harrow knew what Lambert was about to say before he said it.

"That is, if Harrow is willing to take the role of instructor."

Lambert pointed at Harrow, and he felt every eye in the room focus on him. He wasn't sure this was the path he wanted for himself. It was one thing to follow, but to lead? Taken by surprise, Harrow bowed his head as Tor gave him a mighty slap of approval in the back. He glared at the vampire before nodding his head in acceptance. A talk with Pritchard and Lambert seemed in order, and Harrow planned to do it as soon as the meeting broke up.

Lambert nodded back, sensei to student, student to master, or whatever their relationship may be. It was a gray area that Harrow was willing to explore.

Pritchard rose from his seat. "Let me remind you to take all necessary precautions. You're all much more valuable to me alive than dead." With those words, he concluded the meeting. Several people started talking at the same time, voicing concerns and asking questions, which Lambert and Pritchard answered.

Everybody dispersed, leaving Harrow, Pritchard, Tor, and Lambert alone in the room. Harrow walked up and sat on the chair closest to Pritchard. Lambert remained standing, appearing like he was too wired to settle down. Tor sat next to Harrow and clasped his hands together on the table.

"I don't have a problem helping out," Harrow began. "In fact, I'm honored to impart the knowledge Cyrus shared with me, but I have some terms I want to address."

Harrow saw Pritchard's eyebrows ride up, and he sighed. "Terms *already*, Harrow?"

"Yes. I want to be granted permission to go out and help with the patrol and reconnaissance."

"No, not possible." Pritchard's answer came fast enough to alert Harrow that the man had been thinking about it or at least just expecting it.

"Give me one good reason why I can't go," Harrow demanded, not wanting to hear the bullshit about his fragile health or any other reasons that Pritchard might have in his arsenal.

"First." Pritchard held up one finger. "You are needed here for the cure, remember?"

Harrow knew it was coming, but he didn't want to relent just yet. Agreeing to be their guinea pig was proving to have been an absurd idea. It had led him to his frustrating status as a somewhat-endangered species in their eyes.

"Do you still need a second reason? The first one is valid and could stand on its own," Pritchard pushed.

"Just be honest. Do you think you can keep me in here?" Harrow challenged, watching Pritchard consider the question with an even-keeled expression, not even showing the slightest clue as to what his answer would be.

"Yes. You will stay because you know you're better off here than you ever were out there." Pritchard waved his hand, gesturing to the world outside. "But you're a grown man, Harrow. I'm not your daddy, and I can't tell you what to do or what not to do. Your responsibility is toward the people you infected. It's your call." Pritchard sounded as if he wanted to add more but had decided against it.

Harrow stood up without offering an answer. His defiance was now a simmering ache in his gut. The need to go out there burned more than he'd expected. He knew that if he went, he'd be going against Pritchard's will, although he wasn't sure if he would be able to now out of respect for Cyrus. What the hell was he gonna do now?

Tor didn't follow when he crossed the room and walked out into the hall without a word. Good. He wanted to think this through. Alone.

"What the hell happened to you?" Demetrius yelled when he saw Giancarlo emerge from the shadows outside his chamber window.

Swinging the door open, he let his right-hand man into the room, looking from one direction to another to see if anyone was watching them. Demetrius wasn't hiding anything, but it was a habit he'd learned from his father. He'd been around long enough to know that anyone or anything could stab him in the back without provocation, motivated by envy or a lust for power. There were enough reasons to be vigilant.

"Fuck!" Giancarlo screamed as he clutched his bleeding right arm with his jacket. The once-pristine white carpet was now stained with his blood, and more was oozing from his wounds.

Sitting on the duvet at the foot of Demetrius' bed, Giancarlo unwrapped the soaked jacket to reveal what was left of his arm, severed just below the elbow.

Demetrius couldn't hide his repugnance when he looked at the bloodied stump. "Dangeran, right?" he asked, but he knew the answer already.

Giancarlo nodded, looking pale and disoriented. "Stop the bleeding. Do *something*, Boss!" he wailed like a goddamn baby.

"Shit! Who did this?"

Demetrius was already rummaging in the adjoining office, where he kept his suturing kit and bandages, the essential supplies necessary to treat victims of the damning blade that had proven lethal for vampires. He gathered several towels from the bathroom before returning to Giancarlo, who looked ill and ready to pass out.

Contrary to beliefs based on legends, vampires were beings who bled, fed, and slept, just like humans. Vampires would react and die just as humans did. The one exception was that their deaths came from sun exposure or from the Dangeran blade. The real difference between them and their human counterparts was their physical attributes. Vampires were sturdier, faster, stronger, and lethal. Now, with humans getting their hands on Dangeran weapons, it made them dangerous to vampires.

Case in point. To survive a Dangeran-created wound, the vampire must sever the impaled area in a matter of minutes before the poison from the blade spread and killed him or her. Weapons made with this complicated metal were lethal to vampires, but not to humans.

Demetrius worked with rapid movements, stitching the muscles together after dousing the area with an antiseptic that made Giancarlo curse like a sailor. The work was haphazard, considering the enormous loss of blood. It would have to do, and the vampire's healing ability would take care of the rest, though Giancarlo was now short a vital body part that would not regenerate. Demetrius applied Mentha extract to the sewn-up site. It was believed to have a calming, as well as numbing, effect on vampires, not that he'd ever wanted to know firsthand if it was effective or not.

The vampire collapsed on the floor within minutes, still writhing in pain but seeming to feel the fast-acting relief of the extract. His cursing continued with his labored breathing. Demetrius grimaced at the bloodstain on his carpet, certain the cleaning crew would be screaming in disgust.

"Who did this to you?"

Giancarlo, through his immense discomfort, recounted his face-off with a human in the alley. Demetrius listened with narrowed eyes and unwavering concentration. Not liking the fact that humans had already figured out and utilized the deadliest weapon against their kind, he sighed in frustration.

Hunting humans was a sport with which he hadn't bothered, but it might just prove to be a good distraction while he built his army—or was it his father's army? Maybe he needed to find another wingman, since the fucker now staining his carpet would be of limited use to him from this point on.

"Human, huh?"

"You wanted to see me?" Jordan asked once the secretary had pulled the door shut, looking at Pritchard as he rose from his supple leather chair as a sign of respect, as he would have done for any woman. The man was dressed in an impeccable dark suit of expensive quality.

Looking around the commodious office, she began to piece things together. She wouldn't have guessed that the office building was somehow connected to the underground facility. Come to think of it, there had been so many surprises since she'd gotten there, including the whole underground operation, their purpose, and the facility's mixture of inhabitants. Jordan noticed the heavy metal shutters were drawn all around the windows, blocking the sun away. She couldn't help but applaud the human silently for his keen eye for details, whether for his human or vampire guests.

"Yes, please have a seat." Pritchard motioned to the chair in front of his desk.

Jordan sat, crossed her legs, and uncrossed them after a second thought. She hated feeling vulnerable and feminine. Damn, this facility was screwing with her head. It had too much testosterone in one place. She needed to get away. It was as imperative as sucking in air.

"I will cut to the chase. I don't want to waste your time any more than mine—"

"Then spit it out already," she snapped.

Pritchard smiled, unperturbed by her show of impatience.

"I want you to locate the vampire you spoke of, the one who taught you how to fight and made your weapon. I will pay him for his services."

Jordan stared at Pritchard, dumbfounded. What the hell was he asking her? Locate Rohnert? As much as she knew Rohnert would love to help, she was certain that the vampire wouldn't want to be around her, not with the way she'd left him without even considering his offer to be with her, to protect her, and to help her bring her parents' killer to justice. Now it dawned on her that maybe she should've accepted, even with strings attached. He must've known all along that it was Goran who killed her parents. The reason why he wanted to help was still a mystery, however.

That was so not going to happen. Jordan huffed. "What if I say no?"

Pritchard considered her answer. "You can, permitted you have no problem with teaching everyone yourself. Someone has to step up, and we need all the help we can get."

"No can do. I have personal business I have to take care of, and you know it. I've been sitting around here long enough, doing nothing." She made a hissing sound. There was no question in her mind that she needed to go. Everything in this place was making her feel trapped. Harrow and his luscious lips, Allison with her visceral guesses that left Jordan more confused than ever, not to mention the gracious people here who had made her feel welcomed despite her fervent resolve to stay detached.

"Then you go find him." His tone infuriated her. Pritchard's arrogance and superior attitude was irksome. He smiled at her as if sensing her disapproval.

"I won't do it." She shook her head.

"Is there any reason why you're refusing to help us? Perhaps he was a part of your past you don't want to be reminded of?" Astute and imperious.

"No," she denied, crossing and uncrossing her legs before beginning to nervously bounce the right one.

"Then what's your reason behind the denial? You must be able to see that we need help." Pritchard sighed. "This incident with Cyrus won't be the last. I can feel it in my bones. The sooner we get our people ready, the better off we all will be."

Damn, why did Pritchard have to the lay the guilt-trip on her? The last thing she needed was to worry about others. She'd long decided that to create a vacuum, involvement was out and indifference was the key. She shouldn't feel, or care, for them.

"I can tell you where to find him. That's the best I can do." She reached for a pen and piece of paper and scribbled the address with short directions. They could find Rohnert in Harlem, long after she'd left.

"Thank you."

Jordan planted both feet on the floor and rose. "No problem," she replied and walked toward the door.

"Jordan?"

She stopped and looked over her shoulder.

"If there's anything you need, please don't hesitate to ask. We are one family here—your family now. You can count on us." Pritchard's tone was soft, making her resent the situation even more. Why did he have to be so damn nice?

She didn't respond before she closed the door behind her. She'd leave as soon as dusk arrived. It was time to start looking and stop stalling.

Pritchard called with an urgent request to see him, so after hanging up, Harrow took his sunglasses, slid them on his face, and made his way toward the wing of Pritchard's office building.

He saw Jordan exiting one of the elevators just before he heard the ding that announced that his elevator had arrived.

Jordan gave no indication that she'd seen him or even felt his presence. He was certain that she had chosen to ignore him. They hadn't spoken since they'd seen each other the night before. He wondered what her business with Pritchard had been. Maybe it had something to do with Allison, since those two had gotten off to a great start. Whatever it was, it was none of his business anyway. He glanced at the secretary, who lifted her head and smiled in greeting before she led him to Pritchard's office.

She announced his name and then pushed the door open, beckoning him to follow her into the room.

"Come in, Gates." Pritchard leaned back on his chair. After Harrow was seated, he spoke. "How're things with you?"

Harrow lifted an eyebrow, leaned forward, and perched his arms on the desk. He could sense the excitement in the air.

"I have something I need you to do, since you look like you could use some fresh air."

The corner of Harrow's lips quirked up. *Now we're talking.* "What do you want me to do?" he asked.

Pritchard turned his laptop around so Harrow could see the information. Harrow shifted his head sideways and looked at the screen. After reading the noteworthy info, he looked at Pritchard for explanation.

"I want you to go and persuade Rohnert to work for us, alongside you, to train and help the others."

It wasn't a task he wanted to do, but it would get him out of the facility with Pritchard's blessing, which was a good enough reason to agree. "What bargaining chip do I work with?"

"Tell him I will pay, no matter the cost—and mention that we acquired his name through Jordan," Pritchard instructed.

"Jordan? What has she got to do with this?" The mere mention of her name brought tightness in Harrow's gut. He wasn't so sure he liked the idea of Jordan being involved with another man.

"Just do what I say, will you? And tell the guy to treat this as a project. He'll be working for me until it is over." Pritchard turned the laptop around and glanced at the screen again.

"Fine." Harrow got up, not liking his assignment, and headed toward the door.

"Take Tor with you, and leave at sundown. The sooner you get this man here, the better," Pritchard said before Harrow closed the door with a grunt.

Tor was ready and waiting for him when night fell, and they left the facility without much fanfare. They ran east to the address's location and reached the neighborhood in no time. The aromas of various dinner preparations wafted around them. *Dinner,* Harrow thought. He needed to feed soon.

Upon reaching the address, they noted a rundown apartment that had seen better days. The bricks that made up the old building had already reached the crumbling stage, and the paint on the main door was peeling. There were a few kids playing Double-Dutch outside, undeterred by the darkness looming around them. A few looked up with unfeigned curiosity as the two men came strolling by.

The front door was ajar, and they made their way into the complex without a hitch. Harrow pulled a piece of paper from his pocket, checked the number, and slid the paper back. The intense aroma of dinner being prepared mixed with the stale carpet smell wafted in the air as they made their way down the hallway of the second floor.

They stopped in front of a door, and Harrow rapped his knuckles on it. There was no sound movement from inside, which was no surprise, until they heard the cock of a gun when the door opened. A barrel slid through the small opening, coming face-to-face with Harrow's skull.

"What's your business here?" a deep voice asked.

Harrow stepped back, glanced at Tor, and then spoke. He hated to speak to the muzzle of the shotgun. "Jordan thought you could help us." No matter how Harrow hated using her name, he knew that mentioning her name first in this situation would be their best bet if they wanted the vampire on the other side of the door to give them even five minutes of his time.

Silence followed, but the door opened after a few minutes, even though the muzzle remained focused on him. Harrow entered the room followed by Tor, who was palming his Glock and ready for action.

The door closed behind them, and then the sound of the safety engaging on the shotgun alerted that the weapon had been neutralized. Harrow gave an inward sigh. He didn't want to get his head blown off before he could conduct his business.

A figure stood behind them. Harrow and Tor pivoted on their heels and came face-to-face with a rather large, olive-skinned, bald-headed vampire. A tall man, pushing six-foot-four with eyes as sharp as a blade, surveyed them with interest. He was packing muscles everywhere visible, and his chest seemed as wide as the Hudson River. Appearing around forty in human years, the vampire looked good in a scraggly sort of way. Their host and Tor sized each other up. They were almost the same build, reached the same height, and their expressions were guarded and calculating.

Harrow cleared his throat. "I'm Harrow and this is Tor."

The male eyed Tor with narrowed eyes. "Rohnert."

"As I was saying, Jordan gave us this—"

"Jordan, eh?" Rohnert turned to Harrow, sounding like he wasn't sold on the idea of Jordan sending them.

"Yeah," Harrow answered, leaving it to the other vampire to digest the information, even though he was curious as hell to find out about Rohnert's relationship with Jordan. Then again, maybe he didn't want to know.

"How is she?"

The tone of Rohnert's voice softened, even though the planes of his face remained hard. There was a somber lilt to the words that Harrow caught right away. His curiosity spiked.

"She's with us." It was a white lie. Jordan hadn't shown any indication she wanted to stay around, but Rohnert didn't have to know that *yet*.

"Tell me what you want," Rohnert said. He walked across the room and laid the shotgun on a table that was filled with ammunition for various weapons. It also held different types of blades they hadn't seen before, along with several Kalimetal similar to Jordan's.

There was the answer, Harrow thought.

Tor settled on the beaten-down sofa without invitation, and Rohnert shot him a fleeting look. Harrow remained standing.

"We want you to work for us, to help train some fighters." Glancing toward the table, Harrow rested his eyes on the neat row of weapons. "And maybe share your expertise with us."

Rohnert smirked and gurgling laughter followed. Harrow's eyes narrowed, not certain what the vampire found so funny about his statement. He fought the urge to jump him, almost convinced that he didn't like this new acquaintance already.

After a few moments of consideration, Rohnert asked, crossing his arms across his broad chest, "What's in it for me?"

"You'll be rewarded generously—and you get to see Jordan," he added as an afterthought. He regretted it as soon as the words left his mouth. Harrow was certain he saw the vampire's eyes glisten and soften.

It wasn't simple. Nothing ever was. Leaving was the best thing to do, for her and everyone else involved. It was sad to see the gloom in Allison's face as she watched her prepare to depart. Strapping her Kalimetal across her back, Jordan readied herself. It would be difficult to say goodbye, knowing the likelihood of returning was next to nil.

"You will come back, right?" Allison sounded close to begging. Jordan hated the answering ache she felt in her heart. This was the very reason why she wasn't crazy about making friends and getting all warm and fuzzy. She knew leaving was inevitable, and breaking her promise to stay was a reality that was bound to happen sooner or later.

"I don't know." Jordan wanted to lie, but she couldn't bring herself to do it to Allison.

"But you need a home. This is your home. Do what you must, but come back." Allison sobbed. "I'm going to miss you, Jordan. You have to come back here. I *need* you to come back here."

"I'm going to miss you, too," Jordan said, hating the way her voice shook.

"You have to promise me that you'll come back." Allison arose from the corner, her favorite spot in the room, where she had been reading a book while watching Jordan pack.

"You know, if there's a reason for my return, it'll be you. Believe it or not, you're like a sister to me now." Jordan knew she shouldn't have said it. Giving Allison more reason to hope was like dangling bait to a piranha, but she couldn't help it.

Allison wrapped her arms around Jordan, hesitating before pulling the other woman into an embrace. They stayed unmoving. Allison's sobs were the only sounds filling the heavy silence in the room.

"You have to promise me. *Please.*"

The plea broke Jordan's heart. She wanted to flee before she made a vow she couldn't afford to keep, but Allison's sorrow broke her defenses and softened her heart.

"I will—once I get this all figured out," she said. Her mission could take months, years. She could even get killed. It was a whole different ballgame once she was out there. She'd been warned many times about the impossibility of her goal. Goran was a powerful vampire no one ever dared to cross. They were warnings she'd heard but chosen to ignore. Achieving the impossible would make her victory sweeter, even if it meant giving up her life to obtain it.

Jordan shifted to get a good look at Allison's face. "Stop crying, will you? You're making it hard for me to leave," she scolded, shaking Allison in the process.

"Good, then my plan's working." The vampire laughed despite her tears. "Are you going to even say goodbye to him?"

Jordan knew who Allison was referring to, but for the life of her, she couldn't fathom why the question had come up. This solidified her resolve. If Allison could see right through her, then maybe the others would, too. What would Harrow think? She'd bet a rat's ass he'd be laughing at her. Harrow didn't like her, as far as she could see. He didn't even so much as glance her way at all if it was avoidable. It was possible he saw her as a pathetic loser hell-bent on waging an unwinnable war against a powerful opponent. *A frail David to a mighty Goliath,* Rohnert had once said.

"No, why should I?"

"I don't know. Maybe because he cares about you?"

Jordan shook her head at the very idea. It was an absurd thought, even childish. They were vampires, for crying out loud. If they wanted something, they went after it. They possessed the object of their affection, and took whomever they wanted.

"That's a load of BS, and you know it, Ally!" she said and moved away from her friend's embrace. The sooner she got out of there, the better—before she ended up all soft and mushy.

"It's not, and you know it," Allison retorted in feeble protest. "I will miss you, Jordan. I look forward to seeing you soon. Please take care of yourself."

"I will—you, too."

With a heavy heart, Jordan turned, not sparing a one last glance at Allison, and walked out of the room, and then out of the facility—away from the first place she'd called home after a year of a nomadic life.

The sun disappeared over the horizon, replaced by the promise of darkness. She had no idea where her feet would lead her. All she knew was that she had to go. Rohnert was in the facility. She could feel him, and she felt Harrow, too.

Pritchard rolled over, groaned when the intercom crackled, and thought, *There goes my much-needed rest.* Sleep was hard to come by since Cyrus's incident, though God knew he tried to take catnaps here and there. Yet, sleep had proven elusive. He found himself thinking of ways to save as many vampires as he could. Cyrus had once questioned the driving force behind his obsession to save afflicted vampires. Pritchard had answered him, without even blinking an eye, that it was because he didn't want them to go through the fear and pain his wife had experienced and that led to her suicide.

It was plain and simple. Nothing else would bring him more satisfaction and joy than to see his daughter be able to go through her existence with as little threat and pain as possible. And that went for *all* the people sharing his Allison's fate.

Pritchard pushed himself, with a great deal of effort, off the bed. He felt his leg muscles tense as he walked toward the beeping intercom. He was going to meet with Harrow and Rohnert in an hour. At least his boy was able to persuade the vampire to come, even if it was just to talk, for now.

Pritchard was aware that he'd practiced a form of blackmail with Harrow and Jordan to get them to do his bidding. Although, no money was involved, he'd bullied them to do what he wanted. It was for everyone's benefit in the long-run, but he couldn't help the uncomfortable feeling that brushed at him.

The intercom beeped again, and he pushed the white button to allow whoever it was to talk.

"Boss, sorry to disturb you, but I think you might want to know about this," Dante's deep voice stated.

"Go on," he demanded.

"Jordan left about an hour ago, taking nothing with her but her weapon and the ankle bracelet."

Pritchard smiled. There was nothing Jordan or anyone could do to remove the bracelet unless they went through a metal cutter—and not just any metal cutter, but one designed for the anklet itself. At least, they'd still be able to track her whereabouts.

"Thanks. That's good to know. Is Harrow back yet?"

"Yes. He and Rohnert are on their way to the I-room as we speak."

"All right. Thanks."

He pushed the button to end the conversation and got in a pair of sweats and running shoes. The tightness in his back had been bothering him for some time, and a back adjustment sure sounded good at the moment. Still, his needs would have to wait until more important matters had been addressed first.

"What is this that I hear about Giancarlo being hammered by a human?" Goran asked in the assembly hall, where most of the Council members were present. Ten pair of vampire eyes focused on Demetrius.

Feeling like he had been shoved under a microscope, Demetrius squared his shoulders and mustered his most dignified expression. Hell, his father could've asked in the privacy of his chamber, but no, he'd elected to do it in the presence of the other old farts.

The Vampire Council met once a month on the first day of the new lunar phase. With the moon in perfect view, the incandescent glow of the sun provided the background lighting. The scheduled meeting was dictated by the wishes of the Council head. With Goran as the head, he directed the meetings based on his beliefs on development. The legion's goal was to keep on thriving and growing. Goran believed that this particular phase was a good time to plan and introduce new ideas and beginnings.

Most of the members of the Council marked a legacy in the vampire world. The member's father, mother, and their parents before them had, at one point, contributed to the growth, leadership, and absolute promotion of the vampires' way of life. The members resided outside the Council grounds most of the time to protect their legacy should they come under attack. No one knew where they lived except Goran. Demetrius found it difficult not to follow them to find out where they domiciled and what they were all made of.

Three females and seven males, including his father, stared at Demetrius, contempt and doubt written in their expressions. Garbed in their regal black and gold robes, each one represented an emblem of their particular bloodlines. They made Demetrius cringe, despite his growing resentment.

Fighting the urge to clear his throat, Demetrius stood up and addressed the Council with a slight bow of his head. "Yes, he was attacked during a routine recruitment mission."

"By a human? And is it true that Dangeran was the weapon of choice?" Goran drilled a blazing gaze through him, enough to burn him to cinders, if it were possible.

"Yes. It was a human, but Giancarlo was able to bring the man down before he fled to safety."

"Rightfully so. A human wouldn't be a superior being if not for their technology. You must know this already," Goran answered. The disgust in his father's tone was hard to miss. "I want you to beef up your efforts. Make sure you know the reason behind the aggression. These weak humans won't be our downfall or cause our existence to be exposed and questioned. Clean up and do what you must!"

"Yes, Father," Demetrius responded, his head bowed low in reverence.

"And might I add," an older vampire named August interjected, "we don't want to see sloppy work. Train your people well. Remember, good ideas are not adopted right away. They must be driven into practice with patience."

"Yes, my Lord," Demetrius answered through gritted teeth.

If this meeting continued with him stuck in the middle, fielding questions and under close scrutiny, he'd be losing his teeth because he was grinding his molars hard—too hard—to keep from lashing out.

Goran lifted his hand in a gesture of dismissal. Demetrius wasn't a part of the Council, but he had been summoned to appear so that he could be thrust into the hot seat. He again lowered his head before turning on his heel and marching toward the massive, wrought iron doors that confined the Council's assembly room.

"And before I forget," Goran added just before the doors were opened by the guards. "Stop following me. Nothing good will come of it."

"Father . . ."

"You may leave now." Goran dismissed him, and the doors rattled open for Demetrius to make his departure.

On his way back to his own chamber, Demetrius seethed. *How in the name of all-fucking-mighty did he know I was watching him?* Why would his father go to such great lengths to embarrass him in the presence of others? Demetrius wished he possessed the answers, but being a subordinate, he would do as he was told and proceed with caution. Now, he must watch his back more than ever. It seemed like his father was keeping tabs on his every movement. There was just one thing left to do—impress the bloodsucker!

Demetrius appeared like the terminator incarnated. If looks could kill, every living organism in his wake would be guaranteed to die on contact. The menace that rolled in his gut only intensified at the thought of what his father had made sure everyone heard before he'd been dismissed. It wasn't enough that dear old daddy decided to parade his shortcomings in front the Council. Goran had made him sound like the vampire equivalent of Jeffrey Dahmer, stalker extraordinaire.

Still fuming, he walked into the game room, where most of his new recruits were waiting for him. From the way the ten or so vampires scattered around when they saw him, he was giving off the don't-fuck-with-me vibe. The television sat idle as the abandoned games rattled on. Someone was quick enough to punch the off button before Demetrius had to ask. It wasn't a good night. Not by any means.

He sat on the suddenly empty sofa feeling the steam jetting from his pores. *Way to go Daddy. One of these days, you're not going to like what I do to you,* he thought, looking around for a diversion. Neon lights flashed from the Coors sign on the wall, along with another that read TAKE A BITE OUT OF CRIME. Real funny.

He spotted Jethro lurking near the window. A throwback-looking vampire from the seventies, he was sporting sideburns like a bad Elvis impersonator with long, wavy black hair. Jethro could have added a gabardine outfit with a multicolored design to the mix, but he saved it these days to wear as a Halloween costume. Sad to say, Demetrius would have to make do with the fashion faux pas if it meant having the vampire fill Giancarlo's shoes as his wing man. The man had been the brightest among the newly inducted vampires. He'd have to do.

"You, come here."

The vampire gave Demetrius a long, hard look. Obviously not too crazy about the brazen manner in which he had been addressed, Jethro walked toward the sofa without hurry. Demetrius pursed his lips. The man had balls. The attitude will work great for him, if he lived long enough.

"Sit," Demetrius ordered.

Jethro hesitated, but did what he was told, although his expression was one of growing defiance he didn't even attempt to hide.

"Tell me what made you join us," Demetrius commanded as he swept his hand across the room filled with newbies, who were gawking at them with interest. Murmurs started, and Jethro rolled his eyes before he answered.

"Got nuthin' better to do. Got nowhere to live," he drawled in a thick southern accent. Demetrius was thrown off. The outfit and the accent just didn't cut it for him.

Good answer and good profile. Someone with no ties. No one would miss him. *Perfect.*

After half an hour of conversation with the newbie, Demetrius was almost ready to backslap the son of a bitch when Jethro said something that piqued his interest.

"What did you say?"

"I'm dying to get me some sick vampires." He flashed his brand-new fangs along with a smile, displaying crooked teeth in dire need of dental work.

"I guess we'll get along well, then." Demetrius, for the first time since he left the assembly room, gave a hint of a smile. "Just do what I say, and you'll be fine."

Tilting his head toward the rear of the room where most of the new recruits gathered, he addressed the rest of the vampires, many of them young ones dripping with enthusiasm and raging interest. Strength was in numbers, but leading a bunch of newborns into a conflict was a recipe for disaster.

"You will report to Jethro here. He'll be working with you all and passing on routes and assignments. You are not to leave the premises unless it's your scheduled time to go out. Keep your distance from humans unless the situation calls for it. If you have to feed, be discreet. I don't want you motherfuckers to give me, or the Council, a bad name. I have an open-door policy. If you so much as think about making a bad move, I will kick you out the door so fast you won't even know what hit you."

Some immature vampires snorted, but others got his message, loud and clear, and understood that he meant business. Jethro's chest puffed with pride, and he followed Demetrius like a hungry dog after the meeting broke up.

Jordan paused after catching a whiff of a scent that could only belong to vampires. There were several of them loitering in the vicinity of Rockefeller Center. She felt their presence. The skating rink was in full swing, swirls of people going round and round like hamsters on a wheel, laughing, singing tunes, and acting without care. The place was pure electricity, and she allowed herself to relax despite the prickling sensation in her skin.

There wasn't much she could do, given the large human population in her midst. Making sure she wasn't easy to spot, she stayed close to a group of middle-aged humans, pretending she was a part of the crowd, despite the lack of active conversation on her part.

As long as she had been working the area, this was the first time she'd come across a dense concentration of vampire scent. They were very close, but Jordan had no idea who and where they were.

Jordan looked up and saw the prominent statue of Prometheus, who had been diligent in watching over the Plaza for over fifty years. It was a comforting and eerie feeling at the same time. She looked straight at the gilded bronze eyes that seemed to be watching her in particular.

Feeling spooked and silly at the same time, Jordan continued walking the perimeter surrounding the rink. The little shops lining the plaza were already closing for the night. It was about an hour before the rink would shut down, and she'd be free to snoop around.

The night was rather warm and the air dry, which contributed to the restless energy of humans milling around. Pointing her nose up to gather a lungful of air, she caught another trace of vampires, close enough that she should be able to see them.

Glancing in every direction and trying to separate humans from vampires was tough enough, without having to guess what she'd do if she came face-to-face with them.

She wanted one man. Much of the information she'd gathered from conversations with Allison led her to believe that the man she'd been looking for lived somewhere in the general vicinity. The next thing she had to do was to scour the gutters and sewers for secret entrances. This was a task she'd rather not do, but the probability that it might lead to something productive was hard to ignore.

She walked, stopped, and sniffed. There was nothing specific enough to get her all excited, so she kept moving around, pretending to soak in the sights and projecting a smile here and there in an effort to blend.

A gloved hand slipped in hers, startling her. Jordan looked down and was met by the two large, brown, tearful eyes of a little girl with red curls jutting out from the fringes of her Hello Kitty beanie.

"I can't find my mommy." The little girl's mouth quivered.

Jordan released the girl's hand as if her touch had jolted electricity throughout her body. Human contact had become all but a distant memory for her. Moving in the opposite direction away from the little lost girl was the reasonable thing to do, but she couldn't bear the thought of leaving her alone.

Kneeling in front of the child, whose little sobs began tearing at her heart, she attempted a smile.

"You can't find her?" Her voice croaked and sounded a little off to her. Compassion had been long absent from her arsenal of emotions, and this little girl stirred something she'd rather not deal with.

"I—can't find her—I walk and walk—" The little girl sobbed, unable to finish talking.

"Don't cry. I'll help you find her." Reluctant, Jordan held out her hand, and the little girl took it with trust Jordan didn't feel she deserved.

Despite her conflicting emotions, Jordan held the girl's hand as they began walking around. "What's your name?" she asked, trying to engage the child in conversation to distract her from crying.

"Gail."

"Gail, I'm Jordan. Listen, I won't leave you until we find your mommy," she found herself saying.

They moved around, Jordan letting Gail lead her and checking every single female along the way. They scoured the entire rink, relying on Gail's description of her mother, but Jordan gave up after an hour.

Gail was showing traces of fatigue. After all, it was way past her bedtime. It was pointless to look any longer, so Jordan headed to the rink's concourse, where the customer service section was located. A man dressed in security uniform looked up as soon they walked up to the table. He shot an appreciative glance in Jordan's direction before he focused on Gail. There was something weird about the man's behavior that Jordan couldn't quite put her finger on. Her grip on Gail's hand tightened.

"Can I help you ladies?" he asked.

"I found this little girl lost in the crowd. She said she couldn't find her mother."

The man studied them for a few seconds. "Why don't you stay here and wait? Let's see if someone comes looking for her. Happens a lot in crowded places—child wanders, parents get distracted. You know." The security gestured with his hand and stood up. He was tall for a human and well built, as if he'd been spending every waking hour at the gym, pumping iron.

It dawned on Jordan that the weirdness she felt was because the man in front of her was a vampire. Although he was talking in a normal way, she could see his efforts to hide his prominent canines, as she'd been trying to hide hers.

A sudden urge to bolt gripped her, and she returned a shaky smile. "We will keep walking around and check back in a few minutes."

Without waiting for an answer, Jordan yanked Gail a little too hard and walked away as fast as her little feet could manage. It was only when they had been swallowed by the evening revelers that Jordan relaxed her grip on Gail's hand.

She knelt, their faces on the same level. What she was about to say would top the list of stupid ideas. There was no doubt she might regret this decision, but there was no way she would leave a child to fend for herself.

"I want to ask you something, is that okay?"

Gail nodded at her with trusting eyes. The look in the little girls face made Jordan's head spin and her heart aching to hold and keep her.

"If we don't find your mommy tonight, would you like to come and stay with me for the night, and we can look for her again tomorrow?" There, she said it. Question being, was she ready for such responsibility, even for just one night?

"My mommy's name is Annie Butler."

Jordan had no idea why Gail answered by giving her mother's name, but she knew the information would come in handy. All she had to do was have Dante run the name in his database, and she'd find her right away.

"Okay—Annie Butler," she repeated. "So you're Gail Butler, right?"

"Uh-huh."

"You will come with me then?"

"Okay."

Just like that, Jordan found herself hailing a cab after the announcement had been made that the rink would be closing in a few minutes. Most of the crowd had dispersed, leaving the almost deserted area. There was no sign of any woman searching for a child, and Jordan wasn't about to gamble on whether the security guard would soon be looking for them.

Within minutes, Jordan and Gail stepped out of the cab, several blocks away from the facility. Here she was, going back to the facility. Back to see the man she was trying to avoid. Why did her life have to be so complicated?

"My feet hurt." Gail stopped in the middle of the street after they'd walked a block. Jordan glanced at her and sighed. This whole scenario was so out of her league. She picked Gail up and carried her rest of the way.

Jordan waved toward an area where she knew a camera was located within the facility's property. A concealed door opened as soon as they reached underground.

"Where are we? Is this your house?" Gail's eyes, though showing exhaustion a minute ago, widened the minute they'd stepped into the big facility.

"This is my temporary home." Jordan hesitated. She doubted Gail would understand when she herself couldn't grasp the idea.

"It's big! Are you rich, Jordan?" Gail's arm tightened as she snuggled into Jordan's neck.

The sensation of human warmth and touch made her head spin. She'd been making a lot of mistakes as of late. She knew this one topped the charts, but who in their right mind would abandon an innocent child?

"No, this is not mine," she said as she tapped on Allison's door. Doubt weighed on her shoulders, but her inherent kindness was far too great to disregard.

Dante realized the minute he let the cat out of the bag that he had made a big mistake. *Big.* Harrow stared at him as if he was goddamn crazy. In his defense, being discreet, or even being closemouthed, was never his strongest suit. So now, he was in a tight predicament, which had led to Harrow's disappearance. How could he explain it to Pritchard? Who the hell knew?

Harrow strode in while he was giving a full report to his boss, as usual, and overheard the tail end of their conversation. Well, that was putting it mildly. Harrow heard the most important detail. Jordan had left, and it seemed like she wasn't coming back, ever.

Well, with his back planted against the wall and his neck being threatened into oblivion by the furious vampire, Dante sang like a blasted canary, giving Harrow details and offering to help track her down.

"Tell me everything you know if you want to live another day." Harrow's words were spoken quite clear, and Dante knew he was in for a very long night. Not one to be intimidated, he'd met Harrow's fury with determination. Hell, he'd seen so much in his stint at the PD, but he knew a furious vampire when he stared one straight in the face.

The livid vampire wasn't kidding. His eyes said so, and the clenched jaw was real. Dante had to tell him everything if he wanted his head still attached to his body. Plain and simple.

"Damn Harrow, ta—take it easy, will you?" Dante squawked, not getting enough air through the chokehold.

"Where is Jordan headed?"

Harrow's fangs elongated and the slashing sound they made against the vampire's lips were clear to Dante. Taunt him to deny the information, and he'd be testing their sharpness firsthand.

Dante tried prying the hands off his neck, but it was close to impossible to budge an angry vampire, let alone a vampire who was in love. Shit, he wouldn't be the one to separate good people, not if he could do something about it.

"Le—let me d—down." He barely got the words out, feeling the dizzying blackness creeping in on him fast. "I'll tell you what I know."

Harrow's eyes narrowed to slits, but he lowered Dante until his feet touched the ground. Crumbling down to the floor, his legs unable to support his weight, he ended up gasping for air and coughing.

"Talk," Harrow demanded. Dante inched back but gave an abbreviated report of Jordan's departure.

"She just left. It sounded like it's for good. Allison's been crying." Coughing more, Dante paused to give his lungs enough air to work with.

"Good thing she still wore her ankle cuff, so I've been tracking her." Planting his palms on the ground, Dante tried to push his body up, but his knees buckled again, and he ended up back in a heap on the floor.

"Show me where she is now." Harrow lifted him by the arm and half-dragged him to his elaborate workstation.

Once seated and his bearings creeping back in place, Dante punched some keys, and voila! A green dot with Jordan's name popped on the screen overhead. It didn't give Jordan's exact location, but the general area showed on the grid. Good enough. They would just have to hope that Harrow's olfactory sense would shift into overdrive and he'd find her without delay.

There was no messing with Harrow at that moment. Dante assessed him during the few seconds he studied the map on the monitor, baring his fangs in the process. Harrow left in a flash without saying a word, the dust particles swirling around in his wake.

Harrow had become a friend, or whatever it could be called, in the last few weeks. Dante found himself admiring the vampire, despite his earlier reservations. If people, human or vampire, were half as decent as Harrow, life would be easier for everyone. But along with the good, there was the regrettable bad. The balance of life sucked, in Dante's opinion.

Love was a powerful emotion that was bound to make anyone, be it a two-legged, four-legged, day creature, or night creature, move with purpose or react in volatile ways. Harrow was no exception. He'd been watching how he moved around Jordan. The funky way Harrow's body reacted to her presence was funny, but very real.

Now, if he could figure out a way to get his head out of the guillotine Pritchard was sure to use on him. Once word was out that he was instrumental in Harrow bolting out of the facility and blowing off the meeting with Pritchard and Rohnert, his ass would be baking on the hot seat.

Harrow moved fast, away from the facility before Dante changed his mind. It was just a matter of time before the human, as part of his obligations, informed Pritchard that he was outside the gate and sent reinforcements to haul his ass back to the facility. Harrow kept running through the endless blur of New York City traffic. It was a sea of yellow and white cars and continual pedestrian traffic. He didn't care if he was making himself noticeable. He didn't give a damn at the moment.

Jordan belonged in the facility, where she was safe, away from the clutches of the man she was hunting. Tables would turn, he was certain of it. Jordan wouldn't stand a chance against the vampire leader, even though she was a skilled fighter. A searing emotion tore through him. The very sentiment he'd fought so hard to ignore and kept hidden from scrutiny was now visible like a beacon in the dark night sky.

Harrow operated on pure instinct. Closing in on Fifth Avenue in the Midtown Manhattan area, he sniffed the air for Jordan's scent. He caught a faint fragrance of lavender and vanilla, a scent that was uniquely hers.

Vanilla reminded him of the sweet innocence she possessed beneath the iron mask she wore in front of everyone. The sensuality of lavender added to the allure of her undisguised femininity, strong and bold at the same time.

Jordan's scent was so faint that it almost didn't register on his radar, but he caught it. He was close to her, if he could only find her. He dug his heels harder into the dank pavement, pushing his legs to go faster and following his nose.

His eyesight was faulty at best. The most he could do was track the blurred figures that passed in front of him to keep from bumping into people and whatever else stood in his way. He tilted his head sideways from time to time to get a clearer picture of the street signs and other smaller details.

Harrow arrived at the busy Rockefeller Promenade in no time. The activity at the ice skating rink was already in full-swing, and he found himself not only surrounded by hundreds of people, but also exposed for the first time in his life as a vampire. He was out in the open, bathed in the light provided by humongous bulbs, which were bright enough to light a stadium, yet for the first time in a very long time, he didn't care. His one goal was to find Jordan and get her back to the facility where she'd be safe.

He walked around at a slower pace, shifting his gaze from side to side to get a better look at people's faces and expressions. Zipping his jacket up to his neck and hiding his hands inside his pockets, Harrow tried to appear as normal as possible. With the dark glasses concealing his eyes, he felt safe from the scrutiny of the people he bumped into.

Based on the amount of time he'd been walking around, he should have reached the outskirts of the city by now. The rink's hours were coming to a close and the crowd was dwindling by the minute, but Harrow hadn't been able to spot her. Could he have been too late? There was a possibility that Jordan had only passed through and was farther away from this place than he thought.

The feeling of denial was soon replaced by gloom. Had Jordan managed to get under his skin and make him fall head-over-fucking-heels in love with her?

Yeah, that was it. The twisting ache in the pit of his stomach told him the truth. How could he have fallen for her so fast? He was a certified dumbass who should've said something while she was still around. Not that it would have made her change her mind, but at least he could have gotten it off his chest—that very chest that now felt like it was going to explode. Heck, Jordan couldn't even stand him, much less be around him for any real length of time. Who was he kidding?

Damn, dream on. Vampires didn't fall in love like this. They fucked, and they sucked, and they kept going. There was no knight in shining armor giving the lady in his life a happy ending. Hell, he doubted that happy could even be associated with a vampire like him. An ending was all there was, and it all had ended tonight with Jordan gone and him feeling like an empty shell.

Another half an hour passed before Harrow decided it was time to head back to the facility. He sensed danger lurking, and he was not in the goddamn mood to jump or be jumped. With a dejected sigh, he turned and headed back home. Yeah, goddamn home. He had a home now. It was a better alternative to what he'd had before Pritchard took him in.

Harrow felt a large cloud of despair hovering over him. Short of kicking himself in dejection, he watched the throng of people breeze by him with enviable obliviousness and remarkable purpose. The enormous billboards of Broadway were littered with drink endorsements, and neon signs towered overhead, giving an electric feel he'd once loved. This time, it all seemed inconsequential to him.

There were no words to describe his feelings about what could have been. Harrow didn't want to fool himself into believing that Jordan gave a shit about him. She had a purpose, and his life was still a puzzle. He was a mere moth prancing around the light, maintaining a steady flight path with no idea why the hell he was doing it.

"Dude, your Houdini acts are getting on my nerves." The voice came out of nowhere, and so did the vampire to whom it belonged.

Harrow had been knee-deep in a flood of thoughts, unaware that Tor had been following him for some time. Whipping his head in the direction of Tor's voice, he growled in response. He didn't trust himself to speak, knowing full well his voice would betray him. Tor matched his stride and shrugged. Harrow noticed the bulge underneath his jacket, and knew the vampire was sporting heavy weaponry.

Feeling like a big sissy being scolded for bad conduct, Harrow hissed at Tor, flashing his fangs. It was better the vampire get offended by him than to see right through him.

"I don't appreciate you running out like that. Damn, you're getting me in trouble. Pritchard is mighty furious at you, and he is debating on kicking my ass out because I failed to keep an eye on you. So cut me some slack, will ya?" Tor griped.

"Stay out of my goddamn business, you hear? And I don't give a flying fuck if Pritchard serves your head on a silver platter."

Tor laughed, his white teeth glistening in the dark, which increased Harrow's agitation. That kind of laugh made Harrow want to tear Tor apart, one piece at a time. Not only was he sounding like a broken record, but his presence wasn't welcome. It would have been a pleasure to imbed his knuckles in Tor's face.

"Whoa! What's gotten you all worked up? You're not brooding over Jordan, are you?"

Harrow turned to Tor, his features darkening at the mere mention of Jordan's name. *Yeah, add more salt to the wound will you?* "Shut your hole."

"If you, for once, shut the anger meter down and listened for a change, you might find that I am a bearer of good news." Tor chuckled, enjoying the moment.

"What the fuck are you talking about?"

"Well, *your* Jordan is back," Tor told him.

"What?"

"You heard me right. She's back."

Okay, so he'd heard the vampire loud and clear. Harrow felt a slow but deep sense of relief and pleasure at the news. Masking his emotions for his own sake, he took a step toward the other vampire and closed his hands around Tor's neck.

"Heaven help you if you're kidding. I will kill you so fast you won't even realize you stopped breathing."

"Ooooh," Tor taunted and wiggled free from Harrow's grip.

"Consider it a done deal if you're lying," Harrow repeated before he released Tor's neck.

Harrow and Tor entered the facility without another word to each other. When they reached the main lobby, their paths headed in opposite directions. Tor went to see Pritchard, while Harrow headed toward a section of the facility he'd known about but had never visited.

He glared at a camera, knowing Dante was monitoring him, daring the human to stop him. Everyone was aware that with a single flick of a button, Dante could close off a wing not designated for a particular person to enter.

Pushing open the door that led to the extension of the facility, Harrow strode to the wing where he thought he'd find Jordan. It went without saying that he had no idea where to go or which door led where, yet doors kept opening for him, leading him well into the Tacks' private residence.

As he stepped into a foyer decorated with an array of fresh flowers, Harrow heard a phone ring. He hesitated and stared at the phone, which was on the console next to a very expensive, and rather large, Capodimonte lamp. He sensed that the call was meant for him. Should he pick up?

His unspoken question received a quick answer. A door opened and a human female came from what sounded like a kitchen filled with humming of appliances. She regarded Harrow before walking to the table to answer the phone. She spoke in hushed voice before turning to Harrow, handing him the cordless device.

"Mr. Gates, Dante wishes to speak with you," the woman said before disappearing once more into the kitchen.

"Yo," Dante said. "If you're looking for Jordan, she's in Allison's room right now. That'll be the second to the last door on your left. Knock first."

Before Harrow could even utter a word, the phone went dead and Dante's voice was replaced with a humming dial tone. So much for two-way communication. Harrow glared at the device before replacing the receiver in its cradle.

He took several steps to his right and was surprised to find a seating area with resplendent furnishings, from the expensive Savonnerie area rug that covered almost the entire room, to the heavy upholstered chairs that beckoned one to sit in regal luxury, and the tapestry that adorned the wall, two crystal sconces flanking it.

"Nothing but the best for Pritchard," Harrow muttered before advancing deeper into the house.

This place was a total contrast to the stark, sterile, and almost military appearance of the rest of the facility and quarters. This was something fitting for women the likes of Allison and Jordan. Yeah, Jordan would fit well in a place like this. Now, the big question was why she had been willing to leave a welcoming home atmosphere, and trade it for a nomadic life of solitude. Maybe even death. It was puzzling, to say the least, but somehow he knew he had to find out.

Cursing, he strode to the dimly lit hallway. The faint light provided by a candelabra fastened to the wall lent a soft glow to the long passageway, which had several doors that faced each other. Expensive paintings lined the walls. Distracted by one painting in particular, Harrow leaned closer to read the signature on the bottom of the artwork and whistled. *Salvador fuckin' Dali.*

Shit! Could it be? Harrow shook his head and continued on. The Leda Atomica looked like the real thing, and he doubted Pritchard was a man who would go for reproductions. The farther in he walked, the more paintings were revealed. The house was packing expensive artwork that could rival any art museum. Works by the likes of Fourneau, Kahlo, and

Fini were spread out before him, until he came upon the second to last door in the hallway.

Harrow's hearing alerted him to the conversation already in progress inside the room. *It's now or never.*

He took a deep breath before tapping on the door. Traces of lavender and vanilla engulfed him. He knocked once more and heard a light scrape on the door, like fabric had brushed against the wood. Jordan had to be on the other side.

"What do *you* want?" Jordan spoke through the thick wood that separated them. Not the answer he was looking for.

I want you. "I want to talk to you."

"Why?" Jordan's tone gave nothing away. There was no welcoming trumpet heralding a welcome, but at least she wasn't sending him away. *Not yet.*

Feeling like a glutton for punishment, Harrow inhaled, trying to catch even the faintest whiff of her scent. *Pathetic.* He was aware that the camera was zooming in his direction and that Dante was laughing himself to death at the moment.

"Could you just open the damn door?" he demanded.

Several seconds ticked by before the lock disengaged. The door swung open to reveal the most feminine room he'd ever seen in his life. And to think, he'd had two sisters.

Taking a page from Charlotte Moss' gallery, the cool, blue room combined great art with feminine touches. A delicate, king-sized bed sat in the middle of the large space. It was adorned with twigs and roses, along with vine designs climbing its intricate carvings, and it finished with a canopy in a beige, flowery design. The simple designs were completed with rich, textured bedding and mounds of pillows in all shapes and sizes.

Jordan took a step back when he walked in. He looked at her like a hungry wolf that hadn't seen food for days. He devoured her with his eyes, not giving a damn if she thought he was a pervert. Losing half his mind over the past few hours of searching for her more than justified this, and he'd be damned if he didn't enjoy it.

Harrow turned around just as Jordan closed the door. He noticed that she was wearing a pink sleep shirt over her jeans and combat boots. This was un-Jordan-like. *Pink?* This must have been Allison's influence. Harrow had to admit, the color made her look less edgy. What he saw now was a vulnerable, shy, but very attractive woman. The hallmark toughness Jordan exuded was nonexistent, and he couldn't say he didn't like it.

Out of the corner of his eye, he caught a small figure stir and begin to suck on her thumb. Harrow whipped his head around and focused on the little one in the center of the king-sized bed, sleeping like the little angel she appeared to be. Her hair was blazing red, just like Jordan's.

"Who the hell is . . .?" Harrow stopped, confused. "I—didn't know you had a kid."

Allison laughed from the corner, where she sat sprawled on the floor. A discarded book lay next to her. Harrow hadn't seen her when he walked in, although he knew that this was her bedroom.

"You're a funny one, aren't you?" Allison chuckled.

"Somehow, it wasn't my intention to be humorous."

Harrow couldn't take his eyes off the little angel sleeping on the bed. Her face was framed by lovely red curls, and she continued to suck on her thumb. The peaceful expression on her chubby face made it difficult for Harrow to remember what he had come here for.

"Well, do you want me to leave so you can talk to Jordan?"

Allison jumped to her feet with the grace of a ballet dancer, and Harrow was taken aback. The whole time he had known Allison, she hadn't exhibited any characteristics inherent to vampires. Her movements were devoid of the speed or lithe movements associated with their kind.

Jordan glared at Allison. "You stay here and watch Gail. Harrow and I will be in the sitting room." She turned to Harrow with an expression he couldn't quite understand. Her eyes were expressive, but the grim lines around her mouth gave another impression. "I have to change. Can you wait for me there?"

Harrow nodded and swept one last look at the slumbering girl before letting himself out of the room. Confused, he walked the length of the hallway to the sitting room. He sat on the chair he'd seen when he first walked in and tested it for feel. The cushion took his weight without a problem. He may have felt regal perched on it, but no amount of regality could ease the tension in his muscles when he thought of the possibility that he would make an ass of himself in front of Jordan.

A few moments later, Jordan breezed into the room, bringing with her the aroma that left Harrow licking his lips.

He noticed right away that she was now wearing a black, long-sleeved shirt that defined her figure. Harrow also realized, by the look on her face, that she had erected walls around herself and had every intention of shutting him out.

This was going to be a long night.

"Is there something you need to tell me that can't wait 'til morning?" Jordan asked. Sitting on a chair next to a little corner table that separated them, he found that he was facing the tapestry on the wall, which showed a knight holding a flower.

Cliché much? Yeah, sure.

"There is . . . You may find this ridiculous, but I'm going to say it anyway. I don't expect anything from you except to listen. I have to get this off my chest before it kills me. I followed you when I found out you left."

"Why would you do that?"

Though the question sounded like an accusation, Harrow didn't miss the gleam in her eyes. He regarded her with his head at an angle, not wanting to miss whatever expression might cross her face when he started baring his soul to her.

"Because you belong here." *With me.*

"What are you talking about?"

Enough with the questions already, Harrow wanted to say, but he couldn't. Instead, he marched right in front of the firing squad and said the words he had been afraid to say out of a sense of self-preservation.

"I don't think I can live without you." The words sounded off. "Heck, I don't possess a romantic bone in my body," Harrow blurted, not feeling confident at the way he'd said it. Hell, up until recently, he'd thought of women as a good fuck and nothing else. Sad as it sounded, that had been his way of life for a very long time—until now.

Harrow sighed, and then held his breath. Now, that hadn't been so hard. So why was it that he felt like a daft piece of worthless shit when she didn't respond? Jordan looked at him with bewilderment, along with some stronger emotions that flashed across her face.

Pulling the sunglasses from his eyes, he placed them on the little table, not wanting to hide behind the dark lenses despite the grim sight he presented. He locked his gaze with Jordan's, refusing to let her hide behind the pity she might be feeling for him.

"Why would you say such things to me?" Jordan asked, while her eyes searched his face, then focused on his lips, and returned to holding his stare again.

"I mean it, Jordan. The moment I realized you left, I cursed myself for not telling you any sooner. I have nothing to offer. I'm sick, and I don't deserve you by any means. All I want is to see you here, safe."

After his pathetic monologue, he saw her mouth twitch up. She was laughing at him. *Just great.* He was not only appearing weak in her eyes, but like a loser too. God, the dictionary wouldn't even come close to listing every abysmal word that could be attached to his name at this moment.

"I don't know what to think, Harrow." Jordan stared at him.

"You don't have to say anything. Just say you won't leave."

"I can't."

Harrow gritted his teeth, feeling his fangs puncture his lip.

"You know you can't take *him* alone."

Jordan straightened her back, looking like she'd been sucker punched in the gut. She jutted out her chin in a convincing way that would lead one to believe she could make it happen.

"I can, and I will."

"I'm here, and I'm willing to help you out."

"No!"

"Don't be stupid. You're looking at a death sentence, Jordan," he ground out. "It's a suicide mission, and you know it."

"It's my mission, and if that's how it'll end, then so be it."

"You're a stubborn woman who cares so little about her own life." Harrow huffed and pounded his fist on the small table, sending his sunglasses rattling to the floor. He didn't bother picking them up.

"And you care for something . . . for someone who doesn't want your help."

Ouch. Her words were worse than any physical blow he'd received in the past. They stung, and as much as he tried to hide their effect on him, it proved difficult. This made him more pathetic, even in his own eyes.

"And you'd do best to mind your own business," Jordan added.

"Funny, I've always said that to people who think they know what's best for me," he laughed bitterly.

"Then you should practice what you preach."

"Somehow, I knew you'd say that. Well, I can't stop you if you want to head to the slaughterhouse, but you can't prevent me from caring, or from trying to keep you from going."

"Don't even dare try to stop me, Gates. I swear I will kick your ass." *Again.* She stood up and turned to leave.

He knew she'd tacked on an unspoken word there somewhere. He winced. This was going all wrong. How could she have such little regard for her own life? It was a question he wanted to ask her, but judging by the way she looked and sounded, all hostile and unreasonable, he knew it was something he shouldn't say aloud.

"Whatever, Jordan, but know that you won't get away from me so easily," he replied with enough force to send a clear message.

"Leave me alone, will you? I don't need your help. I don't care how you feel about me. I don't need anyone in my life. I don't care about anything but getting my hands around that bastard's neck." Jordan walked out of the room, leaving Harrow in stunned silence.

Her words burned. Harrow opened his mouth to speak, but she'd made her point clear. She wanted nothing to do with him. Her point was clear, and it hurt like hell.

Demetrius and Jethro sat at a local piano bar, looking casual just as they had for the past week. A part of their new MO was to scout the local dives, bars, hangouts, pool halls, and even karaoke bars. The pair studied the vampires around them—their tendencies, their habits, and whatever else they liked to do as soon as darkness loomed.

It was not difficult to blend in with the rest of the patrons. They dressed similar to the crowd who frequented that type of joint. They pretended to talk, even if they would rather have remained quiet, to gather the quality information they needed.

It was a sneaky idea to dress up, but it got Jethro to shed his godforsaken clothes. Demetrius was sick and tired of the vampire's wardrobe failure. Jethro was a walking fashion disaster with his taste for anything out of date and loud, be it a design or a color. The 1970s blast from the past look just would not work for Demetrius anymore. His eyes were not made for constant offensive visual assault, but that was what he had been enduring thanks to the flared pants, rayon flower-power shirts, and Afro-like hairstyle the other vampire preferred.

Tonight, they were both sporting Versace cable sweaters. Jethro's was a pumpkin hue, and Demetrius had stayed with his favored black. Both men paired their sweaters with jeans to complete the GQ outfit. Money was no object, and Demetrius liked spending Daddy's money.

"So tell me, what's your story?" Jethro asked, popping an olive in his mouth. The vampire loved his martinis, the dirtier the better.

Demetrius cocked his head in the vampire's direction, not sure what had brought about the question. Though they had only been working together for two weeks, Demetrius had found Jethro clever, sharp, and seemingly trustworthy. The latter attribute was still debatable; time would tell if the decision to replace Giancarlo had been a smart move. Of course, it was. He needed his men geared up and ready to go, with all cylinders clicking. Snorting at the idea, he chose to come clean with the vampire.

"Well, I'm the eldest bastard who's waiting for Daddy's demise so I can rule the world." He laughed.

"No kiddin', Boss?" Jethro popped another olive in his mouth, rolling it inside his mouth. "I wonder what your Daddy looks like."

"You got to be special to warrant *Daddy's* audience," Demetrius replied. His father seldom ventured out of his chambers, except to attend the monthly meeting or to check on his collection of women. His harem. "For now, just be happy you're looking at the next big thing."

Jethro chuckled. White teeth gleamed like those glow-in-the-dark sticks children waved around during Halloween.

Demetrius stretched his legs under the table and leaned back. He folded his arms across his chest and tried to enjoy the music, tuning out the noise of human chatter. Jethro sat ramrod straight and continued to watch all the comings and goings inside the club.

Checking his watch, Demetrius saw that it was close to midnight. This was the usual time when the vampire population deemed it safer to go out and mingle—not that there was a threat to them. It was amazing how humans had very little inkling of what lurked around them, sharing their oxygen.

They had an equal opportunity existence—live and let live. Except the vampires needed to feed from the human bastards, and that was where equality ended. The live bottom feeders would continue to give the vampires nourishment until the end of time. Even when the human food source was gone, Demetrius knew, they would persist. Their kind were sturdy enough even with good ol' Satan staring them in the face.

Jethro had asked what Demetrius's story was. He wished he could be more honest with his answer. Yeah, everyone had a life story. His wasn't a tearjerker spawned from a goddamn soap opera. He was the firstborn son. One would think he would have graces falling at his feet like a miracle, but Daddy-O had other plans for him.

He was bred to fight and had learned from the best vampires out there, whatever his father's influence could arrange. Rohnert had been the toughest vampire of them all, but he'd disappeared without a trace. No Dear John letter or even a farewell fuckin'-see-you-later note. The vampire had dissolved as if he'd never existed in the first place. This made the drama a fuckin' tearjerker, since Rohnert had always treated him better than his own father had ever done.

Well, Demetrius had turned out to be a good fighter after all, thanks to the abbreviated lessons of his teacher before he disappeared. Demetrius did what was expected of him and laid the royal red carpet on the ground his father walked on. He worshipped his father with the loyalty of a dog, yet his god-worship was ignored, and he was treated more like a dog than a son.

Nothing he ever did was good enough. He was given an inch whenever possible, but he was never worthy of a mile. He was often humiliated for the smallest mistake, even those beyond his control. Yeah, loyalty and hero-worship were overrated.

If he wanted out, he would have taken off in a heartbeat. However, no, his own covetous nature dictated that he stay and endure. He knew his time would come, but only if his blasted father wasn't always one step ahead.

Sure, he was quick, sly, and lethal. If he'd inherited even a pinch of his father's powers, he'd be hopping like a bunny onto greener pastures, but he lacked the extra sense his father possessed, the gift to read people's reactions, and the pureblood borne to supremacy.

There was no use lamenting over things he could not control. He was better off honing the talent he did have and be smart about it. If there was one thing his father lacked, it was the ability to plot with skill and an evil heart. This was a gift from his mother. She had given him the steeled persistence to thrive and to carry on, traits he knew would bear sweet fruit in the future.

"Hey, Boss, you okay there?" Jethro had been watching him for several moments, not recognizing the fire in his eyes.

"Yeah . . ."

Demetrius turned his head toward the window just in time to catch a glimpse of two vampires strolling past. A male and a female out for an evening walk. How fuckin' sweet. Demetrius felt his stomach twist with aggression at the unmistakable signature of disease and stench of the ailment. He could spot them a mile away. Whether it be dark or blindfolded, they stunk to high heaven. Following the couple with his eyes until the window blocked his view, he nodded to Jethro.

"Let's have some fun." Demetrius stood up, gathered wads of bills from his pocket, and dropped a one hundred dollar bill on the table before striding out of the bar, Jethro following at his heels.

He unsheathed a Dangeran knife and followed his nose. The pair turned into an alley, which made it all better for him. No need to subject humans to unnecessary gore. As soon as he and Jethro made the turn, the male vampire jumped on Demetrius, landing a hard kick on his chest. He staggered back, righting his footing fast. It was quite clear the pair was expecting an attack, for the next thing Demetrius realized, daggers began to fly in his direction. With his inherent speed, he avoided every piece of steel headed his way.

That was the problem with these damn knives and daggers. If you weren't hauling a suitcase filled of ammo, you were bound to run out if they didn't hit the target on the first attempt. Now it was Demetrius's turn to wield his ammo against the male vampire. In reality, one blade was good enough to do the job. Demetrius tossed the knife in the air, caught it, and flicked it toward the male vampire. The metal flew so fast that a human eye could not have tracked it. Even before the vampire had a chance to counter-attack, a gaping hole fizzled in the middle of his abdomen, followed by a snapping sound as his body disintegrated, leaving nothing but ashes and his knife on the ground. And there was something else . . .

"Well, what do we have here?" Demetrius bent down and retrieved his knife, hot as an ember, as well as what looked like a bracelet of some sort. It was metal and bore the logo TE. He fingered the engraved letters and wondered what they meant. Demetrius glanced back at the ashes, glad there wasn't a dead body on the ground. It was best to leave the authorities out of this. No clues, no trace. *Wonderful.*

Jethro had his hands full as it was. The female had engaged him in skilled hand-to-hand combat that was worthy of applause. The vampire was exhibiting some serious martial arts talent.

As strong as Jethro was, the female stayed with him, and it was looking like it would have been a draw had the female not fallen for one of his trick kicks. He dangled his foot in front of his body and when the vampire lunged at him, he sidestepped and gave her a flipping combo that hurled her to the ground. She got up, but she wasn't quick enough. The dagger Jethro thrust into the center of her torso kept her down. With the same crackle and sizzle, her body turned to ash, just like her boyfriend's.

"Damn, and she was purty," Jethro mocked, looking down at the fragments of what had once been a vampire.

The sound of footsteps approached, and they knew their time was up. Time to disappear.

"I'm not one to tell people what to do, but this is insane, Jordan." Pritchard's voice was clear. Resonant. Condemning. He paced the floor without even sparing a glance in her direction. Lambert stood in one corner and watched the exchange with bored curiosity.

Under normal circumstances, Jordan didn't fidget under pressure, but she knew the big mistake she'd made. There was no going back now.

"If you found a little girl, lost and scared, would you have left her alone in a big city?"

Pritchard sighed, closed his eyes, and began shaking his head.

Score! Jordan knew Pritchard's kind nature wouldn't allow it. She decided to tug at his kind heart, pushing her luck a little if need be.

Pritchard stopped pacing and glared at her. "I'd take her to the police station and leave her there where social services can take care of her."

"You think I'd march inside a room full of cops with weapons and expect to come out alive? You gotta be kidding me," Jordan protested.

"Maybe not a police station. You could've left her outside and called the station or something. Hell, I don't know." He raked his fingers through his blond hair, leaving some strands sticking out.

"That's pretty original, Pritchard."

"Just in case you haven't thought about it, you found the girl around the vicinity of a suspected hidden Council location. The girl sought you. You, of all the people out there. Don't you think it's a little suspicious? Think about it. Someone could have planted that girl to lure you into taking pity and bringing her home, which at the moment is here."

"What makes you think I haven't thought about that? If you must know, I went to security to inform them that I had a missing girl. What do I find? A vampire security guard. Weird? Yeah, no doubt."

"Fine . . . maybe leaving her was not the best way, but for heaven's sake, you brought her here. Who knows what kind of chaos will follow because of it?" Pritchard started pacing again, before walking to the bar and pouring himself a drink. Bringing the glass to his lips, he tilted it and drank it down in one swig. He put the glass down and looked at Lambert. "Am I the only one who thinks this is a bad idea?"

Lambert let out a long and unhurried sigh, a clear sign that he was weighing the situation before he spoke. "I think the girl's clean, Pritchard. I mean, she's what? Six years old?"

"That's what she told me. And Pritchard, she *is* human. What do you think, they hardwired her?"

"I don't know what to think anymore. I'd hate for something bad to happen to her, but this is not an ideal place to have a youngster running around."

Jordan could sense she was somehow gaining solid ground in her fight to keep the girl until her mother was located. She glanced in Lambert's direction, but the human just stared back at her. No help there, but at least he'd sort of stood up for her.

"I plan to look for her mother. In fact, Allison and I Googled the mother's name already. I won't stop until I find her."

"You better not, because if you don't find her, you'll be playing *mom* for a long, long time." A wicked gleam lit up Pritchard's eyes.

An uncomfortable feeling washed over Jordan. Was her Good Samaritan act going to blow up in her face?

"Then I'd better go and find Annie Butler." Jordan rose to her feet, feeling the tension in every muscle of her body. This was going to screw up her plans, so she'd better get on to finding the woman before she found herself a reluctant guardian. Halfway out the door, she heard Pritchard laugh, and Lambert joined in.

Bastards!

"Look man, I think we started off on the wrong foot here," Rohnert said. The class he taught with Harrow had ended, and his feet were now spread in front of him on top of the desk. It had been a week since he'd agreed to the teaching stint at the underground facility. Students came and went, human and vampires alike, throughout the day. The classes were divided between martial arts training and weapons training, which they taught alternately.

Harrow grunted a response from his seat behind his own desk, across from the other vampire.

"I think there's more to it besides my unorthodox welcome wagon back at my place," Rohnert continued.

Harrow shrugged. "I'm sure you'll be telling me whatever is on your mind."

"You don't like me, do you?"

"If you're asking me to go out on a date, sorry, bro, but I don't roll that way."

Rohnert snorted at his first whiff of Harrow's famed sarcasm. People around the facility seemed to gravitate toward Harrow in spite of his thorny way with words, but it was something Rohnert didn't want to have directed at himself. In their line of work, so to say, getting attached was perilous. One day you see a person, and the next day, who knew? It was a fact of life. They fell like flies if they weren't careful.

That was what had happened to two of their very own. Dante had tracked the two latest recruits, a couple who had fizzled off the radar. He'd confirmed that they had been obliterated and were, therefore, out of commission for good. The danger was that the ankle bracelets they'd worn hadn't disintegrated and might be in the hands of the people who were on the hunt for them.

All of them.

Rohnert shifted his legs before planting his bare feet on the wood floor. He stood up and walked over to where Harrow was sitting. He pressed both palms on the table and leaned forward, crowding his space. "I think you know I dig the opposite sex. And I'm almost positive that is the reason behind the animosity between us."

"Do enlighten me."

"It's quite easy to read you. You came to my apartment against your will. You gritted your teeth when you mentioned *our* Jordan's name."

Our? Harrow raised an eyebrow at the word. He straightened on his chair and leaned forward to meet Rohnert's face, so close that they almost rubbed foreheads. He jabbed a finger in the other vampire's chest. "What does that have to do with anything?"

"Whoa, man. Take it easy." Rohnert backed off a little, but not enough to leave much space between them. Eyeing the finger on his chest, he hissed. "It's very obvious that we dig the same female, and I can't blame your good taste, my man."

Harrow's eyes blazed behind his sunglasses. This, he now knew, was the reason behind Pritchard's insistence on mentioning Jordan's name. The vampire was after Jordan. Moreover, how Pritchard knew about this was a mystery Harrow had every intention of unraveling.

"Stay away from her," he warned. He felt every single one of his muscles start to coil with unfurled anger.

Surprisingly, Rohnert smiled. It was a somber smile that conveyed not only gloom, but also a lifetime worth of memories one could not begin to understand. Rohnert walked away, masking the transparent emotions that were written all over his face.

"I don't have to. Jordan took care of that for me. Believe me, the female can take care of herself."

Harrow hesitated. That revelation and Rohnert's tone validated what he'd suspected about Jordan—the woman meant business. Nothing and no one would stand in her way of achieving her goal. They had both been shown the highway and kicked to the curb. The puzzle was starting to piece itself together. No wonder Rohnert had agreed to come—he wanted to see Jordan, even if it meant he was going to start hurting all over again.

Damn. Weren't they a bunch of pansies, jonesing after the same woman? To make matters worse, it sounded as if they'd both pledged their existences to protecting her. Harrow had a newfound respect for the other vampire, and he felt a slight shift when some of his anger was replaced by pity. Yeah, goddamn pity for them both.

Harrow flinched before he spoke. The whole idea sucked. "So Jordan gave you a no-go, too?"

Rohnert turned and faced him from across the room. "Yeah, the woman is stubborn to a fault. But who could blame her?" Rohnert shrugged. "She's not going to let anything derail her plans. I'm telling you as I see it. Jordan won't stand a chance. I've known all along it was Goran she sought."

"You knew?" Harrow huffed. "What do you mean?"

"Goran and I go way back . . . don't want to talk about it right now, but all I can say is he is just too powerful and too smart to beat. One vampire, even a determined and lethal one at that, won't be enough to take him down. But now that I know where Jordan is, I'll be damned if I let her get herself killed."

"Then that makes two of us."

Harrow knew the future was as murky as his eyesight, but hell itself wouldn't be able to stand in his way and prevent him from protecting the woman he loved.

The statement elicited a bark of laughter from the other vampire. "Then we are in agreement that we are on the same team? That's all there is to this whole situation." Rohnert strode across the room, back to Harrow's side, hand extended. "And may the best man win?"

Harrow clasped the hand and smirked. "If there's even one of us lucky enough, but sure, I'm up to the improbable challenge."

Instead of Rohnert letting go of his hand, the vampire pulled him to his feet, and they stood face-to-face, the desk providing an insignificant barrier between them. Rohnert was a foot taller than Harrow, bigger in build compared to his trim body. They began sizing each other up as any normal red-blooded males would do.

"Why don't we work off this aggression?" Rohnert asked.

"Suit yourself."

Harrow followed Rohnert to the center of the room, and they began squaring off with hybrid martial arts movements. Their movements were precise, quick, and measured. Rohnert exhibited vast knowledge of the art form, but Harrow held his own, kicking and smacking the vampire several times in the neck and shoulder.

"So this teacher of yours is out of commission?" Rohnert asked in between grunts. The interchange between them was noteworthy, and soon enough, several spectators gathered around them, including Lambert, Tor, Holt, and Drake.

"Yeah, my man is fucked up, but he's resilient. The bastard isn't one to quit on us. I'm sure he'll be back soon."

It was all wishful thinking on his part. Last time he'd seen his friend, Cyrus had still been flat on his back and unable to do much. Several surgeries were lined up for him.

Harrow shot a front kick, which landed on Rohnert's chest. The vampire staggered backward but regained his footing, and they faced off again. Harrow was moving side to side, aiming, and jumping before Rohnert launched a double roundhouse, catching him on the lower torso and blasting him across the room. He ended in a heap of his own limbs against the wall.

Rohnert followed and offered a hand. "That's good to know. I heard a lot of good things about the human," he said.

Harrow took the outstretched hand and jumped to his feet. Instead of letting go of Rohnert's hand, he twisted the vampire's arm and pinned him against the wall. Their bodies pushed against each other, and he whispered in the vampire's ear. "He *is* a good man. Now, why don't you teach me that Kalimetal shit you're so good at?"

Rohnert grunted while he struggled against the firm hold Harrow had on him. "You have an odd way of asking a favor, my man. But okay, just be sure you learn fast. I'm not the most patient teacher when it comes to the Eskrimas."

"Meet eager and willing," Harrow retorted and released Rohnert's arm. He was surprised a moment later to find himself collared against the wall. Snickers coming from the men watching them rose above the sounds of the vampires' efforts.

"You'll be my second student. Watch every movement so you can teach others. Consider it an honor."

Somehow, the statement didn't sound like bragging, but just stating a fact. Harrow bowed and with a blink of an eye, Rohnert had already gathered two metal sticks similar to those Jordan had. The sticks were tossed Harrow's way, and he caught them with both hands.

Rohnert waved at the audience. "Sorry, folks. This will be a private session for now."

Lambert narrowed his eyes good-naturedly before nudging Tor and the others toward the exit. "You better learn good and fast, Gates," Lambert called before yanking the door shut.

Rohnert motioned for Harrow to follow him to the center of the room. He moved in front of Harrow and maintained a three-foot distance between them. "This is what I want you to remember first—the three key elements to learning Eskrima are fluidity, rhythm, and timing. There are few sharp, sudden movements. Instead, you're using smooth, flowing transitions from each movement to the next. The flowing skills are the most important, and the most difficult, to learn and apply.

"Respect for the master is a very important part of the training. The physical and spiritual aspects of Eskrima are nurtured at the same time. As in the former days of Eskrima, secrecy and self-control are stressed. It is only during public demonstrations that the student is encouraged to share their martial knowledge. In olden days, many of the old Eskrima Masters would choose to die with their martial art knowledge rather than teach it to someone who might disgrace or dishonor them. Remember, always respect the art and the master. You understand?"

"Yes," Harrow answered. No wonder the vampire was hesitant at first to share his knowledge with others. It wasn't a question of selfishness, but more of pride and high regard for the martial art form.

"I will introduce the art by teaching you the basic stick exercises." Rohnert began demonstrating the twelve basic offensive strikes. "These are practiced at length before you are permitted to advance to the twelve basic defensive blocks."

Harrow nodded his head, trying to store all information in his hard drive for later use.

"After we practice and I feel you're comfortable, we will move to the more advanced forms, which use two sticks."

They practiced the basic movements and strikes over and over, and Harrow found himself engrossed and captivated by the art form.

"You're learning quite fast. That's good," Rohnert commented as soon as they switched over to the defensive blocks.

"Thanks. Call me Mr. Sponge." Harrow chortled. Without a doubt, he was not only fascinated, but the art also had caught him hook, line, and sinker.

Rohnert laughed a little. "One of the more exciting forms is 'one for one,' in which a strike is delivered and blocked by the opponent, who follows with a strike to the closest area immediately after the block. There are many variations, such as hand-against-weapon and hand-against-hand. The most advanced forms of Eskrima are the counter-for-counter movements. The loser is determined when he cannot counter the other's move."

"Is there any particular reason why you adopted this particular martial art form?" Harrow asked as he repeated the strikes Rohnert had demonstrated.

"I was already fascinated by Eskrima and had fashioned my own weapon. After I left the Council, I went crazy and traveled the world, looking for the meaning of the new life I was facing. I ended up in Asia, where I was taught the tricks of the trade by fellow vampires."

There was a hint of amusement in Rohnert's voice as he walked down memory lane. Harrow got more and more interested in the vampire and his background.

"Vampires? Are we in abundance?"

"Believe it or not, we are everywhere. Like ants. Like light and darkness. Like cold and heat and—"

Harrow cut him off. "I got it . . . know what you mean."

"Well, I went to China, the Philippines, and Korea, where I learned different arts of self-defense. At first, it was just for entertainment purposes to pass the time, but later, it became a passion. I couldn't stop until I'd learned everything under the sun." He smiled, and then tacked on, "No pun intended."

"Interesting. Are you telling me that you haven't had any students other than Jordan and me?"

"Aside from you and her, yes. Well . . . there was one, but I called it off when I realized the intention, or shall we say the *purpose*, wasn't virtuous and noble."

"Is that what you are? Noble?" Harrow asked, interested.

"I don't know if that's what you'd call me, but I don't want this knowledge used for anything but good."

"Then why'd you teach Jordan?" Harrow stopped and waited for Rohnert's answer.

"Because I . . . Hell, can we change the subject?" Rohnert asked. He pressed his eyelids together as if expelling a burst of bad memories he'd rather forget.

"Sorry, that was none of my business. I don't have the right to ask."

"No problem."

Harrow changed the subject. "Who was the one you didn't continue to teach?"

"Demetrius. Goran's son."

"What the fuck?" Harrow saw red upon hearing the name of the vampire.

"Are you shitting me? What do you mean, Goran's son?" In a few quick steps, Harrow knocked Rohnert to the ground. "What a lousy claim to fame."

"Hold your horses, vampire!" Rohnert shouted and flipped to his feet. He squared his shoulders and fixed a challenging stare in Harrow's direction. "I told you, Goran and I go way back, and I still don't want to talk about it."

"The hell you don't. Does Jordan know about this?"

"What she doesn't know won't hurt her," Rohnert bit back. "If you ever lay a hand on me again, I swear to God, you won't live to see another day."

"You just make sure she doesn't get hurt." Harrow was dead serious.

"I wouldn't be here if I didn't care."

"I'm glad we're clear on this matter. If you think for one minute that your threat has any effect on me, you're mistaken."

Harrow strode out of the room without waiting to hear another word from Rohnert. As much as he wanted to hate the vampire, his gut feeling told him to trust the damn guy.

"You've been quiet. Want to talk about it?" Allison asked, eyeing her friend with keen interest that was well blended with worry.

"It's nothing," Jordan answered. She took the trench coat that was hanging on the wing of an armchair and headed for the door. Her weapons were already strapped to her body. "I have to go. Watch Gail for me, will you?"

Allison nodded. They both listened to Gail, who was in the shower singing a song by her much-loved Justin Bieber. The tune had been rattling against their eardrums for the last two days, but neither one had the heart to ask the girl to stop. Jordan sighed before she pulled the door closed behind herself.

It had been two days since she'd brought Gail home, and a trip back to Rockefeller Center to find the girl's mother had proven fruitless. There was no trace of Annie Butler anywhere. They had Googled the girl's mother, and most of what the search engine produced was Facebook and Twitter accounts. The woman's last post had been the day she'd disappeared.

"Going to skate with my baby girl," her status on Twitter had said. "Enjoying the rink with Gail," was posted on Facebook with a picture of the two of them, big grins on their faces. Few people commented, but after that, there were no further postings on either of her social network accounts.

Dante had supplied their address. The apartment checked out clean— nothing out of the ordinary. No forced entry. The place looked like it hadn't been lived in the last few days. Dirty dishes were sitting in the sink, an open box of cereal was on the counter, and leftover food languished in the refrigerator. There was unopened mail on the counter, the dates stamped on the envelopes several days past.

The living room was barely big enough to fit a loveseat and a little recliner, and it was sparsely decorated. The only thing that livened up the drab room was the countless pictures of Gail and a few of mother and daughter together. Just like Gail, Annie was a certified redhead, and she was beautiful. At the very least, it was good that Jordan now had a face to go with the name. There was no man in any of the pictures. Jordan wondered whether Gail had a father looking for her.

She made her way toward the hall that led to the bedrooms. Clothes were strewn all over the two bedrooms, and the windows were firmly locked in place.

Where had Annie gone? Damn it. Jordan reached into her trench coat pocket, retrieved a tiny phone, and autodialed Dante's number. "Can you tell me where Annie Butler works? Maybe I can check there, too. This place is clean. I don't see anything to suggest foul play." She paused and waited while Dante recited an address from the other end of the line.

"Okay, thanks. Yeah, I will let you know if something comes up." Jordan hung up. She checked the place one last time before she went out of the front door and locked it behind her.

Annie Butler was a server in a twenty-four-hour café not too far from the apartment. Jordan reached the place within a few minutes. Seated in the booth next to the window, she ordered a cup of coffee from a bored-as-hell-looking server with bubblegum-colored hair. Jordan couldn't blame her for her lack of interest. The place had a dingy atmosphere with peeled moss green paint. The whole thing screamed "Remodel now." The customers, or lack thereof, seemed more on the broke side of the wage scale.

The server came back after a couple of minutes with her piping hot coffee in a ceramic mug that had seen better days. The veins running across the mug spoke of too many trips through the dishwasher. "Anything else you need, sweetie?" the server asked as she smacked her gum.

"I'm looking for Annie Butler. Have you seen her around?"

The woman looked at her through narrowed eyes. "The boss is looking for her, too. She was supposed to work two nights in a row. She hasn't answered her phone, and it's so unlike her not to call if she wasn't coming in." She shrugged, looking guilty for saying more than she'd intended, before she walked away

Jordan nursed her coffee as she watched throngs of people walking by. New York City at any time of the day or night was always buzzing with activity. There was never a dull moment.

Back to square one. The woman had disappeared without a trace. Jordan had no leads left to go on. Hating the idea of keeping Gail and being tied down, she decided to convince Dante to get some inside info from the police department. A list of dead females would help. Maybe he could secure a copy of Gail's birth certificate as well so that Jordan could find the biological father.

The whole concept was too taxing even to contemplate. However, if this would get Gail back to people who cared about her, then Jordan had no choice but to go the extra mile. She fished for her phone inside her pocket, flicked it on, and hit redial.

"Dante, can you get a hold of Gail's birth record?"

"I already did. I checked the father. His name's Daniel Butler, and he has been dead for over two years. Accident at the construction site he worked for," Dante said from the other end.

"Damn it!" Jordan exclaimed before slamming the phone. She took the mug of coffee, emptied the remaining contents, and dropped an Abe Lincoln before striding out of the coffee shop and into the cool, dark night.

Jordan hugged her dear old trench coat around her body before joining the foot traffic. She made her way toward the direction of her favorite bench by the river. As soon as she sat on the bench, her mind wandered to Harrow while she watched the light play from the buildings across the river. Why did he have to pull such a stupid stunt on her? Baring his feelings like it should matter to her?

The thing was, it did matter. Unlike Rohnert, she'd felt something akin to attraction for Harrow, instead of the fatherly or brotherly shit she'd wanted to use as an excuse. Having never been in love, Jordan had no idea how to explain the stupid flutter in her stomach. The dime store romances that had been her mother's favorite reading material would doubtless tell her that she was falling for Harrow.

Her mother had been a hopeless romantic, just like her father. She had taken after them, until . . . How sad that she couldn't afford to feel that way now. Love, lust, or anything in between had no place in her life. The trouble was that Harrow had gotten under her skin, whether she welcomed it or not. There was no question that she'd fight it. Besides, what would be the point of falling in love? Vampires didn't build lives together. They couldn't make plans, dream realistic dreams, aim for the stars, or even make love.

Now, that was a stunner. Why was she thinking along those lines? She dug deeper into her soul. It wasn't even to be considered. The fact remained that he was infected and she would be, too, if she ever decided to . . . *Hell, no!* Jordan shook the thought and the vision of Harrow out of her head and tried to focus, but to no avail. If she claimed he didn't affect her—that he didn't make her toes curl and make her ache for fulfillment—she would be a liar.

He was much too gorgeous, and he had no idea. The day she'd found him killing the punching bag in the training room, her defenses had broken down. She wanted to feel his body against hers, his mouth caressing hers, and to tangle her fingers through his unkempt hair. He was gentle by nature, a far cry from all the other men with their thundering testosterone in the facility. Although, he had been a laughing-stock after she'd beaten the crap out of him, she had no doubt Harrow could hold his own. He could take on any of the others without a problem.

But enough of Harrow . . . Yeah, enough of him. He had occupied her mind every single minute of the day, and Jordan hated every infinitesimal moment of it. She had to get him off her mind, because there would be no chance of them being together, not by any means. The same went for Rohnert, too.

Yeah, she loved Rohnert, but like a brother. The man had taught her everything she knew. He loved her without reservation, despite her anger and careless disregard for her life, but she'd left him because she couldn't handle his infinite kindness and the affection she couldn't afford to reciprocate.

She avoided him like the plague when she knew he was close. Maybe one of these days, she would open the big dam of her feelings and let him in. *Maybe . . .*

Damn. Her mind was playing tricks on her. Jordan had enough baggage to last a lifetime—and now there was Gail. What was she going to do with the child if she couldn't find her mother? Was she going to be stuck with her?

Heaven forbid. She had long lost the power to care and give a shit about anything or anyone in particular. She wouldn't allow the girl's doe-eyed look and cherubic face to sway her firm resolve.

Jordan sighed, a long exhalation that she hoped would ease the constriction in her chest. Nope, didn't work. Gail . . . God, the little girl was a gem.

After a quick shower, Harrow proceeded to the laboratory after getting a message that Leroy wanted to see him. He knocked before pushing the door open to Leroy's lab, which he'd started calling the Rat Lab. The good doctor had tons of paperwork piled up to his nose but smiled upon seeing Harrow.

"C'mon in, my boy." The doctor stood up and walked around the desk to give Harrow a bear hug, which he reluctantly returned.

"You rang?" Harrow asked, sitting on the chair offered to him.

"Yes, yes." Leroy pushed his glasses back up his nose, tossed his book aside, and gave Harrow his full attention.

The lab was already empty, working hours having ended about an hour ago. Leroy had stayed behind to have a little tête-à-tête with Harrow and to give him a full report on his research. Pritchard had suggested that Harrow should know the ins and outs about the ongoing research.

Leroy picked up a remote-like device on his desk. He pressed a button, and the lights went out, leaving the desk lamp the sole source of illumination in the room. "Look at the far end of the wall." He pointed at an empty expanse of plaster.

Harrow pulled the sunglasses off his face and focused on the white wall. A retractable visual screen slid down when Leroy pressed another button, and then a slide appeared on the panel with a graph and several drawings. They were funny-looking drawings, and Harrow squinted to get a better look at the words and pictures.

Leroy got up and walked closer to the screen. His head was illuminated by the light glowing from the projector. "You're aware that I've been working on the blood you supplied me, right?" he asked.

Harrow nodded.

"Well, I started with the very basic . . . It was stupid almost, but I wanted to make sure I covered all the bases." Leroy pushed his eyeglasses up his nose again.

"Uh-huh." Harrow waited.

"I tried mixing your blood with the different blood groups—O, B, A, and AB—to see what yours reacted most violently to as far as feeding the disease." Leroy pointed a stick to a graph that showed the different levels of effects. Each blood type was numbered on a scale of severity from one to ten.

"See this one?" He pointed to blood group O. "There is not a whole lot of difference when it came to reaction. O is almost the same as A. It leads me to believe that my earlier theory was correct. Any blood type boosts the flare-up."

Leroy pointed to a picture resembling a paisley pattern, a twisted teardrop shape with little hair-like follicles sticking out. "That is your cell, when it's inflamed and lacking enough blood supply. Once you feed, the follicles calm down, kind of like you're combing them off." He pointed to the next picture, which showed a teardrop with fewer of the hair-like protuberances. "The papilla is satisfied with the blood supply, whatever type it is."

"Okay. Where does that leave us, then?" Harrow tried to follow and believed he had a decent grasp on what the doctor had said. The scientific mumbo jumbo was a little out of his league.

Leroy turned the lights on and flicked the screen off. He walked back in Harrow's direction after grabbing a bottle of pills from the counter. "Here, take this," he said.

"What is this?" Harrow asked, shaking the bottle, which was filled with pink tablets.

"Those are pills that are on the market now. They contain Lentivirus, which is used to treat HIV."

Harrow shot Leroy dagger glares. The kind doctor held his hands up, and his face broke into an apologetic grin.

"I know, I know. I'm not saying you have it, and we know you don't. I have to see if your particular virus will react to the medication the same way as the virus that medication was meant to control."

"Fine. Just because you're nice and asking." Harrow smiled at the doctor, whom he'd grown fond of.

"Thanks. Take the pill once a day. We'll give you a week, and then we'll draw blood again." Leroy gave Harrow a fleeting look of compassion. His wrinkled forehead smoothed a bit when he smiled.

"You're welcome." Harrow stood up and held his hand out to the doctor, who shook it firmly.

Harrow was almost out the door when Leroy called out. "Oh, I'm curious about the diet of that girl of yours."

"Don't tell me you're another one to gossip, Leroy," Harrow scolded the older man, who chuckled apologetically. "Just in case your sources forgot to tell you, she told me straight up to fuck off."

"Huh?" Confused, Leroy scratched his head.

"She told me that she doesn't care about me."

"I'm sorry to hear that." Leroy sounded like he meant it.

"It's okay." Even if it wasn't okay, what could he do? Beg?

"What I wanted to ask you is whether you can follow her when she goes out. I have a feeling she's feeding somewhere." Leroy sounded conspiratorial, and Harrow's interest was piqued.

"Why?"

"She hasn't touched any of the blood supply allotted to her ever since she got here. And the few times she's stepped out, even though we were tracking her, we didn't know her exact location except that she went somewhere deep in the forest."

"And you want me to follow her and report back to you?" Harrow didn't savor the idea of following Jordan, but just like Leroy, he was curious now.

"Yes, please."

Harrow slumped next to Dante, glued to the screen monitors while tracking Jordan's movements within the facility. At this point, Harrow was permitted to move unrestricted among all available sources of information and devices in the facility. There had been no resistance from any member, be it vampire or human, to his ascension through the ranks. In fact, Tor celebrated the news, which still left Harrow gritting his teeth to this day. Tor's claim to fame was that he served as the official babysitter to one of the biggest bosses in the facility.

Harrow had met with the lawyer and the accountant, together with Pritchard and Allison. The meeting was informative, overwhelming, and weird. The weirdness came from the fact that the lawyer Jeffrey and the accountant Claude stumbled through their words several times. Harrow couldn't help but wonder what Pritchard had told them about him and Allison. The V-word hadn't been disclosed or the weirdness scale would have been off the charts.

Provisions were made, and arrangements were set. Allison and Harrow were named joint vice presidents, sharing equal rights in running every holding of Tack Enterprises, with Lambert and Cyrus to serve as representatives during meetings and presentations.

Harrow chuckled several times when he saw both men's hands tremble while they held their pens to sign Pritchard's instructions. Pritchard darted knowing looks Harrow's way several times as if warning him to keep his mouth shut.

At last, the meeting had adjourned with a noticeable sigh of relief from both men while they gathered and fumbled their things. They stumbled in hurried footsteps to the helipad for their ride back to the city. It was clear that Tack Enterprises was so big that both men were willing to override their fears and discomfort for the lucrative account. Pritchard Tack was so big that everyone clamored for his business, and once you'd gotten it, it would've been a damn shame to let it go.

"There, she's about to go—east wing." Dante nudged Harrow, pointing at the screen where a green dot moved in the direction of the exit.

"Thanks." He slapped Dante on the back, causing the human to mutter an oath. Chuckling, Harrow made sure his weapons were secured and strapped on his back before gunning into the stairwell and toward another outlet that would take him closer to her path.

Closer but undetectable, he hoped.

Armed with a device Dante had supplied him—a little GPS-like gadget that gave both their locations—he followed her like a predator stalking its prey, like a damn moth attracted to a flame.

Tracking Jordan using the device was seamless as she moved with the speed of a Jaguar on the prowl. Harrow was able to keep up without much effort.

It didn't take long until Jordan entered the foot of the Catskills Mountains, with Harrow following close behind. They ran into the mouth of a thick wilderness, far from the city where the voices of Mother Nature and her legion of creatures were all that one could hear.

Within minutes, Harrow had turned the device off, preferring to use his ears to follow Jordan the rest of the way. She was in his visual range, but with his faulty sight, he depended on his scent tracker and hearing to guide him. The moon shone down, lending an erotic feel to his task, and Harrow felt the desire within him grow.

Jordan crisscrossed the forest floor with ease and familiarity. Harrow noted the grace with which Jordan moved, the vibe she exuded with every jump, skip, and hop. A loose excitement hummed when she ran and turned.

Harrow was beginning to enjoy himself, just watching and listening to her. He was careful with his every move, avoiding the faintest sound that would give his location away.

He was also enjoying the feel of the wind against his skin. The amazing scent of the firs, cedars, cypresses, and junipers, and the musky smell of the mosses surrounding them provided a backdrop he hadn't experience before, always having been a city boy at heart. Everywhere he looked, he saw green, smelled lush vegetation, and heard the different symphonies provided by the forest's inhabitants.

Jordan seemed in tune with her environment. There was a primal, instinctive movement about her enticing Harrow to look even closer. He heard several animals skidding somewhere close by, when Jordan abruptly stopped. She tilted her head in one direction and began stalking, her bare hands constricted into claws and fangs fully elongated.

She picked up her pace, and Harrow matched her movement, still maintaining a safe distance between them and making his advances with very little sound. He watched her lunge at an oblivious group of white-tailed deer grazing on beds of plant life. Catching one, Jordan wrestled the powerful animal to the ground with very little effort, exhibiting tremendous hunting skills. The instinctive way she moved was electrifying, sending chills up and down Harrow's spine and arousing desire deep within him.

Upon pinning the animal down into submission, Jordan sank her fangs into its neck with enthusiasm and raw hunger. She was a sight to behold, and Harrow felt his body react to her moans of satisfaction, amorous heat pulsing like hot wax.

Jordan tugged, sucked, and pulled at the deer until its struggle ceased. Her body shifted around the animal's body until she'd drained it dry. Harrow felt his own breathing become labored in response to the passion he was witnessing. There was nothing more enthralling than watching a vampire moving with languid and sensual prowess.

Harrow closed his eyes and felt desire wash over him. This vampire had his number, and he was as helpless as a newborn baby around her. He was surprised to find that the vision of her feeding on animals exuded the same sexuality as if she'd fed on humans. Harrow could feel his body responding with insuppressible need.

He sensed a slight movement around him. By the time he opened his eyes, it was too late to react. A hand slid around his neck, and a knife was poised at his throat.

"I don't appreciate being followed." Jordan hissed in his ear. The aroma of the blood from her breath wafted through his nostrils, causing his insides to do flips and turns.

"You feed on animals." It was as a mere statement, though it sounded like an accusation. Jordan, seemingly offended, pressed the knife against his skin. A prickling sensation began where the tip of the blade touched his neck.

"You have a problem with that?"

Jordan pressed the knife harder against his neck, and Harrow realized that one wrong move would make him crackle, sizzle, and disappear. He lifted his hands up, palms out in surrender. There was no point in aggravating her more.

Without a word, Jordan released him and pushed him to the ground. He landed face-first, his chest hitting the earth with a loud thud. With the blur of movement, she sheathed her knife and pulled her Kalimetal from their straps. Harrow had a few seconds to react when she lunged at him, weapons in striking pose.

He flipped up and landed on his feet, unsheathing his own Kalimetal and bursting into a defensive position. Jordan stood steady with the tip of one metal pointed in Harrow's face. Her fangs flashed a sign of aggression, and Harrow responded, his lips curling to expose his own.

Jordan struck her metal stick downward, aiming toward his lower torso, and he parried with his right. Jordan returned with an upward strike toward his face, which he blocked with an upward strike as well. She jumped and landed behind Harrow, and he pivoted in one quick motion, following her every move. Jordan returned with a third attack, taking aim at his neck. Harrow sidestepped and struck back. She let out a gasp, knowing Harrow was going to cut her neck into pieces with the metal. Instead, he struck at Jordan's head and cut a big chunk out of the length of her hair.

She screamed in anger as her hair flew down to the ground, each tendril flying like a feather, taunting her. Harrow's laughter was that of obvious delight in scoring against her.

"You're a son of a bitch," Jordan rasped. Her eyes flashed in anger while she positioned herself for another attack.

"I'm just defending myself." He mocked, repositioning his body defensively. "You're not thinking clearly, Jordan. You're letting your anger rule you. Think and breathe deep."

Somehow, his words infuriated her further, and their movements flashed in one fast blur. The sounds of metal against metal reverberated through the dark forest, clashing against their laborious grunts as each strike was met with another. Jordan attacked, and each hit was met with a clean block. She was showing signs of frustration, and he sensed it from her body language. Even though she was aggressive and strong, her anger was getting the best of her.

"I think we should stop this before someone gets hurt. These weapons are lethal, and I'd hate for you to be injured," Harrow reasoned.

"Talk is cheap. Show me what you've got," Jordan snarled. Her eyes snapped with intense emotions that Harrow couldn't quite comprehend. Was she upset because he'd followed her? Or was it something else? He knew the answer would help, but it didn't look like she fancied chitchatting, and he wasn't about to have his balls served on a platter. So he'd fight her until she gave up or he give in. Even if they had to go at it all night long.

So far, he was reading her like a book. Rohnert had been right. React fast, try to read your opponent, and anticipate their next move.

Jordan lunged again, striking horizontally at his abdomen, but Harrow sidestepped and kneed her in the stomach before punching his elbow into her arm, forcing her to release one weapon. Jordan cried in pain and staggered forward. With quick movements, Harrow rotated his body, using hers as a spinning point, and swept the other metal from her grasp.

Jordan recovered fast and repositioned herself in a fighting stance without any weapon, legs spread apart and fists jabbing in his direction. Her eyes burned with unconcealed rage, but there was something more. Harrow could sense that there was some frustration in the mix.

"Stop your madness, Jordan. You're going to get yourself killed," Harrow demanded, feeling his anger surfacing at the ludicrousness of the situation.

"You learned fast, and now you can gloat while you finish me off!" Jordan roared.

"You think I would do that?" Harrow answered back.

"Why not? I expect you to want to prove your point."

"I have nothing to prove to you."

That much was true. He wanted to protect her, but she wasn't seeing it that way. Jordan was too stubborn for her own good. If there was anything he wanted to show her, it was how much he desired her, how he wanted her in his arms and not flat on her back with a weapon staring down at her.

"Then fight me. Show me what you're made of," she taunted.

Harrow tossed all the Kalimetal on the ground and faced her. Bare hands, he could do.

Jordan snarled in anger and threw a punch to his face, which Harrow blocked. He shifted his weight onto one leg, wrenched her arm, and twisted her around. He pinned her arm behind her, while one arm slinked around her neck and drew her body closer. He could feel the contours of her body straining against him, but his firm hold disabled her movements. He moved his mouth to her neck, breathing against her skin.

This was an opportunity of a lifetime. To sink his teeth into her exposed jugular had be the most erotic exchange there was between vampires.

But it wasn't right. He'd infect her, and that was the last thing he wanted to do. Nevertheless, her bare neck teased him, inviting him. Jordan squirmed against his touch. Her grunts encouraged him to show her how he felt.

With tremendous effort, Harrow willed himself not to succumb to his nature. Instead, he grazed her neck with his mouth, enjoying her flowery scent without hurrying. He sniffed as much as he could before he kissed her neck and hurled her to the ground. His mind reeled and his body jerked, rebelling against his decision not to take her. There was nothing he'd rather do, but it wasn't right. Not like that—not against her will.

Jordan recovered and snapped her body back up, but her expression had changed. The anger had simmered down to be replaced by bewilderment. Something in her face questioned why he hadn't finished her off.

"As I've said before, I can't live without you."

Harrow would have loved to give her more reasons, to let her know that he was in love with her, but as she'd said, talk was cheap. So he said no more.

Jordan glared back at Harrow after he threw her on the ground. Her dinner was ruined, her clothes were dirty, and her appetite was gone, all of which added to the resentment she felt for him.

Her rage, compounded by self-loathing for the way she'd overreacted, pushed her to take out her frustrations on him. Jordan couldn't think straight. She had attacked him without provocation, and he'd let her get away with her rash behavior.

"Here." Harrow offered her a hand.

When she hesitated, he dropped on his knees. "Jordan, I'm sorry if I ruined your evening."

Why in the hell was Harrow apologizing? Oh, God, this wasn't what she had been expecting. She wanted to hate him, because if she didn't, she'd fall for him . . . which was a tad bit late.

"I . . . Harrow . . . I'm sorry for the way I behaved. I don't know what's gotten into me." She couldn't meet his eyes. Heck, she couldn't see them anyway under his dark glasses.

"Jordan, I had no right to invade your privacy."

His face softened, and Jordan found herself mesmerized by the gentle movement of his mouth when he spoke. Before she could stop herself, she reached out her hands to his face and laid them on the frame of his glasses. She felt Harrow tense. This was a night when all her emotions were in tumult, leaving her dazed and confused.

"I want to see your eyes," she whispered.

"They're hideous."

Harrow started to move away, but she held his face steady.

"No, they're not."

Harrow hesitated before nodding his head.

Gently, she pulled the glasses off his face expecting him to be looking back at her. Instead, his eyes were closed. His lids pressed tight with the long, thick lashes providing the cover.

"Harrow, I want you to look at me . . . *please*."

She recognized the unknown territory where she treaded. It was a place she'd never wanted to see herself, yet she couldn't fight the pull. To be frank, she was not sure she even wanted to fight it any longer.

Like a veil opening up to her, his lids lifted to reveal the eyes that had once scared the hell out of her. At this moment, all she could see was a man who was just as vulnerable as she was—someone who harbored the same fear and uncertainty. His eyes were tempting her to get lost in them and to see herself as she never had before.

"Your eyes are beautiful," she murmured. Her hands remained on either side of his face, refusing to let him look away.

"You're being kind. I know what they look like." Shame laced his tone, but she shook her head.

"I don't think I've seen you up close like this."

"Jordan, please don't do this to me." Harrow glided his face closer to hers, almost touching.

"What am I doing to you?"

"I can't be this close to you and not want to kiss you or touch you."

"I—I want you to touch me. Kiss me."

Just like that, she went and jumped to extremes. All her reservations were thrown out the window. She'd be damned if she would wait a minute longer for the chance to taste those lips. Jordan felt his muscles tense at her invitation, and she could hear her heartbeat like it was the only sound in the world while she waited for Harrow to react.

They remained half-sitting on the forest floor in silence. Harrow seemed to be debating what to do next. His inner struggle caused his jaw to flex.

At last, his hands moved up to the small of her back and pressed her closer to him. Her hands slid from his face and clasped together behind his neck.

"You have no idea how much I've wanted to do this."

Instead of kissing her like she'd expected, Harrow's mouth landed on the base of her neck, where he caressed her collarbone with his lips, stroking, feeling, and touching. Jordan felt a flame flicker to life, igniting a desire deep within her as his mouth teased her. If this was what heaven was all about, Jordan wondered what had kept her outside its door all this time.

She shuddered with every touch. Her body arched when his hands grazed her waist and started feeling her up and down. His fingers traced the contours of her body. Groans escaped her lips, and Harrow's breathing came in quick spurts, sounding like his tightly lidded self-control was waning and slipping from his grasp.

"Love me," she moaned. Her fingers tangled in his luxurious hair, feeling the strands' silkiness between her fingers.

Groaning, Harrow moved his mouth over her chest, planting kisses everywhere his lips could touch. His hands snaked inside her thick coat, and then found their way underneath her T-shirt. The warmth of his touch seduced her even more, making her want to feel him inside her. His lips were smooth as silk as he burrowed his head deeper into her chest. She wrapped her legs around his waist and sat on his thighs, feeling him shudder.

"This is not right, Jordan," Harrow murmured in ragged breaths. His hands stopped wandering inside her T-shirt and reemerged.

Jordan's body sagged as if life and air were sucked out of her. "What could be so wrong about this?" She could still feel the warmth of his mouth on her skin, and her temperature rose at an alarming rate. *Why stop now?*

"I can't have you. You and I can't happen. I'm not safe."

Harrow's chest heaved. His gray eyes were now flashing white, and his pupils dilated as he expelled a deep sigh. Jordan knew that the fleeting moment of ecstasy between them had ended. Whatever happened between them had been rolled back and sent packing to the what-could-have-been file.

"Harrow . . ."

Jordan knew that Harrow could see the hunger in her eyes. She was desperate for the promise of physical intimacy he no longer offered. Time stood still while she relinquished her desire, what was once a dream turned into nightmare filled with regret. Still holding her body, his fingers rubbed her back, giving her a chance to absorb his words and make her see the idiocy of her hopes. All she could do was stare at him.

As if he'd read her mind, Harrow answered the silent questions that had been nagging her since he'd abruptly withdrawn.

"Jordan, for Christ's sake, don't look at me like that. Hell . . . I want you like I've never wanted anyone. But this isn't happening." Harrow pursed his lips, and she could imagine his internal battle. He touched her face, his thumb fingering the contour of her mouth. "If I have to cut off my hands to keep them from tearing your clothes apart, I will do it. I have nothing to give you but this damned disease. It's not a gift I want to give to the woman I love."

Jordan felt her desire evaporate under the blast of temper that flared inside her. *How could he tell her he loved her when he hardly knew her?* Hell, he wouldn't even take her when she had all but thrown herself at him.

Jordan sprang away from him in one quick move, wrenching her trench coat across her body and walking away. She wanted to hide the hurt he'd inflicted on her and block the thrilling sensation of his hands on her skin from her memory.

"*Love me?* Damn you, Harrow," she cried. She attempted to pick up her weapons, which no longer held the invincibility they'd once offered. Her feet were heavy underneath her, telling her that it was wrong to walk away.

Just like that, Harrow was next to her, gripping her elbow and turning her to face him. "Jordan, how can I make you understand?" Desperation was written all over his face.

"What am I not getting here, Harrow? It's clear that you're playing with me. You wanted to see how I'd react, didn't you?" she screamed. Unable to stand still, she yanked her arm out of his grasp, torn between wanting to rip his clothes off and walking away.

"Look at me, Jordan," Harrow ordered. When she didn't look up, he asked again. "Please, look at me."

She did, although her whole being was already geared to run away from him as fast as she could. He was quicksand, waiting to suck up her whole body and soul. If she wanted to salvage whatever was left of her pride and her heart, leaving was the smart thing to do.

"Look at me. As much as I want you, being with me will condemn you to a life of pain and suffering. If you hate where you are now, you have no idea how much worse it would feel to be in my shoes. I don't want this for you, Jordan. Please believe me."

Although she hated to listen to the voice of reason, there was truth in his words. Jordan knew how the disease worked. She had seen how it ravaged everyone in its path. Granted, Harrow was looking healthy now, but one incident could trigger a flare-up and turn everything around in a snap.

Harrow reached out and tilted her face up. She met his unflinching gaze and saw the honesty in his eyes.

"Where does this leave us?" She couldn't hide the quiver in her voice. This was the very reason why she had never wanted to let her guard down. Being involved with another person spelled trouble, and it would only complicate her already-shambled life.

"I don't know, believe me. I didn't plan for any of this to happen, because I have nothing to offer you. God, I tried to stay away from you, but the more I tried, the more I found myself drawn to you."

The weight of her emotions was hard to bear, and she felt her body sag into him. He wrapped his arms around her, while he spoke soothing words in her ears. Jordan tried to make sense of the whole situation. She still could run away. She was good at it. It was what she had done with Rohnert, and it hadn't been difficult. Then again, how could she group how she felt for Harrow in the same category as Rohnert?

Could she run away from Harrow and deny herself the chance to be with him? Even if it was just to touch and feel him next to her? "I'll take whatever you can give me," she sobbed against his chest.

"Jordan . . . I can't be that selfish," he protested.

"Yes, please be selfish. If that's the only way we can be together."

"Oh, Lord, Jordan . . ."

If she had been in her right mind, she would have backed away from him, reneged on everything she had said, and run away as far as she could. However, here she was, offering all that she had to him, throwing a year's worth of planning down the drain to forge a relationship with a man who wouldn't be able to take what she had to offer.

Truth was, she was out of her mind. She was tethered between insanity and irresponsibility, but damn her plans to hell. Jordan would have to figure something out later, but for now, this was right. Everything felt right. Having Harrow with his arms wrapped around her and shielding her from her own demons was a good reason enough to throw her cares away. Alarm bells clashed with a deafening warning, but she couldn't ignore her feelings any longer. Newsflash in a big neon sign—she was in love with Harrow.

Jordan allowed the revelation to sink in. Why couldn't she think straight? All she could see was how good it was to be with him, even if their relationship was laden with restrictions.

She sighed. She was one big mess of contradictions. Right, wrong, run, hide, hate, and love. What was she supposed to do?

Harrow picked up their weapons from the ground and held his hand out to her. His smile was captivating and full of promises. Jordan realized what she'd always wanted as soon as she placed her hand in his. She had wanted to be with him.

"Let me show you a piece of what I once was before this madness started."

Demetrius and Jethro used the gate that would lead them to the Council's lair underneath the ice skating rink. The gate, a mere blur of lines even upon closer scrutiny and undetectable to human eyes, had been around for centuries. Their own growth had paralleled that of humans, and their kind had seen the birth of modern civilization and the rise of New York City to prominence in the worlds of art, fashion, finance, and politics.

It was a strategic location for maintaining geographical and social control. Despite its close proximity to humans, it was expected to play a big part in their predetermined existence.

The entire assembly was quiet. Demetrius entered through the side entrance meant for other members of their vampire community. He had decided against taking the entryway intended for the Council members and their families to minimize the possibility of bumping into his father after the Council meeting, where he had been embarrassed without cause in front of the esteemed members.

The wooden flooring creaked underneath his soles as he hurried to his bedroom. Jethro followed him until they reached his door.

"Run an ID on this." Demetrius tossed the piece of metal he had found at the scene to Jethro, which the other vampire caught and inspected. "Get to it as soon as you can. I want to know what those two vampires were up to."

"Yessur. Right away, sur." The way Jethro pronounced the word made Demetrius wince before he pulled the door shut behind him.

"Nothing like a warm shower to finish off an eventful night," he said aloud to himself. He headed straight to his large state-of-the–art, walk-in closet. The Council house, as well as the rest of the quarters, which was decorated in a lavish Gothic style and preserved in such a magnificent state, left him flat. He was your regular contemporary Joe. Straight, clean lines would do it for him. Demetrius's room was a modernist take on essential, uncluttered, and the aesthetic beauty of what was both pleasant and expensive. His wardrobe was made of cedar wood. The luxurious closet holding his tasteful clothing was operated by a remote-controlled wall unit that rotated all his clothing for selection.

Clothes and accessories had been an obsession for him, although a distant second to pleasing his father. They were like an aphrodisiac that healed his soul and boosted his ego. Demetrius stripped his clothes and was down to his boxers when he heard a slight movement coming from the direction of his bed.

"Sounds like you had a busy day," the sultry voice belonging to his mother said. She was sprawled on his bed, her remarkable body waiting for him while her glorious mane of red hair was splayed over his pillow.

"Mother, you startled me." Demetrius snapped his fingers, and the lights on the sconces responded, illuminating the entire bedroom.

"How is my boy?" Melissa asked as she snapped her fingers and the lock on the door engaged. Another flick of her fingers drew all the heavy draperies shut, just the way she preferred them to be.

"I'm fine, Mother."

Demetrius walked toward the direction of his king-sized Louie XV-style bed, feeling the rush of adrenaline receding. He climbed onto the bed and settled on top of her with his legs on either side of her body. Bending down, he kissed her on the forehead. She responded with a moan when he glided his lips down to the curve of her nose, to her mouth, which he seized with his own.

"Oh, child, you kiss so reverently," she breathed, pulling his body closer. "I can smell the remnants of death on your hands, my son," she whispered.

Melissa clapped for the lights to dim until they were mere silhouettes in the darkness. Demetrius took his Mother's blood, which she gave as if she was presenting an ice cream to a sullen child. It took the tension out of his system, leaving his coiled body all slackened and feeling content.

"Only because you're a stunning creature."

Drinking her blood was always a beautiful and special occasion, not only because she was a rare beauty who possessed indefinable strength and copious charm, but also because she made him feel revered and exquisite. They shared a bond not just of blood, but also of deep-rooted resentment against Goran's blatant disregard for their affection and loyalty.

"Drink from me." Melissa tugged at his arm. "You must be hungry."

"My soul isn't. I got to slay a parasite tonight," he bragged. "Those pathetic characters didn't see us coming. I'm famished, but somehow, humans don't hold any appeal for me tonight."

Melissa tangled her soft-as-silk legs with his strong ones and pulled herself on top of him. She leaned forward and angled her neck to his face. Demetrius gathered her hair in one hand and latched his mouth on her pulsing artery. The first tug was the sweetest, when the first drop of blood slithered down his throat and the fresh taste began coating his mouth. The rest of his body awakened. Sucking harder, he could hear Melissa's moans as she arched her body with each tug and pull.

"Take as much as you want," she whispered. The blood she fed from was of his father, who was as pure as they could get, and that reality alone made his body shudder. Demetrius felt a small amount of satisfaction at the recompense their actions signified as he smiled to himself.

He had always liked his females willing, and he'd taken them fast. He pulled and sucked harder, feeling the blood glazing his system, jerking life into his depleted body. His mother's grace and natural gentleness made this a blessed event that left him always craving more. Demetrius considered this a spiritual experience. The blood offering was as benevolent as God himself was, and Melissa always obliged. Their rendezvous behind Goran's back added to the sweet rapture of it all.

After yet another satisfying encounter, Melissa wrapped the fine material of her robe around her beautiful body, kissed him on the forehead, and slipped out of his bedroom.

Smiling to himself, Demetrius walked into the shower for his much-deserved cleansing. While the warm water cascaded down his taut body, the evening's earlier encounter came to mind. The vampires they'd eliminated had been armed and competent fighters. Even with the rather brief run-in, he knew they were afflicted, but there was something about them that struck him as odd. Was it the remarkable absence of active lesions, or the fact that they posed an actual threat to him and Jethro?

Most diseased vampires were known to retreat and shut themselves away from the eyes of the general population, except for a few dim-witted bastards who didn't know any better. There was a nagging suspicion at the back of Demetrius's mind that the tides might be turning. These poor excuses for vampires were now fighting back and making their stand against his father's decree that called for their extermination.

The mere thought of killing more bugs and ridding the earth of them brought tingles of excitement from his spine down to the soles of his feet. He'd be willing to build a bigger army to squash them out of existence and send them all straight to hell.

After his glorious shower, he donned a silk bathrobe, grabbed his cell phone from the table, and speed-dialed Jethro's number. The vampire picked up on the first ring. Demetrius was beginning to believe that Giancarlo's demotion had been a sound choice.

Jethro was not only an accomplished fighter, but also a damn loyal and smart vampire. He followed orders like they were his bible, and he kept Demetrius's subjects in line.

"Jet, did you find anything?" He pressed his back against the mattress and enjoyed the feeling of the satiny cushion on his skin.

"Well, boss, it could be anything. There are a few leads I've gathered that are worth taking a look at. TE could mean so many things. Here're a few of the names or acronyms I found. Throat Erosion, which has something to do with firearms, then there's Technology Evangelist, which sounds like religious shit. Ya know, like a sect?"

"Keep going," Demetrius ordered.

"There's Team Europe, which can mean anything, not just the team sporting crap. Could be a cult or a 'beat the devil' organization, for all we know." Jethro let out a throaty laugh, sounding amused at his own sick humor. "Then there's Tack Enterprises. It's a heavy duty, 'hold your pants or you'll drop them with envy' type of company. The owner, Pritchard Tack, is a longtime New York City resident and a multibillionaire who supplies sniper rifles to the military. And there's Terrestrial Entity, which I think is suspicious. The website is pretty weird, some jacked animal on the web cover, blood and all that gory stuff. Okay, let's see . . . what else do I have here?"

"I will let you get all the details together. Check them out if you have to, and report back to me with whatever you think is important. Don't bother me with stupid stuff."

"Yessur. No worries in that department. Anything else?"

"Get some boys out tonight."

"Right away, sur."

"They know what to look for, right?"

"Yessur."

"Get them in bigger groups, and tell them to concentrate within the city. Have them prowl the back alleys, but make sure there's more than four per group. Judging from the two we nailed tonight, I have a feeling there are more well-trained vampires out there and they're somehow connected to this TE."

"Okay. Would that be it?"

"Yeah." Demetrius flicked the phone off and thought more of his mother, Goran, and the vampires they'd sent to kingdom come.

"Where are you taking me?" Jordan asked as soon as they'd reached the heart of the city's theater district. Harrow had been quiet during their run from the forest, and Jordan had stayed to herself, trying to reorganize her whirling mind.

Things had happened a little too fast. Not only had she tried to talk Harrow into taking her, but she'd almost spilled her guts out to him. Not your typical Jordan approach, but she seemed to have no control over her emotions where Harrow was concerned.

Harrow, except for holding her hand, had not attempted anything remotely close to sexual throughout the duration of their short trip. He would glance at her from the corner of his eye, but he hadn't uttered a word until they reached the theater row.

"I want to show you a special place for me. Where I've always felt like I belonged," he answered.

"Oh."

Nothing else came to mind until they stood outside a well-known landmark, the Ethel Barrymore Theater. Then everything clicked into place, like puzzle pieces meeting the rest of their connections. Jordan remembered

Harrow and Allison's conversation about their mutual passion for theater and acting.

"This is where I used to work a long time ago," Harrow said, sounding proud.

The wistfulness in his tone brought a familiar pain to her heart, reminding her of her own life that had been cut short. The theater, with its exterior modeled after the designs of Roman public baths and a two-story terra cotta grillwork screen, was closed for the night. A few lights were left blinking in the front of the imposing edifice, giving it an eerie effect. The marquee glittered against the darkness while they made their way toward the rear of the building.

Harrow brought her hand to his lips and kissed it once before he let it go. "Be right back," he said. He scaled the side of the concrete building until he found a window and went through the opening like a thief with a purpose.

Jordan found herself glancing left to right, feeling like a criminal. The alley was deserted, and she doubted very much that anyone would come strolling by.

The sound of a door creaking open brought Jordan into an instinctual defensive position. Harrow emerged from the back entrance, which was marked CAST MEMBERS AND EMPLOYEES ONLY.

"Come this way," he said as he ushered her in.

From the back entrance, they made their way through the empty building, Harrow seemed caught in a whirlpool of memories. They reached the dark lobby, where marbled walls and golden doors greeted them. Without needing the aid of light, Harrow pointed to pictures in a glass enclosure that displayed a photograph of the theater's namesake, who had been a famous actor and a household name in the 1920s.

"Do you miss acting?" Jordan asked. Their shoulders were touching, and she could feel the tremors that rocked his body.

"Like a flower misses the rain in the dead of summer," he answered. There was a tinge of mournfulness in his voice that prompted Jordan to reach out to him.

She placed a hand on his cheek, and he leaned against her touch. His eyes closed briefly. In the darkness, she could very well see the sadness in his face, catching a momentary glimpse of a broken man. It was a side of Harrow she hadn't seen before.

"This was your past. There must something worth looking forward—"

"Just you," he murmured.

Harrow took the hand that was touching his cheek and kissed her palm again.

"Harrow, I don't know what you expect from me, and I don't want to disappoint you. I've been out of touch, and all this is new to me."

"Nothing about you could ever disappoint me, Jordan. Nothing."

Nothing? She couldn't say the word out loud for fear of ruining this picture-perfect moment.

She stood on the tip of her toes and reached her mouth to his, brushing a light kiss against his lips. The intense emotions were creating havoc inside her, making it difficult to think straight. Sensing her turmoil, Harrow took her hand and led her through the double doors.

The interior of the theater took her breath away. "This is amazing." Her eyes were diverted upward to the massive, crystal chandelier that hung in the middle of the room. Next scanning the entire room, the most elaborate element she noticed were the boxes, where columned porticos stood amid the sunburst of pattern. Even in the darkness, Jordan could make out the intricate details in every carving, the decorative arches and combined décors of the Elizabethan, Mediterranean, and Adamesque styles.

"Let's sit."

Harrow led her to the center of the orchestra seats. He sat down, facing the creased, dark red curtains that hid the stage. Jordan sat next to him on the velveteen seats, no longer fascinated by the grandeur around her but more interested in watching Harrow.

She watched his chest rise and fall with his even breathing and the way his eyes darted around with fondness and remembrance. There was nothing she could offer him at that moment except a squeeze of his hand to tell him without the necessity of words that she was there for him.

"Do you mind if we stay here for a little while?" Harrow asked.

"Not at all. We have more than four hours before sunrise."

Jordan leaned her head on his chest, despite the arm of the seat that divided them. Harrow lifted her hand and guided her to sit on his lap.

"I won't do anything you don't want me to do," he whispered.

"I will let you dictate the tempo for us," she answered. There was nothing else she could say. Harrow needed to set the limits between them, and demanding more might push him away.

"I just want to hold you in my arms, smell your hair, and listen to your heartbeat. These are the things that would give me the greatest joy."

Jordan was left pondering his statement as she snuggled into his embrace. He'd mentioned the three senses available to him, with the absence of sight and taste. It was clear to her now how it was going to be with him, the limitations and the sacrifices they both had to make. Was she okay with it?

The answer was clear—yes. She'd have him any way she could, any way he'd offer himself to her. This was more than she'd ever expected out of her life since her transformation. If this was as good as it could get, she was lucky to have someone to love and someone who felt the same way about her, regardless of their imperfections.

The sound of silence that cloaked them was comfortable. Harrow's hand ghosted across her back, rubbing and running circles with his palm outside the material of her shirt and coat. Even with the layers separating their skin, Jordan was aware of the warmth radiating between them. How she wished they could be doing more.

After several minutes, Harrow broke the quiet.

"What are you thinking about?

"Everything," she said before exhaling. "I have the tendency to live inside my head a lot. I haven't done a lot of talking lately."

"Does that mean you want me to shut up?" The hint of a smile laced his voice.

"Heavens, no. Ask me anything you want. I'll answer if I can." Jordan tilted her head so she could watch him.

"Fair enough. What was it like for you growing up? Where are you from?"

A deep sigh escaped her lips. Talking about her past was something she hadn't done, and she wasn't sure if she could go through remembering the whole ordeal again.

However, as the first words came out, the rest flowed like a raging river that had been unleashed for the very first time. Jordan told Harrow about her family. She spoke about the loving parents who had imparted not only their love for the outdoors, but also for life itself. The thought of how happy and complete their lives had been, until the moment their nightmare began, brought her comfort.

She hurried through the account of her parents' death, the man who had taken their lives, and her own bitter and painful transformation. Harrow held her hand as she spoke of the whole past torment, occasionally murmuring soothing words when she faltered.

Each spoken word, as she said it aloud, reinforced the fact that her parents were gone. And she . . . well, she was sort of alive. The paralyzing fear of knowing what she'd become had been buried deep, to be replaced by a resolve that had spawned the retribution she now sought.

"I'm sorry about your parents. It must have hurt to watch them go through what they did." Harrow tightened his arms around her, but somehow, she felt liberated to have spoken about the ghosts of her past. The sense of relief was gratifying, as if she had finally been released from the multitude of emotions that had once been her prison.

"I think I ought to thank you for asking me about them. I have never spoken to anyone about what happened that night and how I came to be." Then Rohnert came to mind. "At least, not in such detail."

"No thanks necessary. I'm glad you shared a piece of yourself with me," Harrow whispered. He spoke with so much tenderness that it brought moisture to Jordan's eyes. She blinked back the tears and smiled.

Harrow lowered his face to the base of her neck and skimmed his mouth along her skin. Every touch left a tingle in each spot against which he'd trailed his lips. Jordan smothered a moan and closed her eyes. She expected more from him. She wanted more. However, his caress stopped soon after, and he buried his face in her hair.

"As much as I want the pleasure of making you mine, there isn't any way around this . . . this . . . unimaginable disease. I won't risk it," he said.

"We don't have to do anything. I'm here. You're here. We can talk." Jordan tried to hide her disappointment with a smile.

She felt him sigh into her hair. "Explain to me what I saw back there in the forest," he mumbled.

"I've never fed on human blood. Ever," she said, not sure if it was something she ought to be ashamed of. It was a piece of humanity that she still clung to, a small part of her old life she wasn't ready to let go, and she was certain she never would.

"Ever?"

"*Ever*. When I woke up after I was turned, the forest offered me the first drop of blood that made the difference between losing my grip and keeping a small part of me."

"How can you take it? Has there ever been a time when you were tempted to feed on a human's blood?" The surprise in Harrow's expression was unmistakable.

"I don't know any better," she answered. Harrow's brows furrowed in disbelief. "Let's put it this way. How can you miss something you've never had before? Animal blood has been my diet ever since I woke up after my change," she explained, and she watched while confusion and awe graced Harrow's face.

"When I was watching you, there was something erotic and titillating about the whole act of feeding on an animal. It made me think of how much we should enjoy what we eat, guilt-free." His eyes darkened at his statement.

"Why did you follow me?" She finally asked the question that had been burning at the back of her mind. Harrow must have better things to do with his time. He had training to conduct and affairs to take care of since Pritchard had relegated some of the facility's responsibilities to him.

Harrow sighed as if torn between telling her the truth and keeping something from her. "Leroy wanted me to see what you're up to, since you never took the blood offered to you."

"And being the Boy Scout that you are, you did what was asked of you?" she teased, and then smiled. There was something about Harrow's inherent goodness that attracted her to him, no matter how hard she resisted. It was like opening a present with every expectation of something good, only to find out that the present inside was much better than she'd hoped.

"When it comes to you, there's nothing I wouldn't do." He smiled in return before he closed his eyes and rested his head on the back of the seat. They spent the next few minutes in peace and quiet, listening to nothing but the steady rhythm of their heartbeats.

She felt her eyes began to close. Sleep beckoned her, and she succumbed to its invitation.

"Jordan?"

"Hmm . . ."

"It's time for us to go," Harrow whispered, not wanting to jolt her out of the restful sleep she'd been enjoying for the last two hours. He would have loved to stay longer, but considering the time and the fact that they'd been out the whole night, it was time for them to head home. Since his cell phone was turned off, he could picture Dante and Tor shitting in their pants with worry.

Jordan's eyes flew open as if she had committed a crime. Disoriented, her hands reached for her weapons, which were sitting next to her. She jerked up onto her feet in hurried and awkward movements, making Harrow laugh.

"Are you always this jumpy in the morning?" he teased. His mouth broke into a lopsided grin. Behind the smile he wore, he realized how aroused he was by Jordan's vulnerability. Wrong—and yet, it turned him on.

"Not usually." She laughed, despite herself. "I don't fall asleep for longer than an hour."

He was pleased by her admission. Until tonight, Jordan had been a mystery to him. She'd kept to herself, made little effort to socialize with anyone but Allison, and had been rather aloof since her arrival at the facility. Harrow took her hand, and they walked out of the theater the way they had come in.

Once outside in the cold winter night, their nostrils were filled with the scent of the holidays that was already marking the air. They looked around and took stock of their immediate surroundings before proceeding into the back alley. This was a faster route to take instead of hassling with the busy main streets. With minimal lighting coming from a lamppost at the end of the alley, they covered the length of the darkened little street with quick strides.

They were almost out of midtown when they heard several footsteps about to cross their path. Sniffing the air, Harrow knew what was coming their way. He let go of Jordan's hand and unbuttoned his jacket in preparation. His weapons would best serve them if they were ready for action. He noticed Jordan did the same with her trench coat. Another set of footsteps registered from behind. Harrow glanced over his shoulder and saw a figure following at a slower pace.

"There are five of them," Harrow muttered under his breath. "Be ready."

A few feet more, and their paths crossed at an intersection. Four men stopped several feet from them. They were obviously not of the humankind, to judge from their arrogant demeanor. Harrow and Jordan braced themselves for an imminent brawl.

Harrow stopped and spread his legs apart, letting his instincts get a read on the vampires standing before them. He was getting all jacked up for a fight. Jordan stopped next to him. Her behavior was unruffled, and he could feel the humming of excitement rolling off her.

He took a quick peek at the vampire trailing them, who at that moment stopped in his tracks, as if waiting to see what was going to come down.

"What can we do for you ladies this lovely evening?" Harrow asked, sounding deadly calm and collected.

"We noticed—actually, sniffed—something rotten. The scent of a dead man walking to his grave," one of the vampires said, while the rest snickered and laughed.

"I don't see anyone rotting here, at least not yet, but that can be arranged very soon if you suckers don't get out of our way," Harrow answered. His eyes blazed with anticipation.

More laughter sounded. "You can go, but we'd like to keep the woman," another replied.

"How about I clip that tongue of yours before you piss me off?" Harrow unsheathed the Kalimetal from his back. The stunning and incandescent glow created by the light hitting the blades stunned the vampires to inaction as Harrow and Jordan inched forward, but it only took a few seconds for them to regain enough of their composure to move forward.

"Sick vampires should go to hell. Leave the woman with us. There are a lot of things we can do with her," one vampire taunted as he jerked his hips forward.

Jordan sensed the inevitable showdown that was about to take place. She unsheathed her weapon and took another step forward. "You're boring me to death with your small talk. Why don't you put your money where your mouth is, and let's get this over with?"

The four vampires flashed their fangs as they pulled different weapons, waving them in front of Harrow and Jordan. Five vampires against two tilted the odds in their favor, and it showed in their confident behavior and swaggering.

Harrow observed them and anticipated their movements. One vampire, who seemed too overexcited to wait for the order, jumped up, somersaulted in the air, and landed in front of Harrow.

Harrow pointed the Kalimetal toward the vampire when he landed, and he shifted as the vampire moved. He kept at the impatient vampire, turning and twisting his weapon with every step. From the movement of his opponents, he could tell they were inexperienced.

Newbies.

Quick, but awkward, the vampire lunged at him. All Harrow had to do was to strike the vampire on the head. Presto—the vampire convulsed and fell headfirst to the ground. There was nothing much one could do when a Dangeran hit a vital part of the body. The fizzling, firecracker-like routine started before his body fragmented into ashes.

Jordan's head whipped in Harrow's direction when she heard the crackling that was followed at once by a sizzling sound. One down, four to go. She shook her hips and teased the remaining vampires with her *come-hither* impersonation.

Nostrils flaring, all three ran toward Jordan while flinging a shower of knives and throwing stars her way. Moving at lightning speed, Jordan jumped into a series of somersaults, avoiding the weapons shooting toward the direction where she used to be.

Heads tried to follow her quick movements, and Harrow took the opportunity to strike another vampire into oblivion. It was like the sound of music to their ears when the crackling and fizzing broke out. Three more to go.

The panic that gripped their attackers' faces was unmistakable. One vampire threw a knife at Jordan, but she waved her weapon to deflect it. Harrow engaged the other by jumping in front of him. His execution was precise, his Kalimetal crisscrossed to ward off any sharp object thrown his way. He kept walking forward while the vampire backpedaled closer to the wall. Cornered, the vampire snarled before pulling a dagger and lunging at Harrow over and over. Every thrust and shove was avoided. Harrow kept the vampire trapped with nowhere to go.

Like an animal, the vampire was striking out with blind movements, confused and very much afraid. Harrow couldn't help but chuckle at the lost cause standing in front of him before he struck the vampire with a direct hit to the chest. Another sizzle sounded and was followed by a pop. Two more, and that was it for the night. It was time to take his girl home.

He glanced over at Jordan, who was toying with her opponent. She showed off an arsenal of jumps, flips, and turns. He had to admit she looked confident—borderline cocky, even.

Harrow turned to check out the fifth vampire. Upon making eye contact, the vampire must've realized his time was coming up. As fast as his feet could take him, he scrambled away, looking very much like a bunny on crack. Harrow decided against leaving Jordan and didn't follow in pursuit.

"This is fun!" Harrow grinned and started wiping the grime off his weapon onto his jeans before replacing it back on the strap. Adjusting his jacket back into place, he leaned against the wall to watch Jordan.

One more to go. Harrow paid attention to Jordan as she and the last remaining vampire circled each other. Her opponent hurled throwing stars in her direction, but Jordan sidestepped and avoided the barrage coming her way.

"I'm getting bored here," Jordan taunted the vampire. The enraged vampire's eyes flashed with fury, but there was something else—*fear*.

"I love fear," she said.

"Fear is what I will see in your eyes when my dagger is gutting your stomach."

"You wish."

The vampire skidded to her left, catching her off guard with a sweep of his leg under her.

Instead of falling over, Jordan jerked her body upward and jumped away. The vampire leapt to his feet, dagger in hand, and lunged while her back was turned to him. As if she had a pair of eyes in the back of her head, Jordan pivoted fast and avoided being struck. With a quick succession of movements, Jordan swung her Kalimetal while the vampire feverishly evaded her attacks. They went at it for some time, Jordan whipping her weapon, her opponent dodging and eluding. It wasn't a surprise that the vampire couldn't sustain his defense against the barrage long enough. For her final act, Jordan raised the blunt tip before striking him in the neck.

As soon as metal met the skin, the inevitable happened. Crack, sizzle, pop, and he checked out for good.

"I doubt anyone will miss him." Harrow laughed.

"I doubt it." Jordan smiled. "Let's go home."

A thundering voice came from the roof. "Bravo, bravo." A shadow in the darkness until he emerged, Tor had a big grin plastered on his face, just like a proud rooster looking over his chicks. The vampire landed next to Harrow with a soft thud of his boots on the ground.

"Have you been there a long time?" Harrow asked.

"I've seen enough of everything." Tor's lips twisted, and he gave Jordan a sweeping bow of his head.

"What have you seen?" Glaring at the bigger vampire, Harrow took Jordan's hand and tucked her in his arms.

Jordan chuckled at Harrow's obvious possessive reaction.

"I'm your babysitter, remember? Just don't expect to lose me so easily. I saw what I needed to see. Let's just leave it at that."

Judging by the thinning of Harrow's lips, Tor knew he had to clarify his position. "I left you guys alone in the forest and didn't even peek inside the theater, okay? Geez, give me a break, will you?"

As much as he wanted to congratulate his friend for landing a great catch, Tor held his tongue. All he could think of was the cruelty of their fate and how they could be likened to Romeo and Juliet—twelve versions of screwed. Tor chuckled at the thought. With Harrow's raw temper and his advanced skills in fighting, he didn't feel like testing him right this minute. There had been enough fighting for one night.

"I'm getting sick of you following me around," Harrow complained.

"Hey, you can run and hide, but I'll find you, my friend. So get over it." Tor turned and headed toward the end of the alley. "You guys had a very long night. Time to park your ass and get some rest."

Jordan chortled at his statement, and Harrow clapped him on the back. "Shall we?" he said and started walking.

They followed him toward the busy part of the city, where they walked the stretch of countless blocks in silence. Tor kept his mouth shut as they maneuvered through throngs of late-night foot traffic. He couldn't help but glance sideways at Harrow holding Jordan's hand and felt sadness creeping in. Sure, he was happy for Harrow, but he couldn't ignore the envy that he felt. All things considered, it was a nice evening for a stroll, except the lovebirds made him sick to his stomach.

They reached the facility within minutes of brisk walking. Running would have been a better outlet for Tor since he hadn't been able to participate in the slaughter. He planned to expel some of his aggression on Rohnert, as soon as the vampire was off his teaching schedule.

A sudden blast from his past rattled him. Serene, warm, and beautiful, Tor saw Jessie in his mind's eye as if she were standing before him. She was smiling at him as if he'd had nothing to do with the misery that had been inflicted on them both. Memories from his past life shot through him like bolts of lightning. It jolted him out of his comfort zone, pummeling the walls he'd built around his frail mind to keep the memories from haunting him. He had a date with the treadmill as soon as he got his ass inside the gym. Being around Harrow and Jordan was a bad idea, no matter how happy he was for them.

"Tor, did you swallow your tongue?" Harrow broke the silence just before they reached the elevator.

Thank God, he'd have the room all to himself today. He could see that he wasn't going to be good company.

"Nah, just don't feel like singing right now. By the way, Cyrus was asking for you," he said as he made a mad dash for the stairwell, aching to get away—away from the reminders of the past, and from what he'd once had.

"I knew it!" Leroy jumped out of his chair and started jerking a poor version of the *Cabbage Patch* dance, making himself look more like a fool than the respectable scientist his subordinates respected. They stared at him with amused, you've-got-to-be-kidding-me expressions.

Harrow laughed, unable to hide his amusement at Leroy's comical attempt to dance. "Leroy, what's the big deal?"

Leroy stopped and peered at him as if he'd lost his mind. "What's the big deal? Boy, let me tell you about a theory I want to try—if you're still willing."

Harrow removed his glasses and examined Leroy closely. "You know I trust you, but if it kills me . . ." He was surprised to find that he meant the words. *Trust.* An emotional compromise he hadn't had the luxury of allowing himself to feel before, not with what he'd gone through in all the years of hiding and running. It was an illogical emotion that could lead to exposed vulnerabilities but would also take him to the crossroads of predictability and reciprocity. Damn. Why did life have to be all about choices?

He'd trust Leroy to do the right thing. He trusted Pritchard to lead them to a safer future, trusted Tor with his life, and Jordan with his heart. Jesus

Christ, he felt like a child open for the world to take advantage of, with nothing but swaddling to cover his ass.

Was he ready for it? In hindsight, this meant he had to give in order to gain something. All he could hope for was that none of his trust issues would blow up in his face.

"I promise it will be worth your time," Leroy said, settling down from his jubilation.

"It better be, or else. I'll string you upside down if I grow hair all over and start scratching like a rabid animal."

"There's no guarantee about growing hair," Leroy teased.

"Tell me what I have to do."

"Let me work out some details, and I'll call on you once I'm ready to try the experiment."

"Why does *that* word scare the hell out of me?" Yeah, sure. Being a lab experiment would do that to any person, even a vampire.

Leroy chuckled. He moved across the room until he reached a computer at the corner desk, passing the counter that held countless vials being used for experiments. With a glint in his eyes, he punched some keys, and the printer started humming. He picked up the printouts once he was done. Harrow could imagine what the good ol' scientist had in store for him.

"This"—he waved the papers at Harrow as if they could satisfy Harrow's curiosity—"is what I have been working on."

"Why don't I leave you to your mad skills and scheming so I can visit with Cyrus?"

"I will call you once I'm confident about the whole idea." Leroy waved his hands before Harrow disappeared through the door.

Harrow left the laboratory feeling rather edgy, pondering what Leroy's experiment entailed. At this point, he would do anything to get rid of the disease or even just render it dormant. He couldn't lie that his eagerness was just as much about finding a cure for his disease as it was about allowing himself to have his way with Jordan. The woman occupied his spectrum of thoughts literally day and night. She was all he could think of, leaving no trace of the self-preservation instincts with which he'd long surrounded himself.

Not bothering to knock, he pushed the door open to the recovery room where Cyrus had resided the past two weeks. Lying flat on his back with multiple tubes running in and out of his body, Cyrus turned his head in Harrow's direction when the vampire walked in, his expression that of a disgruntled soldier aching to plow the battlefield.

"Good morning, Sunshine."

"I fuckin' can't even scratch my butt without these damn machines beeping like I'm committing murder. What in the hell is good about that?" Cyrus grumbled, his voice drowned out by the clicking noises coming from the different gadgets all around his bed. He seemed to be on the fast track to recovery if his humor was intact and kicking into high gear.

"It can't be that bad. At least you get to eat all the Jell-O you want."

"Fun," Cyrus mumbled. He shifted on his bed before being attacked by a series of ear-piercing beeps that could rival the Emergency Broadcast System warning on television.

"What is going on here? Haven't I told you not to move?" the sleepy doctor yelled from the door, looking like she'd run a marathon from her office to Cyrus' room just to answer the irreverent beeping.

Shelly glared at Cyrus before crossing the room to jab a finger on a blinking button. The annoying beeping stopped. The resident doctor had done miracles on Cyrus' injuries, and she had been a permanent fixture in the facility. She had been there to run a battery of tests on Harrow when he'd first arrived. Health-wise, he had checked out okay, but the woman's sharp eyes and no-nonsense attitude had given him the heebie-jeebies.

Shelly acknowledged Harrow's presence with the raising of an eyebrow.

"I feel like a goddamn prisoner with my every movement being tracked," Cyrus retorted.

"Welcome to my world, buddy," Harrow jibed, and Cyrus shot him a don't-fuck-with-me look.

Shelly walked over to Cyrus and pointed to the call button on his bedrail. "This button is to call on us if you need anything. Your wound is still healing, and the last thing we need is for it to open back up and start bleeding," she scolded.

Harrow couldn't help but snicker at Cyrus' dumbfounded expression when he stared at the doctor. In Cyrus' defense, the man was used to giving orders, but not taking them.

Shelly turned to Harrow. "If you can make sure he doesn't do anything stupid, I will let you visit with him longer than I allowed the others."

Cyrus groaned, and Harrow nodded his head, thinking, *This is one hell of a doctor, ordering him around.* "Sure thing, doc. Anything else?"

"Yeah, his lunch is coming. Do you mind feeding him?"

She had to be kidding. Harrow laughed and waggled a finger at her. "Aren't you a tough cookie?"

"I have to be. Dealing with big babies and stubborn vampires can suck the life out of you." She paused and chortled. "No pun intended."

"I'm not a child who needs to be fed," Cyrus complained, but Shelly wasn't listening.

The door creaked open, and Rohnert strode in, confident and relaxed in his sweats, his shaved head glistening in the shine of the overhead fluorescent lighting. The manner in which he entered and cast a glance in Cyrus' direction told Harrow that the men had gotten acquainted. This didn't surprise him in the least.

"Another visitor? My, my, aren't you feeling special today?"

Shelly wasn't looking at Cyrus. Instead, her gaze was fixed in Rohnert's direction. It was like witnessing love at first sight, except the affection went just one way. Rohnert, seeming oblivious to the tongue-tied human who was ogling him, walked across the room and settled on the opposite side of Cyrus's bed.

"I can smell love in the air," Rohnert said. His gaze fixed on Harrow.

It took Harrow a few seconds before he realized that Rohnert wasn't talking about Shelly. He was referring to their conversation not too long ago about Jordan, and how it would be if she ever decided to be with either of them. Harrow was taken aback by the bluntness of the other vampire's statement. "Your words were 'may the best man win,' and he did."

"And I meant it." Though the words were spoken in honesty, he detected a glimmer of resentment and jealousy. "As I said before, my vows remain. Nothing's changed."

A man of few words, Rohnert nodded at Cyrus, and the two exchanged a knowing look that made Harrow feel like an outsider.

Harrow shifted his stance and placed his hands in his pockets. "Thanks."

Rohnert bobbed his head in his direction before turning his attention to Cyrus. "I'll be ready when you are," he said.

"Ready for what?" Shelly found her tongue and intercepted the subtle nuance of the exchange.

"None of your business, Doc," Cyrus retorted. He shifted in bed, and a blaring noise started shrieking again like an emergency door. Shelly gritted her teeth and punched the button once more.

"Aren't you a tough cookie?" Rohnert spared a glance in Shelly's direction, as if noticing her for the first time.

"So I've been told," she snapped before turning to Cyrus. "If I so much as hear that you've lifted a finger to do anything stupid, God help me, I will put cuffs on all fours and restrain you in bed."

"The hell you will," Cyrus challenged, squaring his shoulders, and the beeping blared again.

Shelly let out a long exasperated sigh and jabbed at the button again, glaring at Cyrus before walking out of the room with a final threat. "Try me."

That left the three men in the room glancing at each other, startled by the spirit of the woman who had just left, before they burst out laughing.

"Jordan, are we ever going to find my mommy?" Gail took Jordan's hand as they walked through the hallways of their new home. Although Gail had shown remarkable resilience for a child whose future was still a big question mark, there were moments when sadness got the best of her.

The sobs that followed were hard to ignore. Jordan had no answer to give. Gail's mother could have ended up dead somewhere in a gutter. She had disappeared without a trace, and there was nothing to indicate what might have happened to her. And who had the heart to break such heart-wrenching news to a child when there was no solid evidence to back it up?

Jordan knelt down until she was at Gail's eye level. She placed her hands on the girl's shoulders and gave them a squeeze. "I've been looking for her, but I can't find her. I went to the place where she worked, but nobody has seen her. Do you mind staying here with me until we find her?"

Gail's eyes were like sprinklers, spouting tears one after another, while she nodded her head. Jordan's heart broke for the little girl, and her fears surfaced with greater intensity. A victim in another sense, she knew how it felt to be alone. Feeling her resolve strengthening, she made a silent vow to ensure that Gail wouldn't experience the sorrow of being alone, even if it was temporary.

"How about I take you swimming at the training center?" Jordan tried the tactic her father had used on her as a child when he wanted to distract her.

As sad as it had been a moment ago, Gail's face now lit up like a Christmas tree upon hearing Jordan's invitation. Then her smile slipped away. "But I can't go swimming, Jordan," she cried.

"Why is that?"

"Because I don't have a bathing suit," Gail whined.

"Baby, we can take care of that. Why don't we go shopping for the stuff you need? We can get some clothes and shoes, and you can pick out a bathing suit, too."

Another set of Christmas lights lit the girl's face as she jumped up and down with glee. "Yes! I love you, Jordan." Gail hugged Jordan, causing her to tumble backward. The little girl was oblivious to the immense affect that her words had on Jordan. It was not a good idea for Jordan to involve herself with another relationship she would have a tough time disentangling. She already had Harrow, which was enough. Besides, goodbyes sucked.

"Shopping? You're going *out* to shop?" Pritchard spat the words like bile twisting in his throat. The absurdity of the request threw him off guard. He'd had a long day, and the last thing he needed to hear was that his daughter was going out to shop in New York City.

"But, Daddy, you told me to live my life. And I'm trying to . . ."

Pritchard couldn't argue with what he had told Allison in the past. He wanted her to lead a normal life after the tragedy she'd had to face, and there was no way he could take back his words. But shopping? How many troubles out there could besiege two women and a little girl? Plenty. The answer was on the tip of his tongue, but he checked himself.

"Since when did you enjoy shopping? As far as I can remember, you've been buying your clothes online," Pritchard said, running his fingers through his hair.

"That is because we have Jenny as our personal shopper," Allison said.

"Damn it," he cursed. "You know it's dangerous out there. Anything could happen."

"We're just going shopping. Buying clothes shouldn't be treacherous, Daddy. You can call your friend at Saks Fifth Avenue and have him close the store early so we can have a private time without all the hassles you're imagining."

Pritchard thought about it. Surely, Eli would be happy to do it for him, even given the short notice. He glared at his daughter, who gave him a sweet smile he hadn't seen for a very long time. He was a sucker for his ladies. If her mother had still been around, he swore he'd still melt at the very sight of her smile. Her requests were commands he couldn't turn down.

"Fine . . ."

He picked up the phone, and his secretary came on the line right away. "Get Eli from Saks for me, please." Pritchard waited a few minutes before his phone rang. His friend was already on the other line. After the pleasantries were exchanged and his request was granted, he hung up.

"You have the store for three hours tonight, beginning at seven o'clock. I hope that's enough time for you ladies to get everything you need."

"Oh, thank you, Daddy! You're the best." Allison jumped off her chair and skittered around the table, throwing her arms around his neck.

Indeed, he was a big sucker for a huge smile from his daughter. Pulling her down to sit on his lap, he whispered in her ear, "One condition."

"I knew it! It wouldn't be you to let me go without conditions." Allison laughed and narrowed her eyes at him. She had no reason to wear sunglasses around him like Harrow did, and in the latter's case, it was a matter of old habit. "Tell me."

"You'll go in a convoy. Harrow and the rest will be going with you," Pritchard said, feeling a little more at ease knowing Harrow, Thor, and Rohnert would be more than adequate to provide security for the women.

"Harrow's fine. Who are the others?" Allison asked.

"Don't worry about them. Just enjoy yourselves, hurry back home, and show me what you got," Pritchard said. He would've loved to join them if there hadn't been a meeting with some bigwigs in half an hour.

"Thanks. You know I love you, right?" Allison pecked his cheek and danced out of his office like the little spoiled girl he'd once known. Wasn't he glad she was back?

Heck yeah!

"What the hell are you talking about?" Demetrius rose from his chair inside the Blanch Room, where a group of humans were about to be introduced to a vampire's life. Screams and cries of desperation coming from the poor souls mingled with the hollering of the vampire who had rudely interrupted them.

Demetrius glanced at his watch and cursed. If what he was thinking was true, the vampire that had arrived was the lone survivor left of the group that had departed just two hours ago.

The young male vampire, one of the five Jethro had sent out to do the patrol, had burst into the room looking horrified. He screamed the words out as if the mere memory was killing him, piece by piece. *Neophyte.* This was to be expected when novices were left to fend for themselves.

Jethro stepped in after assigning another vampire to resume the blanching. Shrieking resumed, and they were forced to move away from the ear-splitting noise around them. Jethro dragged the vampire with him.

"Talk," Jethro ordered when they reached the patio, which overlooked . . . well . . . nothing. There wasn't much to look at when you're deep underground and your neighbors were nothing but tunnels, sewers, drains, and pipes.

The vampire couldn't even talk straight. His words were coming in garbled flurry, tripping over each other in his haste to tell the story.

"Calm down," Jethro threatened as Demetrius looked on. They were both getting more impatient by the second.

"We went on patrol, just like you instructed. The—the others—we were in the city. I was following them when we all caught a whiff of that nasty sick scent you warned us about." The vampire paused to catch his breath. His eyes darted left and right, as if he were expecting to be jumped at any moment.

"Keep going," Jethro urged.

"Well, we saw this male and female walking in the alley, and we split up. I brought up the rear while the others took the front, hoping we could trap them. Strength in numbers, the element of surprise, remember?" Those had been Jethro's exact words when he'd sent out the five-man unit.

Jethro nodded with annoyance. "Don't stop."

"So a fight broke out after we taunted the male and threatened the female. The weapons on those two vampires were out of this world. I've never seen them before."

"What weapons are you talking about?" Demetrius sprang up like a slinky.

"Two stick-like metals, long. They swung around, sideways and forward. It was like poetry in motion, because they were good at it. And once they hit the guys, they just sizzled out! As in gone. *Poof!* I know the weapons were made of Dangeran. I'm sure of it!" The vampire shivered, and his eyes bulged with fear.

Metal sticks, as in Kalimetal? Demetrius couldn't wrap his mind around the information he'd been given. Could it be? He knew of but one vampire practitioner of such martial arts. It was a dying discipline, and only a few were still practicing, as far as he knew.

Rohnert. The vampire who had disappeared without a word.

The name came like bad news with wings. Demetrius was sick to his stomach, and he felt like he had been stabbed in the back. How could Rohnert have taught others when he'd halted Demetrius's instruction? Was he unworthy? The vivid memories he had of the vampire were some of his most cherished ones. The news cut him like a knife.

Deep. Betrayed.

He paced around, seething. This was unexpected. The project he thought would have be so easy had taken a nasty turn. To find out a dear friend was involved added to the complications. He didn't know whether to get pissed or cower at the news. Rohnert was as good as they could get. The vampire, with his vast fighting knowledge and bloodline, would be a welcome addition to any group. There was no doubt in Demetrius's mind that Rohnert was an asset anyone would kill to have fighting alongside them. Too bad he had gone to the other side.

Preparations had to be made. A bigger army had to be assembled now, more than ever. It was a desperate venture that needed to be completed soon. Build them, teach them, and arm them. And Goran had to be notified. Projects of this magnitude shouldn't be done behind his back, and besides, Demetrius needed the financial backing, as well as the manpower to fulfill his plan.

"Sur, is everything all right?" Jethro asked, leaning against one of the concrete posts and looking at him. The young vampire was nowhere in sight. He'd most likely slipped away when Demetrius was pacing, caught in his internal monologue.

He needed Jethro's help in many respects, but breaking the news to Goran was his job. Anger seeped into him like leaden sap. "Finish the blanching, and keep adding more. I want you to keep at it until we have more than fifty. You need to train them all. Rotate your best men, and give them the patrolling assignments while we build up. This will be an all-out war. I can feel it."

Jethro looked lost for a few moments, as if he couldn't follow Demetrius' train of thought. Even though he was not quite certain what war Demetrius was talking about, Jethro didn't ask any questions.

Good boy, Demetrius thought. The few questions he was willing to answer were those of dear old Dad. The sooner he got in his father's good graces, the better the outcome would be. This was one plan Goran wouldn't be able to negate. If Demetrius had read his father right, betrayal was one thing he wouldn't tolerate.

Rohnert had betrayed their long-standing friendship, and that constituted an all-out war in Goran's book.

"Right away, sur," Jethro said.

Moving with purpose, Demetrius opened the door to the blanch room, where the cries for help had diminished. The remaining sounds now were the pounding of hearts about to give way, the chattering of teeth, and the occasional shifting of bodies on the floor. The process had begun. In a few days, they'd be ready to create more. Demetrius took the stairwell that would lead him to his father's chamber. He checked his appearance in the hallway mirror. His red hair was pulled away from his face, and his eyes gleamed blood red. His mother's blood had done that to him.

Demetrius smoothed the wrinkles in his mouth, plastering on a smile he didn't feel. He needed confidence before facing his father, or else he'd be read like an open book, and that was the last thing he needed.

Bracing himself, he strode to the carved door and pounded on it with his fist.

"Come in," Goran's deep voice answered.

"Father," he began as soon as he'd pushed the door open. The scent of lust still hung thick in the air. This was not a surprise, but his father was alone, so the female must have left before he'd arrived. "I have some news for you."

"Ah, news. I hope it's good," Goran parroted.

His father was lounging on a chaise, his velvet robe in slight disarray. Demetrius noted. Goran must have caught him staring, because he straightened the lapel and tightened the string around his waist. "Sit."

Demetrius lowered himself onto the single chair opposite the chaise. He sat straight and fixed a smile on his face. Better to get the information out instead of throwing in a little chitchat he wasn't in the mood for.

"I sent some scouts out tonight, and one of the five came back with grave news."

"Grave?" The black eyebrows rose. "Tell me."

After giving a full report of what had transpired according to the survivor, Demetrius watched his father's unflinching face as he shifted on the chaise.

"Rohnert," Goran said.

"That is my suspicion as well, Father."

"What do you plan to do?" Goran asked, unruffled.

"I will create more vampires—"

Goran cut him off. "Let Hamilton help you. He is on regular patrol with some of his men, and he has taken out his fair share of those diseased abominations. He'll be an asset to your group."

Hamilton. They couldn't come any cockier and confident than that son of a bitch. The vampire, just because he was in Goran's good graces, talked and walked like he was untouchable. Nevertheless, how could Demetrius deny his father's direct order? The mere thought of working with the bastard made him want to spit blood.

Goran might have sensed his hesitation and spoke before his son could say anything. He got up, walked over to his study, and retrieved a cell phone.

"Hamilton will be instructed to work with you. You call the shots, and he'll follow orders as you give them. Is this acceptable?" Goran's lips twisted.

One step ahead. Always. "Yes, Father."

At least, he would be in charge and the bastard would have to follow his orders, whether he liked it or not. Score one for his father.

"You may take your leave. Give me good results." Goran waved his hand in dismissal. That was it—the short time the bastard was willing to give him. "And stop drinking from your mother if you want me to spare your life a moment longer."

One fuckin' step ahead. Every single time. Demetrius bowed his head lower than he'd ever done before.

As soon as his son left, Goran dialed Hamilton's number and gave the vampire the four-one-one on his latest assignment. "Make sure my son is safe at all times. He resents my trust in you, and it's understandable. He is impulsive and feels slighted easily. Report back to me when necessary. I expect nothing but good results from you both."

Why wasn't he surprised that Rohnert had turned against him? The vampire was straight as an arrow and held no loyalty to anyone but himself. They've fought together during the Great Vampire Revolution in the early sixties, and Rohnert had fought valiantly alongside him in more ways than one. He swore no allegiance then, except to what he believed in—that the race had the right to coexist with all species. That was the extent of his participation in the past. *Vampire with a conscience*. Such a waste.

When Goran solicited Rohnert's help to train Demetrius, he had seen the bond he'd shared with his son and assumed that would seal the deal, but Rohnert had disappeared after finding out the reasons behind the preparation. Obliterating their own kind for reasons beyond their control wasn't what he'd signed up for. That was the motivation behind Rohnert's stepping aside and his refusal to impart any more of his craft. Goran respected his decision because of their friendship. He'd halted any active pursuit in deference to their amity.

To find out that Rohnert was now participating in an effort to oppose him was unacceptable. Goran pounded his fist on the table. This deliberate treachery would not be tolerated. If Rohnert was willing to throw their comradeship out the window, then by all means, out the window it would be.

"Shopping? Fun!" Jordan muttered, realizing the little shopping trip she'd planned earlier was turning into one big fanfare, complete with security escorts. All she'd wanted was a quick getaway to buy Gail's essentials and to return to the facility before anyone sent out a search party. Letting Allison in on the details had been a big mistake. A huge one, now that Pritchard had made a big deal of the little trip they'd planned.

Of course, the boss didn't do things halfway. He marched to his own tune, blowing every single thing out of proportion, just like this little shopping trip. Of course, Allison should notify her father, but this was just too weird for Jordan.

Knowing who would be their entourage made her cringe. Not only were they in a convoy on their way to Saks Fifth Avenue department store, but also the whole shop would be closed for their own private shopping spree. Her plan to just get in and out of Macy's had been thwarted, and there was an entourage to boot, which just exemplified Pritchard's outrageous nature.

Harrow squeezed her hand and gave her a peck on the cheek before they got into the three-car convoy. "It's going to be fine. Relax, okay?" She nodded, knowing how silly it would be if she made a big deal out of it. Allison and Gail were excited, and she didn't want to suck the fun out of their high, so she kept quiet and offered Harrow a wan smile. He took the passenger seat in front, and she, Allison, and Gail took the rear passenger seats. She saw a glimpse of Rohnert before he got into the first car, and Tor took the car behind them.

Rohnert. She'd managed to avoid the vampire ever since he had joined them in the facility. She wasn't even sure she wanted to talk to him. What in God's name would they talk about? Jordan knew, by the expression on his face, that he'd caught a glimpse of Harrow's kiss. Harrow hadn't mentioned what the vampire knew, and Jordan wasn't even sure why she was stressing over it.

Gail was bouncing off her seat like a wired Mexican jumping bean. "Jordan, Allison said I could get whatever I want. Is that true?" Gail asked. Her expression radiated pure energy and disbelief.

Jordan rolled her eyes at Allison, who was dressed in tight black leotards paired with a long gray sweater that reached her thighs and pointed, high-heeled boots. Dark-as-night sunglasses completed her outfit. No doubt, it was more of a necessity than a fashion statement. She needed to conceal the regression of her irises. Allison smiled like a Cheshire cat and stuck her tongue out at Jordan before answering. "Of course, darling, anything you want."

Jordan shot a warning glance her way before answering Gail's question. "Yes, if that's what she said."

"Yippee!" The little girl kept bouncing, and Harrow laughed with open adoration. Jordan had seen his eyes sparkle whenever he was around Gail. Heck, everyone's eyes sparkled when she was around. The girl had the power to make the hardest of hearts melt with her pure charm and angelic presence. Even Pritchard had been noted asking for her quite a few times.

The dark tint of the Suburban made it difficult for Gail to see their whereabouts, so Jordan told her that their car was making its way down the ramp leading to another entrance to the store. This underground entrance was meant for employees and delivery personnel only.

Rohnert jumped out of the car first and held the doors open for them as they made their way to the stark hallway where rows of Bundy clocks were located. The few employees scattered about were ordered to move away by the countless men in security uniforms.

After the basement had been cleared, Harrow, Tor, and Rohnert took over. Gail's eyes grew as big as saucers and she squealed with delight as soon as their private party entered the main lobby, catching everyone by surprise.

"This is beautiful. It looks like that Swarsh store," she remarked.

Her incorrect pronunciation of the world-famous flagship toy store made everyone laugh, including the store manager, who was making his way toward their group. Dressed in an impeccable gray suit, Eli extended his hand to Allison, a wide grin on his face.

The behemoth department store promised ten levels of shopping luxury. The ground floor alone was a shopper's paradise dedicated to cosmetics, perfumes, and spritzes guaranteed to overwhelm one's olfactory sense. Several sales attendants smiled as the group looked around the store, waiting to serve them.

Allison placed her gloved hand in Eli's, and the manager shook it with eagerness. "Welcome to our store, Ms. Tack. I'm pleased to be of service to you and your party. If there's anything you need, let my assistant know"— he gestured to a woman in a light beige suit, who in turn smiled at their group—"and she'll make sure you get everything you require."

"Thanks, Eli." Allison smiled and nodded at Gail, who was growing more impatient by the minute. Gail would've sprinted toward the escalator if Jordan hadn't had a tight hold on her hand. "She is going to need a lot of clothes."

"We will take care of her." Eli beamed and directed them with a sweep of his arm toward the escalator.

"Are we all going to the same department?" Harrow whispered in Allison's ear when they started following the manager and his team of sales associates. "Because if you're planning to go your separate ways, I will have Tor follow you around."

"I will go with them first." Jordan watched as Allison glanced in Tor's direction, and she couldn't help but chuckle when she noticed Tor staring at Allison as if she were the most delicate thing he'd ever seen. Allison subsequently squirmed.

Jordan fell one step behind and matched Allison's stride as they headed to the foot of the escalator. "Are you okay?"

"Why wouldn't I be?" Allison asked.

"I swear I could hear your heartbeat like it was tolling in my ears." Jordan laughed and peered at Allison before Gail pulled her hand, urging her to hurry up and get to the escalator.

She heard Allison muttering under her breath, "No, it wasn't."

The shopping experience was twice as fun due to Gail's nonstop gushing, squealing, and jumping around. The three of them sat on a plush sofa inside the dressing room while the rest of the men stood outside, looking both amused and uncomfortable at the same time. Their massive presence was intimidating enough to keep the sales associates moving as if they were walking on eggshells.

Innumerable outfits were presented to them in different colors, patterns, and styles. When Gail was whisked into the dressing room by two women, Jordan wandered into one of the other dressing rooms to check her appearance in the mirror. Unlike Allison, who appeared as if she'd walked out of a fashion magazine, Jordan had settled with her usual tight jeans, black T-shirt, and black trench coat.

Her hair had been swept into a severe ponytail, and her face was as fresh as the moment she'd washed it that morning. Plain and very simple—that was who she was. She had no intention of changing her style, despite Allison's repeated prodding.

"Jordan, we are going to stop by the ladies' department after this." Allison snuck behind her, and she looked back at her from the mirror.

"No, we're not," Jordan retorted.

"Yes, we are. In fact, they are waiting with several styles and sizes picked out already." Allison laughed, and Jordan spun around.

"What for?"

"I'm planning to host a surprise party for Dad, and I need you all to clean up. So that means you need something nice to wear to the party." Allison jutted her lower lip forward in one of her rare displays of imperious attitude.

"Whatever," Jordan answered, walking toward Gail's dressing stall. "Are we done yet?"

"Almost." The sales rep answered while Gail giggled from behind the curtain that separated them. One of the women attending to Gail smiled at Jordan and shrugged her shoulders in amusement.

A few minutes later, Gail burst out of the dressing room in a red dress paired with black tights and black patent leather ballet flats with a bow. She twirled around and modeled the outfit for them. Allison nodded with approval, while Jordan shook her head in amazement. The dress emphasized Gail's red tresses, which one of the women had secured with a matching red barrette, making the girl look older than her age. She was beautiful—quite adorable.

"Do you like it?" Her eyes twinkled with excitement.

"You are the prettiest girl I've ever seen," Allison answered.

"Jordan?" Gail twirled in her direction.

"Adorable. Allison is right." Jordan beamed.

As if their compliments weren't enough, Gail rushed out of the dressing room and located Harrow, who was standing outside hanging out next to Tor. She gave another twirl.

"What do *you* think, Harrow?"

Gail was fishing for more compliments, and she got what she wanted when Harrow exclaimed, "Aren't you a thing of beauty? That is perfect for you, sweetheart." Harrow bent down and planted a kiss on Gail's forehead before picking her up around her waist to twirl her several times.

Gail snaked her arms around Harrow's neck, and kissed him on the cheek just before he set her back on her feet. Tor shuffled his feet, seeming uncomfortable with the whole display of affection, but he smiled when Gail looked up to him.

"You're as cute as a button," Tor offered.

Harrow laughed and smacked his back, trying to ease the tension that had started to build up and was showing in Tor's expression. "Lighten up, buddy. I thought you enjoyed shopping," Harrow teased.

"If I was getting my own duds."

"Good, you'll get your chance later," Allison said as she walked out of the dressing room, followed by Jordan and the sales associates, who were carrying a handful of clothes for Gail.

Tor narrowed his eyes at Allison, but he said nothing. Harrow began following the women, and Rohnert shifted from his position across the room. Jordan noticed the blatant distance Rohnert had placed between them. She remained quiet during the entire shopping process while she and Allison were taken to the dressing rooms, where a variety of outfits with labels she'd only seen across the pages of fashion magazines was waiting for them. *Prada, Escada, Louis Vuitton, and Chanel.* Enough to make a woman's head spin.

Shoes in different styles, heel sizes, and colors were thrust into her hands. Before she knew it, she was holding two garment bags and ten pairs of shoes, and she had no idea when and where to wear any of them. The single purchase she cared about included leather jackets, a trench coat, and two pairs of lace-up leather boots without heels that were comfortable enough to run in.

An hour later, the men, through Allison's insistence, were treated to their own shopping nightmare. Harrow, Tor, and Rohnert were whipped into dressing rooms with multiple outfits that made them flinch with obvious discomfort.

"I guess we are done here?" Harrow asked when they were allowed to walk away from the torture chambers, where the three of them had been held captive for over thirty minutes.

"I guess we are," Jordan answered with relief in her voice.

"Now, that wasn't so bad, was it?" Allison laughed.

"I've never seen someone spend a hundred thousand dollars in one sitting!" Jordan exclaimed, but Allison waved her off.

"I wouldn't know. I've always been at the mercy of Daddy's personal shopper." Allison laughed and slanted a quick glance in Tor's direction, who in turn looked away. Jordan didn't miss the subtle act and smiled to herself.

Just as they were walking out of the department store and heading to their waiting cars, Harrow's phone rang. He glanced at the caller ID, and flicked the phone on.

"Lambert, what's up?"

His brows scrunched together while he listened to the other man on the line.

"Give us a few minutes, and we'll be there," he said and hung up.

"Rohnert, take the women home." Rohnert nodded with understanding. "Tor and I will head over to see Lambert. Backup is needed. We'll take one car, just in case. Dave, meet us at The Corpus, park in the alley." He spoke to one of the vampire drivers, who nodded back.

"In case of what?" Jordan was at Harrow's side in a heartbeat.

"Of transport," he replied, already moving across the parking lot, flanked by Tor.

Jordan was poised to move when Rohnert clamped a hand on her arm to stop her. He didn't say anything, but his eyes told her not to follow. Despite her inner struggle to dismiss his warning, Jordan found herself conceding, and she followed Allison and Gail to the waiting car.

The trip from the department store to the shady part of Brooklyn took less than five minutes when one was gunning at a blurred pace Harrow and Tor had set.

The pair flashed their fake ID's at the door attendant and didn't encounter any resistance from the throng of people waiting when they sized up Tor's imposing figure the minute the vampires cut in line.

The nightclub, as promised, was dingy to all outward appearances, and the interior wasn't much better. The rundown structure was coming apart at the seams, peeling paint and crumbling bits of concrete blocks evident everywhere.

Adjusting his eyesight to the dimly lit room, Harrow spotted Lambert in a huddle with Drake and Holt.

"Damn it, he should know better than to come here without a vampire escort," Harrow muttered, and Tor exhaled in response. They crossed the room toward the bar where the three were situated, glaring at a group of six vampires who seemed like an excitable media. A team of undoubted neophytes appeared to be ready for a fight.

Lambert looked over his shoulder just in time to see Harrow parked behind him. "Glad you girls made it here fast," he said.

Drake and Holt nodded and exchanged fist bumps with Tor, who towered over them all. "So what do we have here?" Tor asked, jaw twitching for some action he had been denied for some time now.

"Those vamps are ganging up on some humans on the other side of the room." Lambert pointed with his mouth in the direction of the same six vampires Harrow had spotted when he'd arrived.

"Holt intervened, and so did some other humans, so the group took a little breather, I suppose. But I can smell a massacre later, and as you can see, we were outnumbered two to one until you guys arrived." Lambert appeared perplexed. "If it weren't for my own orders to keep a healthy group of vamps and humans on patrol, we would have gunned them down already."

"Maybe we can start to boogie now," Tor piped in.

"We should wait until one makes a move, how's that?" Harrow said, and Lambert nodded in agreement. Holt and Drake were twitching in anticipation. Their eyes were glued on the group of vampires that was harassing the humans.

"From what I can hear, they're here on the prowl to increase their numbers," Harrow said. His ears were trained on the mixed exchanges going on across the room from them.

"I don't have a problem with the whole turning humans into vampires shit, you know, but I don't believe in bullying humans into submission. I'm sure there are a lot of people who wouldn't mind going through the change of their own free will." Lambert gritted his teeth, throwing another glance across the room.

Without a word, Lambert stood up and walked to the group that was circling two human males, who looked scared shitless and lacked the courage and the numbers to fight back.

"Ladies, why don't we ease up on the gentlemen here?" Harrow heard Lambert say to the leader of the group, a stocky vampire with a bad haircut and an attitude to match.

The vampire turned around and looked Lambert up and down as if measuring the size and length of his coffin. Harrow inched forward but didn't show himself to the group. Holt and Drake flanked Lambert on either side, and the vampire leader coughed a mocking laugh.

"You think I'd listen to you?" the vampire asked, turning his attention to Lambert. The human was taller, and the natural skills of the vampire had to be taken into consideration. One on one, it could fly, given Lambert's talents and dexterity.

"You should," Lambert chided. "And may I remind you, we're among humans here. Maybe we should take this conversation outside so we can properly address the issue."

"Sure. Why don't you lead the way?" The vampire asked and signaled his entourage to follow.

Lambert strode to the exit door with Holt and Drake, who were already resting their hands on their holsters. The group followed close behind, and when they were free of the building, Harrow and Tor shifted into stalking mode at once.

In the darkened alley, Harrow could make out the parked black suburban waiting for them. Dave the driver was nowhere to be seen, but Harrow knew his ass was parked somewhere where he could strike if needed.

Lambert turned around, and before he could say anything, the vampires flaunted their fangs at him.

"I don't think talking would do the trick here. Why don't I just sink my fangs into your gracious neck and get it over with, since you interrupted my dinner in there?"

Lambert backed off a step, and Holt and Drake pulled out their weapons, pointing their guns at the vampire's head. Harrow knew it was time for them to lock and load as he and Tor came into view. He unsheathed his Kalimetal, and Tor brandished his newly polished axe with a menacing smile.

"Let's dance," Harrow invited and pointed one metal toward the leader, buying Lambert time to pull out his own weapon. The vampire laughed and then sneered at Harrow.

"So you're the sick one they've been talking about," he stated, pulling out two daggers from his waistband while his cohorts wielded different weapons at the same time. Harrow inventoried the weapons pointed at them and assessed the situation.

"At your service," Harrow bowed.

Harrow knew this was going to go down quick. He'd have to fight fast and gun several down to keep his human friends safe. No matter how good they were, vampires were still faster, and time would work against them.

A barrel disengaging sounded, and the scuffle broke out when a bullet struck the first victim.

"Fuck!" Harrow saw Holt clutch his abdomen and fall to the ground, but before Holt succumbed to his injury, he aimed his gun at another vampire and pulled the trigger.

From that moment on, Harrow hauled ass as he struck the leader with his weapon before the vampire could even jump away from striking distance. Tor threw his axe at one of the vampires who flanked the leader, striking the vampire in the head before the familiar crackle, sizzle, and popping followed.

Drake pulled the trigger just in time to protect himself from a vampire who jumped in front of him.

From the corner of his eye, Harrow saw Dave pulling Holt out of the danger zone, carrying the injured man to the suburban, and speeding away.

Lambert saw an opening and threw a dagger straight into one vampire's chest. Harrow took the last one by surprise when he jumped behind him while the vampire aimed his knife in Lambert's direction. With a mighty swing, he lashed his weapon across the vampire's back. A whizzing and sizzling sounded before the four of them looked at each other and what was left of the six vampires' residues on the ground.

Tor had a mean grin in his face. Drake was shaking under his skin, and Lambert whipped his head in Harrow's direction. "Thanks," he muttered.

"Don't mention it. Shall we?" he asked, ready to go home and see what was happening with Holt and his injury.

Rohnert hung up the phone as soon as Harrow told him what had gone down, and he rushed over to the clinic to alert Shelly of her incoming patient. After a series of knocks were left unanswered, he pushed her office door open and found her inside, sleeping on a makeshift cot.

He walked over to the cot and caught a whiff of her sweet breath when he knelt down next to her. Her hair was in utter disarray, as if she hadn't had a chance to run a hairbrush through it for who knew how long. Even in her sleep, Shelly's facial expression was that of weariness, looking like she was ready to jump at a moment's notice. Hardly the rest a human needed to stay alert and to be on top of her game. Rohnert had to remind himself that Shelly had admitted that she was a tough cookie. He had to give her that.

He didn't want to disturb what little sleep he knew she was getting, but he had no other choice. Rohnert could hear the noise emanating from the screeching tires in the garage. Dave would be bringing Holt in any second now.

Rohnert gently nudged Shelly's shoulder. "Dr. Anderson," he whispered.

Shelly stirred and shifted her body, but her eyes remained closed. Rohnert tried again. This time, he shook her shoulder with a little more force. "Dr. Anderson, wake up."

"Hmm . . ."

"Dr. Anderson, we have an incoming patient," he said louder with another tug at her arm, which he noted felt warm against his touch. Like a bolt of lightning had struck him, he let go, and he gave her shoulder another shake instead.

Shelly jumped up as if her ass was on fire when the words finally registered. She focused on Rohnert and turned beet red.

"I'm sorry. Have you been here for a while?" she asked. She fumbled with her hair and snapped a tie into a ponytail. She moved fast for someone who had just been awakened. Rohnert stifled a grin and nodded his head.

Grabbing her stethoscope from the table and shoving it inside the pocket of her green scrubs, she headed for the clinic. Rohnert followed as they made their way from her office to the little trauma room. Dave was unloading Holt on the table, and several nurses were already scrubbing in at the corner faucet.

Shelly sprang into action at the sight of the blood dripping from Holt's body, and sleepiness was swept off her face.

"Oxygen!" she yelled and moved to the faucet to scrub, while a nurse rushed to follow her order and placed a mask on Holt's rapidly paling face. He moaned.

Rohnert stayed in the background, away from the action, away from the blood, and away from the woman who was now moving in a fast, efficient way.

Scrubbed, gloved, and ready to go, Shelly pressed a remote and the intro to Queen's *Bohemian Rhapsody* floated from the speaker system. With the assistance of two nurses, Shelly cut Holt's clothes off and began the painstaking task of removing the bullet that was lodged in his abdomen.

With nothing else to do, Rohnert slipped out into the hallway and decided to wait there instead. He could hear the music as if he was still in the room. The doctor was tough as nails, and nothing seemed to faze her. *Good thing*, he thought. The facility needed someone who could take a lot, considering the mix they got going in there.

Jordan was running out of the elevator by the time Rohnert caught her scent, and he felt himself straighten against the wall as soon as she walked up to him.

"Holt is injured?" she asked.

Rohnert nodded, not knowing what else to say. His eyes were fixed on Jordan. Her eyes were alive now, and the usual frown lines across her forehead were absent. She looked different. *Happy.*

Jordan, in turn, studied him. She moved closer as if to touch his arm, and he recoiled. This was not necessary. One touch and he knew his defenses would crumble down like they were made of sand and not hardened steel.

"I just wanted to say . . . I'm glad to see you're here," she said and searched his face.

His expression softened, and he sighed. "I'm glad to see you're all right. And happy," he added as an afterthought.

Jordan showed signs she knew what he was talking about. "Thank you. I guess you could say I am."

"Harrow's fine. They're on their way back here, if you were wondering," Rohnert offered, changing the subject.

Jordan smiled, relieved. "I know. He called me, too."

Various orders could be heard slinging from Shelly inside the OR while she continued to work on Holt. Rohnert couldn't help but smile at the spirit of the female doctor. He knew that Holt was in good hands.

Even before he could say anything, Harrow, followed by Lambert, Tor, and Drake, stepped out of the elevator and came gunning through the hallway in big strides. Harrow stopped next to Jordan and gave her a peck on the cheek.

Rohnert turned to hide the flinch that came with Harrow's affectionate display. His emotional wounds were still fresh.

Grim, Lambert nodded to no one in particular before he and Drake walked in the clinic.

"I'm going to my room. Just let me know what's up with our man as soon as you can," Tor said and strode away.

The phone ringing offered a much-needed distraction from the awkward air around them. Harrow pulled out the phone from his jean pocket. "Yes, Leroy?"

"I think I've got it. When can you come?" Leroy declared from the other end of the line, excitement evident in his words.

"Just give me a few minutes, and I'll be right up." Harrow shut the phone and held Jordan's hand. "I'll be back soon."

Rohnert watched Harrow leave and wondered what else there was left to say to Jordan as they waited in silence for news about Holt.

Harrow strode into the laboratory after a quick shower. Leroy stood up and gave him a shaky smile as soon as he walked in. He took one good look at the doctor, thinking the man had been pulling far too many late nights on prolonged experimenting and research. Leroy's penchant for extensive studying and perfection was impossible to ignore.

Leroy's hair was an absolute mess and his white coat wrinkled and unbuttoned, showing his wrinkled beige slacks and striped polo. Huge circles rimmed his eyes, but there was also a glint of enthusiasm in them.

"What's so important that you can't wait to tell me about?" Harrow sat on a stool next to the stainless steel counter, which held an exorbitant number of vials filled with red liquid. It was easy to guess that the liquid was blood.

Leroy pulled pieces of crumpled papers from his pocket and smoothed them out on the table. "I think I may have some answers for you. It's just a theory I've been toying with—not sure if it'll work until tested."

Harrow gestured with his hand for Leroy to keep talking.

The doctor climbed onto the stool and moved the paper in front of Harrow, who now saw that a few formulas and some notes were written on the page. Harrow looked closely, but most of the handwritten notes were illegible, even allowing for his bad eyesight.

"Until you came back and told me about Jordan consuming animal blood instead of human blood, I didn't think animal blood was nutritious enough for vampires to live on." Leroy paused as if trying to organize his thoughts. "You know, this process got me all fired up. It's weird enough that I don't know all the effects blood has for your kind, so please excuse me if I babble sometimes."

"No problem, my friend, take your time." Harrow laughed, sensing the charge of animation coursing through the human's body.

Leroy flashed an awkward smile before he proceeded. "Now that it's definite that animal blood has enough nutrients to sustain a vampire, as in Jordan's case, I went ahead and did some tests. Of course, the results are inconclusive until we conduct the tests on you."

"What do I have to do? Drink animal blood?" The idea wasn't as repulsive as it sounded. Maybe put it in a sippy cup, and he'd do just fine. Harrow chortled at the thought.

"Well, that's the general idea, but allow me to tell you why I think it'll work."

"Shoot."

"To begin with, your virus . . . err . . . disease is very much dependent on the blood that you drink. It's understandable, because that is your lifeline, your life force. Without it, you waste away until the disease incapacitates you, right?

"Yeah?" Harrow tried to follow. "One request. Dumb it down for me, will you? I wasn't a science geek growing up." He laughed. "No offense."

Leroy rolled his eyes at the deliberate jab. "Fine, dumbing it down. Well, animal blood has almost the same characteristics as yours and ours. On intake of human blood, the virus consumes all the cells in the blood that you drink. It satisfies you. Therefore, the lesions are also satisfied. That explains why they diminish and the flare-up goes away. However, the human blood cells do not contain the X-protein that the animal blood has.

"I'll call it an X-protein for now. I don't have a scientific name for it because this is new to me, and to anyone else out there." Leroy waved his hand excitedly. "Your body takes human blood, which is what it's used to, feeding and keeping the virus active and running. Human blood triggers action on the virus, keeping it alive.

"My theory is—the animal blood's X-protein, upon ingestion, gives the opposite effect. Your virus, like the animal blood, is a foreign matter. They are both threats to your system, but combined together, they don't impede on each other. The X-protein neutralizes the virus on contact, so it halts the virus into dormancy. Your immune system sees the animal blood as food and does not push it into any adverse reaction. It just might work, if the process goes down the way I predict it should. I think it will keep working as long as you maintain the animal blood diet." Leroy drew a long breath before exhaling, his whole body shuddering with the effort.

Harrow's head shot up. The idea, even if it sounded strange, might just be the key to unlocking the cure for the virus. How bad could it be? He had been dealing with the disease for some time, and he had seen himself in the worst possible light. He had experienced the pain and burning of the hellish lesions. If this half-baked theory worked, then there was hope for him—hope for them all.

"What do I need to do?" he asked, feeling a thrilled rush just considering the possibilities of a pain-free existence and the vulnerable state he'd be happy to leave behind.

"That's the thing I want to talk to you about." Leroy's expression turned somber. "This isn't going to be easy on you."

"Name it." No measure of uneasiness could quell the optimism Leroy's theory had embedded in Harrow's brain already.

"I want to test it when the disease is in its most active state."

Harrow shifted in his seat. "What does that entail?"

"Let me remind you that this is just a theory. I could be wrong, okay?" The man's earnestness urged Harrow to take the plunge into unknown territory.

"Don't worry about me. Let's do what we have to do."

"What if the outcome is not what you wanted?"

"How much worse off could I be?" he asked. His outlook was never promising to begin with, so how bad could it go?

"I hope not too much worse." Leroy offered a shaky laugh.

"Tell me what you're thinking."

"You won't feed for the next week or so."

Harrow winced. *Oh, not a good plan, but okay, maybe there's a light at the end of the tunnel.* "Do you have any idea how bad it gets?"

"Sort of. That's why I wanted to make sure you're up to it. If anything, I can get another subject—"

"No . . ." He sighed and ground his teeth. *Crap! This would be painful . . . but hey—no pain, no gain.* "Leroy . . . just make sure you keep me inside a room where no one can touch me, or better yet, where I can't touch them. Extreme hunger and pain can make us lose focus, and there's a possibility we can attack anyone because of deprivation."

"I won't let you wait a moment longer than is necessary." Leroy jumped off the stool and walked to his computer to punch in some information. "I have to give Pritchard a head's up."

"So the scenario will likely be?"

"Starve and experience pain. Then I'll take blood samples before I let you drink the animal blood."

It sounded so simple, so easy—if Harrow could but lead himself to believe that it would be a walk in the park rather than more like trudging through hell's gates and back.

"So I'll stop feeding from now on. In a week's time, you tie me down, lock me up, and don't do anything stupid so I won't." It wasn't a threat, but more of a warning. A big neon sign that read, CAUTION—MAY BITE WHEN HUNGRY.

"Blast those idiots!" Demetrius exploded.

The news of losing more vampires sickened him. Hamilton must realize that he had to know every movement within their group. That meant every single one. Hadn't his father made it clear that he was the leader?

There had been an obvious breakdown in communication, or better yet, Hamilton was not conforming to his father's orders. It wasn't a tough task to follow. Let Demetrius make the decisions on whether their men should be out there.

Now, another six had bitten the dust. No news, and no trace. Wasn't that just dandy?

Demetrius paced the empty Blanch Room. By his father's order, he'd stopped creating new vampires until they straightened out the growing rebellion within the infected vampires. It was an order he was aching to defy, but he had no balls to act on that urge. Son or not, his father would not tolerate that level of betrayal.

Rohnert. If he could find and nail the guy, then he'd be walking his merry way toward Daddy-O's good graces again. Maybe if he served Rohnert's head on a silver platter, then his father might ease up on him. Demetrius sat down, the forced inactivity giving him a dismal sense of frustration.

So far, Jethro had come up empty in the research department. There were no solid leads to take them anywhere, though two of the names he'd mentioned had drawn Demetrius's attention. Sometimes, when you want something done fast, you have to do it yourself.

"Sur, do you want me to call on Hamilton?" Jethro asked. The vampire sat on the steps just below his Bergere chair, waiting for an order. It had been dead for them, and the inaction was making the vampire antsy.

Demetrius stood up and walked to his room in a hurry. Jethro trailed him like the most loyal dog there was. He marched straight to his desk and pulled out a pad and pen.

"No, I think we'll keep that damn vampire in the dark. We'll use his men but leave him out of the operation."

"Sounds good to me." Jethro smiled. His crooked teeth bordered by long fangs were an irritating picture, but it was the kind of distraction Demetrius needed. "I never liked the dude anyway."

"Here's something to keep you busy. Go to this address and pick up some boxes for me." Demetrius scribbled down an address and gave it to Jethro. "Tell the man that payment will be wired to him."

"No problem," Jethro said.

Demetrius powered up his laptop and waited. As soon as the web browser was available, he typed "Tack Enterprises." A company logo graced the screen—the letters TE in a heavy font of camouflage green. He clicked on home, and a picture of the company's owner and CEO came up.

Rich son of a bitch.

He read through the company's introduction, the online brochure, and its products. Nothing out of the ordinary, but he had a feeling that something was off.

He typed the man's name, and presto! Several articles about Pritchard came up. He had a wife and a daughter. Both were works of art in the beauty department, not that the man himself wasn't good looking. The odd thing was that the article mentioned both women had been attacked during a shopping expedition, but no other news reports followed except that they both had disappeared.

All articles pertaining to the attack and their disappearance were either marked as "page not existing" or "exact match not found" or they had been taken down altogether.

Dead end.

It could be if one were easily discouraged. Demetrius went through tabloid reports. The family was filthy rich, and tabloids had exploited their story. There were reports and speculation that there had been a vicious attack and that Pritchard had been devastated. The man had disappeared from public view afterward, and no further reports had surfaced about him or his family.

The rumors led some people to believe that the multibillionaire was suffering from grief and had chosen to become a recluse. Demetrius stared at the few pictures that had circulated among the tabloids and scratched his chin.

What if his hunch was close to the truth? Maybe his intuition was playing tricks on him, but he had always followed his gut. Most times, he found it gratifying to be proven right, and he felt this was one of those days.

He pulled out his cell phone from his pocket and dialed a number. It was time to give someone something important to do. "Zane, I need you to pay someone a visit." He smiled at the idea forming in his head. The visit may just give him the clue he needed.

Everyone was seated in the I-room when the door swung open and Cyrus hobbled in, looking every bit like a fugitive. He was pushing an IV pole, clutching his abdomen, and looking over his shoulder at the same time.

There were about twenty vampires and twelve human fighters present altogether, three of them female. Most of them got up on their feet when Cyrus walked in. Harrow clapped him in the back, and Lambert chuckled.

Judging from the way Cyrus threw himself into the chair between Harrow and Lambert and flinched, the effort of getting himself out of bed and into the meeting room had sapped him of all energy—what little he'd had to begin with.

"Don't even bother with the lecture," Cyrus warned when Pritchard leaned forward, resting both hands on the edges of the table and glowered at him.

"I wonder sometimes if you have a death wish, my friend." Pritchard shook his head and straightened. "As I was saying, we are going by the last intel we gathered. Much of the vampire concentration seemed to appear and disappear around the area of Rockefeller Center—in around a three-block radius.

"Lambert is suggesting at this point that we halt all involvement with other vampires. We don't want our injuries piling up."

There was a collective response, ranging from approval to discontent. The likes of Tor and Drake and a few other vampires wanted action and a chance to fight for whatever suited their motives. Others looked relieved. Fighting and constant surveillance could take its toll on anyone, vampire or human. Rohnert stayed quiet while he leaned on the wall at the farthest end of the room.

Lambert rose and coughed. "I made the mistake of getting our group into a scuffle with a bunch of vamps a few nights ago, and for that, I apologize."

The room fell silent. Lambert looked miserable, and Harrow tapped his shoulder.

"It's okay, man. You didn't expect Holt to get clobbered," Harrow offered, and Lambert winced.

"I think that's what we should do right now," Pritchard continued. "We will resume recon, and if we find diseased vamps, we bring 'em in. Other than that, we must lay low for now. And there are a few things I want to address."

There was a shifting of bodies, rustling of chairs, and expectant breathing. Pritchard smiled. Weren't they all getting antsier by the minute?

"Leroy thinks he has something worth putting into testing. Of course—"

The sound of the door creaking open stopped Pritchard midsentence. Jordan walked in and sat in the first available chair.

"Sorry, I'm late," she murmured.

Pritchard acknowledged her apology, and Harrow inclined his head in his direction.

"What is she doing here?" he whispered.

Having Jordan in the meeting was something Harrow hadn't been expecting. He didn't fancy the idea of his woman fighting alongside them, and more so, her finding out about the testing about to take place. But what was he thinking? There was no way he could keep her in the dark. For her not to find out what he was about to do in this cloistered facility was next to impossible. Just like bored housewives, the fighters loved to gossip.

"She wanted in, and I'm afraid I can't keep her out any longer. Besides, this is an effective way to persuade her to stay here, where she's safe. Don't you think?" Pritchard, as usual, had his bases covered.

Harrow seethed. "I don't want her fighting."

"I think we should let *her* decide what *she* wants to do," Jordan said from across the room, throwing glares in Harrow's direction.

Tor chuckled.

"Let's keep the bedroom drama in . . . the bedroom?" someone yelled, and the rest of snickered in response.

Harrow glared back in Jordan's direction, but he clamped his mouth shut. This was best handled away from prying eyes. He ground his molars, trying not to display an undue reaction for everyone to witness. Whoever said it, was right. It was better to leave some things in the bedroom. Pillow-fuckin' talk would just have to wait.

"Where was I?" Pritchard chuckled before continuing. "As I was saying, Leroy is onto something. He has high hopes it'll work. And our very own Harrow has offered to be the first to do the test."

"About damn time," someone chimed in.

"Wait . . . what are we talking about?" Jordan stood up, a baffled expression on her face.

"Oh, Christ, woman. If you came on time, you would know what we're talking about," one vampire hissed.

Harrow felt his muscles twitching, and he sprang to his feet. As quick as lightning, he stood next to the vampire and breathed down his neck. "You might want to watch your words, vampire," he warned.

Just as fast as he'd moved, Tor was standing next to him to restrain him. Tor dragged him back to his chair. "Easy there, my man," Tor said.

Harrow sat down, feeling like he was going to explode. Maybe it was the fact that he hadn't gone to bed that was making him irritable and ill tempered. He tried to catch a glimpse of Jordan, but all he could see was her standing with hands on her hips.

Pritchard held his hands up to quiet down the roomful of now-twitchy vampires and humans. "As I was saying, Leroy started his experiment on

Harrow a few days ago. We'll get an answer in two weeks tops. We'll know by then if we can give it a go for everyone else."

"What type of experiment?" Jordan asked, her voice sounding labored, as if air was being squeezed out of her.

The kind of experiment I don't want you to witness, Harrow thought to himself. This was the reason why he hadn't told her in the first place, even though he'd had several chances to do so. He knew she'd freak out, just the way she was sounding now.

Harrow stood up and strode to the back, not caring what everyone else thought. All he could see was Jordan and her misery at having been kept in the dark. "Let's talk outside." He took her elbow and ushered her out the door.

"What is he talking about?" Jordan turned and squared her shoulders as soon as they were alone in the corridor. Her eyes were flashing confusion and hurt at the same time.

"I stopped feeding several days ago, and I will not feed until symptoms and lesions have returned. This will mark the beginning of the active stage of the disease. At that point, Leroy will give me animal blood to see if his speculation holds water."

"And this . . ." Jordan paused, her breaths coming in quick spurts, ". . . piece of information I don't deserve to know?"

Tears burned in her eyes. Her silent question was loud enough for Harrow to hear. How could he not trust her enough to tell her?

"Jordan, you already have enough on your plate with Gail and all. You don't need this shit on you—"

Jordan cut him off. "Let me figure out what shit is good for me, okay? I'm sick of this protective crap you keep pulling on me. I'm a big girl, and in case you haven't noticed, I can take care of myself." Waving her hand in frustration, she walked to the end of the hall and back. Harrow leaned against the wall, easing his fingers along his temple, where a throbbing pain had started.

"You have a way with words, don't you?" he retorted, his tone sharp. "Okay, fine. I should have told you, but it's no big deal. I'll be okay after that." He downplayed his fear, making himself believe it was going to be easy—that he could pirouette his way out of the experiment without a hitch.

"You don't know that." Jordan scrubbed her tears with her jacket sleeve. "What if the animal blood doesn't work and you're starved beyond repair?"

Harrow stepped forward, close to Jordan but without touching her. He didn't want to invade her space, with her being pissed and all. "All I have to do is take human blood again, and all will go back to normal. There's nothing to it, Jordan." He tried to placate her.

"If that's the case, then I will be with you throughout the whole process —"

"No!" he snapped. "No one should be with me past the first week. It's dangerous." He held her face with his gloved hand. Jordan shook her head at him before lowering her eyes to the ground.

"Look at me." She shifted her eyes to meet his. "This isn't a joke. I don't want you hurt. I mean, who knows if hunger would push me to take you, and with the whole world watching?"

Jordan swayed at the thought. He could take her if he wanted, because she wanted it, too. Harrow breathed deep, catching the shifting emotion in her.

"You can't change my mind. I insist." She leaned closer and kissed his lips.

Harrow drew back with difficulty. The woman was pushing his limits. "I won't let you. Can't you understand this is a test, an experiment? Nothing is written in stone. Things can go wrong."

Jordan wrapped her arms around his waist, trapping him. "Please—I want to be with you," she begged.

"Woman, you're stubborn."

"Yes, and I will wear you down until you say yes."

He sighed. "It's going to be Leroy's call."

"And the man won't be able to resist my charm," she said with a sudden gleam in her eyes. There was no doubt she'd win Leroy over, and that made Harrow uncomfortable.

"Let's go back in." He brushed a feather-light kiss against her temple before he turned her around in the direction of the meeting room.

Pritchard flicked a knowing look at them when they reentered. "I will be entertaining a big client for several days. This is pretty big, as big as the military account. If negotiations go well and we land their business, I think I'll take a little vacation."

There was loud applause that rippled across the room, and Pritchard laughed.

"Long overdue, boss," one person teased.

"Sure is," another agreed.

"Thanks. I'm in dire need of a rest. If all goes well, I may take a prolonged vacation." He winked and tapped the table. "If no one has any questions, then this meeting is adjourned."

Heads shook, and everyone piled out of the room within the next few minutes. Cyrus and Lambert stayed behind.

"Cyrus, you better listen to Shelly," Pritchard started, but Cyrus raised his hand.

"Don't, boss. I'm going crazy in that room. The woman is driving me nuts. She's always telling me what to do. She even wants me to try this cracked diet of hers. No meat and eat nothing but vegetables and tofu. Can you believe it?" Cyrus complained and shook his head.

Lambert snorted and crossed his arms across his wide chest, while the others hooted in laughter.

"I'm just saying, take it easy," Pritchard said. "And there's nothing wrong with being healthy and eating less meat," he added.

"Hell, no. I happen to love meat, and there's no chance I'm changing my diet." Cyrus shook his head.

"Fine. It's your call." Pritchard sighed and changed the subject. "What I want here is to fill you guys in. Allison and Harrow have met with our lawyer and accountant, and I expect both of you to be their counterparts in dealing with the outside world."

They nodded in understanding.

"Details have been ironed out, and your contracts and compensation are already on paper. All they need are your signatures."

"Boss, you know . . . money has been the least of our concern for some time now. We're here because this is our family." Lambert grunted, uncomfortable with any display of deeper emotion.

"I know that, but you have families and I want them set for life. I value your friendship and services. More than you'll ever know." The part about family was bullcrap. Lambert was given up for adoption, moved from one foster home to another until he was old enough to fend for himself, while Cyrus remained tight-lipped about his personal life and had assured Pritchard that no one would miss him. Both men were perfect for the job because they had no emotional ties with the outside world.

"Okay, enough of this emotional crap. It's giving me the creeps." Cyrus attempted to push his body up, but a bolt of pain from his wound made him slump back down in the chair.

"Shall I carry you bridal-style?" Lambert asked.

"Want my fist lodged in your throat?"

Pritchard's laugh echoed across the room. What would he do without his loyal friends? The duo was like the brothers he'd never had.

"Get out of here, and stay out of trouble," Pritchard admonished just before the door closed behind them.

Harrow woke up with a rattling pain inside him. It was a pain he knew too well, and it had come back with a vengeance. This time, he made an effort to ignore the gnawing ache that emanated from the center of his body, radiating pulses throughout his system.

He turned to check the time—eleven in the morning. *Shit*. He'd only been asleep or just unconscious for forty-five minutes.

Back in the day, pains like these were ignored and suffered in silence. With his inability to move in the daylight and the fear of capture at nighttime, his chances to feed and eliminate the torture of his wounds were few and far between. He'd suffered every time it was time to feed. He had been hunted, and his odds of survival back then were slimming down with each passing day.

The steady and rhythmic snoring that came from the other side of the room kept him on edge. Tor was dead to the world, and Harrow knew he'd go crazy if he spent a moment longer listening to the hoarse noise. He found himself twitching with each passing second. Sleep, in times like these, wasn't going to come even if he beseeched the higher powers for it.

The throbbing from his lesions promised longer days and nights ahead. It had been over a week, but it felt like it had been months, or even a year, since he'd last fed.

Picking up the phone, he punched three numbers and waited. A clipped voice answered. "Yeah."

"Rohnert, spar with me again before I go crazy," he grumbled.

"Sure, meet me in the training room in ten." Rohnert hung up the phone.

Harrow got up and walked to the closet, pulled out a matching pair of sweat pants and shirt, and got out of his mismatched pair. Making as little noise as possible, he picked up two of the wooden Arnis they often used for practice. The use of Kalimetal was confined to actual patrols and during real fights since the blades were lethal upon contact.

He checked his arms. The wounds were getting bigger, deeper, redder, and nastier. The mere sight of them gave him pause. Soon, he wouldn't even be able to go out. The sores were repulsive, guaranteed to drive everyone away.

His cheeks were reddish and welts were prominent along his jaw and down his neck. The lesions were increasing in size at a steady rate. A ski mask would be a more appropriate cover to wear if he wanted to get out of his room over the next few days.

"Where in the hell are you going? It's the middle of the day, for crying out loud," Tor groaned in the darkness.

"Gotta let off some steam," Harrow said before he pulled the door shut behind him.

"Ready?" Rohnert asked as soon as he made his way into the training room. The vampire was dressed in a white t-shirt, nylon basketball shorts, and sported a headband on his head, the kind Dai-Sensei's from all over wore.

Harrow dropped the Arnis on his desk and moved to the center of the room, where Rohnert was waiting for him. They bowed facing each other and readied their fighting stance.

Sparring with Rohnert was an effective tool to pass the time, just as it had been over the past week. Since patrolling had been rotated among the others, Harrow had been feeling like a caged lion, dying to blow off some frustration.

As they went at it over and over again, Harrow channeled his energy away from the stinging hunger in the pit of his stomach and into the non-stop kicks, jabs, socks, and punches.

They were evenly matched—his speed to Rohnert's experience, his raw talent to Rohnert's perfected art form, and his strength to the vampire's power. It was finesse and skill against grace and expertise, and whichever way it seemed, they always ended in a draw.

Their grunts and grumbles were the only sounds attesting to the competition while kicks were blocked, jabs were repelled, and punches were deflected.

Even when it came to using the Arnis, Harrow's confidence was remarkable as their sticks clashed and struck each other. It was apparent that Rohnert was enjoying himself, too. By the end of the third hour, they took a break, drank some water, and wiped off the steady stream of sweat drenching them.

"Thanks for doing this," Harrow said after taking a big gulp of water. He sat next to Rohnert on the floor, where the vampire was stretching his legs.

Rohnert snorted. "I don't like getting my butt kicked, but it's all good." The vampire stole a few glances Harrow's way as he wiped his face, trying to be discreet about it.

Harrow sighed. He was back to the old drawing board. His appearance was garnering stares, disgust, and pity. No fun, but that was the story of his life.

"Don't even think that's how I feel about you," Rohnert said, averting his eyes in another direction. "I'd heard about it before I got here, but I haven't seen it."

"You read minds?" Harrow asked, startled.

"Nope, but your expression was screaming the words out."

"Yeah, that's me . . . fuckin' Mr. Open Book."

Rohnert laughed in mock humor. "You want to talk about it?"

"Do I want to talk about the pain? Hell, no. I just want it out of my mind before I go mad. That's all."

"It's going to be worth it. All these sacrifices you're making," Rohnert responded.

"How in the hell would you know?" Harrow felt the raging thirst at the back of his throat, and he swallowed hard. Twice.

"She supports you, she understands, and she's behind you one hundred percent. So that makes it all okay."

Flabbergasted, Harrow stared at the vampire. "You have no idea how bad it is for me." How in the hell could he talk about how much he wanted her, to be with her, and take her all in. He had no idea.

"I think I do. Our frustrations lie in the same area. We both like what we can't have. Except . . . you know she wanted you back."

"Damn. It sucks either way, doesn't it?"

So Rohnert had been hurting. It wasn't an alien feeling, hankering after someone you couldn't have. The vampire was right. Harrow was better off. At the very least, Jordan had expressed her affection for him. But tell that to a hungry dog who wanted to sink his teeth into a bone that kept being dragged away every time he moved an inch.

"Not as piss-fuck as it is for me."

"Life isn't fair." Harrow sighed. The image of Jordan strangled his brain. Every single day he saw her, he had to deal with the tight, choking reality of being with her, but not enough.

"Tell me about it."

They lapsed into silence, both lost in their own steamrolling train of thoughts. A movement by the doorway brought them out of their stupor. They looked up to see Jordan and Allison peek around the door.

Allison smiled and spoke while Jordan hung back. "Are we disturbing you?"

Harrow smiled and waved them in. "No, we're just taking a break. C'mon in."

Rohnert drew a sharp breath, but he kept his expression light. He glanced at Allison and Jordan, offering a little smile when they sat on the mat next to the men.

"I wanted to let you know what my plans are for Daddy's surprise birthday party."

Allison had made no secret of her plan to throw a party for her father during their shopping trip in the city weeks ago. She wanted a formal gathering, which was to be attended by employees and special friends of Tack Enterprises. The guest list would encompass both the humans and the vampires in their facility. After all, Pritchard was turning fifty-five, an age when most people were still grappling with life's challenges. He'd built a multibillion dollar empire and had a host of other successes under his belt. It was a fitting tribute to have all his beloved people share the day with him.

"What do you have in mind?" Harrow watched Jordan, who was quiet as a mouse, sitting still next to Allison.

"Well, I talked to Darryl."

All three vampires lifted their eyebrows, not having the slightest clue who Darryl was. Allison laughed.

"That's right, you guys don't take advantage of the meals here, but you should. Darryl is one of the best chefs in the city."

"Sure, Ally. Like we'd dine every night like humans and compliment the man on his Veal Parmigiana." Jordan laughed.

Rohnert shifted and sat cross-legged. "I, for one, don't mind human food. I enjoy the taste, although it doesn't do much for me," he said.

"Me, too, but I have to keep up the pretense for Darryl's sake. He's been with us for as long as I can remember, and it would break the old man's heart if I didn't sample his daily offerings." Allison giggled.

You had to love the woman. She was a breath of fresh air for the ones who'd been there, sweated it out, and done that.

"Then we shall eat what he offers us," Harrow said. The mere mention of food made his stomach growl, although he was thinking along the lines of velvety, sweet, thick blood. He licked his lips.

"When are you planning the party?"

"Three weeks from now. His birthday is a few days before Christmas. So I figured we could even tell him it's the company's party, except it isn't."

"Where do we come in?" Harrow asked. The roaring in his stomach made it impossible to think straight.

"What I want is for the guys to take him out for a happy hour of some sort. Maybe Lambert and Cyrus can handle that, while we get the place ready. You know with Dad and his cameras, it's going to be hard to hide even the little things."

"Don't I know it," Harrow agreed.

He felt his stomach heave—he was having one of his physical reactions to hunger. A bad one. Harrow got up and wobbled.

"Whoa, are you okay?" Rohnert grabbed his arm, and Harrow recoiled.

"I think it's best if I go now."

"Are you okay?" Jordan ran to him, wrapping her arms around his waist and offering support.

"Don't touch me." He pushed her away.

"Why?" Her face flushed.

"Can't you see the damn wounds? They aren't safe. I'm not about to let you find out the hard way, Jordan!" he lashed out, but he felt bad right away for taking it out on her.

Just like that, he went from Jolly Harrow to Little Grumpy. "I'm sorry. Fill me in with the details later." She fell back a step and watched him walk out of the room.

Minutes later, he staggered inside the laboratory, finding Leroy buried in a pile of reading materials. The room hummed with excitement but silenced when everyone got one good look at him. They knew, and yet they stared. *What a circus!*

"Leroy!" He shouted to get the man's attention.

Leroy looked up, startled, scrambled to his feet, and rushed to Harrow's side. He put his arms around Harrow's waist and urged him to transfer some of his weight on him. "Are you getting close to your limit?"

"I'm headed into hostile territory. Lock me up, now." It wasn't a request —it was an order.

Leroy cursed and took him to a room with reinforced glass windows. It was a room that had been reserved for testing. One-way glass windows were meant to allow the doctors to study their subject. *Perfect!*

"Jones, get me some towels and a spit bucket," Leroy called to his assistant, who bolted in and out of the room in haste. The young man came and placed the towels and bucket on the table next to a bed.

The room was bare, with white walls, white sheets, and white everywhere. Harrow lowered himself onto the bed just as his body started shaking. He felt his knees give way right as his butt met the cushion.

"Get out of here, and don't come back until it's time for me to feed. Better yet, don't come near me. It's best to stay away." Harrow was beginning to feel the chills that he hated with a passion. The room felt cold. "Turn the goddamn heater on."

"But . . . I have t—to draw your blood." Leroy stumbled through his words.

"Get an infected vampire to do it. Don't even dare play hero on me now, okay? We talked about this before."

Leroy stumbled out of the room as the vents started blowing warm air that neither comforted nor helped with the chills. Harrow threw the blanket around his back and faced the wall. This was going to be a very long day.

Curse this disease to the high heavens.

"Harrow, I will be watching you the whole time, my boy." Leroy's voice piped in through the speakers mounted on the wall, and he didn't even have the strength to nod his head. The symptoms would go away in a few minutes, he hoped.

"I've been waiting for your call," Demetrius said as soon as Zane's call came through. "Tell me what you found out about our reclusive Pritchard Tack."

Zane was half human, half vampire—an anomaly of nature. Unlike him, Zane could go out during the daytime and hadn't developed fangs like the rest of them. There was no logical explanation or any clinical justification for why he was different. He just was. Born to a human woman who had died during his birth, he was just like his father in many ways. Tall, extremely attractive, red hair, and with dull, reddish eyes, Zane looked like he had more than enough to drink and exuded vampire qualities. He was nimble, possessed speed, was strong, and had a huge lust for blood. He was Demetrius' pride and joy, as well as his secret. Goran had yet to discover his lasting legacy.

Zane cleared his throat. "I had several meetings with Mr. Tack. At first, I placed a call and introduced myself as the COO of gran . . . I mean, your father's organization. Mr. Tack encouraged my queries. After all, our needs are quite large, and it's a big account anyone would love to get their claws into."

Demetrius felt his heart race while Zane chronicled his visit with Pritchard Tack. "Our reclusive billionaire is using a different office now. I was flown to the new building by a helicopter, blindfolded.

"Total secrecy. When I got to his office where he is now based, I could see the Manhattan skyline, so I am certain it wasn't as far away as I thought it would be. Plus the ride only took about fifteen minutes. If I judged it right, the helicopter was circling to throw me off as far as location."

"Hmm . . . interesting."

From the way Zane made it sound, Pritchard Tack was hiding something. Demetrius's curiosity was piqued to the max. What could the man be hiding?

Zane continued, not even waiting for an invitation to go on. Excitement was radiating in the timbre of his voice. "We discussed products, prices, and delivery goals. The man is thorough, if nothing else. With his reputation, he could deliver what he promises, twelve crates in a few days. I didn't see anything else worth following since I was granted limited access as far as mobility within the office building."

"Anything else?" Demetrius asked.

"I don't know what to call it, but I could sense there was more to the office building than what my eyes could tell me. I did check the hardware you showed me, but their company logo is different from the insignia on the metal bracelet.

"I think I'll be able to tell you the general area where I think the facility is located, but I can't be certain. The man had several private guards watching my every move, even during our meeting. He is what you might call very jumpy. There were several interruptions during our meeting, but his replies were cryptic, so there was no giveaway there."

"Well done, Zane. How about I take you out to dinner tonight? We can talk about it more and maybe scope the general vicinity after."

Demetrius might as well be looking at Zane in person, because he could imagine him smiling, looking quite smug at having been able to please him. "Sure, that'll be nice, though I still prefer red juice, you know." Zane chuckled and hung up after they set the time and place.

Demetrius nudged the mouse, and the computer monitor buzzed to life. He typed the name Tack Enterprises again and stared at the monitor for some time. His mind roared into overdrive. "What could you be hiding, Pritchard Tack?" he asked aloud.

He pushed a quick dial to call on Jethro, who got there in just a heartbeat. "Jet, we are going to scout a place tonight, but we'll have dinner and drinks before that."

"I'll be ready, sur. Any particular costume you want me to wear?" Jethro asked, aware of Demetrius's abhorrence of his fashion choices.

"Dapper is the word. If you don't know what it means, Google it."

"Leroy, how long has Harrow been sleeping?" Jordan walked in but did not spare even a brief glance in the doctor's direction. Her eyes were rooted to the sleeping figure on the bed, curled and in apparent distress, even in his slumbering state.

"He had been pacing for the last hour before he lay down and fell asleep not a few minutes ago. I think it's exhaustion that finally got to him." Leroy walked up next to Jordan and stood beside her.

Jordan touched the glass, aching to touch Harrow himself. It had been three days since he had confined himself in the room. She had been watching him every moment of the day, except when she had to check on Gail. Jordan had been torn between her concern for Harrow and her responsibility to Gail, which she had delegated to Allison, who had been eager to step up to the plate.

As much as she wanted to get closer to him, she restrained herself to accommodate his wishes. It was awful enough to see him suffer, but the thought of him suffering alone made it unbearable for her. Several times, she caught herself crossing the line of doing what she wanted as opposed to what he'd requested of her. Feeling the ache deep in her heart, she wanted to touch him, to comfort him.

"This is killing me, Leroy," she said.

"I can see that." Leroy reached out and placed a warm hand on her arm to comfort her. The act in itself brought back memories of her father's touch, his caring spirit, and his sympathetic nature. The recollections stirred within her made her flinch. With regret and deep longing, she ached for one more moment to see her parents again, to have another chance to feel their love, and to witness their smiles. Every memory had been blurring with the passage of time, and she feared that soon, she'd forget about them.

Jordan snapped her mind out of the pool of yearning she was swimming in and refocused on Harrow. He started jerking on the bed, his body flopping around like a fish out of water.

"I don't know how he can take this suffering." She cried, and hot tears stung her eyes. Jordan hadn't been one to cry, but watching Harrow had raked up weird feelings inside her. She now knew what love was. It knew no boundaries. It was about the joy of giving, without expectation of return. It was willing to overlook faults, shortcomings, and differences.

Leroy was concentrating on Harrow, tabulating his movements as if he were counting every single twitch, jerk, and groan. He took notes of the regularity of the vampire's breathing, as well as the development of his lesions. The doctor had also been in that room for days, only taking off when Jordan pushed him to take a short break or a catnap. Jones had filled in for him, too, when Pritchard visited, and they watched him together.

At one point, everyone in the facility had taken turns watching over Harrow, and it wasn't because they wanted to gawk at the circus freak. They did it to offer support and encourage his sacrifice. Even Cyrus came and spoke with Harrow a few times.

Jordan had been in the forefront of it all. She spoke with Harrow, assuring him that she wasn't going to step out of the facility to hunt without Tor or Rohnert, telling him stories about Gail and her swimming lessons, and when Pritchard wasn't around, she gave him the full details of the party preparations.

Dante popped in several times when he found someone to cover for him. This was the type of people they worked with—good ones. They were caring people, just how a family should be.

"It's just a matter of hours before we give him what he needs. It may be a shock to his system at first because he's not used to it, but I'm hoping he'll take it well. But for now, I need his blood drawn."

"Let me do it," she offered, ready to grab the syringe and the vial from Leroy. Jordan would not take no for an answer, and she knew her expression was enough to tell Leroy that she would do it whether he agreed or not.

Leroy hesitated, and Jordan turned her palm up without another word. After a few seconds of deliberation, he dropped them in her hand.

"I'm going to buzz you in. Here's a pair of gloves. Wear them even before you go in."

After Jordan was prepped on the extraction procedure, Leroy punched a series of numbers, and the door opened with a shrill sound like an electric can opener.

"Be careful," Leroy reminded before she walked in, and the door closed behind her. A distinct, cloying smell hit her. The scent of raw meat came to mind. She inhaled and got more of the distinct odor. It smelled like fresh blood, with a diminutive scent of decomposing flesh. An odd combination.

Harrow looked up at the sound of her footsteps, his eyes unfocused. His sunglasses were on the table, and his eyes were almost opaque in color when they settled on her. He sat up on the bed.

"Jordan, please go away." He hissed and moved back when she approached. Her movement was slow and calculated. She was unwilling to startle him into action.

"Darling, I need to draw blood from you," Jordan said, as if appeasing a crying child with sweet offerings.

His fangs were incredibly long. She wasn't sure if she was imagining it, but she thought she saw them throb right before her very eyes. It had been almost two weeks since he'd last fed, and it looked like he had reached his limit.

Harrow licked his dried, chapped lips and inched away from her. The lesions on his arms, legs, and around his neck were raw, almost glowing red and had grown bigger. He gritted his teeth as if to dispel the demons of his disease. Jordan was certain it had something to do with the burning pain from the wounds as well as the pang of hunger. Starvation was a tough opponent, because it would eat you up alive and spew out your carcass after it finished you off.

"Make it quick, because I'm trying hard here." Harrow appeared bone tired, his tone weary as he held out his arm after he made sure she was wearing gloves. "Move fast," he reminded her as he eyed her jugular. The pulsing clearly began to excite him.

"I know you won't hurt me." She kept her voice low and held his arm. He was burning hot, and she felt like her hands would melt on contact. Harrow rested his arm on his thigh as she tried to keep her hands steady.

Harrow drew in a deep breath before exhaling with a curse. "Hurry up, Jordan."

Once she stuck the needle into his skin, Harrow hissed and began twitching again. After she filled the evacuated collection tube with blood, she pulled out the needle and applied a little pressure to the entry site with her finger before taping it up.

"Get out now!" he screamed. "Now!"

Before she stepped away, she held his gaze for a moment and whispered the words she'd been dying to tell him.

"I love you, Harrow."

Time stood still as soon as the words were out of her mouth. Harrow's breathing slowed, and his twitching ceased for just a moment. "I love you more," he said. "But please, get out of this room now."

He didn't scream the order, he whispered it as if it was a last ditch effort before he turned savage. Jordan walked out the door, which Leroy held open for her. Her heart was aching, but at the same time, it was soaring. How could her heart sing and lament at the same time?

She was out of answers. Helpless, she watched Harrow slump back onto the bed, lying on his stomach as he clutched it in pain. His mouth gaped wordlessly while he fought the torturous, invisible enemy.

Leroy took the tube from her hand and tossed the used syringe inside the biohazard bin. He turned the mike on and spoke to Harrow. "Give me an hour to see and get confirmation, and I'll bring you what you need."

Waiting was a slow, brutal process for Jordan and Harrow. The passage of time was at a snail's pace, while their frustration and impatience climbed at a fast rate. Leroy came back an hour after he'd left, and in his hands were bags of blood.

He opened the door and left the bags on the table in one quick movement. Harrow took the bags right away, and Jordan saw him empty them, one by one. There was something sensual in the way that he sucked down the blood that made her body respond. The realization of how much she wanted to be with Harrow was an unnerving, but pleasurable, thought that she couldn't just push away.

"All we have to do now is to wait and see," Leroy said with an inaudible sigh.

A few minutes after feeding, Harrow fell deep into an exhausted slumber, and he slept like a baby. No doubt, it had something to do with his exhaustion and sated appetite. He'd gorged on the bags of blood like there was no tomorrow. Afterward, lethargy had claimed him and he'd conked out.

How the feeding would affect him was the million-dollar question. Leroy and Jordan stood like expectant sentinels as they watched Harrow, but their own state of fatigue was hard to deny. Jordan offered the first watch together with Jones, who had spent as much time in the room in observation as Leroy had.

Jordan wrapped a blanket across her shoulders. At some point before Harrow fell asleep, he requested that they crank up the air conditioner. Her breath blew thick fog, and she felt icicles forming on the tip of her nose. It was plenty cold, but Harrow was burning up. If this was the only way he'd be comfortable, she'd be happy to bundle up like an Eskimo.

"How is he doing?" Rohnert spoke from behind her. How he could sneak up on her without making the slightest noise was still a mystery to her. The vampire had a canny gift for stealth and suppression that was yet to be rivaled. He looked at her with a veiled expression. Whatever he was thinking, it was masked with the determined set of his jaw and his narrowed eyes.

"He took it like a trooper. For now, we're in watch-and-wait mode." The words came out clipped, and she saw Rohnert's features soften.

"He's the last known Boy Scout here, or out there. I'm sure he'll be fine." He gave her a small smile, and his hand landed on her arm and gave her a gentle squeeze. She took comfort from the action. He was a fine being, a gentleman, and a great friend to Harrow—even to her. Despite her negative response to his affection in the past, he remained tight and loyal.

"Thanks. Look, Rohnert. I appreciate everything that you do for us . . . err . . . for me. You came here even though we both know it was the last thing you'd want to get involved in. I . . . I just want to—"

"Jordan, don't." He stopped her when she placed her hand on top of his. "It's cool, really."

Jordan nodded. Though much of what she wanted to tell him would remain unspoken, she had a feeling that Rohnert had accepted defeat with grace and that things between them were going to be okay. She drew a deep breath and returned her gaze to Harrow when he stirred in the bed.

"Looks like our boy is coming back from the dead," Rohnert said, pulling his hand back.

Jordan stepped forward, pressed a button, and spoke into the intercom device perched on the wall. "Harrow, are you okay?"

Harrow opened his eyes and blinked. He then blinked again, as if trying to focus his sight, glancing up at the speaker at sound of her voice, and she grew fearful. Something wasn't right. She could feel it.

"Jordan?" He sighed, and his fangs extended.

"I'm here, Harrow." She was already making her way inside the room, despite Rohnert's disapproval. He walked behind her with his hand poised on his holstered weapon.

Harrow fumbled when he got up on the bed and groped for his sunglasses on the nearby table. He covered his eyes just as she walked up to him. The scent of the fresh blood and putrid flesh had been replaced by the fragrant and captivating scent of cured meat. The intense scent lingered around her as Harrow shot to his feet.

The aggressive display didn't deter her from moving within inches of him. He reached out his hand to touch her face, as if he wanted to see her. She stiffened when his fingers grazed her cheek. *He can't see me?* Feeling as if a bucket of cold water had been emptied on her, she shuddered at the horrific implications running through her head.

"Harrow, can you not see me?"

"I can . . . It's the same thing almost—but there are rings around your face, everywhere—like a halo surrounding my eyesight." He shut his eyes, hard. His eyelashes fluttered, and his eyeballs rolled underneath their lids.

"Harrow, what's wrong then?" She reached out and cupped his face with her hands, angling it down to her.

"I don't know—it's a weird feeling. I can't explain it." He shook his head and then glanced around the room.

"What is it?"

"There's a weird onslaught of energy in me." Harrow closed and opened his eyes, then tilted his face in a way she knew he could see her best. "But you're still as beautiful as ever."

He pulled away.

"Harrow, stop fooling around. What I want to know is if you're okay. Are you hungry? Do you need to feed?" Jordan stood on her toes and brushed her lips over his mouth. In spite of the electric-like current she sensed from him, she was not afraid. He was throwing off a myriad of emotions. One of them was aggression, which didn't make sense to her.

"No, I don't feel hungry at all."

His hand started gliding over his arms, inspecting the lesions by touch. His fangs contracted back to their normal size after a few minutes.

Rohnert shifted next to her. She knew he felt the undetectable change in Harrow, too, judging by the way his hand tightened around the push dagger. She could tell that Rohnert was prepping for a fight.

"Rohnert . . ." Harrow's eyes flickered to Rohnert's locked grip on his dagger. "That isn't necessary. I won't attack anyone."

Rohnert hesitated. "Welcome back, buddy," Rohnert said, but his grip didn't relax. They clapped palms before Harrow collapsed back onto the edge of the bed. Rohnert walked to the direction of the door and leaned against the doorjamb.

Jordan flipped open her phone and dialed Leroy's number. "He's up." She sighed and turned in Harrow's direction. "He says he feels weird. I don't know. Just get here as soon as you can."

Within minutes, Leroy poked his head through the door, looking every bit as if he'd just jumped out of bed and thrown his coat over his striped pajamas.

"Harrow . . . are you feeling all right?" Leroy nodded to Rohnert, who moved out of the way to let him pass through the door.

Harrow's fangs flashed at Leroy before the impulse buried itself when he realized what he'd done.

Leroy stepped back and raised his palms as if in surrender. Confused, Harrow buried his face in his hands, embarrassed at his unexpected reaction.

"It's okay, Harrow. Let's talk." Leroy pulled up a chair and propped it in front of Harrow's bed. He looked pointedly at Jordan and Rohnert. "Do you mind giving us some time to talk alone?"

"No problem." Rohnert took the hint and disappeared, but Jordan hesitated.

Harrow lifted his head and gave a Jordan a pleading look. It was then that she turned on her heel and left. As difficult as it was to leave Harrow, she knew he needed the privacy after what he had gone through over the past two weeks, bearing the pain for everyone to see.

Leroy took out a pen from his breast pocket just as Jordan closed the door behind her. The feeling of dread enveloped her as soon as she walked out of the laboratory. Her questions were all lined up, but this wasn't the right time to ask them. Harrow needed to get his strength and bearings back and figure out what type of changes he was facing. For the meantime, she intended to distract herself from the nagging uncertainty of his situation. She found herself wandering to the training room, where she discovered Rohnert alone.

"Can you help a friend pass some time?" she asked, not knowing what response awaited her.

Rohnert looked up and smiled. "Sure thing. Get your Arnis and let me kick your butt as payback."

After a grueling afternoon of sparring and Arnis dueling with Rohnert, Jordan walked out of the training center tired and drained but satisfied. True to his word, Rohnert had kicked her butt more than once and had mopped the mat with her face several times. It'd be safe to say, though, that she had gotten him a few times, catching him by surprise and employing one or two tricks she'd learned on her own.

Not one to use her feminine charm against the opposite sex, she'd learned men almost always hated to hit a woman. This was their Achilles heel, the inexorable weakness in their arsenal. On several occasions during their sparring, Rohnert would catch her in a vulnerable position and would ease up on the use of force, and that was when retaliation was the sweetest.

In one quick and decisive move, she spread her forefinger and middle finger as the striking point, while the rest were curled in a fist. With a quick thrust, she targeted Rohnert's eyes, pointing to the area above his eyebrows. A sharp stab rendered him useless for a couple of seconds, enough to buy her time to strike him down.

He fell for the trick, twice. The other time a single finger got him on the solar plexus, and it was satisfying as hell. Rohnert bowed to her at the end of their afternoon workout, a validation that he was pleased with her performance and capabilities.

"Jordan, can I go to the park?" Gail ran to her as soon as she entered the bedroom. Allison looked up from the desk and rolled her eyes.

"She's been bugging me all afternoon," Allison complained.

"How come we can't go out in the mornings or in the afternoons? Why do we always go out at night?" Gail whined, tugging at Jordan's jacket while she tried to get her attention.

Jordan knew it was a matter of time before Gail started asking questions —questions she was not prepared to answer. Even if she had the answers, she knew Gail wasn't ready for the truth. She was young, too young to know and understand the complexity of the situation and the nature of the people surrounding her.

For the time being, ignorance was bliss, and she'd protect Gail's innocence until she could no longer sustain it. Until then, Gail would have to believe in whatever lies and cover-ups she could come up with.

She walked to her closet with Gail dogging her, still tugging at the edge of her jacket. She unloaded her Arnis, propping them against the wall, and turned around to sit on her haunches. It was necessary to be at Gail's eye level. "Baby, didn't I tell you that I have too many things I have to do in the daytime, so it's only at night I can go out and do things with you?"

"Yeah, but—"

Jordan in a stern tone cut her off. "No buts, Gail. You'll have to make do with the toys we got for you."

Gail's lips trembled and her eyes started brimming with tears. "But I'm bored now," she cried, and Jordan regretted the tone she'd used.

Jordan racked her brain for ways to make up to Gail for her reprimand. She shot a quick look in Allison's direction for reinforcement, but the other woman was busy leafing through catalogs. There was no mistaking it had something to do with the party that she'd been so caught up in planning and preparing for over the last few days.

"How about if I ask Uncle Lambert and Uncle Drake take you?"

Gail, at one point, had questioned Jordan about her countless 'Uncles and Aunties.' Jordan had evaded the question like the plague, muttering excuses that these were people close to her and that they should be addressed as such.

"But I want you and Dad—I mean Harrow, to take me," she sobbed.

There was no missing the word. Gail had expressed her desire to call Harrow *Dad* in the past, and Jordan had often chastised her. Harrow wasn't her father, and besides, she wasn't even sure how Harrow felt about Gail, though anyone could see how Gail's presence had made even the toughest men in the facility weak in the knees.

"Harrow is working on a project, and I need a shower. Let me call Uncle Lambert right now, so he can take you." Jordan hardened her tone again and steeled her heart. As Gail sagged against her leg, nodding a weak acceptance, Jordan retrieved her cell phone and dialed Lambert's number.

After arrangements were made and Gail had been whisked away by the two humans who promised her an afternoon of fun in the park, Jordan allowed herself to breathe a sigh of relief. Sometime soon, Gail would be asking questions again. Nevertheless, for the time being, Jordan celebrated the little triumph of evading yet another tough question. She shoved the thoughts away and dragged herself inside the bathroom for a much-needed shower.

There were many things that needed answers. In the forefront was the nagging uncertainty of her existence now that Harrow was in her life. How could she make herself leave, and would he ever understand?

Tough questions needed straight answers. She would have to make that call very soon. Jordan looked at her reflection in the bathroom mirror and couldn't recognize the image of the woman staring back at her. This woman had fallen in love, and now she had a decision to make—two decisions that were guaranteed to hurt her and the people closest to her in the meanest possible way. Her chest ached and burned like someone had poured scalding water inside her as she stepped under the lukewarm spray of the shower.

Dinner with Zane was as blissful as blissful could get. There hadn't been many chances to get away and meet each other on a regular basis for the past twenty-five years of the boy's life. Yes, in his mind's eye, Zane would forever be a little boy to him. He had been a well-kept secret from everyone but Melissa.

His mother, the single soul who knew of Zane's existence, had safeguarded his secret. Somehow, by sheer luck attributable to his son's anomaly, Goran's internal radar had missed one important detail. His father was not in the know, and that was how Demetrius preferred it.

Though Melissa hadn't gotten the chance to meet Zane, she was all too aware of his importance in her son's life and was happy for him.

After dinner, they rode in Zane's brand spankin' new Porsche Carrera GTS convertible. Packing all the bells and whistles from the leather interior package to the sports rims, the car was smokin' hot. This was a car lover's dream, and a perfect gift for his one and only child. The joyride excluded Jethro, who had to fend for himself and find his own way back to the Council headquarters.

Dressed in an impeccable dark Gucci suit, Zane was the epitome of the city's elite. A strikingly handsome man and a spitting image of his father.

They looked more like twins rather than father and son. Showing off his new toy, Zane drove around the city, the Bose sound system blasting AC/DC's *Highway to Hell*. Speeding and weaving in and out of traffic, they made their way across the river to the location where Zane suspected Tack Enterprises was located.

After half an hour of cruising and looking around, they spotted the structure he was almost certain was the office building he had been taken to. Demetrius took pictures and surveyed the area, taking note of the address, the cross streets, and the other key interests worth jotting down in his memory bank.

There was a general feeling of being watched, tracked down, and followed while they circled the streets encompassing the Tack Building. The feeling stayed with Demetrius until they turned onto another street that led them away.

Zane volunteered to park the car at a favorable vantage point, produced two sets of binoculars, and offered one pair to him. It was a moonless night, and their stealthy location wouldn't give them away. They moved to the front of the convertible and leaned against the hood.

"Let's watch from here." Zane popped the binoculars and started scanning the areas around the building. It was getting quieter by the minute, and there was no reason to believe that anyone could bust them for sightseeing in the dark.

Demetrius focused his attention on any activity from and around the building. There was no movement in or around the structure. He waited, while Zane did the same.

He lowered the binoculars and relied on his vision to scan their surroundings. There was nothing for miles away, not even the slightest movement. The stale night offered nothing but chilly air blowing in every direction. All of a sudden, there was that acrid scent wafting in their direction, the reeking and stomach-churning stink he knew all too well and could detect from miles away. There were some sick vampires moving around in the area—quite a few of them, judging by the degree of the stench that assaulted his nose. There were four of them not too far from his current position.

Good thing he didn't leave home without his guns. This would be easy. Too easy. His body hummed as he filled Zane in on the details. They hid behind the car and waited as the reeking odor became stronger.

He pulled two handguns from the holster inside his suit and handed a Beretta to Zane. "Here's a gun. All you have to do is point at the chest and let it do its magic. We have to move fast, get them all before they even know we're here," he whispered.

He checked his own Smith and Wesson with its attached silencer, praying the noise wouldn't attract attention to them.

As the foul odor got closer, his guess was confirmed. Four vampires came into view, walking as if they were in Central Park, oblivious to their presence. He nodded to Zane just as the group moved closer to their parked car. By the time one of the vampires even noticed their presence, they had pulled the triggers and bullets raced, hitting their targets in the chest. The popping sounded, and two vampires fell. Before the other two bolted, the next round got them straight in the back. Two more rounds of popping followed as the Dangeran bullets performed to perfection.

"Follow and cover me," he instructed Zane, and they ran to the disintegrating bodies before the crackling, popping, and sizzling sounds had ceased. All they could find by the time they reached the nonexistent bodies were the expected ankle bracelets on the ground.

Demetrius retrieved the anklets while Zane provided cover. He collected all four accessories and found the trademark he was looking for. Even in the dim lighting, he recognized the logo TE.

"Let's go," he said. He whipped his head from side to side, willing his hearing to decipher if more company was coming. So far, there wasn't any more of the repulsive scent.

"What are those things?" Zane asked as soon as they got in the car. He drove the length of the deserted street that took them back to the city.

"I think those sick vampires reside somewhere in this general area, and this, boy, is our key to the question. I'm positive there is a connection between those sickos and our dear Pritchard Tack. I'm certain of it." He fingered the metal bands before slipping them inside his coat pocket.

Zane shot quick glances in Demetrius's direction, fascinated by his candor. "Did you expect we'd be running across some vampires back there?"

"I don't know about you, but I could feel some serious surveillance." Demetrius said as the car slowed to a stop in front of the Rockefeller Center.

The streets were still littered with holiday shoppers and window shoppers alike. The area buzzed with the holiday spirit. All the window displays were flashing signs of big sales and slashed prices meant to lure the smart, and the not-so-smart, consumers. Christmas decorations reflected the crazy, electric holiday bustle. Wreaths and lights, as well as glittering reindeer and holly, proudly hung from each lamppost that surrounded the block.

"I get that, too, but don't worry. I'll gather more information if I can." Zane put the car in park as Demetrius stepped out.

He leaned on the passenger window. "Don't even worry about it. I think I got what I need. I will call you again if I have a project for you."

"Sounds good. I will wait for your call."

"Thanks for the four-one-one. I'll be in touch soon." Demetrius leaned forward and gave Zane a pat on the back.

"Thanks for the dinner, Pops." Zane grinned before he shifted the car into drive, accelerated, and sped away with a wave.

Demetrius hurried down to their secret entrance and got to work on his computer right away. He downloaded the picture from his camera phone and studied the exterior of the building. Plugged the address into Yahoo maps, he clicked on "satellite view" before zooming in on its general location.

The building was the only one within a three-block radius. Lots of vegetation surrounded the area, and there was a big parking lot on the right side of the building. With its odd, circular shape, it faced the Manhattan skyline, glowing like a lone jewel in the vast empty surface.

There was an odd feeling he couldn't quite put his finger on as he focused his mind to spit out the little noticeable details, the vast and empty lot next to the building, the distance of the office building from the other structures, and the fences surrounding the wide and vacant space. He stared at the screen. Why would a man of Tack's status choose to hold his lucrative business away from the city's main drag?

Unless he was hiding something. Now, that was a thought Demetrius lingered on. Why had Tack flown all his potential clients in instead of having them come to meet him?

The anklets meant something to Pritchard Tack. Demetrius inspected the accessories and made a wild guess. It had to be . . . it's gotta be.

If there was anything he could credit himself with, it was his relentless pursuit and patience in seeking answers. The nagging feeling was there for a reason. Penetration would be the key, and it wouldn't be difficult once he'd set the wheels in motion.

He leaned back against the supple leather chair and rested his hand at the back of his head for support. Why had he zeroed in on this Pritchard Tack in particular from among the other leads they had? Easy . . . the son of a bitch was filthy rich, and he could buy his way into anything his heart desired. He'd lost his family . . . or had he really?

It was like a whole quiz sheet of questions, and all Demetrius had to do was fill in the blanks. He had the answer right at his fingertips, and yet he couldn't quite make heads or tails of it. What would a man like Pritchard Tack want? And why?

Demetrius let the questions roll around in his head, dissecting, arguing, and presuming. He could always march in there in the middle of the night and see what he would see. Yeah, that was the easiest way to go about it. Sherlock Holmes would be put to shame by the time this little project was over.

Jordan and Allison had been meeting in secret with Darryl to plan menus and seating arrangements. The mix of humans and vampires would be challenging as far as meal preparations, but Darryl was more than willing to rise to the occasion.

After all, this was for his longtime employer and friend. Nothing could be more satisfying than to help with a momentous occasion such as this. Allison was turning tables to keep everything hush-hush. With all the hand-written invitations out and RSVPs returning with a quick turnaround, the last thing left to do was to get Pritchard out of the building so the rest of them could get started on the final prep and the decorating.

"The menu is set," the aged gentleman announced as he rushed around his desk, sat down, and spread a printed paper on the table. "We are having terrine of foie gras with rhubarb gelée, spiced apple chutney and a slice of toasted *kougelhopf* served with French string bean salad as an appetizer. Then for the main dish, I'll be preparing roasted milk-fed veal chop with an aged Parmesan cheese crust and onion ravioli with pistou in a sage reduction[1]." Darryl stopped to watch Allison lick her lips and laughed with gusto.

"Desserts will consist of Raspberry Napoleon, raspberry coulis, and rhubarb ice cream. The only difference will be that our vampire friends will have a small tureen of blood on the side—warm or cold, depending on their preference—to be poured over the meat like *aus jus*."

"God, Darryl, you're making my mouth water. I'm sure anything made by you will be divine." Allison teased the celebrated chef. He blinked before accepting the compliment with a gracious bow.

"Thank you, mademoiselle," Darryl chirped. "If there's anything else you wanted to add, just let me know right away so I can make the necessary adjustments."

"I sure will." Allison smiled sweetly, a smile Jordan knew so well. Her vampire friend was a charmer and could coax even a statue to sing and dance for her should she wish it.

With the food planning all squared away, all they needed to do in the next two days was to wait, get ready, and have fun.

---

1. Featured menu is from the now-defunct L'Orangerie Restaurant in Los Angeles

"How's it going, my man?" Tor asked, watching Harrow as he emerged from the bathroom, a flurry of foggy mist trailing behind him.

"Just weird. How are you doing?" Harrow grunted and twitched a smile with his fangs showing their tips, still reeling from the changes his body was going through. It had been two days since his feeding, and the blasted effects were still causing him trouble, from his shifting eyesight and bipolar hearing to his uncontrolled aggression. Damn, he needed to take a course in Attitude 101.

"Well, let me tell you. I'm bored as hell, and I miss going out with you." Tor smiled, showing a perfect set of pearly whites and a pair of sturdy canines.

"Ha! You wish you could go out with me. But sorry, buddy, this guy is taken." Harrow laughed, walked straight to the closet, and opened it with a curse. He thought about Jordan and how he'd tried to avoid her on several occasions. Harrow had acted like a damned idiot, concentrating on how his body was reacting to her instead of what she was saying. The unwanted feral reaction every time she was around might give him a complex. Now, he wasn't just a diseased freak. He was a diseased horn-dog freak.

"I don't know about you, but I like the subtle changes in you. The gleam in your eyes compliments your arching eyebrows, and that hissing and growling is a total turn-on. And man-oh-man, that tube you're sporting between your legs will soon be a legend." Tor chuckled, getting a kick out of annoying his roommate. He was ready to rock in the brand new outfit Allison had forced on him during their shopping trip. He looked like James Bond, except bigger and nastier.

The dark brown Armani blazer paired with tan slacks and Gucci loafers were a far cry from his usual work clothes of jeans, leathers, and military boots. Looking like a million dollars, Tor lounged back in a relaxed pose as he waited for Harrow to get his shit together for Pritchard's big day. However, appearances could be deceiving, because the vampire was packing some serious ammo underneath his expensive garment. It was like an AmEx card. You should never leave home without it.

"Yeah, whatever, laugh all you want." Harrow looked over the choices. There was not much there except the suit Allison had encouraged him to buy. The Dolce and Gabbana narrow pinstripe grey wool suit with a slim-cut, notched-lapel jacket was paired with flat-front trousers that had been tailored to perfection. It made him look like a sleek panther, hugging his lean but powerful, elegant body.

He shrugged out of the towel wrapped around his waist and pulled on crisp, brand new CK boxers from the drawer. Next came a simple white shirt, open at the chest. He opted out of wearing a tie, thinking the thing would be much too restricting around his neck. The outfit fit like a glove, and he felt like a champ as soon as he put on a pair of black Bruno Magli leather shoes to complete his ensemble. He took two push daggers from their vault and inserted them in the suit's inner pocket before grabbing a Glock and placing it inside his waistband. Now, he was almost ready.

He crossed the room, heading to the bathroom to check his attire in the mirror. As soon as Tor saw him, he let out a whistle. "Damn, step aside Bradley Cooper, I think a new babe magnet is in the house."

"Shut your grill, will you? You're beginning to get on my nerves," Harrow warned.

Nevertheless, when he caught a sight of his reflection in the mirror, he was pleased with his appearance. Well, it turned out he tidied up real good. If his hair would cooperate, he'd be the complete, spruced-up package. He ran his fingers through his longish hair and fingered it into place, the curls of his blond locks touching the collar of his white shirt.

Harrow finished off by adding sleek black sunglasses. He strode out of the bathroom feeling good about himself. The lesions were already in the mending stage, fading into a pinkish tint that was almost unnoticeable.

"Ready?" Harrow asked, and Tor stood up, appraising him with a stupid grin on his face. "Don't say it."

"Fine. Let's go." Tor chuckled.

They met the rest of the group in the lobby of the office building. Cyrus and Lambert both sported fine Italian blazers over their dark slacks and looked very much like the guys from *Miami Vice*, except bigger and meaner looking. Cyrus's movements were still feeble, although God knew the man was trying hard to suck the pain in. Yeah, being stabbed deep in your abdomen would make movement hurt like a bitch for anyone.

Rohnert had opted for the more subdued attire of a black wool vest and pants over a stark white shirt with a lavender tie. The man looked lethal, despite the elegant exterior. Judging by the bulges underneath the vest, he was packing, too.

Pritchard arrived just as they were teasing each other over their cleaned-up act. His light grey Zegna striped suit in wool and silk fabric had been paired with a khaki striped twill and fancy silk tie, making him into a walking mannequin of glamour and impeccability. The one thing missing was a bow, and he could be presented as a grand and very expensive package any woman would love to unwrap.

Amidst the manly whistles of appreciation, Pritchard downplayed the rascals hounding him. "Ready to paint the town red, boys?" he asked, adjusting the lapel on his jacket.

"As ready as we'll ever be." Harrow checked the time on his cell phone. Thank God for the longer winter nights. They had more room to move. Six in the evening, and the ladies had three full hours to move and get stuff ready.

This was going to be an interesting boys' night out. Three humans and three vampires made for an unusual mix, but the rest needed to be given ample time for preparation for the surprise party.

A black stretch Hummer was waiting for them in front of the lobby, and each man climbed in like eager teenagers embarking on their first outing. The mood was charged, and everyone seemed relaxed, banking on having a good time.

Allison had taken care of the dinner reservation at Le Bernardin, which granted them a cozy and exclusive private room decorated with black and white balloons. After the chef had presented them with options under the strict orders of Allison, the three vampires opted for a rare Filet Mignon, and Pritchard went for the chef's choice of dinner offerings.

Afterward, servers dressed in pristine white suits came in with bottles of Cristal and Dom Perignon Rose. Bottles popped at the same time, and the merriment began as soon as the appetizers came and tongues started to wag.

Harrow clinked on his glass as he stood up. As soon as Tor and Lambert ceased yapping, he raised his flute to give a toast, belatedly remembering to remove his sunglasses.

"Ahem . . ." He cleared his throat, and everyone laughed.

He looked at Pritchard and spoke unrehearsed, but the words came from the heart.

"Over the past few months, I often wondered where I would be if you hadn't found me. Most likely, I'd be lying next to a ditch or disintegrated and forgotten in time. You're a gift from heaven, if there ever was one. I'm one lucky SOB that you didn't give up on me.

"Now, I look back, and I see what has drawn me to you, aside from the fact that you refused to let me go out there and threw away the key." Everyone snickered.

"You are the kind of man who sees the good quality in a person despite their current predicament or their lot in life. You're a lifeline for those of us who are trying to get a grip on life and a light in the deep, dark hole we were in.

"I think it is safe to say that I speak on behalf of us all gathered here when I tell you that none of us could hope to find a better friend, a protector of our interests wherever they lay, and a director who would take us to a better place than we've ever been."

"Aye, aye." All the guys saluted, and Pritchard smiled in acknowledgment.

"Happy Birthday, Pritchard! May all your wishes come true, my friend, and may the Gods of fortune keep smiling down on you for the rest of your life. We can't ask for a better friend."

Harrow raised his glass in Pritchard's direction, and everyone else did the same before taking long gulps until their glasses were empty.

Backslapping and awkward hugging followed, and then Pritchard rose. "That was a touching rendition of the Godfather, my friend, thank you." Everyone laughed.

"I could never be happier. I am surrounded by men whom I not only with trust my life and that of my daughter, but I also consider myself lucky that each one of you came into my life. You are my family, and fate couldn't have been kinder to me. Thank you from the bottom of my heart. Now drink, and let's party until we drop."

As their main entrée was being served, the conversation moved to sports, Ultimate Fighting Championship, action movies, and the latest Playboy Bunny—anything a full-blooded American male would be interested in.

As more bottles were popped open, laughter became boisterous and good-natured teasing floated around. Tor was in his element, as well as the usually quiet Rohnert, who started up with knock-knock jokes. The time passed quickly while they all had fun, and before they knew it, they were faced with the difficult decision of having to call an end to their outing so that they could move on to the real, big party.

Jordan was frantic, thanks to Allison's hyperactive mood and Gail's excitable antics as she ran around the room, singing, dancing, and babbling nonstop about her first grown-up party ever.

If this was how a mother felt with a young one, then Jordan was in big trouble, because as young as she was, the little girl was depleting every bit of energy she had. Not that she wasn't up for it. It was just—just something not for her.

What if it was time for her to go? What if Annie Butler was around and demanded her daughter back? What would she do? Damn her if she would be able to handle the separation that way. It was best if she did it on her own terms. Jordan called the shots. Either way, she knew it would kill her.

Then there was Harrow. How in the name of love could she love him and yet plan on leaving him behind? *Wretched* was a good name for her, a tag most appropriate for someone who toyed with another person's feelings before leaving him high and dry.

She was taken out of her self-deprecating trance when she heard a noise coming from the closet. She ran and found Gail pulling her dress off the hanger.

"What do you think you're doing, missy?"

"I want to change now." She kept tugging at the hem of the dressHer eyes implored Jordan to help.

"If you change now, that means no more ice cream or snacks for you. We don't want stains and stuff on your dress."

"Okay, no more ice cream." Gail bobbed her head up and down, willing to accept any condition to get what she wanted. Jordan exhaled before removing the dress from the hanger.

Gail removed her T-shirt and shorts, jumping up and down in the process. "I'm ready, I'm ready."

Jordan unzipped the dress and lowered it onto the floor so that Gail could hop through the opening. She pulled up and zipped the back together. She could see Gail's excitement in the gleam of her eyes as the little girl tried to jump up and down to see herself in the bathroom mirror.

"Here, let me help you up." Jordan picked up the little girl and propped her on the granite vanity countertop. Both their mouths gaped open as they looked at Gail's reflection in the mirror.

"You're so beautiful." Jordan gushed.

"I like the dress, Jordan." Gail's smile was as wide as the Pacific waters. An ocean of contentment and pleasure crossed the little girl's face as she stared back at herself in the mirror.

"You are the best-looking angel I've ever seen."

It was not an exaggeration, because the dress complimented the red curls cascading from the side of her face down to her shoulders. The little ribbon tie in the back gave a slight shape to the ankle-length dress, and the elaborate off-white embroidery on the chest lent the outfit a dainty contrast to the fabric color as well as her hair.

Gail smiled, pleased with herself. Jordan worked to tie an off-white ribbon around her hair, which showed off her cute little face even more.

"I want my shoes now," she demanded.

"Gail? What did I teach you to say?" Jordan raised a reprimanding eyebrow.

"Say please. Please?"

"Get your tights and your shoes from inside the closet for me, please."

She lowered Gail, who skittered across the bathroom and into the bedroom like a live rocket and was back before Jordan could even count to five.

"Here." She panted, handing her off-white ballet shoes with half-inch heels and matching off-white tights.

They worked on the getting Gail into the stockings. Her squirming wound up being helpful, making the process of pulling up the tights easier. With the outfit completed, she gave Jordan a tight hug. "Thank you," she said, beaming before running out of the room. If Jordan was a betting woman, she'd put her money on Gail showing her dress off to any available soul she could find who would be willing to give her a compliment.

With the live rocket out of the room, Jordan had a short moment to ponder the recent changes in her life before she had to start putting on a little makeup and getting into her own gown. Yes, she was going to wear a God-forsaken gown, because Allison said so.

And yes, she'd agreed—or more accurately, she had let the vampire talk her into it. If it had been left for her to decide, a cocktail dress would have sufficed, but no. Just like her father, Allison didn't do things halfway. It always had to be the best—the one that would make a statement.

As Jordan finished the final touches on her makeup, she added a sheer lip gloss to complete the ethereal look Allison had taught her. Her hair was pulled into an elegant chignon that highlighted her thin, long neck. She felt naked with her hair styled away from her face. *One night. This all will be over in one night,* she reminded herself again.

She glanced at the garment bag hanging from the sill of the doorway. It read Versace, a name she'd only read in fashion magazines and on the

Internet back in her college days. Not by any means a household name, the dress was breathtaking, expensive, and so not her.

It demanded refined movement, an elegance she didn't possess, and confidence she lacked. Feeling like an impostor, she slid the zipper down and felt the luxurious material in her hand. Splendid and soft, the fabric screamed classy.

With a sigh, she took it out of the bag and placed it on the bed. Jordan pulled out the box of stiletto heels Allison had purchased, black platform shoes that boasted crystals and five-inch heels. Wondering what type of mishap she'd create wearing them made Jordan want to cringe. She was tall enough that wearing heels was never a need. This would test her balance and her endurance, and it was anyone's guess on how long she'd stay vertical, instead of facedown on the floor.

Slipping into the gown was like sliding into another persona, and she couldn't decide whether she was okay with it or not. She walked to the bathroom to check herself out, and the first few steps proved that she had a long night ahead of her. Each step was labored and unnatural, making her feel like she was going to tip over, like a toddler learning to walk—difficult, scary, and yet exciting.

Her breath caught at the sight of the woman staring back at her. The long, bustier dress of delicate, knitted pink and gold metal mesh hugged her body like a second skin. The bodice was finished with an intricate weave of drapes and pleats. The dress was stunning on her, if she could just muster the guts to admit it.

The color of the gown emphasized her creamy complexion and added more fire to the color of her hair. She'd never thought she'd see the day when she looked and felt glamorous.

After doing a last minute check in the mirror, Jordan grabbed the little purse Allison had bought for her. She walked the length of the hallway up to the adjoining office building where the party would be held. The grand conference room would be transformed into a Las Vegas casino, completed with slot machines, card tables, roulette wheels, and actual dealers Allison had hired for the night.

Jordan walked into the most elaborate room she'd ever seen in her entire life. Allison, who was already dressed like a Roman Goddess in her white floor length one-shoulder gown, was busy considering some last-minute details with Darryl. She looked up and beamed the moment she saw Jordan headed their way.

Darryl found his tongue first. "*Mademoiselle, vous regardez ravissante ce soir.*" He took her hand and kissed it.

Jordan laughed. *What the hell did he just say?*

Allison hugged her and whispered into her ear, "He said you look ravishing tonight," and laughed.

The ringing of Allison's phone afforded Jordan an opportunity to collect herself, not being someone who was used to compliments. It wasn't easy to hear others telling her she looked good after a long solitary existence.

"They're here. They took Daddy to his bedroom first so he could freshen up." She rolled her eyes. "But Harrow, Rohnert, and Tor are on their way. Let's get ready, guys."

Allison and Darryl scrambled away as if their derrieres were on fire, and Jordan was left in the middle of the room with no idea of what to do or how to act. She turned around just in time as Harrow, Rohnert, and Tor entered the room.

Lord, have mercy! she exclaimed to herself when she took one good look at Harrow walking her way. With rattled nerves, she smoothed a wisp of hair that had fallen loose and tucked it behind her ear. Her eyes ravaged him. She had known he was an attractive man, but she had no idea how fine looking and virile he was—a stud in every meaning of the word. Jordan felt weak in the knees and stumbled forward by the time he reached her. Harrow reached out and circled his arm around her waist. She caught a whiff of his scent, and it sent her mind and core reeling.

It was criminal to be that sexy and beautiful at the same time. Jordan inclined her head to get a glimpse of his face when he didn't say anything.

"Har—row? Is everything okay?"

He was staring at her in a way she hadn't seen before. It made her uncomfortable, on the edge of fright that he found her appearance distasteful, possibly thinking she was better off the way she looked every day instead of the glamorous impersonator standing before him.

"Harrow, please say something," she begged. Her hand tentatively reached up to remove his sunglasses so that she could witness his disgust firsthand.

Say something, you idiot.

Harrow had his arm around Jordan's waist, and he was devouring her with his eyes. Words eluded him. All he could do was stare at her, drinking in everything about her. His mind was wrapped up in the wish that he could sink his fangs into her to taste her sweet blood. He needed to take her somewhere private and unwrap her like gift on Christmas morning.

What the hell was going on with him? Where had all these thoughts come from? For a second there, he'd looked like he was ready to eat her, a rabid dog salivating over a bone.

"Harrow, what's going on?"

Jordan's voice finally penetrated his clouded mind, and he righted himself. He eased his hold on her waist enough for her to stand on her own, not that she'd needed his help. He was the one who felt like he was going to crumble any time. Harrow didn't let her go. He couldn't. If sniffing her was the only thing he could do, he would inhale all of her like the dog he was.

"Y—you are so . . . beautiful." He stumbled through his words. His eyes drank every single bit of her like she was a vintage wine, including the sediment, every little particle he could get.

Jordan let out a sigh of relief before she braced her hand against his chest. "I think you ought to look in the mirror. I have never seen a man as gorgeous as you are."

That made him smile despite the boogie-woogie that was happening inside. He felt like a grand perv because he wanted to touch every single part of her body and dip his hand in between the mounds staring back at him, covered halfway by the off-shoulder knockout she wore.

"Jesus Christ, Jordan. You're perfect." He let his eyes linger on her bosom. Harrow did what he knew she'd allow him to do and ran his mouth along the side of her neck, skimming, touching close enough to taste. "Oh, Lord, you'll be the death of me."

Jordan seemed jazzed by the lavish attention. She arched her back, willing her body to meet his demands right that very minute.

Someone cleared their throat . . . more than once before they ended their make-out session. Harrow growled at the intrusion.

"Easy there, boy." Tor patted him on the shoulder before sweeping an appreciative gaze at Jordan. "You are a vision of loveliness tonight."

Jordan laughed, her expression revealing that Tor's words had surprised and pleased her.

Harrow pulled Jordan closer and glared at the vampire. "Back off, my man," he warned.

"Sure thing, man, but I want to remind you lovebirds that you make me sick with all the PDA in the middle of the dance floor."

Jordan and Harrow blinked, looked at each other before their gaze swept across the room. Everyone they knew, and some they didn't, were looking at them with unconcealed interest and amused expressions.

"Holy cow," Jordan muttered and blushed.

"I love you, and I don't care who's watching," Harrow whispered, but he whisked her to the side when Allison made a signal for the lights to be turned off. The room was suddenly pitch black, and the sound of shushing hissed across the room.

The door creaked open. Lambert stepped in first and held the door for Pritchard. Once Pritchard walked in, everyone jumped up and screamed surprise at the top of their lungs. The lights blinked on and bathed the room with light as the slot machines sprang to life.

Pritchard stopped mid-step, hands on his waist, but his face was all smiles and radiating with pleasure. He made a sweeping bow in front of all his well-wishers before he was engulfed with hugs and kisses, which were initiated by Allison. The moment between father and daughter was a tender scene worth remembering for the night, aside from the lovely woman in his arms, Harrow thought.

Looking at the tables filled with guests, the headcount tipped over the one hundred mark. Darryl could be seen moving about and helping serve the guests, even though it wasn't in his job description. He'd promised a divine feast, and he delivered.

Although the men had already eaten, they couldn't bear the thought of not tasting Darryl's creations, so they ate for the second time that evening. The blood *aus jus* was a big hit among the vampire guests.

After dinner was served, guests mingled and started to enjoy the slot machines and table games. A DJ began to play popular dance music while Pritchard and Allison made their way toward Harrow and Jordan's table, where they were joined by Tor, Rohnert, Leroy, Shelly, and Gail.

"You guys think you're slick. You led me to believe that party at the restaurant was my birthday celebration." Pritchard looked very happy and gave his daughter a kiss. She giggled.

"Well, it was, except you have another one," Tor answered.

"I'm glad you liked your surprise, Dad."

"I love it, my dear. This would rank up there as one of my most memorable birthdays."

Fast, upbeat music started playing, and Allison looked at the dance floor, which had started to fill up with couples, feet tapping to the beat of the music. Leroy stood up and began to talk shop with Pritchard, so Harrow took the opportunity to kick Tor's shin under the table.

"Ow!" he yowled.

Harrow didn't say a word, but his head was pointing and nudging in Allison's direction.

Tor glared at Harrow for a moment before he eased himself out of his seat and walked over at Allison's side.

"Care to dance?" he asked, looking uncomfortable.

"Sure."

As the two disappeared among the throng of bodies dancing and jerking to the music, Shelly spoke up. "Rohnert, would you like to dance?" she asked. From the expression on her face, she was not sure what the answer would be.

Rohnert, who had been content to be silent for the last hour, nodded and got up. He held his hand out to Shelly. She took his outstretched hand, and like the perfect gentleman that he was, Rohnert led Shelly to the dance floor.

Harrow seemed satisfied with his matchmaking skills as far as Tor was concerned. He grinned at Jordan. He hadn't let go of her hand all evening. Stroking and rubbing his thumb on her palm, he was happy to bask in their close proximity.

Just as the song ended, a slow song began, and Harrow knew he had to show off his two beautiful redheads. "Ladies, shall we?"

Gail bounced up and down on her chair in pure excitement, and Jordan couldn't help the sheer joy that wrapped itself around her like a warm, security blanket. She got up while Harrow picked up Gail. He led them both to the dance floor, one female on each arm.

They shuffled the girl around while Harrow enfolded his arms around them both, and they swayed to the sound of the gentle music that drifted around them. They looked very much like a tight, solid, family unit, and Jordan's heart ached. Harrow's eyes were closed, and he gave off the impression of contentment and satisfaction.

"Harrow?"

"Hmm . . ." Harrow's eyes remained closed.

"Can I call you Daddy?" Gail asked.

Harrow's eyes shot open, and he looked at Jordan, who had stiffened, before directing his gaze at the little girl. His voice was even when he answered.

"Sure. I would love it." He kissed her on the forehead, and his arms tightened around them. "But don't you think that when you have a daddy you're supposed to have a mommy, too?"

What a loaded question. But who cares?

"I want Jordan to be my mommy, because we can't find my mommy." Gail's eyes held the innocence and expectation that melted and tore at Jordan's heart at the same time. "I can have two, right?"

"Sure you can. There's no rule that says you can't have two." Harrow smiled encouragingly and looked at Jordan for confirmation.

The uncertainty he saw in her face gave him pause. She wasn't ready for any of this, and the idea might scare her away. However, it was too late to back off now.

He felt Jordan's body became rigid, and he began rubbing her back in rhythmic motion, hoping she'd get the message.

"Gail, let's give Jordan some time to think about it, okay?"

Gail nodded and burrowed her head in Jordan's chest. It took a few moments before he felt her relax again. He didn't stop rubbing her back until the music had stopped and they had to go back to their seats.

Allison was left at the center of the banquet room and called for Pritchard just as a birthday cake was rolled on top of the table next to them. She urged all the guests to gather around the table, after which everyone started singing the birthday song. Pritchard blew out all fifty-five candles, and a loud hooting and clapping followed.

Just as everyone was returning to their seats, a human security guard positioned at the front lobby scrambled over to Cyrus and Lambert's table. Judging from his appearance and the terrible shaking of his body, Harrow realized that something was up.

At that point, Cyrus called him to come over, along with Tor, Drake, and Rohnert. When the seven men ran out of the room, Jordan instructed Allison to hang on to Gail, and she followed behind them. She clutched at her purse, which held a little dagger that fit inside.

"What's going on?" Tor asked, releasing the buttons of his blazer and reaching for his Glock.

Rohnert answered. "I can sense an unwelcome presence. Arm yourselves."

Each one of them produced a weapon and began moving in measured steps—quiet, stealthy, and calculating. Before they could move further, they saw Dante streak past the lobby, gun in hand, followed by another security guard. They disappeared into the first floor hallway.

Cyrus pointed to his eyes and then in the direction of Pritchard's office. Rohnert and Harrow took the front, while Tor flanked Harrow. At the same time, Cyrus, Lambert, and Drake surrounded Pritchard.

"I think you guys will need this." Jordan's voice was low enough not to catch attention, and they all pivoted to see her carrying their choice weapons. She threw Kalimetal in Harrow and Rohnert's direction, and there was an axe for Tor and more guns for the three humans.

Harrow's expression was grim when he realized Jordan was going to join them. He had a big problem with it, but this wasn't the right time to address his male pride. As soon as they turned the corner, they heard Dante's order ring out.

"Don't move!"

Several shots rang out before they got a chance to reposition themselves and get a better look. They heard grunts and more popping sounds, and they all ran to the open doorway, where the security guard's body lay crumpled on the floor, blood dripping from a chest wound. Rohnert acted fast and pulled his body out of the way.

They heard skirmishes inside and jumped when bullets started shooting like darts in their direction. Harrow, Rohnert, and Tor were able to clear the doorway and jumped for cover behind the set of lounging sofas inside Pritchard's office, while Cyrus was left outside with Pritchard, Jordan, and Drake.

"Pritchard's hit, Pritchard's hit." Drake's voice drowned out the sounds of the guns firing.

Harrow felt his blood surge to a boiling point at Drake's announcement. He looked at the others and communicated with hand signals. Rohnert flashed all five fingers twice giving them a heads-up of how many people to expect.

Tor and Lambert would provide cover while they attacked. Harrow gave a signal, and as guns started firing, he and Rohnert jumped from behind their cover and ran toward the direction from which they were certain the others were hiding.

Their planned surprise attack was met with an equally surprising number of men in front of them. Two were planted in front, and several others flanked the man in the middle. Crap, it was a vampire in the middle. In fact, there were vampires everywhere.

"Rohnert, why am I not surprised to find you here?"

"Demetrius . . ."

"You left without a word and abandoned me. Then, I heard that you taught—" He threw a disgusted look in Harrow's direction and spat. "You taught this diseased piece of shit the art form."

"It's my business whom I deemed worthy of the art, Demetrius. I never hid that fact from you or your father." Rohnert's tone was smooth as silk and dead serious.

"Then we shall find out how good you all are."

Before Rohnert could respond, a vampire with a sad imitation of Elvis sideburns jumped in front of him, looking every bit like he was dying to get cremated. They engaged in a circling pattern while the funky-looking vampire sneered at him. They were almost the same size.

Rohnert moved fast. His opponent held a gun and a dagger in one hand. Such close quarters made him queasy about the gun. He had to get rid of it fast. With surging adrenaline, he punched both Kalimetals forward, landing on the weapons and missing the vampire's hand by mere inches. The weapons flew in the air, and Rohnert threw one Kalimetal in one hand so fast the naked eye couldn't even follow the movement, and he caught the dagger by the handle and the gun by its muzzle.

The funky vampire staggered from the impact and the juggling act, but he recovered fast. He lunged forward, but a quick swipe of the Kalimetal across his torso sent him reeling back. And what do you know? He crackled, sizzled, and went buh-bye.

"Who is smirking now?" Rohnert chuckled before letting his index finger roll inside the trigger guard, blowing on the muzzle and then sliding the gun into his waistband. Wheeling around, he next engaged a young vampire, handing the boy a quick death by slinging a dagger at him when he wasn't looking.

Harrow was focused on Demetrius, while Tor took the distractions everywhere as a cue to come out of his hiding spot.

With his axe poised, Tor stepped out and got busy with a vampire who took him for a monkey bar, hanging on his neck and trying to pull him down. Tor swept his hand over his head, grabbed a handful of the vampire's hair, and jerked him away.

"Ow!" The vampire howled as Tor popped his axe on the man's head before he could throw a punch.

"Damn, it's not even the Fourth of July," he said as the fireworks exploded before his eyes.

Jordan emerged from the door as sounds of metal hitting metal continued. She glanced at Harrow when a bullet zipped by her line of vision. She pivoted to face the shooter. No wonder he'd missed. The recoil was too much for him to handle with one hand.

"You must be the lucky one Cyrus busted, huh?" She smiled at the one-armed vampire and flashed her fangs.

"Shut up." His lips curled up and exposed long-ass fangs that would have put Dracula to shame.

The vampire aimed the gun in Jordan's direction. Before he could fire another shot, Jordan cartwheeled toward him in a blur, kicking the gun away from his shaky grasp. He clasped her ankle and spun her around. Jordan rolled her body, unsheathed one Kalimetal, and struck him on the leg. The vampire fell to the ground, his eyes mirroring fear, and then more fear at the sizzling sound.

"Don't worry, I won't let you suffer." Jordan flipped her body upright before striking his almost-mutilated body with two slashes, creating a letter X. She didn't even wait to watch as she turned around to hunt for her next victim.

Harrow was fighting an even battle against Demetrius. The vampire had a dagger, and as fast as Harrow moved, striking his Kalimetal forward, Demetrius evaded with faster movements. Grunts and groans were echoing in the room as each vampire was engaged with one or two opponents.

Harrow stopped tracking Jordan's movement and focused on Demetrius after realizing the vampire was as well-trained as he was. Each strike was deflected, and each hit was blocked.

They went at it for some time before Harrow decided he was better off closing his eyes and feeling the vibe off the vampire. Sounds of moving feet and shuffling bodies were all around him, but he singled out his opponent's movement.

They pushed, kicked, and shoved, each trying to beat the other at their game until Demetrius was cornered by the glass of the window. Harrow thrust his Kalimetal and struck the vampire on the arm. The sizzling sound began, but before he could finish off the vampire, Demetrius twisted to the side, lunging forward and thrusting the dagger deep into Harrow's abdomen.

Oh, fuck!

His energy started to wane at once, and he could feel his strength draining as if he was a faucet turned on full blast. Harrow summoned one last call to his depleting oomph, lashed out with his weapon, and struck the vampire in the chest.

The last thing he remembered was the crackle, sizzle, and pop before he stumbled backward and fell to the carpeted floor.

"Harrow!" He heard Jordan's hysterical voice and other frenetic shouts before his lights were turned off. Black was all he could see, and then he heard a click.

"Jesus Christ," Tor shouted as he finished off his second kill for the night and ran toward his fallen brother's body. The other vampires were eventually killed, and the rest of their team had arrived to finish the clean-up. Everything had happened so fast, his mind still reeled from the incident. How the vampires had found them and penetrated the building was a question he'd kill to get answered.

Amid the chaos, he dropped his axe and pulled Harrow's body from the floor, slung him over his shoulder, and raced toward the infirmary. This was a nightmare of gigantic proportion.

Jordan was right on his heels, tears streaming down her face. She kept chanting Harrow's name over and over again.

They reached the infirmary, where a preternaturally calm Shelly was working on Pritchard. There was blood on her dress and a bleak expression on her face. The clinic held four beds. The second one was occupied, but the body lying on it was covered by a bloodied white sheet.

Tor laid Harrow's body on one of the narrow beds, shooting a glance across the room at Shelly. "Doc, anyone else we can get in here to help Harrow?" Shelly, who was still working on a pale, almost gray, Pritchard shook her head and a sob tore through her. The machine attached to their boss had flat-lined and the shrieking sound wailed, deafening and frighteningly real.

Tor looked down at Harrow and knew he had to do what he could at the moment. He started pumping on Harrow's chest and began CPR when he felt the vampire's heart falter and stop.

"Harrow, my man, stay with me." He grunted with each pounding effort. "Stay with me, damn it!"

Jordan shivered against the cold air that blew from the air conditioner vents, but she didn't budge from the chair where she had been sitting for the last six hours. No one and nothing could make her move away from Harrow.

Sometime during the course of the trance she'd been in, someone had placed a jacket around her bare shoulders. Her gown, now ruined, was stained with blood, but she dared not move. She had to be around when he came back to them.

After several hours of grueling surgery, Shelly had removed fragments of Dangeran that were lodged throughout his abdomen. The dagger had splintered, throwing pieces of the Dangeran all over his stomach region. Each removal was painstaking and slow, causing Harrow to go into cardiac arrest twice. He was losing a lot blood, and a transfusion had to be done during the operation.

It was a lucky break when Jones stepped in and volunteered to help out, suggesting that animal blood be transfused instead of human blood. It was still a mystery to them all how Harrow was reacting to the new diet, but the biggest mystery that now boggled their minds was how did he escape the wrath of the Dangeran? Not that they had a problem with the end result. Harrow was alive, and that was all that mattered.

"Jordan, would you like to take a break, and I'll stay and watch him?" Tor's voice drifted from behind her, and his warm hand squeezed her shoulder.

"No, I'll stay with him."

Tor eased back and leaned against the wall with a sigh. The man, for once, was at loss for words. Nothing could be said that hadn't been said before. Fear and uncertainty ruled, and silence engulfed them, trapping them in a nightmare that held no promise of better days ahead.

Her tears had dried out. Marathon crying could do that to a person, and she felt drained, like she'd gone through a wringer. Jordan's muscles ached everywhere, her back was stiff, but most of the pain was concentrated around the area of her heart.

Like her, Tor hadn't left Harrow's side, even with all the commotion and heartbreak happening around them. He stood next to her, quiet, unmoving, and just as heartbroken as she was. The only thing that filled the long stretch of silence within the stark white walls around them was the steady beeping of the machines hooked up to Harrow's arms and torso.

Jordan had no idea what the machines were for or what the readouts meant. All she cared about that she didn't have to hear the flat-lining sound. The scary as hell wail of someone in distress. The sound that signaled the time was gone and the person was no longer there.

Shelly had done everything within her power to remove the poison of the Dangeran. Time would tell the true extent of Harrow's injuries. There might be permanent damage, Shelly warned, but with the nature of Harrow's condition, there was nothing much she could offer anyone but a little sliver of hope that at the very least the Dangeran hadn't popped him out of existence like it did the others.

Jordan held Harrow's hand like it was her own lifeline. His clammy hands were almost lifeless in her grasp, and fear shook her to the very core.

Life would never be the same for her. Harrow had changed her and the course of her destiny.

Oh, Christ! Please come back, Harrow. Just come back to me, she pleaded.

Jordan watched his face, ashen and sunken. His eyes were shut tight, given the morphine pumped into his system. It was a good thing that his body took the painkillers, and there had been no adverse reaction as far as she could see. However, as Shelly had cautioned, there were no guarantees as far as potential side effects, given that Harrow seemed like he had gone through some internal changes in the past week.

As if on cue, the doctor walked into the room. This time, she was out of her cocktail dress and garbed in scrubs with stethoscope hanging around her neck. Her eyes were bloodshot from lack of sleep and from crying. There were serious bags underneath her eyes when she flicked a glance at Jordan before she started checking the machines for readouts.

She initialed the paper feed, turned to check the amount of liquid in the IV bag, and adjusted the dose. "Is there anything I can get for you?" The effort it took for Shelly even to speak was all too obvious, but she managed to keep her voice from cracking. She still maintained a professional façade, even if it was obvious she was a total mess inside. Shelly lifted the sheet that covered Harrow's body and slid it down to his thighs.

"No, thank you," Jordan answered, trying to keep her voice as even as she could.

Shelly inspected the bandage wrapped around Harrow's stomach and noted some blood seeping through the saturated white gauze. "I have to change his dressing."

Walking toward the sink, she pressed on a walkie-talkie and called for a nurse on duty. After snapping on surgical gloves, she and the nurse worked on removing Harrow's bandage, shifting his body from side to side. Harrow was dead to the world. The stimuli didn't rouse him from his deep sleep at all.

After the bandage had been changed, Shelly tossed the gloves in a biohazard container, jotted down some notes on a clipboard, and left the room after nodding in Jordan's direction.

It had been like that for the next day. With him in a drug-induced sleep, Harrow's breathing was the only good news to which Jordan could cling. At least he was alive and breathing. It was a consolation she would consider a victory until he was back on his feet again.

What they had thought would be a perfect night had been turned upside down, shifted into a nightmare that none of them could have ever imagined happening. The whole facility had been thrown into fits of fury and tumult. No one could make sense of the events that had led to the attack.

The facility, now in total lockdown, appeared to be a just remnant of its former self—quiet, mourning, and vengeful.

The stench of death still hung in the air. So much blood had been spilled.

A knock on the door shook her out of her reverie. She looked up and saw Rohnert at the door. He walked in, his face a tight mask of emotions Jordan knew so well.

"Has he come around?" His eyes flickered to her hand that clutched Harrow's, and his features softened a fraction.

"No."

"Jordan . . . I'm so sorry," Rohnert offered and sat on his haunches until he was at her eye level.

"You have nothing to be sorry about."

"I feel like I brought them here. Demetrius wanted me. That's why he came." Rohnert's voice was barely audible, and if she knew him at all, he was beating himself up for what had happened.

Jordan's gaze left Harrow's face to focus on Rohnert. There was guilt in his eyes that she didn't understand. The lines in his face were deeper, harsher. His jaw was clenched so tight, it looked like it could crack at any time. Repugnance shone on his face.

"You heard what he said. He was surprised to find you here. If there's anything, we can be glad that you taught us what you did. It helped us in our time of need. Don't beat yourself up over this. I'm sure Harrow would feel the same way."

"I don't know what to say." Rohnert dropped his eyes on the floor and sighed. Unshed tears were threatening, and his lids closed to keep his emotions at bay.

"You don't have to say anything right now. Just promise me that when the time comes, you will help me hunt the father down. His family owes us —all of us—so much. I think it's just and right that we collect what is due us."

There was a slight twitching in Rohnert's jaw. He looked up and locked eyes with Jordan. "You have my word," he answered.

"Thank you."

Rohnert reached out and patted Jordan's arm before he got up and positioned himself next to Tor. They leaned against the wall in agreeable silence.

Jordan had no idea how many more hours passed or when she fell asleep, head bent over the mattress next to Harrow's body, still clutching his hand.

When she woke and looked up, she found Rohnert and Tor fast asleep, still leaning against the wall, but slumped on the floor. Jordan checked the time on the wall clock. She'd been out for three hours. Harrow hadn't roused from his drug-induced sleep.

With as little noise she could get away with, she let go of his hand and tiptoed to the bathroom. She needed some time alone to collect herself. Tears were long gone and dried up. Jordan looked at herself in the mirror. Her mascara had smeared under her eyes. She turned the faucet on and washed away the remnants of her party makeup, scrubbing her face with hot water until it felt raw. After she wiped her face with a paper towel, she sat on the toilet, rested her elbows on her knees, and covered her face with her hands.

God, she had no idea how long the wait would be, but it didn't matter. She'd be waiting for him however long it took. *Then what?* the nagging voice in the back of her mind asked. *Are you going to wait for him forever?*

A slight movement in the room brought her on her feet so fast. Tor and Rohnert were surfacing from their sleep, stretching, when she came back into the room. Harrow was squirming under the sheet, his eyes pressed together as if in pain, and his hand was reaching out for something.

"Do you want me to call Shelly?" Tor volunteered.

"Yes."

She ran to his side and clasped his hand in hers. The moment their hands touched, he relaxed and sank back to sleep. By the time Shelly arrived, he had already returned to his deep slumber. The doctor checked his vitals and left without a word, and Rohnert followed after her.

The room once again fell into silence, Tor taking a seat across from Jordan, arms across his chest. He, too, looked like he was going to drop at any moment from exhaustion, but he wouldn't leave her side except for a brief period when he had gone to check on Allison.

Several times, Harrow drifted in and out of consciousness. He would squeeze her hands in the process, relaxing once more when she squeezed back.

"Harrow, I love you, baby." She had no idea how many times she whispered the words in his ear, and she didn't care. She'd say it over and over.

She must have fallen asleep again, because the next time she surfaced, she felt Harrow's hand on her head where it rested next to his side. He was rubbing her head, as if comforting her.

"Harrow, oh my God, you're awake," she gasped and shot out of her chair. Jordan pressed the call button to summon the nurse, or Shelly, or anyone.

Harrow knew it was Jordan next to him, even if he didn't open his eyes. Going by her scent and the even breathing, she was asleep. He could recognize one other person just by the snoring. He knew Tor was in there, too, wherever he was. Harrow's lids felt like they were made of lead and opening them became an effort.

A sharp pain shot up in middle of his body when he tried to move. Sinking back into the pillow, he took his time, regulated his breathing.

Then everything came back to him. The night out with the guys, seeing Jordan in her knock-out outfit, kissing her, Gail calling him daddy, Pritchard blowing out the candles, and being called to respond to intruders.

They had been intruders, all right. Vampires, the fighting, and Pritchard getting shot. *Shot!* Harrow's eyes flew open, despite the weight they bore, and he winced in pain. The slightest movement caused his body to convulse. Whatever it was inside him was jacking him up real good.

"Prit—chard! Wh—where is Pritchard?" His voice was hoarse, and his throat felt like it was on fire. Dry, his tongue was thick and uncooperative.

It took a few minutes before he could focus his eyes on Jordan's face. The halo in his vision had remained. Turning his body in her direction felt like a bitch of an effort.

"Please don't move," she ordered, and he felt the mattress dip when she sat on the edge of the bed to lean closer to him. She kissed him on the lips, refusing to look him in the eye.

"Jordan . . . where is Pritchard? He was shot. I remember now." His tone was gravelly, and his throat ached. He tried to swallow, but the little movement made his insides scream in pain.

Jordan glanced across the room. He could tell by the expression on her face that she was seeking confirmation and reinforcement from Tor, although following her gaze proved to be a tough act, given the state his body was in.

"Jordan, why won't you answer me?" he implored.

"He—Ah, I . . . Pritchard didn't make it. He passed away yesterday."

A sob escaped her just as Harrow's body began to quake. Harder and harder, his body shuddered until his tears spilled out. *Wasn't life a bitch?* Just when you thought everything around you had fallen into place, someone decided to pull the rug out from under you and fucked you real hard.

"I have to go and see Allison," Harrow said.

It was his third attempt to get out of bed, and his agitation had been rewarded by more shots of sleeping medicines, courtesy of the female doctor. Shelly didn't even bat an eye, scolding him several times when he insisted on getting up and she knocked him out like a violent animal.

"Oh, no, you don't."

Tor muscled Harrow back against the mattress and held him down until he gave up. Yeah, the vampire must be feeling real good about himself right now, getting the chance of a lifetime to push him around.

"I have to see if Allison's okay."

"She's fine . . . or least, she's dealing. Harrow, I've checked on her several times, and Shelly has given her a healthy dose of sedatives to calm her down. Peyton is watching over her right now, as well as Rohnert," Jordan told him.

She wiped the sweat off his forehead. Feeling trapped, he struggled, but Tor pinned him down. "Damn you, let me go. She needs me. She has no one. Can't you see that?" Fresh tears trickled down his cheeks, and he brushed them away angrily.

"I know how you feel, Harrow, believe me. I'm hurting, too. You're not the only one who loved the man." Tor rubbed his eyes, blinking back unshed tears. "But you have to think, you're *the* Pritchard now. What good will you be to us if you're not one hundred percent?"

Harrow stilled. "If that's the case, then I'm ordering you to let me go."

"No can do. I'm on strict orders to keep you in bed."

Tor kept his hands clamped on Harrow's shoulders, keeping his weak struggles at bay. *Just great!*

"By whose orders?"

"Mine. Until I've said you're good to go, you're going to be in that bed for as long as it takes your wound to heal." Shelly grinned.

Such arrogance. "You can't make me stay against my will. Doesn't anyone get it? Allison needs me. We have to address our situation here. I have to talk to Dante and review the tapes with him."

The room grew quiet, and it took Harrow a moment to realize they were keeping something from him. "What the hell is going on?"

Jordan shot a nervous glance at Tor, who looked at Shelly. The doctor shook her head and tried to fade in the background, which added to Harrow's confusion.

He repeated himself. "What is going on?"

"Dante was our first casualty. By the time we pulled him out of the room, he was long gone." Tor broke down.

Shelly began to recite the number of shots it took to kill Dante, but Harrow tuned her out. Dante had been a fine man and a friend. What in the world had happened that night? What had gone wrong?

"And Harrow . . . I hate to break this to you after all that you've gone through, but Leroy is dead, too." Jordan tried to break the news as gently as she could.

"Jesus Christ."

What followed next was a tormented cry from a grief-stricken soul. Harrow howled like an injured animal, and just like one, Shelly had to put him out once more. He thrashed around in great rage and wailed in misery until the drug took over and respite was given, yet again.

༫ༀ

Allison woke up in a haze of foggy thoughts. The room was dark and quiet. She remained unmoving, feeling her body trapped in a sluggish state. After a few minutes, memories came flooding back to her, along with the reason why she was in such a condition.

Her father . . . she cried out. Her father was gone. It was her fault. If she hadn't planned the damn party, her father would still be alive. She'd exposed them all, handed three people she loved their death sentence. She'd killed them. It was her fault.

The pain mounted by the second. She had been instrumental in the deaths of three people. How could she have left them vulnerable? Tears . . . her tears couldn't bring them back. No amount of tears would be enough to change their fate now. How could she have been so cruel?

Each realization hit Allison with the intensity of a wrecking ball. A punch of madness hit her, along with a big dose of self-loathing and guilt.

"Allison, is there anything I can do for you?" A hand shook her out of her agonized state, and she lifted her tearful gaze to Peyton. The vampire had been sitting with her for several days now while others attended to Harrow and the rest addressed the security situation.

What can anyone do for me? Her mind wanted to scream the words out. Instead, Allison shook her head. *Breathe, Allison, breathe*, she ordered herself.

Harrow. She had to see Harrow. He was the only one she had. She couldn't breathe. It felt like her heart was being crushed in a vise, the pain doubling inside her, making sure she suffered the same fate she had bestowed upon the others.

"Take me to Harrow."

Allison snaked her legs out of the sheets, and she pushed herself up and stumbled forward, her head feeling woozy. Peyton's hand braced her and settled her in a sitting position.

"Why don't you rest some more?" the vampire asked, her crimson eyes showing kindness Allison knew she didn't deserve.

"No, please take me to him."

Allison planted her feet on the floor, ignoring the shaky sensation in her head, and got up. The room danced around her. She closed her eyes for a moment and pushed back the faint wave of nausea that hit her, taking her first step. Her legs wobbled.

Peyton sighed and wrapped her arms around Allison's waist. "Put your weight on me."

Together they walked out of her room and made their way toward the clinic. Allison prepared herself for the scorn and hatred everyone would throw her way. She deserved it, and more.

"This time, you'd better not stop me, or so help me God, I will kill you with my bare hands," Harrow warned Tor the moment he surfaced from the drug-stimulated sleep he'd been subjected to a number of times.

"Hey, my man, I'm just following your doctor's orders," Tor answered.

Tor backed off for the first time in two days since Harrow had come out of his mini-coma. He knew the vampire was dealing with the situation as best he could. Harrow had a big lump lodged in his throat, ready to cut off his circulation any time, and he had to do something about it. Anything to keep his mind off the madness and the loss.

"Harrow, please. You shouldn't be up on your feet yet," Jordan said, her hand touching his arm in protest, but she didn't restrain him.

"No . . . there's so much that needs to be done, and I can't be lying on my back any longer." He pushed Jordan away when she attempted to make a move.

Harrow swung his legs toward the floor, and his head felt like it was going to fall off his shoulders. The pain in his stomach rendered him immobile for a few minutes. He sat up and braced his hand on the edge of the bed as he tried to suck the pain in.

"Harrow, please, won't you listen to me?" Jordan implored.

Tor shook his head in disgust and went back to his usual place leaning against the wall.

"I can't call a meeting in here, lying down like a piece of worthless meat!" Harrow screamed in frustration. Why wouldn't anyone listen to him? There were many things that he needed to address before he could even think of convalescing.

Just as he was planting his feet on the cold linoleum, Allison walked into the room, assisted by Peyton. By the look on Allison's face, Harrow knew she'd been crying. Hell, they had all been crying. Harrow knew how hard it must be for her.

Peyton led Allison to his bedside, and she stood in front of him, barely noticing the other people in the room. This was the first time they'd seen each other since the horrible incident. She swallowed and watched him while she struggled to keep her tears from falling.

"Ally . . . I'm so sorry." Harrow's voice croaked. He reached out for her.

"Harrow . . ." Allison sobbed and rushed over to his waiting arms, right in between his parted legs, and buried her face on his chest and cried . . . and cried . . . and cried.

He rubbed her back and let her cry her brains out. As much as he hated to cry in front of Allison, it was hard to stop. He felt his heart threatening to break again. Harrow choked down the emotions and kept rocking Allison until her sobs began to wane and all that was left was a silent whimper.

Harrow had no idea how long they had clung to each other before the last of their tears had been shed. He continued to rub her back. That was all he could do. He didn't even trust himself to talk without running the risk of breaking down again.

When the last hiccups receded, he tilted her face up to him. "You and I . . . and the rest will get through this. I'm with you every step of the way."

Allison's mouth trembled. "It's my fault, Harrow. If I hadn't plan the party . . . none of this would have happened. Daddy would still be here . . . and Dante . . . and Leroy . . ."

Allison's anguish was heartbreaking, and he held her again. "Shhh, you mustn't say that. None of this is your fault. No one knows why this thing happened, but sure as hell, I intend to find out."

Harrow wasn't even in the least comforted by his own words, because he was at a loss. This felt like just the beginning of a nightmare that neither of them would be able to walk out of easily.

"Harrow, I don't know what to do." Allison sniffled.

"I don't either, but let's make sure your dad gets a proper burial first. We'll figure out the rest together."

That sounded like a plan, if he just had an idea where to start. Somehow, knowing what to do or not, he had to get the ball rolling. The sooner he started, the better off they all would be.

"What can I do?"

"Well for starters, let me get into the shower, and I'll meet you and the rest in the I-room in an hour. We can make the decisions there."

Allison forced a weak smile and nodded.

"And do me a favor. Feed first. I can smell your hunger, and I don't want you to think on an empty stomach. Peyton," he summoned the vampire, "please make sure Allison feeds and keep watch over her."

The vampire nodded and helped Allison up. After they were gone, Harrow let out a fierce sigh, one that tore at his chest and told him he was in pain, but alive. Hell itself wouldn't keep him from finding out where those bastards came from, and what else they had going for them.

It was his vow in Pritchard's name—the man who had given him hope. Now that very hope would light the way to seek out the truth in the midst of the insanity that had befallen them.

An hour later, Harrow, with Jordan and Tor at his side helping him remain upright, walked into the I-room as several heads turned in his direction.

Grim nods of acknowledgement were offered, but no words were spoken. Most of the people he'd called upon were already seated, waiting. Allison sat to his left, while Cyrus took the chair to his right.

With a heavy heart, he called everyone's attention. "We are gathered here tonight so we can decide what path we'll be taking now that Pritchard is gone. But before that, Allison and I wish to bury Pritchard."

Allison stifled a sob, and Harrow reached over to cover her hand with his own. "Arrangements will be made as soon as this meeting is over. Is there anything you want to add, Allison?"

She looked up at him with a grief-stricken face, and he squeezed her hand. "Go on. This is not going to be easy, but your father, I'm sure, would have wanted to see you step up," Harrow whispered.

Allison stared at Harrow for a long time, as if begging him to lend her his strength. After a few moments, she began to speak in a quivering tone, her lips trembling at the effort.

"I . . . I'm so very sorry for what I have put you guys through. You have —"

Everyone cut her off, speaking at the same time, denying her of her misplaced apology.

"Allison, none of this is your fault," Cyrus said.

"No one is at fault," Tor echoed.

"You had your father's best interests at heart, and he was happy dancing with his daughter on his birthday. Don't forget that, ever," Rohnert offered.

"We are in this together, Allison. We are your family, too," Jordan added.

Lambert reinforced everyone's sentiments. "You have nothing to worry about where we are concerned."

Allison swept her eyes to each and every one. There was an undeniable surprise written all over her face at their willingness to forgive her. Harrow nudged her gently to say something.

"Thank you," Allison responded. "I want my father buried here in the facility. I am sure this is where he would have wanted his resting place to be. As for the Dante and Leroy, we have contacted their families, and they will be given a proper burial whenever those arrangements are made. Cyrus and Lambert, since you are the ones who can represent our family here, you have to attend the funeral for our two beloved."

Cyrus and Lambert nodded grimly, and an expressed sadness rippled across the room. The mournful mood lay thick upon them, and Harrow let a respectful amount of time to pass before he spoke again.

"I want our facility on total lockdown until we can watch the videos of the comings and goings from that day. I want to study each video. In the meantime, I will call on our lawyer to contact clients and announce Tack Enterprises will cease production until further notice. Is that agreeable, Allison?"

"Yes. Do what you think is best, Harrow."

Harrow nodded his head in acceptance. "Next, with Dante and Leroy gone, I need suggestions on who will take their places." Harrow looked at each person as they began ticking names off one by one.

"How about Jones? He was working with Leroy during your testing period," Jordan suggested.

"Let's put Rayce in Dante's position. He's adept with computers and the rest of the technology. I've seen him crack some codes Dante challenged him with. The kid is pretty good. I think he can do the job, and maybe we can get him an assistant, so he isn't overwhelmed," Lambert said.

"Sounds good. Can you get on that, Cyrus?"

"Right away," the man answered. "In the meantime, what do we do with the employees?"

"Give them an extended leave with pay until we figure out the holes. I don't want anyone leaving without my knowledge or yours."

"Yes, sir."

"And don't call me that. It's Harrow, for everyone. Nothing changes here. You guys clear on that?"

"Yes." Cyrus lowered his head, and everyone agreed.

"Good. I think we're finished here. Get some rest. I know the last two days have been hell for everyone involved. I will talk to Jones.

"Anything else you want to add, Allison?" Harrow glanced at her. Though she seemed frail now, Harrow knew she'd be okay. He believed it, because he saw strength in her.

"I wish to learn from Cyrus and Rohnert, from you all. If that is agreeable to everyone?" she asked and looked around tentatively.

Harrow smiled to himself. Yes, she would be all right—no doubt about it. "We'll talk about it when the time comes. I also just want to make one slight change. Tor will be assigned as your personal bodyguard."

Allison began to protest while Tor shifted uncomfortably in his chair, but Harrow cut her off, throwing a glare in his friend's direction.

"That is what I think we need to do here. I won't gamble with your life at any time."

"I'm sure Tor has better things to do," Allison protested again. "Maybe Peyton can do it."

"Tor will be happy to watch you, my dear. Won't you, Tor?" Harrow asked, watching the vampire grind his molars before answering.

"Sure, it will be my pleasure."

"Now, I guess we are done here. Get some rest, and I will let you all know when Pritchard's funeral will be once we have the arrangements made."

After everyone but Jordan had left the room, Harrow let his crumbling emotions out in the open. His shoulders sagged with the weight they carried.

"Come here." He lifted his hand and reached out for her.

Jordan walked over to the chair next to him, sat down, and took his hand in hers. He shook his head and patted his lap. "Sit here, please."

When she did, he wrapped his arms around her waist and turned her to face him. He kissed her on the lips before the waves of emotion took him by surprise, and he broke down and buried his face in the tangles of her hair.

"I thought I'd never see you again," he said after he'd regained a decent amount of composure.

"I was always with you," Jordan whispered.

"Thank you," he answered.

They held each other for a long moment, taking comfort in the warmth the other had to offer. There were many things racing through Harrow's mind, questions that needed answers, and he decided it was time to address one nagging fear he'd had after learning of Leroy's demise.

What in the hell would he do now? What would happen with the research? Would he be suspended on a pendulum of uncertainty now that Leroy was gone?

"Let's go see Jones," he said.

Pritchard's funeral was the exact opposite of what the mogul had enjoyed when he was still alive. His love affair with the extravagant, superfluous, or anything out of the ordinary was toned down to a muted minimum. It was not what one would have expected for a multibillionaire who had taken life by the balls, seized each given moment, and squeezed every last drop out of the life he led.

Nevertheless, the services and the funeral, even in their simplicity, were befitting for a man who was so loved, remembered, and who would be missed. The mournful weeping of the violins throughout the subdued ceremony and the coinciding snowstorm were a testament to heaven's grief at the loss of a beloved man, father, and friend.

The services were held on Christmas Eve, four days after his death on his fifty-fifth birthday. The irony sucked in the deepest sense. Not an eye was left dry, not one heart left unpierced. They buried Pritchard Tack at the unused subterranean level of the facility, now designated as his resting place. Amid the howling of the wind and the pounding of snowfall, he was laid to rest in the hastily excavated earth, witnessed by all who loved him.

Allison eulogized her father, and the whole scene was gut wrenching enough to stay with the mourners long after her last words were spoken.

Hours after Pritchard's interment was over and everyone had left, Allison and Harrow stayed behind, sitting on the white chairs and staring at the newly packed grave in silence. Allison shivered.

"Allison, I think it's time for us to go." Harrow brought his hand around her shoulder, pulling her closer to him. She welcomed the warmth but hated the fact that it wasn't her father providing it.

She stifled a sob. The tears hadn't been all cried out. More came, flooding and drenching her eyes until they were raw. She heaved and coughed, not wanting to give in to the panic attacks that had threatened to drown her for the past few days.

"No . . . I'll stay. Go on." Allison pulled away and lifted her tear-stricken face to meet Harrow's sunken face, cupping it with her trembling hands. "Thank you."

Harrow shook his head and tipped her chin closer. "Please don't thank me. I'm here because your father believed in me. We're going to honor his memory by moving forward and continuing what he loved doing. I'll be with you every step of the way," he whispered.

"But you have your own life. You have Jordan. I can't tie you down by expecting you to give up your life to continue Daddy's project."

Harrow gave a deep sigh. "I gave him my word, and I will stand by it. I hope Jordan will find a reason to stay. But that's beside the point. I'm here because I want to be, and I'll be happy to care for you as my sister for as long as you will let me."

"Oh, Harrow . . . I don't have any words to tell you how I feel . . . but thank you. From now on, you shall be my brother, not born by blood but by love and sacrifice. I'll cherish you for as long as I live."

"Thank you. Now, let me be a big brother and tell you that you need to get some rest. I'm calling a meeting tomorrow, and I want you to be there when I make the announcement."

Allison's eyes expressed curiosity, and she offered a little smile at the order. "I'll be there."

"Good girl. I think Pritchard will be happy for us both. I wish he was here to share the joy . . . but I know he is here in spirit. He always will be."

Harrow let go of Allison and pushed himself up with difficulty. It had only been four days since Demetrius had almost killed him, and his insides still felt like a freight train was barreling back and forth. The pain hadn't subsided, but he had declined any more sleeping pills from Shelly. He swore the doctor enjoyed bullying her patients around.

Blowing a kiss to her father's grave, Allison turned to Harrow. "Here, why don't you put your arms around me? God knows you're stubborn as a mule. I don't know how Jordan puts up with you."

Allison took his arm and placed it on her shoulder, and they began walking back toward the elevator. Each step created a spark of pain that shot from Harrow's stomach to everywhere else blood flowed.

"I don't know for sure that she still will."

His tone startled him. Who would want to follow orders from a pansy who sounded like a lovelorn puppy as he did? One thing was for sure— there would be no stopping Jordan. She was hell-bent on exacting her revenge on the bastard who had taken her family. Not that he could blame her, but he was still hoping he would be a good enough reason for her to stay.

"I'm sorry. As a general rule, I don't wear my heart on my sleeve."

"Don't apologize—it's one of your more endearing qualities. You're just like Daddy. You love fiercely and give love freely."

Indeed, he gave his love to others without restraint, and he had gotten Jordan's love in return. Could her affection override her need for revenge and make her stay with him? That question confronted him like a fist in between his eyes. Jordan's reality was different from his. She existed because she had a goal. He existed just because he wanted to. Was that so bad?

He loosened his tie and unbuttoned his shirt. It had been a long-ass twenty-four hours, and God knew his wound had yet to fully heal. The throbbing ached like a mother. Shallow breaths worked. It was the only way he wouldn't be rendered useless.

Not bothering to turn the lights on, he walked over to his bed, dying to surrender to the exhaustion of the past few days and go to sleep. He was dead tired and felt it in his bones, but his nose caught a scent, albeit belatedly. It was an all-too-familiar scent, and his nostrils flared. He dragged his tired ass as fast as he could toward the inviting aroma.

Harrow strained to see with his faulty eyes and was able to catch a figure sprawled on his bed. He angled his face sideways to get a better view. *Holy Moses!* His jaw dropped open as if a lead weight was pulling it to the ground.

His eyes popped out. Jordan was on his bed, *naked*! There was nothing on the woman—not a bra, not a bikini, not even a weapon. Her beautiful red hair fell around her face like strings of Christmas lights, and he couldn't take his eyes off her glow-in-the-dark form. As if flashes of lightning had struck him, his body jerked forward like it had a mind of its own, and it led him to her.

It took a titanic effort to stop his body's response to the visual stimulus —from latching onto Jordan and doing everything he'd always imagined could happen between them if he hadn't been a walking plague.

"What are you doing here, Jordan?" He jerked away from her.

"Harrow . . . would you care to join me in *your* bed?" Damn, even her voice sounded naked, if that were possible. Her tone was sultry and inviting, sucking him toward her like a damn vacuum. Everything about her screamed different. For maximum invite, she spread her legs apart just enough for him to want to take a peek.

"Jordan, are you out of your damn mind?" he rasped and staggered backward until his heel hit the foot of the sofa. Harrow stumbled back, hitting ass first on the floor. A jolt of pain shot up from his abdomen, radiating throughout his body. He cursed at the pain between his legs rather than the pain from his hard landing.

Jordan shot up and ran to his side. "Harrow, are you okay?"

As she leaned forward, he couldn't help looking at the sensual way her breasts jiggled with her movement. Her hair fell over her face, and he caught the scent of vanilla. When she reached out her hand to help him up, Harrow recoiled, feeling like a live grenade ready to explode.

"Don't touch me."

She pulled her hand away and watched him push himself up, using the sofa as a steadying aid. He stood up and towered over her. For once, she looked vulnerable without her weapons and clothes. But he had to give her some credit. She didn't cover herself.

Confusion graced Jordan's face. "What's wrong?"

"You're naked," he barked.

"I thought you'd never notice."

She had the audacity to blush. Damn her for creating a mammoth confusion inside his sweat pants. God, he was a sick bastard, reacting to a naked woman like a first-timer. He hadn't been in a situation like this in over a decade. No wonder it felt like his first time.

"Will you put your clothes on . . . *please*?" he added for good measure.

"I thought it would please you to see me like this." Hurt began to seep from her pores, palpable and accusing.

"Damn it, Jordan, I'm not dead. Any living, breathing male would love to see a naked woman waiting in his bed. But that's beside the point. You put on your clothes, and let's talk."

"*This* is how I wanted to talk." She swept her hand along her body invitingly, undeterred by his refusal.

"Put on your damn clothes, Jordan. I'm not kidding here." Harrow felt like sagging to the ground. He had no idea how long he could hold back the wild trampling horses inside him, wanting to take a free rein on what was being offered to him.

"Nor am I," she said.

"For Christ's sake, what has gotten into you?" He shoved her away and staggered toward the bed. Jordan brought her hand up and placed it around his waist, and her body brushed against his. Although he was clothed, he could feel the heat from the slight friction. By the grace of all that was good and holy, he felt like he would burn alive just by the mere touch of her hot flesh. Considering he was fully dressed, his imagination was going to eat him up and spew him out if he didn't get away from her.

"I thought this would be a good time for us to lay things out on the table. I want to—"

He cut her off. "Talk in the nude? Woman, just in case you haven't gotten the memo, I'm not primed for pillow talk or . . . or . . . any of this." He waved his hand in frustration, feeling his anger simmering.

"Harrow, why are you being difficult?" Jordan didn't falter, keeping her body as close to him as possible.

"I'm being difficult?" Harrow snorted and lowered his pulsating body onto the mattress. He pushed her hand away and leaned against the headboard with a sigh. "If you want to talk, let's talk, but please cover your body now, before I do something I'll regret."

"I thought you loved me."

Jordan stated the question, plain and simple. Harrow shot a glare in her direction before his gaze slid down, lower . . . until he was staring at the taut mounds that heaved up and down, and then further south to her flat stomach. Hungry for more, he gorged his eyes on the center of it all. *Nice and easy*, he told himself as he dealt with the herculean effort of making himself stop.

He panted, and his voice came out ragged. "You know I do. But you can't tease a dog with a bone knowing he is on a mechanical diet. For the love of God, Jordan, will you stop pushing me over the edge?"

A sob tore out from her before she leapt, grabbed her coat, and ran out of his room. Even if his whole damn body wanted to take her, it was best to leave her be.

Breathe. Yeah, keep breathing. He urged himself to stand down.

"Harrow, Jordan left. No words whatsoever." Rayce sounded nervous over the phone.

He should have known. "Thanks. I'll take care of it." He rang Rohnert.

"Yes." Rohnert sounded as tired as he was.

"Man, get her back for me. I'm afraid I won't make it very far." God, wasn't he screwed, asking the vampire for help, knowing how he felt about Jordan. However, he had no other choice. If there was anyone who could talk some sense into her, Rohnert was the man.

Summoning all his will to calm down, he reached for the laptop and powered it on.

The throbbing between his legs was more pronounced than the pain caused by his wounds, and yet they both ached like a mother. He had to take shallow breaths so the damn pain wouldn't render him useless.

He looked at the laptop that had belonged to Leroy and waited. Jones had given it to him when they'd had their closed-door meeting. He had to give Jones credit. The man had taken the news of his promotion with humility. He'd gone and dived right down to business, sharing his own views of the research that Leroy had worked on with him.

The computer came to life, and Harrow logged in. He clicked on the document marked RESEARCH and opened it.

In bullet points, Leroy had documented his theory and research. Harrow read it again for the hundredth time since he'd gotten a hold of it. He pictured Leroy talking animatedly about his findings and pushing his glasses up the bridge of his nose as he'd done many times in the past.

First was his research on the vampires in general. It was the same stuff Leroy had told him when they'd first met. There were a few added notes, but the ideas were the same. Humans and vampires had coexisted for a very long time.

This, of course, was highlighted and deemed mere theory. Some formulas followed, and Harrow skimmed over the information, not knowing what it meant in the first place.

Leroy had conducted additional research, basing it on Rohnert as his experimental model, after finding out that the he came from a long-line of vampires with no mix of human genes in him whatsoever. In italics, Leroy had written, "*can reproduce.*"

Shelly even had gone out of her way and provided some insights and helpful information on vampire anatomy, based on those she had treated in the past. Everything had factored in his findings. He'd also tested Tor, who was a human turned vampire. Most of his human cells had been taken over by vampire cells. The precise amount of converted cells depended on how long a vampire had been in existence.

Next came his results and Leroy's findings, with a long explanation of his virus, most of which had already been explained by Pritchard when they first met. The one thing Leroy was definite about in all his claims was the success of Harrow's experimentation.

Reading the word *success* brought an immeasurable amount of relief and satisfaction. Harrow squeezed his eyes shut, feeling like the whole trip to hell and back had been worth it.

The animal blood had neutralized the virus and rendered it dormant. Leroy was sure of it. It was deemed safe to purge all diseased vampires of their present diet before administering introduction of the new diet.

Dormant meant the disease would lie in its inactive state, so long as no slip-up occurred. As far as infecting another, it was still up in the air. This was his planned research down the road, although now it seemed like it would be halted for good unless Jones could continue Leroy's research. Harrow could only wish.

He thought about Jordan and how his need for her grew each day. Harrow felt different underneath his skin. Right after the experiment had concluded and his diet had been changed, there had been different sensations to his movement, his tactile functions, his other senses, and even his taste. Overall, he felt better, even if his eyesight had gone a little whacked.

In conclusion, Leroy had found a semi-cure that would alleviate the pain and suffering. If he continued with the consumption of animal blood, there would be a guaranteed quiescent disease.

It felt like a victory had been won to some degree. Harrow let out a heavy sigh before leaning against his headboard. He took out a small piece of paper Jones had given to him, unfolding it and staring at Leroy's handwriting. This, he'd written on the night he died, and Jones had pulled it out of his pocket just before his body had been released to his relatives.

Leroy had been a victim of being at the wrong place at the wrong time. After watching the playback several times, they discovered that Leroy was in the men's restroom when one of the intruding vampires attacked him after he asked who the vampire was and what he was doing there. Harrow's heart doubled in pain as he watched Leroy die on recorded tape. What a senseless murder of an innocent man. He gritted his teeth as his wound throbbed yet again.

Harrow stared at the paper. Leroy had written *Harrow is manifesting animalistic instincts after feeding from animal blood. Coincidence? Maybe, but further blood tests showed another mutation I can't explain. His aggression, his eyesight, the way he explained it seemed two-dimensional to me—like what we believe animals to have. His hearing is far more superior to others after testing. Oh, God, could it be that his virus and the blood, though rendered neutral, were evolving into a sub-species? The possibilities are endless . . .*

Why did it feel like he was on information highway overload? Too many details were pulling at him in different directions, vying for his attention. He couldn't even begin to think where those theories would take him . . . them. It was a sad realization that Leroy wouldn't be around to enjoy the fruits of his labor. Harrow folded the paper and placed it inside his nightstand drawer. This was something he'd discussed with Jones once the smoke had cleared. He wasn't even sure he wanted to share the information with the others yet.

Jordan knew from the get-go she was being followed. Too tired to care, she crisscrossed through town until she got to her favorite spot and sat down on bench overlooking the grand skyline. Somehow, the twinkling lights, even with their brilliance, failed to bring her the solace they had given in the past. She shivered against the cold. The harsh December weather with its pounding snow hadn't let up. Though the winds had eased, she could still feel their fury. The ground was packed with white flurries everywhere.

She squeezed her eyes closed and leaned back, hearing careful footsteps approach.

"I think someone needs a friend." Rohnert's baritone slashed through her tired brain.

"Why did you follow me?" she asked the obvious.

"Because you don't belong anywhere else," Rohnert answered before he sat next to her.

She let out a sigh. "I don't know where I belong anymore. He doesn't want me. I threw myself at him, and he said no." Why in the hell was she telling him this? Harrow was right, what had gotten into her?

She heard him draw in a long breath. God, wasn't this just what she needed? Talking to a man who she knew had feelings for her. Not only had she lost some valuable marbles, but she was also a sadistic wench for pouring salt into the man's wound.

"God, Jordan, you have to be blind not to see how much you mean to Harrow." Her eyes popped open at the slight accusation, and she stared at him. His expression was solemn, and his eyes were fixed on the luminescent display of lights around them. "You have to give him time to grieve and to heal. Harrow is not your typical vampire. The man has a conscience." Jordan watched as a smirk spread across his face.

"I might have driven him away . . ."

"There's no way you can do that. From what I've seen, Harrow has a fierce attachment to you. The vampire would kill for you—bleed for you. I imagine it was sheer torture for him to deny you."

"I can't live without him, either." She cupped her hands over her face, ashamed at her display of weakness in front of her teacher.

"Don't be embarrassed, Jordan. I know how you feel. I see it in your eyes every day." He gave her shoulder a quick squeeze before pulling his hand away and tucking it inside his jacket pocket.

Oh, God. Not only had she turned soft, she also was now reduced to a whining crybaby. It was out of character, but she wasn't sure how much more of this she could take.

A good amount of time elapsed, while they stared at the glowing buildings. It was a quiet that was neither uncomfortable nor unnecessary.

"I think we'd better head back. There's nothing out here for you. You belong with us, with Harrow . . . and even Gail." Rohnert smiled a little, his eyes crinkling on the sides.

"Gail!" How could she have forgotten about the little girl? It was almost dawn, and she wanted to be there when her little angel woke up on Christmas morning to open her presents. Christmas didn't stop for children just because there was chaos around them. She would do anything for Gail, even if it meant allowing the child to call her Mommy. Jordan shot to her feet, grabbed Rohnert's hand, and pulled him forward. "Let's go. I have a child waiting for me."

Rohnert laughed. "Merry Christmas, Jordan," he said.

She pivoted and wrapped her arms around his neck with appreciation. "Merry Christmas, Rohnert—and thanks."

It had been a week since they laid Pritchard to rest. The facility was dead quiet and operating on autopilot with everyone acting like a walking zombie. Harrow spent most of his time in bed, finally giving in to Shelly's constant nagging to rest. His wound still throbbed like a bitch, but he ignored the pain. Neither would he mention the fact to Shelly. He swore that the doctor had a sadistic streak and found pleasure in knocking him unconscious.

Harrow opened his eyes to a start of a new day and was surprised by how long he'd slept. He hadn't planned to sleep, but exhaustion had its claws in him, and he was taken hostage despite his unwillingness to succumb to his body's warning signs.

Tor's bed was still made. The vampire hadn't made it back yet. It appeared that he was taking his new job seriously, camping out in front of Allison's door all night.

Since his schedule was screwed up anyway, Harrow decided to ring Cyrus up and call for a meeting in the afternoon. Shaking off the lethargy, he walked to the shower and let himself relax under the hot spray, feeling his muscles going lax.

After showering, he was putting on a pair of sweats when there was a knock on the door. He hobbled over and opened it. Jordan was waiting for him to let her in.

"Harrow?"

"Jordan."

"Can we talk?" She was in her going out jeans and her trench coat, and she had strapped the holster that held her Kalimetal across her chest.

"Hi. Come here and give me a kiss, will you?" He smiled, guessing she was about to drop a bomb on him, but he was glad she had come back.

Jordan crossed the threshold, framed his face with her hands, and brushed her lips against his. Damn, how he ached between his legs every time she pulled that number, and there wasn't anything he could do about it. Harrow snaked his arm around her waist, and like a greedy mongrel, he drank in as much as he could, feeling the softness of her lips and trying his best to avoid sliding his tongue inside her mouth.

Jordan pulled back, and her expression didn't give her emotions away. He tried to smile, but a grimace showed up instead. Harrow walked over to the sofa and waited for her to close the door. "Please sit." He patted the spot next to him.

Jordan sat next to him, willing calmness within her. *Yeah, that's right, girl—deep breathing will help.* She had bamboozled through the process thinking Harrow would take her with open arms and accept her argument without reservations. She had almost forgotten that she was dealing with a vampire with a conscience.

"You know I love you, right?"

Harrow took her hand and kissed it. She savored the kiss, closed her eyes, and nodded. This was how it was going to be. Going gung-ho on Harrow and catching him off guard didn't earn her a merit badge, she had to let him in on her plans first. No wonder the man had turned her away.

Sexy wasn't going to cut it. Hell, he wasn't going to take her even if she tied a big bow around her body and held up a sign that said "take me, I'm yours." She needed to tell him how she felt and give him no way out on what she wanted to happen. It took a mean dose of reality for her to realize she couldn't live without him. He had to be on his deathbed before she'd accepted the fact that her plans, though important, must take the back seat. She'd be willing to bet her life that she'd be miserable without him. Might as well adjust her plans and tell him what she wanted.

"Harrow?"

"Yes," he whispered.

"There's something I want to tell you." He stiffened, and his hand gripped at hers tight. She winced, but didn't pull away. His eyes fell to their entwined fingers before Jordan tipped his chin in her direction with her free hand. "I want to be with you."

"You are with me," he answered.

She shook her head, making sure he got her entire message by the mere action. He looked confused. "I want you to take me, body and soul."

Harrow's breath stilled. He stopped moving and stared at her, hard, before his anger crackled like kerosene thrown in a bed of fire. "You're insane, Jordan. Insane." He pulled his hand away, stood up, and turned away, heading for the door.

Jordan blurred to the door, impeding his forward march. "No, I'm not insane. I'm in love." Harrow bared his fangs and pushed her aside, but Jordan didn't budge. With her strength and his presently weak state, she was able to get away with it.

"I know you're impulsive and impatient . . . I didn't think I would have to add dumb to the list." Harrow gnashed his teeth, and she could hear the sound of scraping enamel.

"You think insulting me will change my mind?" Jordan smirked, pushing him back farther into the room. "Sit and listen to me. Don't say anything until I'm done talking."

Harrow opened his mouth to blast her, but he snapped it closed again. He let her lead him over to the bed. Eyeing the damn thing like it was made of glass and not meant to lie on, he gave in and gingerly sat down.

Jordan propped a pillow behind him, walked around the bed, and sat on the other side. Yeah, slow and easy. The guy wasn't ready for this, and Rome hadn't been built in a day. Patience was a virtue she'd need to get acquainted with.

She sat next to him—close, but not smothering. "I want to stay with you, here . . ." Harrow opened and closed his mouth fast, but then sighed instead. "I have to admit, I was planning on leaving because I don't want to drag you into my own drama."

Harrow's lips thinned.

"But then I almost lost you, and I figured out that if you lived to see another day . . . and another . . . then I would stay and figure out the rest of my plan later on." Jordan twisted her fingers on her lap, her hair veiling her face. She was about to break the goddamn but.

"But my staying with you won't be like this. Touching, but never owning. Kissing, but not penetrating. I don't want you halfway, Harrow. I want all of you. Disease or no disease. I want you, to be with you."

"Can I say something now?" Harrow pushed the hair away from her face and tucked it behind her ear.

"Not yet. Can't you see? I don't care if I get it. At this point, being with you is what matters to me."

"Jordan, don't you love yourself even the tiniest bit?" She looked up, puzzled at his question. "Why would you condemn yourself to this . . . this life?"

"I love myself for the first time in what feels like forever. Don't you understand? I haven't allowed anything or anyone to get close to me because I didn't want them yanked into this mess I'm living with. My thirst for revenge had ruled over me, and I was willing to throw everything away, including you. But I don't want to live without you, and I don't think you or I can survive it if I leave."

"How can you put a condition on everything?" he asked in a dead voice.

"That is how I am. Take it or I'll leave." She was treading on thin ice. Harrow glared at her, but she met his challenge straight on. "This is how I want it. You and me, together all the way."

"Jordan, please be reasonable. How can you even ask me to be so selfish?" The fingers that rammed through his hair were shaking.

"You won't survive a day without me—I know it. Because you love me, and that protector instinct will kill you once I've stepped out of your life." She sounded almost smug.

"Don't do this, Jordan."

"Harrow."

"I love you so much that it will kill me if you leave. You're right. I won't survive it. But how can you even think of—"

"Stop, just stop," she cut him off. Jordan couldn't take the talking any longer. It was time to start doing . . . each other. She hauled him closer and crushed her mouth onto his, throwing her cares out into the thin air. All that mattered was here, in front of her.

She slipped her tongue into his unwilling mouth. Harrow tried to push her away, but she planted her hand on his back and didn't let him break the kiss.

"Don't," he said against her soft lips.

Jordan wasn't listening anymore. She pushed her tongue in, stroking and probing inside, taunting, teasing, and invoking his lust receptors to respond.

Harrow jerked like a switch that had been turned on. From that moment on, their tongues twisted, fought, and savored each other's taste.

"If we don't stop this now, there's no guarantee I'll ever stop." He framed her face and spoke against her lips.

"I don't care if we never stop. Take me to heaven, Harrow," she whispered.

Judging by the gleam in his eyes, he was going to take her anywhere she wanted. Harrow pulled her closer, and her body molded to his. Slowly, their fire blossomed into a full-blown raging inferno. Each touch unfurled their pent up desires and ignited the flames they could no longer hold back.

Hours later . . .

Harrow smiled into Jordan's hair. What do you know? He'd taken several trips to heaven, and he still had enough gas in him for another run. His wound throbbed, a sick reminder that he should be flat on his back and resting. No can do. The beautiful woman lying naked on his bed demanded of him, and he happily obliged.

"What are you smiling about?"

"I was just thinking what a crafty manipulator you are."

Jordan laughed, a tinkling sound he found irresistible. "It worked, right?" She winked.

Harrow pulled her face up to his, and he stared at her amid the halo and fuzzy eyesight. "You know what? I guess you'll be seeing me like an angel soon," he said. "You'll have the same bad eyesight I have with the halos framing everyone you look at."

"Good . . . the more the merrier. I'm in good company." She kissed him again.

"You wanted me to take you to heaven, but hell was our actual final destination, given how I've infected you."

"Hell, schmell. That doesn't matter to me as long as we're together."

"How can you be so reckless and embrace it without question? I wonder if you're missing some proverbial screws." He felt a decent amount of guilt moving in.

"I'm embracing you, Harrow, and whatever comes with you. As I said, you're who I want. Nothing could make me happier." Her smile melted away his worries.

"Are you going to decide one day that it's time for you to go?" There, he'd said it and sounded like an insecure moron. But he couldn't help it. If there was anything he was afraid of, it was losing Jordan.

"If that day comes, I'll take you with me." She smiled again, and just like that, he was all thawed out.

"You still want your revenge?"

"Yes, and you, Harrow Gates, will be with me when I plunge that dagger into his heart," she promised.

"You know I will be." He kissed her, and another trip to heaven coming right up.

Vroom . . . He accelerated when she pressed her warm body against his already overheating engine. No doubt, this would be one of the many journeys they'd be embarking on together. The glide of her mouth against his reinforced the love she'd promised. Jordan made it so easy.

Harrow smiled and lost himself in her one more time.

The room was filled to capacity. The vampires and humans he had called on occupied all the available seats. Cyrus nodded when they walked in. Tor, with his arms folded across his chest, stood behind Allison, who was already seated next to his newly designated chair. Jones, as he'd requested, was also in attendance.

He sat down with effort, hating the pain that shot through his system with every movement. Harrow looked up after settling rather uncomfortably in the chair. Shelly was right, he should be lying down. This upright business was a bad idea.

"Is everyone comfortable?" he asked, sweeping his gaze across every person in the room.

The group nodded in unison.

"First thing I want to discuss is what I saw on the video tape—in particular, how the vampires got in and what made it possible. They had with them four anklets, the same ones our comrades were wearing the night they disappeared."

"Shit," one vampire cursed.

"Yes, it is," Harrow agreed, and for some reason, everyone laughed. "How they were able to figure out where we were is still an issue I'll try to address. So, with that being said, I will abolish the use of the ankle bracelets for the time being."

"It's about damn time," Peyton hollered in her high-pitched voice.

"But how do we track each other down?" Cyrus asked with a worried frown.

"We don't. We'll have to rely on cell phones as a means of communication for now. Rayce suggested setting up an untraceable number for each one of us. We call each other by way of a code, no name and no other information. This is the only way we can keep our existence safe."

"You have a point, but what if it lands in the wrong hands?" Lambert looked halfway convinced.

"Wrong hands, no problem. Since we are not going to store a name on the phone except codes that correspond to each other, there won't be any danger I can even think of. Nothing in that phone would give our location away. It has a GPS Rayce can use to detect movement."

"Sounds good to me," someone said from across the room.

"Okay, one down, two to go. Our friend Dante didn't see what was coming when he raced across that hall, thinking it was a bunch of burglars wanting of a quick payday by robbing the office building."

"Damn it," Lambert cursed, and his jaw clenched so tight, it looked like it was going to crack into pieces.

"Yes. So I'm thinking that Demetrius didn't get a chance to find out that our facility existed because he went through the office building." Harrow flicked a quick glance at Rohnert, who had been quiet the whole time. The vampire nodded in agreement.

"Now, instead of ceasing production, we will continue with the orders that had been processed already. I'm afraid that if we stop producing, rumors might spread, and there'll be questions about the company that we are not ready to address."

"That sounds logical. I'll have to visit the plant and make sure that productions are timely," Cyrus commented.

"Great. You and Lambert will be our community liaisons, as Pritchard instructed."

"If there are any evening meetings we can rustle up, I'll be glad to help out with that," Allison offered, and Harrow gave her an approving smile. About time the woman said something.

"Last piece of news I want to share with you is Leroy's findings." Harrow hesitated. He squinted to get a better look at Jordan, who was seated at the opposite end of the table. She was looking at the floor while everyone held their breath.

"We're waiting." Tor sounded impatient.

"Well . . . it was a success, according to Leroy. Tests showed that the virus was neutralized. The disease is inactive. It doesn't mean we are *cured*. It only means we got the reprieve we were looking for and the pain will no longer cripple us if we stay loyal to the diet. I don't know about you guys, but I'm ready for a no-pain existence." Harrow laughed, and it broke the ice.

Everyone clapped their hands, and loud hooting and whistles rattled the room. Fists pumping and knuckles bumping continued until Harrow raised his hand to silence the jubilation.

"This doesn't mean you are safe, you know." Harrow let the words dangle in the air.

Some things were better left unsaid. For Christ's sake, he was in a roomful of adults who would know to what he was referring. No need to add insult to those already injured by the unfairness of their disease.

"Well, congratulations, brother." Allison beamed. "I guess I'll be next in line, then?"

"Yes, you are, and we will be working on each one of you until we are all happy and comfortable," Harrow quipped. "Jones will be conducting each treatment, and I'll be helping with that. You guys good with it?"

"Oh, yes!" Several vampires jumped to their feet and hollered in relief.

"All's well that ends well." Harrow smiled. "I believe that's it for now. Cyrus will give you your patrolling schedule. For now, we continue to concentrate on helping our friends out there."

"Alrighty then—I want myself in rotation," Rohnert spoke, and Harrow couldn't help but chortle. The vampire had been itching to go out, and this was a way to say thanks for everything Pritchard had done.

"Put the damn vampire in rotation, Cyrus, before he shrivels up and dies," Lambert joked, shaking his head. Rohnert flashed his fangs in the human's direction, and they laughed.

"That's it, then. More power to each of you. May the spirit of Pritchard guide and watch you. I'm speaking for myself when I say this. I know the man is smiling down at us all right now, knowing that all he'd ever wished for us is now a reality." He glanced at Allison and smiled. "Pritchard didn't die in vain. The miracle he sought is upon us. You are his greatest miracle, and seeing you thrive will continue to bring him joy wherever he is now. Continue what he started and keep doing what he did best—help others. I'm indebted to him. If not for his kindness, I wouldn't be here in front of you, still breathing and living. He gave me the gift of a continued existence without having to fear for anything. For that, I'll be forever grateful to him, and I'll celebrate his life the best way I can. That is, to keep this facility going in the path he envisioned."

They all bowed their heads in reverence, and then they walked out with a bounce in their steps, with renewed spirits and with a brighter outlook. This had been a bittersweet end to a long and arduous journey. Still, the end result had been worth it. This, Harrow was certain, was something Pritchard would say.

Several months later . . .

"Did I catch you at a bad time?" Jones's excited voice came over the line. The human had been working with Harrow on getting the rest of the diseased vampires eased into their new diet and lifestyle. So far, so good.

"No, it's okay. What's up?" Harrow pulled Jordan closer, and her body molded to his without question.

"You know that test I've been working on?"

Of course I do. Harrow held his breath. "Yes."

"Well, there's no hint that she got it. However, please don't think she's out of the woods yet. Moreover, I think it's prudent that we keep this to ourselves. Last thing we need is widespread gamut of vampires mating in our midst. You know what I mean?" Jones chuckled.

"Yeah, I know what you mean."

"Which is rather baffling . . . I swear you guys are just freaks of nature."

Harrow heard no more. Freak or no freak, Jordan was safe, for now. That was all that mattered. "Thanks. Good job, Jones. I'll talk to you later." He threw the cell phone across the bed and laughed aloud.

"What was that about?" Startled, Jordan sat up, gathering the sheet to cover herself.

Harrow pulled the sheet away, raked his gaze down her body, and smiled. "Damn woman, I think you're my lucky charm. You didn't get it. Not a trace—*yet*."

How Jordan could land so quickly on his lap was a trick she'd mastered over time. "I had a feeling that was the case."

She beamed, and all he could think of was kissing her, free from fear and reservations for the very first time. "I still think you're insane." He laughed against her mouth.

Sneak Peek from
Tormented,
the second book in
The Gates Legacy series
by Lorenz Font

"I'm scared," Gail cried when another deafening thud shook the underground facility.

Huddled in the I-room with the others, Allison Tack recognized the devastation of those around her. Her adopted brother, Harrow Gates, and their purebred ally, Rohnert, were conferring on the far side of the room, while Tor hovered in the background like a shadow. Tor Burns, Allison's appointed bodyguard, sent an occasional look of reassurance in her direction, but he did not speak. He must have known that there were no words that could comfort her now. Each pounding, ear-shattering strike that drilled in their ears compounded the atmosphere of regret, apprehension, and loss. A significant chapter of their lives crumbled more and more with every strike of the wrecking ball.

Finality.

Allison watched while the little girl clutched Jordan close, her young eyes reflecting a mixture of fear and confusion. When they'd been unable to locate Gail's mother, Jordan had stepped into the role, and Allison cherished the opportunity to be the adorable girl's honorary auntie. Now, Gail's stubby fingers dug into her new mother's arms, and she buried her face in Jordan's shoulder amid the sounds of concrete and metal colliding.

"Shh. Don't be scared, baby. It's all going to be over soon." Allison reached out to pat Gail's head, stroking the length of her hair to soothe her. She felt Gail's body shudder and heard little sobs escape her lips, but they were drowned out by the relentless sound of the wrecking ball ramming the building.

At the recommendation of her godfather, General Leo Krever, she and Harrow had decided to level the building following the incident that had claimed the lives of her father and their close associates Dante and Leroy. The decision hadn't been an easy one. The building, after all, stood as testimony to her father, Pritchard's, achievements as one of the city's most successful businessmen. Seeing it broken down into nothing more than piles of debris was heartbreaking.

One of the most persuasive arguments for taking such a drastic step pertained to the security of their underground structure. How could they safeguard everyone in the facility after the office building over the underground structure had been breached by Demetrius and his band of vampires? More attacks could come, and this possibility alone was enough to justify the demolition. Without knowing whether the head of the Vampire Council had knowledge of their operation, they couldn't risk another breach. Caution was necessary, since the lives of their people took precedence over any emotional ties to the structure itself. Their continued survival would have been Pritchard's top priority if he'd still been alive, and Allison would see to it that the people and mission her father had loved continued to thrive.

There had been inquiries from all over regarding the whereabouts of her father. So far, Allison and Harrow had managed to dodge the questions with vague excuses. It would suffice for now until more specific questions came up.

Each memory of her father hit her with new pain: dread, sorrow, longing, and remorse. The what-ifs never stopped tormenting her, often leaving her guilt-ridden and filled with shame.

To his credit, her godfather had been fairly active in maintaining the facility's functions following Pritchard's demise. After all, the two men had been close army buddies, sharing horrific experiences together in the army, family holidays and the births of their children throughout the years. Although things would never be the same, Leo's presence had eased the burden of Allison's misplaced guilt. No one except Jordan would ever know that she still lay awake most nights, crying and blaming herself for everything that had gone wrong.

Jordan's amber eyes met her gaze now, conveying reassurance without speaking aloud. *It will be over soon. This is for the best.*

The stress of Allison's situation had taken its toll, and a bubble of laughter rose in her throat. When it escaped, the brittle sound, edged with fear and uncertainty, echoed through the room. All heads whipped in her direction.

Jordan took her hand and squeezed it in a firm grasp, but Allison couldn't accept the comfort her friend was offering. She wasn't entitled to such an emotion. She, who was the root cause of it all; she was the reason three people were no longer among them.

"Allison, are you okay?" Jordan's voice squeaked, contradicting her otherwise calm demeanor.

Despite her attempts to keep her emotions in check, Allison couldn't help but laugh harder, tears pouring down her cheeks. It was a crime to sacrifice innocent lives in order to protect her. Dante, Leroy, and her father would still be alive if she hadn't thrown a silly party, compromising their safety in the process. Now, they were demolishing the building that had been a prominent reminder of her father's pride and hard work. Was she even worth all the trouble her father had gone through? She tried to nod her head in response to Jordan's concern, but her body had begun to shake. Harrow shot across the room and crouched next to her, his expression laced with worry and his body taut with concern.

"Ally, what's going on?" His fingers traced her face, in order to give him the answers his eyes couldn't find. Harrow had the worst vision among all of the infected vampires. With the change in diet, his sight hadn't gotten worse, but the damage had already been done. His white irises dilated when he tried to focus on her. Allison knew him well enough to guess he wanted to gauge her state of mind.

"Harrow, this is unbelievable. All of it." She gestured with her hand, waving it above her head.

Harrow nodded in understanding before gathering her in an embrace. "I know, I know," he said.

Allison knew that he meant to calm her, but lately, each time Harrow held her, a sense of helplessness crept up her spine. The realization that she was weak and in constant need of protection chilled her.

Harrow frowned when she tried to push him away, not understanding that she needed to soothe her frayed nerves. Her friends were looking to her to rise to the occasion. If she allowed herself to succumb to the constant grief, it would forever cement her as feeble and dependent in everyone's eyes.

"I need to think. I have to get away," she said, her legs wobbling underneath her when she stood. Harrow placed a hand on her elbow to steady her.

Tor moved closer but said nothing. Lately, his words were few and far between. It seemed like he had developed the habit of keeping quiet in her presence, although she knew very well his wry sense of humor was still intact.

"Allison," Harrow said, turning her to face him. "It's fine. Go—I'll take care of things here." He turned to Tor. "Take Allison, Jordan, and Gail upstate. Stay there until I say it's safe to come back here. Clear every activity with me first."

The house upstate was one they had recently built and fortified to meet their special needs. Set in the middle of a wooded area with the Adirondack forest in their backyard, the location provided easy access to an abundance of wildlife. After careful deliberation and consultation with Leo, Harrow had bought the land and hired the best architect money could buy. Permits were secured using the General's connections, and building took less than five months. The construction crew worked night and day, and before they knew it, a two-story, ten-room home had been erected, complete with an underground section the size of football field.

"Okay," Tor grunted in reply. His eyes flickered to meet Allison's for a second before he stepped back and leaned against the wall. Yes, Tor Burns and his silences were beginning to irk the hell out of her.

"Rohnert, would you mind keeping the ladies company, too? Maybe take Drake with you so someone can run errands during the daytime."

"Not at all. How about you? Think you can handle everything here?" Rohnert asked, snapping his gaze in Jordan's direction.

There had been a widespread speculation among the fighters that Rohnert could read minds or emotions, although the vampire had yet to make that admission. "I'll stay here," Jordan said before Harrow could speak again, further supporting this belief.

Harrow's lips thinned into a tight smile. "Darling, I think it's best if you keep Gail and Ally company. I'll try to catch up with you guys when I find the time."

The admonishment in his tone was clear, and Jordan sighed but said no more. Her body language made it clear that wasn't what she'd wanted to hear but she'd give Harrow the support he needed rather than argue with him.

Harrow took a few steps in Jordan's direction and kissed her on the cheek before giving Gail a tender pat on the back. "I love you ladies—you know that, right?"

Jordan nodded, her fiery hair swaying with the movement, and tilted her head in his direction. Gail's head, still nestled in the crook of Jordan's arm, bobbed several times.

Another jaw-clenching thud shook them, and Tor sprang forward. "If you ladies are done with your goodbyes, I think it's best if we get ready leave as soon as sundown hits." He strode to the door. "Allison?"

She smiled at Harrow, placing a hand on his arm for a moment before following Tor out of the room.

Left alone, Harrow sat at the head of the table and glanced around the room. The same white walls stared back at him, a quiet witness to all that had transpired in the past months. He grabbed the remote control on the table before sinking back into the chair. The flat-screen television came to life with the click of a button, and the real-time, real-life action unfolded before his eyes. No matter how bad his eyesight, the development outside was as heartbreaking as if he had been standing in its midst, witnessing everything firsthand.

People in yellow hard hats were standing and watching; some were barking orders, others were hard at work. A crane stood next to the building while the large wrecking ball was already hard at work. Harrow pressed a button and zeroed in on Leo, who was standing with Cyrus and Lambert. The latter two men appeared somber; their pale faces, lined with stress and anxiety, showing signs of undeniable sadness. Harrow felt every single one of their emotions. Each one tore through him like a jagged knife, cutting and puncturing his tattered nerves.

Harrow leaned toward the speakerphone on the table. One punch of a button connected him to Rayce, who was now the official tech guy after Dante's untimely demise.

"Rayce." He strained to make his voice sound firm and devoid of emotion.

"Yes, Harrow?" The human's response was quick as lightning. Rayce had been recruited by Pritchard to be Dante's assistant. What he lacked in brawn, he overcompensated for with intelligence. Thin and somewhat geeky, Rayce held his own within the group of snarling vampires and smart-mouthed humans. Dante's protégé was as confident as his predecessor and just as competent. Reeking with potential, Rayce had been a fine addition to their team. Although Dante was missed, he'd left behind a lasting contribution to their team by giving Rayce all the training and knowledge he would need.

"Is it safe for me to go out there?"

There was a long silence. The speaker crackled as the pounding of a keyboard sounded in the background. "We're about to hit sunset in a few minutes, boss. I think you'll be good to go. Just wear those glasses of yours, and you'll be fine."

"Thanks, Rayce. Buzz me out through the side exit. Make sure the women and their escorts are tracked. Call me if there's anything out of the ordinary."

"Will do . . . and Boss?"

"Yeah?"

"Good luck out there. I know you made the right decision."

"Thank you." Harrow's chest tightened. "You're doing a good job, Rayce."

There was another stretch of silence while the speaker idled. It took a few seconds before Rayce answered, "Thanks, Boss."

Harrow got up. He felt for his daggers and the Glock underneath his jacket before picking up his Oakleys from the table—the same pair Pritchard had given him—and putting them on. Harrow strode out of the room and made his way down the long hallway. A few minutes later, he faced the door that would let him out into the twilight. Harrow faced another tie to Pritchard being severed. The man had not only given him and others a chance at a new beginning, but he had been a friend and savior to Harrow.

Melissa walked listlessly around her boudoir, feeling queasiness grip her like never before. It had been six months since she'd last seen or heard from her son, Demetrius. He had simply vanished.

There had been times in the past when Demetrius had found the need to take a breather from his father's relentless expectations and demands. She couldn't blame him for needing to escape Goran's unrealistic whims and summons every once in awhile. Demetrius had gone on prolonged vacations before, but this time he had left without a word. There were times when the need to scream was too great, when she wanted to pull out her hair in frustration.

Caring for Goran's redheaded pets and his children was an item on her list of assignments she was getting tired of, but she didn't have an ounce of nerve to defy him. He trusted her to do things his way, and she had come through for him, every single time. Happiness and freedom had been taken from her, but her son made those sacrifices bearable. With Demetrius missing, Melissa felt the weight of his absence like a ton of bricks bearing down on her body.

She drifted to the porch, her feet heavy, dragging with every step. She opened the french doors, which led to a vast space of nothing—a dead end of walls and concrete. This was the life she knew as the head mistress of

Goran's harem: an existence underground, away from the prying eyes of humans and daylight. Although it was dank, dark, and dreary, it was the best view that could be afforded to the mistress of Vampire Council's leader.

Gathering the skirt of her gown in her hand, she swung herself onto the railing and sat down. She let her feet dangle before releasing the hem of her gown. After yet another day filled with duties and obligations, there was nothing left for her to do. The Vampire Council was settling in for its scheduled slumber, and her silent suffering began again.

She was beginning to hate the endless blur of days and nights spent watching over the needs of Goran's collection of redheaded women and their bastards. It was a big responsibility, one she would rather do without. Too bad she could no longer have children since she had been turned after giving birth to Demetrius. It was so different for the halflings, as they were often referred to by the others. Unlike their purebred counterparts, who were able to procreate at will, the created vampires no longer had that ability. Their biological clocks stopped ticking, halting the progression of life and removing the gift of childbearing. If she'd had a choice, Melissa might have wanted another child with Goran—another child to cherish and love, who could help her pass the time, but it wasn't possible anymore.

Once they were turned, life as they knew it changed. Melissa was just worth the value of the services she provided. When the glitter of her star ebbed, she'd be kicked to the curb and cast aside for another woman with a better shimmer.

Melissa sighed. For now, she remained Goran's favored female, or so Goran kept telling her. His actions so far hadn't contradicted him. If and when that time came, Melissa wouldn't know what to do with herself. Demetrius was the one constant in her life. Without him, there would just be a dull ache in her heart and countless hours of solitude.

She tried to recall any conversation she may have had with Demetrius that could lead her to his location, but she came up empty every single time. He had made no mention of leaving or of a special assignment had might take him elsewhere.

If I could only ask Goran. It was wishful thinking on her part. She sighed. He had been distracted, either by his redhead menagerie or by the Council's demand for a purebred heir. A few times she'd overheard him muttering about being betrayed by someone, but the culprit's identity was unknown to her.

The big question was where Demetrius and his band of vampires were holed up. There were about ten of them who hadn't been heard from since his disappearance. No one from the team he'd left behind had any information. Not even Hamilton, the hard-nosed and irritating vampire, could give her an answer. Melissa recalled her conversation with him a few days back. The vampire had just narrowed his eyes and had shaken his head at her question, acting suspicious of her inquiry.

"Are you baiting me to give you information you already know?" he had asked.

Melissa had felt her blood boiling. "Do you think I would ask if I knew? We're talking about my son here." The rage inside her had neared its saturation point, just like her patience. She remembered crouching and baring her fangs at the impetuous vampire.

Hamilton had sneered at her, mocking her in the manner that had made him hated among his peers, especially by her son. The lone reason she'd gone to Hamilton was the fact that Demetrius had mentioned working with him at Goran's instruction.

"Dial down your anger, woman. If I knew where the bastard went, I would have reported to Goran right away." With those words, Hamilton had strode away, leaving Melissa seething with anger and back where she started, with no leads and her hopes diminishing more with each passing day.

Desperation often led people to do stupid things, and she was afraid of reaching that point. She would give Demetrius three more months to emerge from wherever he'd been hiding, and then she would have to act upon what her instincts were already shouting for her to do.

If any unlucky fate had befallen him—*no*, she told herself, *it couldn't be*. Her son was sturdy, a fine fighter, well-trained, and fierce. He would still be out there, burrowed in somewhere on his own. When he came back, she would wring his neck—snap the life out of him for reducing her to this tangled mess of worry. She would not even think twice about taking his life for being so irresponsible and insensitive.

The drive toward the mountains had been uneventful and quiet. Everyone had retreated into their own private thoughts once they'd climbed into the car for the four-hour trip. They had taken a bulletproof limousine, a recent purchase Harrow had deemed a necessity.

Tor reclined in the front passenger seat and rested his head on the leather headrest. Dave, one of Pritchard's rescued vampires, was driving and had been silent since they had left the facility. The same burden rested on everyone's shoulders, and Tor felt it as well.

A partition glass separated the front seat from the rest of the passengers. Tor was not one to worry, especially when Rohnert was around, but given that Harrow had entrusted Allison to him, he had to make one quick check before he slept. He pushed a button, and the glass slid down.

"Everyone okay?" Tor asked. He smiled at the sight of Gail sprawled between Jordan and Allison. Her head rested on Jordan's lap, and her little shoeless feet were nestled on Allison's thighs.

Rohnert turned to face Tor and grinned. "Yes, we are. Get some sleep, my man."

Allison looked away from the window just in time to meet Tor's eyes. She gave him a blank stare, the same empty look she'd been wearing ever since her father had passed away. Tor searched her face until she offered a weak smile.

"I'm fine. Thanks," Allison said.

Only after she'd spoken did Tor nod to Rohnert and roll up the partition glass, sealing him in a semi-private world. He could imagine Allison's pain. Many times, without her knowledge, he'd heard her cry herself to sleep. Those had been the times when he waited outside her door until he was certain she was asleep before he would leave.

Yes, he took his role of guardian seriously, just like he had when Pritchard had given him his first assignment as Harrow's babysitter. Tor had parked his ass in the vampire's grill, not caring about his privacy, intent on just keeping him alive. Harrow had turned out just fine, and Tor took pride in knowing that he had been instrumental in that. They were good friends now; it was hard to believe that Tor had wanted the bastard dead in the beginning. Who would have thought that destiny would have such different plans for them?

Tor looked out the window and let his eyes rest on the looming darkness. The headlights weren't necessary for him to see what was around them. They were in the outskirts of the city now. A few more hours, and they would be in a different place, far removed from the noise and the traffic.

Tor closed his eyes, stretched his legs in front of him, and let the lulling sound of the engine soothe him. He thought about Allison, her unending tears, and the pain of losing a loved one. The sentiment was not lost on him. He'd been there, seen it, and felt every single emotion that dealt with death —terror, grief, guilt, and loss.

No, he wasn't going there. Not this time, after all these years. It had been difficult to bear then, and was even more so now. He tried to pull his thoughts back, but it was too late to prevent them sprinting down the forbidden memory lane. It was a path he dared not visit, if he could help it.

Not that he'd ever stopped thinking of her. There hadn't been a minute that he'd ever stopped thinking of his Jessie. She had become a permanent resident in his mind, occupying each day with visions and torturous memories, good and bad.

Whether it was painful or tender, she invaded all of him. Jessie had a way of reminding him of what he'd lost and what he had done that forever changed their lives.

There was no backing out now as she took hold of him again. He forced himself to relax, despite the tension building in his muscles. *Sleep, Tor, sleep,* he urged himself. He needed a respite from the nagging guilt and his inability to forgive himself.

Tor could envision that day's events as if they had happened yesterday. He had come home from work at the construction site, parking his old pickup in the designated spot of the apartment complex where he lived with Jessie, his wife. He'd turned off the engine, taken off his hat, and laid it on the passenger seat, stepping out into the afternoon heat.

Just like every other day, he couldn't wait to get home and be with Jessie. They could spend a quiet evening over dinner and maybe watch TV before heading to bed. Evenings and weekends with his wife had been the focal point of his life.

He'd attempted not to make the slightest noise so he could surprise her he'd put his key into the lock. Given his size and weight, being quiet wasn't a skill he possessed. At six-foot-three and two hundred or so pounds, he was nowhere near being light on his feet.

He'd grinned when he saw Jessie look up, a smile lighting her face. She had jumped off the couch in her robe and rushed to greet him.

"Darling, I knew it was you out there," Jessie had said, wrapping her arms around his neck and pulling his face down to meet hers. Well, dangling would have been a more accurate term, since Jessie was five-foot nothing and weighed no more than a sack of rice.

"I was trying to tiptoe, but I guess it didn't work," Tor had said and laughed against her mouth. Her sweet scent provoked his overactive libido, and he was certain of one thing alone: This kiss would guarantee a delightful frolic in bed with his wife. Her delectable mouth seizing his was more than he could handle. He was, after all, a sucker for anything Jessie.

"I missed you." Her smile was inviting.

He'd slammed the front door closed with his foot and grinned at her. Tor had closed his eyes, drinking in her scent before capturing her lips. He had cradled her in his arms like delicate china and crossed the length of the hallway to their bedroom in big strides. Even with his eyes closed, he'd known where he wanted to take her.

Jessie had broken their kiss just as they got inside the room to ask, "What about dinner? I made your favorite, Beef Strogan—"

"You're dinner for me." He kissed her again, and Jessie responded with ardent passion.

He held her after he laid her on the bed. With desire pulsating in his veins, he unknotted the tie of her robe like a ribbon on a gift, dying to see what he'd find. She whimpered with anticipation.

Tor lifted his eyelids to take a quick peek, but instead of the fair skin of her belly or the robust mounds of her breasts, Jessie's blood-soaked body greeted him. Her eyes were wide open and unmoving, and her mouth was pinched into a bizarre and painful grimace. She looked lifeless—dead!

"Jessie!" he screamed and shook her, trying to call her back to life. "Jessie!"

Tor's scream still echoed in his ears, and his eyes were filled with tears when he opened them. He struggled against Dave's hand on his shoulder, pushing the other vampire away. "Jessie," he cried out again, expecting to wake up from his nightmare.

The thing was, he was awake but seemed to be trapped in a nightmare—another one of those he wished would no longer haunt him. Tor knew, no matter what he did or how fast he'd run or how hard he tried to forget, the bitter reality would catch up with him and he could only hold the memories at bay for so long. He had to continue living with this torture, a fitting punishment for his crime.

"Tor, are you having a nightmare?"

Dave took his hand from Tor's shoulder when he growled in confusion. There was pounding on the glass partition, and Tor noticed that Dave had stopped the car.

Tor rubbed his face in shame. He hated being caught in a vulnerable state, cornered in a place he didn't want to be.

"No," he said in acknowledgment. *Welcome to my world.*

Acknowledgements

Writing is supposed to be a solitary adventure, mine was anything but that. There was never a dull moment during the days following the conception of this idea. I'm humbled at the show of support I got from several people without resorting to begging or bribery.

Huge thanks to my lucky charm Lucia Morales for the long forty-five nights, when you stayed up with me while I wrote. Your silly chats and pompon waving antics got me through the whole experience in one piece. Woof ya!

Big thanks to Wendy Depperschmidt for supporting me wholeheartedly and for always reminding me that I was on to something good.

Kristen Giles — your cyber hugs never failed to bring smile to my face. Your indomitable pep-talks have kept me together. I appreciate your lightning-fast responses to my chapters and for never once complaining. You're a gem.

What would I do without my techie friend? Claudia Trapp — you're a girl any writer would be lucky to have on her shortlist of supporters. I adore all of your work, most especially the book new covers. You plucked the picture from my mind and breathed life into it.

Judith Somera — Lola, I'm one lucky gal to have you as a friend. I can't thank you enough for listening to my daily rants and for giving me the necessary prodding to focus and concentrate.

Eric Banaag and Ching Yu — Thanks for being my male guinea pigs and for the valuable input.

Bunny — I don't know what I'd do without you. Thanks for believing in me.

My babies, Roma, Frances, and Kevin — This is for you guys; the legacy I've been obsessing over.

And last but certainly not least, Mavvy Vasquez, thanks for everything. I will forever be your Padawan.

About the Author

A professional daydreamer, Lorenz Font discovered her love of writing after reading a celebrated novel that inspired one idea after another. Since being published in 2013, she has been conspiring, butting heads, and enjoying her spare time with vampires, angels, samurais, and other creatures she has created in her head.

Her perfect day consists of writing and lounging on her garage couch (a.k.a. the office) with a glass of her favorite cabernet while listening to her ever-growing music collection. She finds writing urban fantasy exhilarating and places an intense focus on angst and the redemption of flawed characters. Her fascination with romantic twists is a mainstay in all her stories.

Lorenz lives in Southern California with her supportive family and three demanding dogs.